WAVE ME GOODBYE

When war is declared, four plucky girls from Dartford – Grace, Sally, Rose and Daisy – are keen to do their bit for the Home Front.

For orphan Grace, it's a chance to start afresh. She's always had a soft spot for Sam Petrie, brother of Daisy and Rose, but realising that he is in love with their friend Sally, she signs up for life as a Land Girl.

Mucking out and early morning milking come as a big shock; life is harder than she expected and she seems to have ended up on the wrong side of Lady Alice, the formidable owner of the farm.

WAVE ME GOODBYE

WAVE ME GOODBYE

by

Ruby Jackson

Magna Large Print Books
Long Preston, North Yorkshire,
BD23 4ND, England.

British Library Cataloguing in Publication Data.

Jackson, Ruby
    Wave me goodbye.

    A catalogue record of this book is
    available from the British Library

    ISBN   978-0-7505-3897-8

First published in Great Britain by Harper
An imprint of HarperCollins*Publishers* 2013

Copyright © HarperCollins*Publishers* 2013

Cover illustration © Colin Thomas

Published in Large Print 2014 by arrangement with
HarperCollins Publishers

Magna Large Print is an imprint of Library Magna Books Ltd.

Printed and bound in Great Britain by
T.J. (International) Ltd., Cornwall, PL28 8RW

ACKNOWLEDGEMENTS

Many thanks to DAIRY CREST for their receptionists' courtesy, and special thanks to Chris Munn of DC for his help, especially his introduction to the incomparable Tom Phelps. Tom, for his long letter full of detail and for his fascinating book, The British Milkman.

Many thanks to Charlotte Murray of the University of Reading who found several sources for me, and generously offered other help.

Thanks are also due to the friendly and helpful staff at the Museum of English Rural Life.

And thank you very much to Jill Ellis of the Royal Shakespeare Company for help with the correct wording of a quote.

For Barnaby, Stella and Finn with love.

ONE

She had been right to do it, to pack up her few personal belongings and go without a word to anyone, even to those who had been so kind to her for many years. She regretted that: not the kindness, of course, but the manner of her leaving. How could she explain to them that she could no longer bear her present existence, the hostility of her own sister, the uncomfortable, unwelcoming damp little house that she and, she supposed, Megan called home? Even her job in the office of the Vickers munitions factory was unfulfilling. All that had brightened her life had been the friendship of the Brewer and Petrie families, the small garden that she and her friends had created, and daydreams of Sam. Winter frosts had killed the garden that had given her such pleasure, but Sam, who had seen war coming and had enlisted long before September 1939, was with his regiment – somewhere. Useless to daydream about Sam, though, not because she had no idea where he was or what was happening to him but because he loved Sally Brewer.

It was easy to picture Sally, with her long black hair and her glorious blue eyes. Sally, an aspiring actress, was almost as tall as any one of the three Petrie sons, and a perfect foil for Sam's Nordic blondness. How could she, plain Grace Paterson, who did not even know who her parents were, be attractive to a man like Sam? Oh, he had been kind to her when she was a child but Sam, eldest in a large family, had been kind to everyone. What would he think of her when he heard some day that she had disappeared without a word?

Grace sobbed and buried her face in her pillow in case any of the other girls were to come in and hear her. Her conscience, however, kept pricking her and, eventually, she found that intolerable. *You have to write, Grace, you owe them that much.*

She got up, straightened the grey woollen blanket and thumped her lumpy pillow into shape. Right, I'm not going to lie here whimpering, she decided. I will write to everyone and then, when it's off my mind, I'm going to try to be the best land girl in the whole of the Land Army.

She picked up the notebook she had bought in nearby Sevenoaks, and moved down the room between the long rows of iron bedsteads, each with its warm grey blankets, and here and there an old, much-loved toy brought from home for comfort. She reached the desk where, for once, no other girl was sitting and examined the lined jotter pages. Immediately, Grace worried that she ought to have spent a little more of her hard-earned money on buying proper writing paper. She shook her head and promised herself that she would do just that when her four weeks of training were completed and she had moved on to a working farm.

Mrs Petrie and Mrs Brewer won't mind, she told herself.

When had she first met them? More than half a lifetime ago but, since she was not yet twenty, half a lifetime wasn't long. Grace sighed. Ten, eleven Christmases spent at the home of her friend Sally Brewer. Ten birthdays either with the Brewers or with the Petries. But when she thought of the Petrie family, it was not kind, comfortable Mrs Petrie or even her school friends, the twins, Rose and Daisy, who immediately came vividly to life in her mind, but Sam. Sam, who, for all she knew, might be dead.

No, he could not be dead. God would not be so cruel. She closed her eyes and immediately saw him – tall, blond, blue-eyed Sam – chasing the bullies who had pushed her down in the playground. He had picked her up, dusted her down and handed her over to his twin sisters.

So many kindnesses, and she had repaid them by slinking away, like a cat in the night, without a word of explanation or thanks. Again, Grace turned her attention to the notebook and began to write:

Dear Mrs Petrie,
I've joined the Women's Land Army and I'm learning all about cows.

That unpromising beginning was torn up. She started again:

Dear Mrs Petrie,
I am very sorry for not telling you that I applied to join the Women's Land Army. I thought it would take some time and I could tell you but I went in and there

15

were lots of women and eventually this posh lady asked me my age and did my mother know. I said I didn't have a mother. You do know it's jolly hard work? she said after she'd been thinking. I've never heard anyone say, jolly hard. Another lady said, See the doctor now. He was in the next room and I was a bit scared as I haven't ever been seen by a doctor, not ever been ill, proper ill. The doctor looked at me and said, Have you ever been ill, or been in hospital? I wasn't sure but I don't think I have and so I said, No, sir, and he said, Why on earth do you want to join? It's bloody awful work.

Grace stopped and thought hard. Was her simple little tale interesting? Would Mrs Petrie think it odd that the doctor had only asked a few questions and then told her that she would do, whatever that meant, and then had added something about being sure to drink milk?

And how could she explain why she had wanted to join, even knowing that it was 'bloody awful work'?

It was working in the garden, growing the sprouts and things. It's hard to explain but, although it was really hard work, I enjoyed it. I felt

She could not explain the pleasure or the satisfaction that growing things had given her and so that effort at a letter ended in the wastebasket, too. She tried to write to Mrs Brewer and four attempts ended beside the others. Grace stared in despair at the wall in front of her but, in her head, saw only the waiting room of the doctor's surgery in Dartford.

There were several girls and women there, and from their clothes and, in some instances, their voices, Grace realised that they came from what Mr Brewer called 'all walks of life', though so far no one had her accent, which, Megan, her half-sister, always said was half-Scot, half-Kent. Grace waited quietly, head down, until she was called.

The doctor was quite old: he had to be older than either Mr Brewer or Mr Petrie and they would soon be fifty. Had all the young doctors been called up?

'Some simple questions, first, Miss Paterson. Why do you want to join the Land Army?'

'I like growing things.'

'Any experience?'

'I had a little vegetable garden.'

'Splendid? Any illnesses?'

'No, not real illness. Measles once.' Grace had felt the words 'in the convent' forming on her lips. Why had she wanted to say that? She had never been in a convent, had she?'

'Height?'

Since the younger Petrie boys had tried stretching her every so often as they grew up, Grace knew exactly how tall she was, but behind her back she crossed her fingers against bad luck and added half an inch. 'Five feet two and a half inches.'

He looked at her and she breathed in and tried to stretch her neck.

'You'll do,' he said, heavy notes of doubt in his voice. 'Shoe size?'

Stupid to fib here. 'Four.'

'Difficult. Best take all your old socks.'

Grace smiled. Surely that sounded positive, even if her feet were too small to be of any use to the war effort.

'Do you have varicose veins?'

She hadn't the slightest idea what a varicose vein was but said, 'Of course not.' Her reply seemed both to please and surprise the doctor, who was busily making notes as Grace waited in something approaching terror for the physical examination.

The doctor closed the folder. 'Thank you, Miss Paterson. Wait outside, please, and, Miss Paterson, be sure to drink all the milk they give you.'

No physical examination; he hadn't even taken her pulse. If he were to take it now, he would feel it racing.

'You'll do. You'll do.' The loveliest words in the English language repeated themselves over and over in her head.

'Still awake? Want some cocoa? We're making it in the kitchen and they've left us some scones – with butter. Amazing how we're able to squeeze more food in at bedtime just a few hours after a three-course tea.'

One of Grace's roommates, Olive Turner, was standing in the doorway, and the appetising smell of a freshly baked, and therefore hot, scone wafted across the room.

Grace rose in some relief. 'It's hard work and fresh air does it,' she said. 'That smells heavenly.'

'And it's mine,' Olive laughed, and together they ran down the three flights of uncarpeted stairs to the kitchen, where several of the other girls were crowded round the long wooden table. A plate, piled high with scones, several little pots of raspberry jam, each with a land girl's name on it, and each girl's own rationed pat of butter, were clustered together in the centre of the table.

'Home sweet home,' said Olive, as she and Grace found empty chairs.

'My home was never like this,' said another girl, Betty Goode, as she bit into her scone.

The others laughed and Grace smiled but said nothing. The trainee land girls drank their hot cocoa and ate scones filled with farm butter and raspberry jam until their supervisor came in to remind them that cows would be waiting to be milked at five o'clock next morning. Groaning, the girls finished their supper, washed up, and made their way back upstairs to bed.

Grace washed and undressed as quickly as possible. The house was large but the third floor, where the girls were housed, was cold.

'Beds are nice and warm, girls,' their supervisor had said, 'and I'm sorry I can't get any heat up here but the summer class'll be wishing it was colder; hotter than a glasshouse, this place gets.'

The land girls had rather liked the idea of being in a lovely warm glasshouse, especially now, in February, when icy winds found every chink in the walls or the roof. Some had even perfected the art of dressing and undressing under their covers, not for modesty but for comfort. Grace, having been brought up in an almost dilapidated old house with one working fireplace, was used to discomfort, and dressed and undressed with well-practised speed.

'Will we ever be warm again, Grace? My feet are like ice.' Olive, in the next bed, issued her usual nightly complaint.

'Keep your socks on, stupid,' the other girls called, but soon, exhausted by their long day of punishing chores, they slept.

Grace appreciated the warm, woollen, knee-length stockings that had been issued to her with the rest of her uniform. She was not quite so fond of the Aertex shirt; it somehow didn't fit properly and she was glad that, for the present, most of it was hidden under her green issue jumper. She took great care of these clothes. Thanks to Sally's mother, and Daisy's, she had had something brand-new every birthday, even if it was a cardigan that had been knitted from wool that had been used previously. The cardigan was made for her and therefore it did not matter that the wool was old. Women like Mrs Brewer and Mrs Petrie had become experts at 'Make Do and Mend' long before the government posters had come out asking the people of Britain to be economical.

Loud groans emanated from every bed several hours later as the trainees were awakened by the large metal alarm clock that stood in a tin basin so that it would make even more of a racket as it told the world that it was already four a.m.

'My God, why didn't I join the army or become a nurse?' This question was asked daily.

'The army never sleeps and bedpans are a great reason for not nursing.'

'Please, it's bad enough having to get up before the damn cockerel without having to listen to all the moans.'

Grace smiled. She loved the life; she enjoyed being with women who were all about the same age. If all the farms she would work on during this beastly war were like this one, she saw no reason to complain.

The word she heard most often from the dairyman was 'cleanliness'. He wanted the girls clean, their white aprons spotless, and he inspected every girl's hands each time they were in the dairy. The work was hard. The first cow she had encountered had terrified her. This large, warm brown-and-white animal with such lovely eyes had suddenly glared at her as she tried milking it in the way that had been explained and then demonstrated, and had deliberately kicked over her pail, spilling the precious milk, which ran down the drain. The instructor had glared.

'Try to keep hold of the milk, Paterson; there's a war on and we need every drop.'

Now at the end of a week of learning how to milk, Grace felt quite secure in her ability. She could manage to wash the rear end of the cow and its udders before starting either hand or machine milking and the workspace was warm. Cleaning out the parlour after milking was not such a pleasant job. The water was always ice cold and the smell of cow waste was, to Grace, unpleasant.

'Rubbish,' announced George, the head dairyman, his Scottish accent giving the word a fierce emphasis, when some of the girls complained. 'Nowt wrong with a good, clean farmyard smell. Too dainty by half, some of you.'

But if George was difficult to please, he was

also patient and fair, and the girls enjoyed his crustiness.

Milking was done and the cows had to be taken out to fields close to the farmhouse. There was still no sign of new growth and so Grace and Olive Turner were assigned to fork hay into large feeding troughs, back-breaking work but warming.

'Hope they've left us some breakfast,' moaned Olive, as the rumbling in her empty stomach reminded her of the time.

'Warden'll make sure we eat.'

'Happen you're right, Grace, here at the training centre, but I'm worried about postings. I've heard ever so many stories about how mean some farmers are. All they want is cheap labour, and the less they have to give in return the better.'

Grace had also heard scare stories but preferred not to believe them. Farmers were people and there were different types of people: mean ones like her sister, Megan, and decent, generous ones like the Petries and the Brewers. 'Everything will be fine, Olive. Now let's finish this and get back to the house.'

'Wouldn't it be terrific if Wellington boots had fur linings?' Olive – who had just stepped into something that smelled terrible, looked awful, and was very wet and cold – stood on one wellingtoned leg and looked down at the one caught tight in the mire.

Grace helped her pull her boot out and it came with a rather horrid slurping sound. It was quite common to lose boots in farm muck and to be forced to dance around on one leg while trying not to put the bootless foot down. 'Best idea I ever heard, Olive, love. In the meantime, wear more socks.'

'I don't have many pairs, and not thick ones.'

'I'm sure I can lend you some. Brighten up; it'll soon be spring – daffodils, primroses, little lambs. Now cheer up and smell your breakfast.'

They had arrived at the kitchen door and the smell of sizzling sausages came out to welcome them.

'I hope there's enough porridge left for the pair of you, but there are three sausages and so you may have one and a half each in a fresh-baked roll. Luckily for you, I came to make myself a fresh pot of tea,' said Miss Ryland, the manager of the hostel.

Grace and Olive washed their hands in the deep sink and sat down gratefully at the table with their plates of porridge.

'Ambrosia,' Olive said as she finished her bowl.

'I never heard that word before. What's it mean? I'd like to write it to my friend Daisy; she loves learning new words.'

Olive shrugged. 'Dunno, really. Something special, I think. Just heard someone say it when something really tasted good.'

'Ambrosia was a honey-flavoured food of the Greek gods, girls,' said Miss Ryland. 'And if it does for you two what it was supposed to do for the gods, you have years of cleaning out cow-sheds ahead of you.'

The girls looked at her in astonishment.

'Would you explain, Miss Ryland, please?' Grace asked. 'I don't know about Olive, but I'll happily clean cowsheds if it helps the war effort, but for how many years?'

'Ambrosia promises immortality, Grace. You'll live for ever, cleaning up cowpats.'

Olive looked as if she might burst into tears.

'She's joking,' said Grace. 'It's only a story but, just in case, you'd better start knitting more warm socks.'

'Enough chatter, finish your sausages and get on with your next cowshed.'

When they had finished the hearty breakfast, the land girls wrapped themselves up again and left the hostel.

'What's next?' Olive was already shaking with cold. 'When were we supposed to get the warm coats?'

'I hope they'll be sent to us here, but I think Miss Ryland is the type who won't mind if we ask her about them.' Grace looked at her companion, who was almost blue with cold. 'You need to put on two jumpers, Olive, or at least a liberty bodice. Don't you have one of those? If you don't, I can let you have mine when we go back for our dinner.' Grace remembered, all too clearly, how it felt not to have enough warm clothes. Her sister had not been the best provider, seeming to begrudge every penny that was spent on the little girl who, for reasons known only to her, Megan had promised to bring up.

'I did have a nice liberty bodice,' said Olive with a sneeze. 'My mum said, "Take it with you and wear it over your vest," but I'm not a child any more.'

'No, you're a young woman who's catching a cold. Just as well it's a lecture. You can warm up and put more clothes on before the sheep this afternoon. Come on.'

They hurried to the main building where, they were later told, a fascinating lecture on arable farming was in progress but, instead of being allowed to go in, they were yelled at for daring to enter wearing such filthy Wellingtons. 'No one ever teach you to wash off mud before you enter a building?'

'We did,' began Grace, but she was given no chance to explain that the new mud had been acquired on their way to the classroom.

'Never make excuses, and keep your eyes open for pumps. Now get out and get clean.'

They backed out as quickly and as gracefully as they could, washed off the mud and went back in.

Betty Goode was waiting for them, her round rosy face tense with anxiety. 'You missed the first half of the lecture but I'll share my notes. It was an absolute hoot. Did you get breakfast?'

'Yes, thank you, Betty,' said Grace, just as Olive sneezed loudly.

The two other girls looked at each other anxiously, over Betty's head, and Grace made a swift decision, based on her ever-present memories of neglect. It was not just that Olive was sneezing but the girl was shivering and the entrance hall was quite warm.

'I'm taking her back to Miss Ryland. If they call my name, tell them I'll come as soon as I can.'

Olive protested feebly.

'Come on, the rest of the day in bed with a hot-water bottle and you'll shake it.' She smiled. *I'm doing for someone else what Rose and Daisy and Sally and their families have always done for me.*

It was a lovely feeling, until she remembered that she had not contacted her friends. *They're not Megan; they'll forgive me because they care about me.*

She shepherded Olive back to the hostel, where she found Miss Ryland in her office. The manager looked up from the papers she had been reading and was visibly startled by the sight of two bedraggled land girls.

'Why aren't you two in class?' Her usually calm and friendly voice was now quite icy in tone.

Olive sneezed loudly several times in quick succession; almost drowning out Grace's explanation. 'Olive's unwell, Miss Ryland. She's been sneezing and sniffling all morning and so I thought it was better to bring her back and to put her to bed for the afternoon.'

Miss Ryland's well-defined and savagely plucked eyebrows seemed to rise up into her hairline. She got to her feet and stood surveying first the room and then the girls. Olive hung her head. But Grace, although as frightened as she had been as a child when confronted by her older sister, stood her ground.

'And who, Miss Paterson, gave you the authority to decide who does or does not take an afternoon off?'

'She's not taking an afternoon off. I think she's really sick.'

'You're a doctor. Silly me. I thought you were a land girl. You do know that there's a war on and taking time off, without permission...? Or did you ask the lecturer for a pass?'

Olive began to cry. She was shaking. 'Please, it's all my fault, not Grace's. I didn't wear my liberty bodice.'

There was a stunned silence, eventually broken by Grace. 'It's not her fault. She's too sick to make a sensible decision and I don't think Mr Churchill would want her to–'

That was as far as she got.

Miss Ryland was looking at her as if she could not believe her eyes – or ears. 'Enough, you insolent girl. How dare you consider yourself capable of deciding what Mr Churchill would or would not want?' She turned. 'As for you – Turner, is it? – return to the lecture room immediately.'

Olive turned and, without a word, ran from the room.

Grace waited. Long experience had taught her that to attempt an excuse, to say anything, would only make matters worse. Miss Ryland stood, looking down at the telephone on her desk. Was she expecting it to ring or did she mean to make a telephone call, to complain about Grace Paterson?

'Neither of you is dressed for winter conditions,' she said at last.

'We haven't got coats yet. I thought I could ask you about them.'

'Need I remind you that everything is in short supply? If there is some material for coats, surely we want it to be given to the manufacturers of coats for our brave soldiers, who do not have a warm comfortable hostel to return to at the end of a working day. Greatcoats were ordered in plenty of time and will be delivered as soon as possible. To win this war we will all have to be disciplined, principled; we will have to make sacrifices for the greater good and, Miss Paterson, we will have to learn to obey the chain of command and not, do you understand me, *not* presume to think for ourselves.'

She turned and went to the window. Grace stood, wondering whether she had been dismissed or if she was to wait. She did not wait long.

'Come here, girl.' Grace joined her at the window. 'Do you see that building over there?'

'Yes, Miss Ryland.'

'It's a pigsty. Clean it. I expect it to be a shining example of good animal husbandry by teatime. Now get out.'

'Yes, miss,' said Grace, and walked out, closing the door very quietly behind her.

After supper that evening, Betty Goode loaned Grace the notes she had made at the lecture and then she play-acted the lecturer in the hope of cheering Olive, who was lying in bed.

'He was a real hoot, Olive; everything you need to know about farming in one easy lesson. Picture him, not much bigger than me and hands like big hams – do you remember hams in butchers' windows? He's got about three hairs stretched across the shiniest head you ever saw and he's wearing absolutely immaculate dungarees and shoes so shiny you could see your face in them. Don't think he's ever been on a farm, but anyway, this is him, fingers stuck in his braces, striding up and down the lecture hall.

'"Growing crops is simple, ladies. First, plough your field, modern tractor or the magnificent

British horse. Next, harrow it. What comes next? Of course, sow the seed. We has machines as do this evenly nowadays or you can scatter – will depend on your farm. Next, weed as crops grow – the damned things will be the bane of your life. After that, you can leave it to Mother Nature. Water, if necessary. And then, the joy of watching golden wheat swaying in a late-summer breeze or superb English peas fattening on the climbing stocks. Lovely. And what do we do last? Yes, harvest and enjoy the fruit of your labour. Now, ladies, could anything be easier than that?" He did not wait for an answer. "No, thought not."'

Grace interrupted the performance. 'Sorry, but didn't he say, "It's bloody awful"?'

'No, he did not, Grace Paterson. Kindly don't interrupt again.'

They were pleased to see a smile on Olive's pale face.

'I'll continue, Olive,' Betty said, and, taking a deep breath, she got herself back into character.

'"Now should you be asked to plough, here's a little tip. Ladies has delicate 'sit-down upons'. I always suggest a nice, if somewhat scratchy sack of straw, easier to find on many a farm than the farmer's missus's best cushion. Tractors is noisy, slow, and they have a bad habit of stalling, but, on the bright side, you won't get so many horseflies buzzing around you. You will still get them, and wasps and bees buzzing away. Just think of the honey from the bees – can't think why the Good Lord invented wasps, oh, yes, must be fertilising. See, everything in its place. Any questions?"'

'Of course, he didn't give anyone a chance to

ask him anything,' said Betty, 'but said, "Thought not. All right, where are you now? Some of you is pigs, some hens. Have a good afternoon."'

Grace laughed. 'You remind me of a friend who's a real actress, Betty: you're good, isn't she, Olive?'

Olive seemed too weak to reply. She had shivered through the talks on the care of pigs, and the egg producer's place in the war effort – 'a hen will lay an egg if it's properly fed, watered and housed, but you can't order it to lay. She'll do it when everything is right and it's the farmer's job to see that conditions are perfect' – gulped tea at the break between lectures and had then caused a small sensation by collapsing in the lavatory. Miss Ryland had been forced to admit that Miss Turner should be given two aspirins and a hot-water bottle and sent to bed.

Grace, on the other hand, had spent what was left of the afternoon and much of the evening cleaning the pigsty. All bedding and food waste had to be shovelled out, and the floor and walls washed down. George, the head dairyman, pass-ing the pigsty in pitch-darkness and, alerted by the sounds of scrubbing, had slipped in quietly and seen a girl scrubbing the floor in the dark.

'What the hell are you doing?' he shouted.

Grace had no idea how to answer. She was ex-hausted, filthy, and knew she smelled as badly as the sty had smelled before she had begun to clean it.

'I can see you're scrubbing a mucky floor in total darkness. Whose bright idea was this?'

For a mad moment, Grace thought she might throw down her scrubbing brush and run, but she tried to remain calm. 'Miss Ryland,' she almost whispered.

'Ryland? Good God.' They stood in the covering blackness for a few moments in silence and then George obviously came to a decision. 'Go and have a hot bath. You'll miss tea if you don't hurry and I'm sure she doesn't want that.'

When Grace hesitated, he yelled, 'Go!' Then added more gently, 'Now, lassie. Get cleaned up. I'll explain to Miss Ryland.'

Grace, now in tears, had stumbled in the pale light of the moon to the hostel.

Later, as Grace left the dining room, Miss Ryland had stopped her. 'You seem to have misunderstood me this afternoon, Paterson. You must learn to listen very carefully and to follow orders to the letter. Now we'll say no more about the matter and, just this once, I'll make no report.'

Grace could not bring herself to say, 'Yes, miss,' and after nodding abruptly she ran upstairs to join her friends.

She had still not written to her friends in Dartford but she sat beside Olive's bed and thought about them. She compared them with Miss Ryland and castigated herself for being such a poor judge of character. 'I actually thought she was a kind woman, a good and honest woman. Well, she doesn't compare with the goodness and kindness of either Mrs Brewer or Mrs Petrie. I didn't misunderstand her; I understood her only too well. She told a lie.'

'Liberty bodices and woolly socks,' she announced to the unusually quiet room. 'I promised a liberty bodice to Olive.' Then, turning to Olive, she added, 'I think I have a pair of socks I can give you too, once we get you well.'

Other land girls stood up and began to go through their often-meagre belongings.

'Every old lady in my home village knitted me warm stockings, Grace, and I bet there's a knitted vest in here too,' said a slightly older girl from Yorkshire. 'Hate wool against my skin, I do, but what can you say to old ladies?'

'Thank you very much,' chorused several of the girls, and everyone laughed.

'I can't take all this,' Olive wheezed, as knitted socks, stockings, vests and even knickers began to pile up on her bed.

'Don't fret; we'll sort it out. We're all in this war together, aren't we, ladies?' Betty made Olive smile as she pulled on a very large woolly vest over her pyjamas. Then she took it off and held it up. 'Bit too small for me, this one. Any takers?'

Grace, still feeling both angry and unhappy, began to relax in the camaraderie. This was how she had joked with her old school friends. No one would ever take their places in her affections but she smiled as she understood that these young women too would always be a special part of her new life.

Two days later, Miss Ryland admitted that Olive was no better and telephoned for a doctor. Grace and Betty were allowed to stay with her while they waited.

Grace had no experience at all of medical care

and could make no suggestions as to how to bring down Olive's temperature. 'She's burning up, Betty. What can we do till the doctor gets here? Should we take off this heavy blanket?' She made as if to move it.

'No,' said Betty sharply. 'If I remember right, my nan used to put us in cold water when we had a high temperature and then quick as a wink, back into the nice warm bed, just till the temperature broke. I know she shouldn't be in a draught.'

Grace looked around. 'Wish there was a fire-place. I could easily find sticks and branches in the wood. It is a bit draughty.' She walked angrily to the small window and tried to peer out. 'Can't see a damn thing. I'm going to run downstairs to watch for the car coming. I can't just sit here.'

Olive coughed, a loud hacking cough that seemed to shake her whole body. 'I'll be all right, Grace,' she wheezed.

That frightening wheezing had been heard too often in the past few days and, combined with the burning skin that made her attempt to throw off her covers, had added to the land girls' worries.

Betty, who had lifted Olive up until the spasm passed, lowered her down onto the pillow. 'You go, Grace, and bring back three cups of tea. You'd like a nice cuppa, wouldn't you, Olive? See, Grace, she's dying for some tea; me, an' all. Run.'

Grace grabbed another jumper and pulled it over her clothes. There would be time to continue the fight for the promised coats when they had Olive well. She strained her ears to hear the ring of the doorbell but all she heard was the clatter of her heavy-soled shoes on the wooden staircase.

It was too cold to stand on the steps, looking down the driveway for the doctor's car and so she decided to jog down to the gates in the hope of seeing it arrive. She reached the gates without seeing any vehicle of any kind, but as she stopped, leaning against the gatepost to get her breath back, she saw a bicycle at some distance. The bicycle slowly drew near as the rider fought both the wind and the weight of the ancient machine. Disappointment. A woman was riding the bicycle.

Grace had never felt so powerless. Olive needed a doctor, the doctor who should probably have seen her two days ago, but just then the wind blew the cloak worn by the cyclist and Grace saw a bright red lining.

'A nurse,' she shouted. 'Nurse, nurse,' she cried again as, her energy restored, she ran down the road to meet her.

The nurse had no breath left for talking but she handed Grace her medical bag and, her burden lightened somewhat, they reached the hostel together.

Miss Ryland was there to meet her. 'We sent for the doctor. Where is he?'

'You'll have to make do with me; I'm the district nurse, Nurse Stevenson, and Doctor's too busy. Now, if I could see the patient... Honey in hot water with maybe a splash of brandy is the best medicine for colds. I'm sure I didn't need to cycle out all this way. The call came right in the middle of my first-aid class.'

She was making her way up the steps and into the hostel, Grace following along behind, carrying the rather heavy and well-used medical bag.

Miss Ryland decided to be charming. 'We are sorry, Nurse, to tear you away from war work but we too are in the middle of the war effort and the health of our students is, naturally, our first priority. The girl is rather delicate and possibly should not have been accepted into the Land Army, especially in the middle of winter.'

She continued upstairs at the district nurse's side and Grace followed on behind.

Very few of the girls had an appetite for supper that evening. There was a roaring fire in the large room used as a dining room, and a delicious smell of roasting potatoes almost hid the mouth-watering odour of roasting apples, but the room, although filled with healthy and hungry young women, was unusually quiet.

The district nurse had taken one look at the shaking, sweating Olive and, with an angry, 'She should have been seen earlier,' sent her to the nearest hospital.

'Pleurisy?' the girls questioned one another. 'What's pleurisy?'

'Ask Grace Paterson. She were with her. What is it, Grace, something like pneumonia, maybe?'

Grace, who was chopping a roasted potato into tiny pieces but making no attempt to eat it, shook her head. 'Nurse didn't say. I think it's lungs but I've never heard of it. Really sore chest and difficulty breathing; Miss Ryland's gone with her.'

That news had a mixed reception. Most were pleased that the hostel manager had accompanied Olive to the hospital, but some were afraid that her doing so only proved how ill the land girl was.

Voices were raised in anger. 'She's one of the girls without a coat. We was promised proper clothing.'

'Only the latest intake's short, girls,' someone tried soothing frayed tempers. 'And the coats is promised.'

'Come on, ladies, look at the lovely supper,' another said. 'Eat up, that's real custard with them apples. Tomorrow's another day and we don't want no more getting sick now, do we?'

The muttering and grumbling died down as healthy appetites were appeased. Some looked round at the warm, comfortable room, with its fire, its benches and old sofas piled with cushions, the shining brassware on the walls, and reflected that, yes, the work was hard but the billet was a good one. A girl, possibly one who should not have been accepted for such arduous work, was sick, but she was receiving the best possible care. Tomorrow, they would learn even more and, one day, equipped with hard-won knowledge and experience, their lives would be even better.

Grace's dormitory was not so quiet that evening. Well aware of how early they had to be at work next morning, the land girls remained unable to settle down and sat up in their beds going over and over the events of the past few days. Only Grace and Betty Goode, the two most closely involved, were quiet. What was the point of talking and losing sleep? Olive was now receiving the best of care – no one, thought Grace, could have done more than Nurse Stevenson – but hospital staff surely had equipment not available to a district nurse.

The loud ringing of the alarm clock had them stumbling in complete silence to wash and dress as quickly as possible. The working day began after breakfast and Grace was delighted to find that a lecture on crop rotation had taken the place of an on-site class on ditch clearing.

'Great,' said Betty. 'Sitting in a nice, warm classroom has to be better than standing in freezing cold water, digging out who knows what. I found a sheep's head in a ditch once.'

Grace agreed with Betty but, after only a few minutes, she found that her attention wandered to the hospital bed where Olive lay. Was there anything she should or could have done earlier? If she had noticed Olive shivering, if she had insisted that the girl wear more underwear, if they had been given their promised heavy coats – would she now be lying in a hospital bed?

She pulled her wandering mind back to the lecture: wheat followed by potatoes ... or did potatoes follow wheat ... or did it matter?

'You didn't make many notes, Grace,' one of the roommates pointed out as they left the lecture.

'None that make any sense,' said Grace, looking at her lined notebook.

They linked arms and began to walk along to the dining room, where a fire was smouldering in the grate and mugs of hot Oxo or surprisingly strong tea were waiting on the long wooden table. Grace and Betty helped themselves to tea and moved away from the fireplace just as the door opened and Miss Ryland appeared. The room went silent.

Miss Ryland stayed near the door and looked around the crowded room. 'Would the women in room eleven please come to my office?' She moved as if to walk out, stopped, turned and with an unsuccessful attempt at a smile, said, 'Do bring your hot drinks.'

Grace and Betty, in the act of lifting their mugs, immediately replaced them and walked to the door, followed by their roommates. No one spoke as they headed for the manager's office.

It was not a large room: a smallish fireplace – where a meagre fire failed to defeat the chill – an enormous desk, two armchairs, a metal cupboard with a key in the door, and two folding chairs leaning against the wall. There was scarcely enough room for the land girls.

Miss Ryland surveyed them, avoiding direct eye contact, and, at last, straightened up. 'There is no easy way to say this, ladies, but the infirmary rang and ... Olive Turner died early this morning.'

Grace stood transfixed. Dead? How could Olive be dead? She had had cold feet. Her pre-war liberty bodice had been left at home as she had left off her childhood. She heard a voice ask loudly, 'Why?' and realised it was her own. The voice – her voice – went on: 'Why did she die? She caught a cold, a simple cold. Why did it suddenly become this pleurisy?'

The other land girls began to murmur and the murmurs rustled through the room like leaves falling from a tree. Miss Ryland appeared to take a deep, calming breath.

'We women of Britain are all in the army, soldiers fighting in our own way. In another time, it's likely that Miss Turner would not have been accepted into the Land Army. Yes, she had a cold, but it developed very quickly into pleurisy ... with added complications.'

The girls released a collective gasp, looking at one another in horrified disbelief.

Miss Ryland continued, speaking even more quickly, 'The hospital staff did everything they could, everything, but–'

Grace interrupted, 'We didn't. You didn't. You as good as killed her.' Grace could hear her own voice, strident, shaking with emotion. She wanted to stop but the voice – her voice – went on. 'You didn't listen. Why? Because–'

She got no further.

Betty Goode was there, holding Grace in her arms, explaining, making excuses.

'Enough. You are dismissed, except you, Paterson.'

Grace, feeling as if every ounce of strength had left her body, watched the others leave; some sent her sympathetic looks, others looked away as if perhaps afraid of being associated with her and her uncontrolled outburst.

For a time, Miss Ryland said nothing. Grace looked straight ahead. She remembered standing in terror in front of Megan and, before that, surely a long time ago, she had stood in an office like this one – but who had stood talking to her? No matter; pieces of memories came and went and they would perhaps come again and become clearer. She waited as the manager moved to the window, stood there looking out, returned, fiddled with some pencils on her desk. Several needed to be sharpened.

'I would throw you off the course if I could,

Paterson, but somehow you have made a better impression on Mr Urquhart, and he is likely to vote in your favour. Unfortunately, galling as it is, he has more clout.' She moved closer to Grace and stared into her face. 'Listen to me. You go to your room, stay there until teatime, say nothing to the other girls and, for the remainder of the course, keep out of my way, and maybe, just maybe, you'll pass. Now get out.'

Grace walked out, her legs trembling. Had she ever before seen such hatred in anyone's eyes? Megan had looked at her in annoyance but surely never with hatred. She stood for a moment at the foot of the staircase, holding on to the banister, and a small nervous giggle eventually escaped. Who on earth was her champion, Mr Urquhart?

Room 11 was empty. Grace walked over and sat down on her bed. Dead. One moment alive and the next dead. Poor, poor little Olive. Grace could not let Daisy Petrie go out of her life so easily. She got up, took out her notebook and quickly, without conscious thought, scribbled a note to Daisy:

Dear Daisy,
I'm all right. Tell everyone I'm sorry and please forgive me. Hope everyone is well.
G.

She had been thinking of a special Petrie as she wrote.

I'll tell them everything soon, Grace decided.

Having written at last, she felt a great weight had been lifted from her, and she stretched and looked around the room.

Next to her bed was Olive's, with its large pile of extra clothing donated by the others. Poor Olive did not need them now.

'Senseless not to take them back,' most of the others said when they returned to the room after tea. 'Who knows what kind of digs we'll get next month? Might well be grateful for an extra vest.'

Grace left her spare vest and thick stockings on Olive's bed, and sighed with relief when, somehow, a few days before graduation, they disappeared.

By the time the last day of the course came round, daffodils had sprung up all over the farm and a lilac tree near the front gate promised to burst into perfumed full bloom.

'Sorry I won't see that,' said Betty.

Grace and Betty were walking together towards the bus that was to take them to the nearest railway station, where they were to begin their first journeys as fully accredited land girls.

'Golly, Betty, I've done it – *we've* done it. Stupid, but sometimes I believed it was all too good to be true. We're land girls, qualified, and I can almost believe I smell lilac.'

'Happen there'll be plenty of lilac everywhere in the next few weeks,' a male voice interrupted them. It was George, the dairyman. 'I'm taking a heifer over to Bluebell Farm, ladies. Station's on my way, if you don't mind squeezing in.'

'Fantastic,' the girls chorused.

'Even prepared to squeeze in beside the heifer,' Betty said, laughing, but she was quick to scramble up in the front of the dependable old

41

Austin K3, beside Grace.

They drove in silence for a time and it was only when they were on the main road towards the town that George spoke: 'Nasty business over that lassie.'

Their euphoria evaporated and the girls nodded quietly.

'Learn us all to err on the side of doing too much too early rather than too little too late.' He leaned forward and wiped an imaginary speck off the inside of the window. 'Happy with your assignments? Together, are you?'

'Unfortunately, not,' Grace spoke first. 'Betty did really well and is off to a lovely farm in Devon. Me? I didn't cover myself in glory and so I'm off to some farm no one's ever heard of.' She did not add that her relief at the knowledge that she need never look at Miss Ryland again or hear her voice threatened to make her sick with excitement. She wanted to sing, to jump up and down with happiness, but it was impossible to do either at this precise moment.

George's emitting a sound that could possibly have been an attempt at laughter broke into her thoughts. 'Happen you've landed on your feet; you have friends, you know.'

'We all thought that, too, George,' said Betty, 'although she's hard to convince. There's a Mr Urquhart who's been in her corner more than once.'

'Aye. Thrawn bugger, Urquhart. Just be careful to pick your fights carefully, Paterson, and you, too,' he added, looking at Betty. 'Now here's station; out you get.'

The two land girls dropped down to the ground

and hurried to the back of the lorry to retrieve their suitcases. 'Thanks, George,' they said together.

'If you should see Mr Urquhart–' began Grace.

'Expect he knows already, lassie. Cheerio.'

He drove off, leaving the two girls standing looking after him.

'He couldn't be.' Grace continued to look until the dilapidated-looking lorry was out of sight.

Betty started to laugh. 'He could, you know. I bet you half a crown that he's your knight in shining armour.'

Grace shook her head. George was a kind and patient, if demanding, teacher, but a knight in shining armour...? There was no opportunity to dwell on it, though, as there was little time to spare before they caught their different trains.

'You will write, Grace?'

Grace promised, although even as she did, she remembered all the letters that needed to be written. *I will be better organised. I will keep in touch with Betty but, before I do, I will contact all my old friends.*

Only when she was seated in the railway carriage, which was for once not crowded, did she have time to think about her new posting. Miss Ryland had given her an unsatisfactory report and dismissal had been threatened. Mr Urquhart had intervened and, instead, Grace was being sent to a large estate that had only just requested government aid.

'Urquhart thinks you'll do us proud, Paterson,' Miss Ryland had said when she had told Grace of her new posting. 'It's a rather grand estate, owned by a real lord, not that anyone like you is

43

ever likely to be anywhere near him or his family. You're to be given quarters in the main house, somewhere off the scullery, I expect, so you'll feel right at home.'

Grace would not allow herself to be baited. She felt strongly that Miss Ryland was hoping that she would say something that would lead to dismissal but she would not give her the satisfaction.

How could she have taken me in so easily? Grace asked herself again. I thought she was a good, caring person.

Miss Ryland turned away abruptly, as if she preferred not to show her face, stood for a few moments, and then turned again, once more in control. 'You do understand the phrase "grand estate"? Not only is it the seat of a nobleman but also it is extensive. Unfortunately for you, his lordship encouraged the estate workers to enlist and he is now ... rather short of manpower. Possibly several qualified land girls will be assigned there in due course, but meantime, you, a few of his retired workers and whoever else can be found will be working the home farm – and possibly his other farms. Do you have the slightest idea what that means? A few elderly men and Grace Paterson, land girl, will be responsible for the year-round work of a large farm; not only your favourite tasks – milking docile cows and delivering that milk – but cleaning shit-filled byres, and real farming: preparing the soil, ploughing, sowing, feeding, weeding, harvesting. I'm sure you grew up in some mouse-ridden slum but have you dealt with rats, Paterson? And I've scarcely begun. Oh dear, you will be tired. Certainly, there will be no time for sticking your nose in where it's not wanted. Dismissed.'

Now Grace looked out of the window and heaved a sigh of relief. Despite everything, she had made it. She was a land girl and she was being sent to work on a farm. She could handle anything, including rats, she decided with a tiny shiver. Life could not possibly get better. The bubbles rose again and cavorted about in her stomach. This is the beginning of a fantastic new life, Grace, she told herself. Look forward to the future and try to remember only the good things about the past.

TWO

Bedfordshire, March 1940

She had never been so cold in her life. Grace stood in her pyjamas beside her abandoned bed and wanted nothing more than to climb back in. Where were her clothes? It was so dark that she could see nothing.

Don't panic, Grace, she told herself. You're standing beside the bed, and the chair where you put your clothes is... She bent down and felt along the bed until she came to the short iron foot rail. She turned round so as to be facing the head. 'Yippee,' she whispered through chattering teeth. She stuck out her right arm and followed its path till she stumbled against the easy chair that she had nicknamed Saggy Bottom the night before. Her clothes were folded up in a neat pile on the collapsed chair seat. She felt through them until she found her knickers and, as quickly as she could, pulled them on. Next, her thick – and blessedly warm – woollen socks. A cream WLA-issue Aertex shirt and a warm green jumper followed, and, last of all, her corduroy breeches. 'I hate you, silly breeches,' she said as she struggled with the laces at the knees. She had not yet mastered how to get the breeches on or off quickly. Under the door, she saw light shining in the corridor.

'Are you awake, Grace?' called a voice.

'Yes.'

The door opened and she saw a female figure. 'Welcome to Whitefields Court. If you didn't catch the name of the station, it's Biggleswade and we're in Bedfordshire.' She changed the subject very quickly: 'Why are you dressing in the dark?'

The woman did not wait for an answer but struck a match, which flared up for a moment, showing Grace someone probably the same age as her sister, but who was dressed exactly as Grace would be dressed if she could see to wash and finish dressing.

'Why haven't you got an oil lamp?' The woman sounded brusque but kind.

'It wasn't issued.'

A second match flared and the woman walked across to the little dressing table and lit the candle that sat there. 'There, now you can see your way to the lavatory. Don't be shy, girl. We all go. If you're downstairs in five minutes, you can have a cup of tea to warm you before the milking. Otherwise,

46

you'll have to wait till it's finished. Now scoot.'

Grace 'scooted'. Something about the voice suggested that the woman was used to being obeyed without question, and besides, Grace wanted a cup of tea, hot and sweet – well, that would be nice, but hot would do.

She had never washed and dressed so quickly in her life but, carrying her heavy WLA-issue boots, she fell into the kitchen no more than five minutes later. Mrs Love, the woman Grace had met the previous night – possibly the cook or housekeeper – was busy at the large, shiny kitchen range, and the woman who had been in Grace's room was leaning against the sideboard, smoking a cigarette. She looked Grace up and down. 'Give her some tea in a tin mug, Jessie, and she can drink it as we go.'

'Yes'm.'

Grace had never really believed that people actually said, 'Yes'm,' but that certainly seemed to be what Mrs Love had said.

'Don't gawp, Grace, frightfully rude. Now, bring your tea. She'll be back in time for breakfast, Mrs Love.'

Was there a warning note in her voice? Grace wondered, but she took the mug, thanked Mrs Love and followed the other woman out into the darkness. Biting cold hit her like a shovel.

'Where's your greatcoat?'

As Grace stumbled over her answer, the woman interrupted her. 'Don't tell me: wasn't issued. How does this country expect to win a war?'

Grace assumed, rightly, that her companion did not seek an answer to that important question; at least, not from her. She tried to gulp the hot liquid as she hurried, in the pitch-darkness, after her. Must be the boss one from the War Office, she thought. Never thought they'd be awake earlier than the workers, or even here at all. Maybe it's because it's my first day.

A large rectangular shape loomed up before them and a faint glow showed Grace that it was a building. Cows, she realised, lovely, lovely warm cows. Milking was never going to be her favourite job – whatever Ryland had said – but sitting with her head close to a cow's bulky side was warmer than being outside.

The woman from the ministry was as keen on cleanliness as George had been at the training farm. 'We have managed to avoid tuberculosis, foot and mouth, and God knows what other diseases these lovely silly animals get, Grace, and absolute hygiene is the key. There will be a clean overall on the door for you every morning and I will inspect your hands – sorry – until I know that I can trust you.'

'The dairyman at the training farm was a martinet.'

The woman laughed. 'Ah, old George, best man in the business. You can see that we don't yet have the new-fangled milking machine. Neither do we pasteurise, on this farm, partly because our local customers tend to want milk "straight from the cow". They like what they call "loose milk", not bottled, and we do the old-fashioned churns and jugs. As with you and your greatcoat, however, I'm assured that modern methods are on the way. Now let's get started.'

48

Grace looked: there had to be thirty or forty cows waiting patiently to be milked. The byre was full of the sweet smell of hay overlaid by another smell, familiar and not entirely unpleasant but certainly more pungent. She had smelled it often, if not quite so strongly, during her training. 'Ugh,' she said, and buried her nose in the warm side of the cow she was milking.

'All part of the fun of the farm,' said her companion. 'I'll start at the other end, but shout if you need help, and watch big Molly, third down; she loves to knock over the pail.'

Great, thought Grace. Is there going to be a cow on every farm whose joy in life is to kick the milk or me? First day: no breakfast yet, and a cow that plays football. But Molly gave her no trouble, as she worked her way steadily along her line. Eventually, she was side by side with the War Office lady and was troubled to see that she had milked at least five more cows than Grace herself had. Grace watched her surreptitiously, as they worked side by side. What beautiful hands she had. Her nails looked professionally manicured, just like her sister, Megan's, but better. She looked at her own work-worn hands and sighed.

'Problem, Grace?'

'No, miss. I have a school friend who's with ENSA and your fingernails reminded me of her.'

'These won't last long with milking. I should have cut them but hadn't time. And please don't call me "miss". I'm his lordship's daughter. Doing my bit, too. Call me Lady Alice. Now, can you find your way to the kitchen? Off you go. I can spare you for thirty minutes. Back here for deliveries as soon as.'

Grace hurried and her mind was working as quickly as her feet. She had been working beside an earl's daughter. When she did write, she would tell Daisy that. And she was just normal, she would say, slim and elegant, with really pretty brownish hair and the creamiest skin, and knew better than me how to milk. Imagine. War did strange things, did it not? Lady Alice had been wearing a land-girl's uniform, just like Grace's own, with the exception of that lovely warm coat. 'Doing my bit, too,' she had said.

Two men were eating breakfast at the long wooden table in the kitchen and Grace hesitated for a moment.

'If you're here for breakfast, Grace, sit down,' said the cook. 'I'm not handing it to you over there. They're only men, you know. They don't bite.'

One of the men laughed and Grace saw that he was quite young. 'Do join us,' he said. He gestured with his hand, as if to point out the size of the table. 'Sit down as far away from us as you like. We're the unpatriotic conchies.' There was a note of sarcasm in his voice. 'We're what's called non-combatants, but we're important, too, and we don't bite.'

Grace blushed and sat down but chose a chair not far from the older man's place. Conchies? Conscientious objectors. She had heard of these men, whose principles would not allow them to fight in the war. Surely, that did not make them unpatriotic.

'Hush, you, Jack. You're after scarin' the lass,'

the other man said. 'She only arrived last night and probably thought she was going to be alone. We're clearing the ditches, and happen you'll only see us at meals.'

Grace smiled at them tentatively. She was used to working-class men like the older man, but the tall, and somewhat aloof Jack, with his plummy voice, was rather different.

A plate was put before her and she forgot about the men as she looked at it. Bacon, two eggs, some fried potato and a thick slice of bread that had obviously been fried in the bacon fat. She wouldn't mind how much work she had to do if she was to be fed like this. 'Thank you,' she said, with some awe in her voice.

She could not help comparing this table with those in the training school. No named individual pots here, but two large bowls, one full of butter and the other of marmalade.

'There's tea in the pot,' the red-faced cook said as she returned to her range. 'Pour yourself some.'

Grace looked askance at the round brown teapot and wondered if she could lift it up and pour without spilling.

The older man spoke again: 'That slip of a girl'll never lift such a heavy pot. You're nearer to it, Jack, lad.'

Without a word, Jack poured Grace's tea. She was embarrassed to be the focus of so much attention, but she thanked the men for their kindness and began to eat.

For some time, no one spoke, and Grace wondered if it would be thought forward of her to start a conversation. At the training farm, everyone had talked all the time. Why should this farm be any different?

'Clearing ditches must be hard work.'

The men looked at her and then, without a word, reapplied themselves to their almost-empty plates.

The atmosphere in the room, never light, was now really heavy.

'Not hard enough for shirkers,' the cook said in an acidic tone.

The men stilled for a moment and then continued eating.

Grace took her courage in both hands. 'It's one of the most vital war jobs,' she said quietly. 'At the training farm, the lecturers told us that before 1939 more than half of Britain's food was imported. Now, our farmers are being told to double or treble their production, and if the ditches aren't cleared then the fields won't drain and crops will rot.'

Embarrassed, she gulped some tea and stood up to go. The cook stood, arms folded, and the look on her face told Grace that, once again, she had made a bad enemy.

'I'm Harry McManus,' said the wiry older man, standing up, 'and thank you, little champion. Young Jack Williams here was learning to be a doctor and save lives, even ones like 'ers,' he added with a nod towards the robust figure of the cook. 'I were a bus conductor before. Must say, I like being on a farm. How did you get into it?'

'You're all here to work, not chat over the tea-cups,' the cook said, reinforcing her position.

Grace smiled at Harry. 'I volunteered,' she

answered. 'I'm off to deliver milk,' she told the men as they moved together towards the door.

'If her ladyship hasn't froze to death waiting for you.'

Grace gasped and hurried out of the kitchen. Had she taken more than thirty minutes? 'Please, please...' she muttered as, hampered by her heavy boots, she tried to run.

Lady Alice was seated in the delivery lorry, and all she said as Grace climbed in was, 'There's an old coat of mine just behind you, Grace. It'll do for now, but I will ring up about your uniform one. As usual, they'll assure me that it will turn up one of these days.'

She had started the engine as she talked and they headed out of the farm.

'Thank you. I don't mind waiting, Lady Alice.'

'I mind. Wear the coat.'

They drove in silence, Grace going over and over in her head all the things she thought she should have been saying. Seeing Lady Alice in the uniform, albeit a uniform that had been made to measure from finer materials, had made Grace think of all the unwritten words describing her WLA uniform she had intended to write to her friend Daisy. She had intended to say it was smart and attractive. In fact, it was ugly, utilitarian and quite inadequate for winter conditions. Her shoes were extremely heavy: wearing them all day exhausted her and she often had blisters on her heels and her toes. But at least no one else had ever worn these clothes; they were hers.

'Cat got your tongue?' asked Lady Alice eventually. 'Relax, girl. Now, when we get to the village – which is called Whitefields Village, by the way – you take the measuring can, which is beside the churns in the back, fill it with milk, and then go to the first house. Knock, and if no one answers, walk in, the door will be open, and the housewife's measuring jug will be on the sideboard or the table. Fill it, come out and go to the next house. There will probably be one or two people up, having breakfast, getting ready for school or work. Just say, "Hello, I'm Grace," and you'll be fine. Any questions?'

'No, Lady Alice. Thank you for the coat.'

'"The labourer is worthy of his hire." Right, I'm stopping here. Coat first and then the milk.'

Grace stretched in the general direction of her employer's pointing finger until her hand met something soft. She grasped the material and pulled.

'You'll need two hands, Grace; it's bigger than you are.'

Grace pulled with both hands and, eventually, the coat gave up the fight and fell over into the front seat. Grace looked at it in awe. 'Lady Alice...' she began.

'It's twelve years old, Grace. I trust it will keep you warm until the Requisitions Department has its house in order. Now, for heaven's sake, girl, put it on and deliver the milk.'

The dark brown skin coat was fur-lined and very heavy. The weight surprised Grace as she struggled into it. It was so long that it reached nearly to her ankles and, initially, made walking rather difficult. Grace felt sure that, even if she were to lie down in the street wrapped in this wonderful coat, she would still be cosy and warm. The thought made her smile. 'But I'm not going to experiment,' she said aloud as she reached the first house. She knocked, opened the door and found herself in a small, dark room, where the smell told her that the fire had been banked up with potato peelings in a futile attempt to keep it burning until morning. She made out the shape of a jug on the wooden table top, filled it, and hurried out as quickly as possible. She had been brought up in poverty and the sight of it was just as depressing as it had ever been.

A gas mantle lit the next small house. A tired-looking woman was bending over the fire where a pot bubbled.

'Oh, thank you, miss,' said the woman with a smile. 'You're new. Where did the other girl go? Woman really, much older than you. I'd enlist myself if I didn't have three upstairs waiting on their porridge.' She stopped stirring and stood up. 'And another one on the way. There's the jugs. I take two lots on a Friday; get my sister's lads for their dinner.'

Grace filled the jugs, smiled at the woman, said, 'See you tomorrow,' and hurried back to the milk lorry.

'I should have warned you about Peggy; she'll talk your head off given half a chance. Nice woman and a good mother but we don't have time to chat. I suppose children are more difficult than animals because they certainly let one know when they're hungry. Not being a mother, I can say that animals are just as important. Does that shock you, Grace?'

There was no time for Grace to answer even if an acceptable answer had occurred to her. Megan had certainly thought anything and everything more important than the one child she was supposed to look after, but not everyone was as selfish as Megan.

Lady Alice knew the area well and effortlessly manoeuvred the lorry and its rapidly diminishing load up and down dark, narrow streets and alleys, until the last customer in the grey-stone village had been served.

'Can you drive, Grace?'

The question surprised Grace, who, eyes closed, was drifting into a doze.

'No, Lady Alice. I can ride a bicycle and I'm not afraid to dangle on the broad back of a shire, but that's as far as it goes.'

Lady Alice made a very unladylike noise. 'Should we ever need to deliver milk on horse-back, I'll remember your talents, but we really need someone who can drive. Otherwise, I will spend the rest of the war driving a milk float.'

Grace thought of her friends, Daisy and Rose Petrie. Both of them could not only drive but also maintain car engines. Their father and their brothers had taught them. 'Do none of the men drive, Lady Alice?'

'Just how many men have you seen on the estate, girl? Most of our young unmarried men enlisted after a rousing talk in the village hall. Saw them-selves coming home heroes, I think, God help them. The married men stayed. We have a few middle-aged farm hands with a wealth of know-ledge and experience between them, and several retired men who've come back. They live either on the estate or in the village and most work a full day. "Farm work keeps you fit", could well be a slogan. Not one has even driven a tractor.'

'The two men–' began Grace.

'Are you deaf? There are no...' Lady Alice paused, thought, and began again: 'Sorry, Grace, you mean the conscientious objectors. I'd forgotten about them. Like you, they have just arrived. Yes, they're men, and I suppose you're right and there's a good chance that the student one can drive. They are, however, supposed to cut down trees and dig ditches – very sensible use of a medical student, don't you think?'

Grace hoped she was not expected to answer that question, although there was something in Lady Alice's voice that made Grace wonder what her employer was thinking. She herself thought that a medical student would be more sensibly employed studying medicine, but who was she to say?

The pale grey light of early morning was beginning to spread itself across the sky. Grace sat up, anxious to get a proper look at the house where she was now living. The night before, she had been aware only of a huge mass at the end of a driveway that had to be longer than Dartford High Street.

'Golly,' she said as the great building revealed itself. Now she saw that the splendid sandstone building consisted of a magnificently proportioned central wing, standing proudly, and almost defiantly, between two other wings, which stood back from it a little, as if assuring the central building of its importance. The exquisite whole, its

57

many windows looking out over possibly hundreds of acres of gardens and rolling farmland, was in the style Grace was later told was Jacobean. As it was, she could only gasp and admire. 'That's one house, for one family. It's bigger than all the houses on our street stuck together.'

Lady Alice glanced across at her. 'Quite something, isn't it? One never really thinks about the house one lives in. Whitefields Court began as a monastery in the sixteenth century. My family was given it, and most of the land, villages etcetera around it, for reasons best left quiet, just before Henry the Eighth died.' She stopped in the driveway, as if to see the house better. 'Most of the land has been sold off, of course. Frankly, I'm never quite sure whether that was a good or a bad thing – being given the house, I mean, not selling the land or poor old Henry dying.'

'But it's beautiful.'

Lady Alice started the engine again and swept past the shining windows on the front, carrying on around the building to the kitchen entrance, where she parked. 'Beauty doesn't keep out rain. Right, out you get. Lunch is at one, in the kitchen, but now I want you to go to the tiled barn near the dairy. Bob Hazel, one of our senior men, is waiting there to show you the home farm and give you an idea of what will be expected of you. I'll see you in the dairy tomorrow morning.'

She raised a hand, either in dismissal or farewell, and walked off towards the rear entrance. Grace, conscious of the waiting Bob Hazel, hurried to the barn.

At first, she was sure the building was empty. It

was very quiet, peaceful really, and there was a pleasant smell of hay, although, from where she stood at the entrance, Grace could see no evidence of bales. 'Hello?' she called. 'Mr Hazel?'

'So, you're our land girl? Well, I'm not likely to make rude remarks about your size, knowing full well that small packages often hold the best presents.'

Grace stifled a laugh, for the old man who had appeared from behind a large container was scarcely an inch taller than she was and just as slender. The hand that gripped hers, however, was hard and strong. She looked into his face and saw strength there and tolerance.

Too fast, Grace. You judge too quickly and you're usually wrong.

'Good morning, Mr Hazel.'

'Hazel's fine, since I hear tell I even look like a nut.' He looked her up and down. 'Had much experience?'

'Four-week course, sir ... Hazel, and I once had a try at growing vegetables in the back garden.'

He was silent for a moment and Grace looked down at her booted feet.

'Come on then. I'll show you round. You'll get plenty learning here. How did your garden grow?' he asked with a little smile.

'Frost got some.'

'Happens.'

Hazel was a man of few words.

The next few hours left Grace both exhausted and stimulated. The home farm covered almost two thousand acres but the seemingly untiring Hazel assured Grace that she had not, as she

59

thought, walked every acre of it. She had seen vast neat acres of young crops, several fields that still had to be cleared and ploughed, grazing cows, hedgerows already in bud, trees that had to be hundreds of years old, ditches in various conditions, a fenced area where several pigs lay happily snoozing in the dust, a few cottages, each with its own well-cared-for garden, and a multitude of farm buildings, both ancient and modern.

'Somehow, we have to get most of the land into production, Grace. We've sold off or slaughtered most of our animals, but the cows are very important, and the pigs. I've got some hens in the garden and, if I have more eggs than me and the missus need, then I bring 'em up here. We grow wheat, potatoes, barley, beets...' He stopped talking, and Grace was saddened by the look on his face.

'When I started here, more than forty years ago now, this place was a paradise. We grew everything, even had peaches and melons. Ever had a peach, Grace?'

'Tinned, yes.'

'Then, believe me, you never tasted a peach. Off the tree, warm in your hand from the sun through the glass, you bites into it and the juice, sweetest juice you ever tasted, runs down your chin. Now we has to do basics and I hasn't got the manpower. If 'is lordship were 'ere, maybe we'd get more done faster, but Lady Alice works as 'ard as me, for all she's a lady. She has got us a tractor. She drives it, bless her, and is teaching me, and that will speed up ploughing. There's a new one ordered for you – a Massey-Harris. Know anything about them?'

'I can't drive.'

Hazel's thin face wrinkled with laughter. 'God love you, you don't drive this model, you guide it.'

Grace tried to smile. At least the sun was now shining and areas of the estate were absolutely beautiful; they had walked the length of a brook and seen masses of tiny yellow primroses and even clumps of pink ones. Grace had bent down in wonder to see these exquisite little flowers and wondered if she would be permitted to pick some for her room. She felt that somewhere, a long time ago, she had seen such carpets of spring flowers.

Couldn't have been Dartford, she told herself, although there were primroses on that farm I trespassed on with Daisy. She tried to bring back the memory that, annoyingly, hovered just out of reach, but Hazel's voice interrupted her. He was pointing to a small cottage.

'That's mine; me and the missus lives there. No electric yet, but we'll join the grid same time as the oldest part of the Court. Can't wait. We have in the back some rabbits, an' all, and I grows flowers in the front: roses mostly, but I love chrysanthemums; have a great show in the autumn.'

'I look forward to seeing them,' said Grace.

A look of doubt crossed the old man's face. 'I doubt you'll last, Grace. Too much work...' He stopped, as she was obviously about to argue with him. 'I can see you're a worker and, happen, we'll be able to get a bit done but, with the best will in the world, unless they send more land girls, or prisoners even, there's just too much work. His lordship expects to take in refugee families – plenty of rooms, but a lot of them are empty – and he hopes as some will be of help on the farms.'

61

'A place this size must need dozens of workers. Lady Alice said all the young men enlisted.'

'His lordship was called to the War Office and so we hardly see him now. He pops down of a weekend to give her ladyship a bit of company of her own sort but he's committed to the war effort. Probably shouldn't tell you, but the young man as Lady Alice walked out with enlisted as soon as war was declared and most able-bodied men around here did, too. Better chance of getting the service they wanted.'

'But farming's a reserved occupation.'

'And very dull if you're just doing it because it's a job. You has to be bred to it, I think. The young ones liked the uniforms, the chance to see the world. I were like that myself in the Great War and what I saw of the world was blood-soaked trenches. Best day of my life was the day the war ended and I could get back here.'

'And you've lived here all your life?'

'Apart from the war. Born here, like my father, my grandfather and as many greats back as we can name – happen as long as the earl's family. Backbone of England, we are. What more does a man need than a good wife, a good job and a decent employer?'

How wonderful to be so contented, Grace thought, as she listened to him.

'Where are the farm workers now, Hazel?'

'You'll meet them all when we has our dinner. I make up a work roster with Lady Alice every Friday evening and that tells us where we're supposed to be. Mrs Love can read and she has a copy in the kitchen.' He looked at Grace questioningly for a moment. 'You getting along all right with Jessie? She's a good woman, a widow woman, and 'er son went off to join the navy.'

To Grace, he sounded as if there might be some doubt about Grace's relationship with the cook. Grace did not want him to be concerned. 'Of course, Hazel, fantastic breakfast she made.'

He seemed happy with that answer. 'Good. She can be a tad snippy at times, worries about her boy, you see. Don't remember when she last heard from him.'

Grace nodded. She could understand that. But his remark reminded her that before another day dawned, she must sit down and write to her friends in Dartford. Why didn't she write letters? What held her back? Her friends would love to hear all about Lady Alice and Hazel, and even lovely old Harry and ... Jack. Grace found herself fascinated by Jack, his beliefs, his obvious education and culture, his voice, more like that of Lady Alice than of old Harry. The Petries, her friends? How often had the four of them vowed that they would be friends through thick and thin? And yet, she found reason after reason to avoid sitting down and writing letters.

'I'm ashamed of myself,' she said aloud, as Hazel went to check a field gate was fastened. 'All they gave me was happiness and a kind of security and I thanked them by leaving like a thief in the night. Surely, they won't forgive that.'

THREE

Grace had worked up a healthy appetite when they eventually returned to the house for dinner. Again, she looked at the mass of the building. So this part, the huge kitchen, the bedrooms above it, was contained in the oldest part of the great historical building. She shivered with delight. The history of England was all around her. She washed her hands in the deep stone sink in the scullery before walking, with Hazel, into the kitchen.

Bob Hazel greeted Mrs Love, who stood before the great iron range, stirring something appetising, and then he turned to the men who sat on either side of the long wooden table. 'This here's our land girl, Grace Paterson. She's not had much farming experience but was highly recommended and we're lucky to have her. Don't have to ask any of you to give her a hand when you see as it's needed.' He ushered Grace to the seat on his right. 'Sit yourself there, Grace, and I'll work down the table and back up t'other side. First, Walter Green, head dairyman and does pigs, too. Dave Semple, Esau Youngman and Maurice Fox, general farm work. There isn't anything they don't know about the land, so don't be shy of asking. Jack Williams and Harry McManus, you knows already; they're doing a grand job and we're all pleased they're 'ere.'

Did Grace detect a stern note of warning in the

older man's voice and, if so, who was he warning?

Three of the four men whom she had not met before appeared to her to be older. Each one had to be fifty at the very least but, like Hazel himself, had a look of physical strength. The dairyman, Walter Green, who nodded to her with a shy smile, was younger, but he too looked so healthy that it was difficult to calculate with any real accuracy.

No one spoke while Mrs Love put a large plate of thick vegetable soup in front of each person. In the middle of the table were two round crusty loaves, which Hazel cut into thick slices. Grace was delighted to see a plate of golden curls of fresh butter; someone, probably Mrs Love, had made a real effort to make the table appealing. She remembered her arrival at the nearest station where she had surrendered a half-coupon for a sandwich that was spread with butter. Mrs Love, however, had taken her ration book without comment. Happily, Grace helped herself to a piece of the fresh bread when the plate was passed to her. After the soup, almost a meal in itself, came a dish of minced sausage meat, onions and dumplings. This too was tasty. They finished with tea and a slice of sponge spread thinly with marmalade.

Grace was to be very glad of the filling meal as, immediately after dinner, she spent two hours weeding a field of young corn. Hazel gave her a short hoe called a paddle, explained how to use it, reminded her that she needed to be back at the milking parlour at half-past three for the afternoon's milking and left her alone. She stood at the edge of the seemingly endless acres of corn and looked around. Row upon row upon row stretching out on all sides. She had a fantasy that she would become lost in the field and never be seen again.

'Well, you'll jolly well have to be found by three thirty, Grace Paterson,' she told herself, 'or Lady Alice will be looking for you.'

She spat on her hands as she had seen Hazel do and began. Some time later, her complaining back forced her to stop. She yelped in pain as she forced herself to straighten up. A quick glance at her watch told her that she had thirty-five minutes to find her way back to the byre, where at least thirty cows would be waiting for her. She longed to be sitting down, her head pressed close to the warm side of a healthy cow.

'I have never been so tired in my entire life,' she said aloud, and was startled to hear her voice in the vast stillness. All afternoon she had heard nothing but the sound of her paddle raking the weeds from around each plant, and the occasional hum of a flying insect.

Grace looked down the row she had been weeding. She was distressed to find that she was scarcely more than halfway along. Did her schedule state that she should return to her weeding after the milking or was she involved in a second milk delivery? If so, when was she supposed to weed the field? The days were growing longer. She could weed before tea, and after, too, she supposed. Apart from the ache in her lower back, Grace had felt only happiness as she weeded in the soft spring air, but now a frightening vision of weeds growing faster than one girl could pull them out stretched before her. Hazel would be angry – had he not already said the work would be too much for her? And what would Lady Alice say?

'You look tired, Grace,' was what she did say when Grace met her in the dairy. 'Weeding can be hellish but, on a brighter note, believe me, it would be so much worse if you were taller.'

'Yes, Lady Alice.' Grace replied without thinking, but Lady Alice merely walked to the head of her line of healthy cows and began to work.

For the rest of the afternoon there was no noise apart from the swishing sound made by the milk as it was directed into the pails, the shuffling of hoofs, the constant chewing from the animals and the clatter of filled pails being moved around on the stone floor.

At last, all the cows were milked.

'We'll drive them down to the east field, Grace. Walter will take over in here. How much of the weeding did you get done? Finish a line?'

Grace felt a blush of shame spread across her face and was surprised to hear Lady Alice laugh.

'Poor Grace. I'm teasing. Two of the men are already there. Get yourself a cup of tea and then give them a hand until dinner.'

What did she mean? They had had dinner hours earlier.

'Tea, Grace, the evening meal,' said Lady Alice, who had obviously correctly interpreted the puzzled look on her land-girl's face. 'My family talks about breakfast, lunch and then dinner, with afternoon tea, of course, between lunch and dinner. Don't worry, you'll learn a great deal more here than how to poleaxe a pig. Go on, girl, a cup

of tea will revive you and there's a piece of chocolate, not much, in the pewter beer mug on the
right-hand side of the mantelpiece; help yourself.'

Chocolate. When had she last treated herself to
some chocolate? Just the thought of it was making her mouth water. Grace hurried off to the
kitchen and was delighted to find it empty. As
always, the heavy teapot was on the hotplate,
together with a spluttering kettle of boiling water
for those who preferred a weaker brew. Above it
on the carved stone mantel stood a very old and
very large beer mug. Had Lady Alice been teasing or was there indeed a delicious treat inside?

She reached up and took down the beer mug.
She lifted the lid, looked inside, and, yes, there at
the bottom lay something in a paper wrapping.
Tentatively, Grace put her hand in and pulled out
the paper. She smelled it. Chocolate. What did
she want it to be? Cadbury's Whole Nut, Milk
Chocolate, or their Coffee Cream, or, no, even
better, Duncan's Hazelnut? She unfolded that
paper to find two sections of Barker and Dob-
son's Fruit and Nut.

'And just what do you think you're doing?'

The unexpected voice surprised Grace so
much that she flinched, dropping the chocolate
almost into the fire.

Mrs Love was glaring at her and for a second
Grace quailed before her. She shook off her fear,
bent down and picked up the chocolate. 'I was
helping myself to her ladyship's chocolate to have
with my tea but, as it happens, I loathe fruit and
nut.' She dropped the chocolate and the paper
into the waste bin that stood under the sink and

walked out of the kitchen without another word.

Her bravado lasted until she got outside and then her legs started to tremble. 'I've done it again,' she muttered. 'I am really good at annoying people. Where will I end up this time?'

As she walked quickly back towards the cornfield, Grace fought back tears as the realisation hit her that she did not want to leave this place, that already she liked Hazel and Lady Alice, even if she did have her dinner at teatime.

To add to her feelings of isolation, it started to rain and, by the time she reached the field, the rain was so heavy that she could barely see. She had learned on the training farm that 'inclement weather' was not an acceptable excuse for stopping working and so she tried to count down the rows to see where she had started and where she had left her paddle.

'It's here, love.' One of the older men had appeared out of the deluge.

Grace, trying desperately to remember which one he was, took the paddle and thanked him.

'Esau Youngman,' he said. 'Easy to remember – I'm oldest.'

Grace laughed and a smile lit up his craggy features. 'A bit easier in the rain. Very devil to dig out when frost's on the ground. Why don't you finish this row and I'll do next?'

Esau worked so quickly that soon Grace could see only a vague outline as he moved rapidly along his row. She tried to copy his action but missed the weed completely and decapitated the plant.

'Damn.'

She tried again and hit her own shin. She

winced and decided that she could not become a master weeder on her first attempt. She was surprised, however, to find that the more she worked, the more efficient she became. She did hit her legs now and again but, when she did hit the corn, it was no more than a glancing blow from which the plant seemed to recover. The afternoon and the rain went on. She finished her first row, quite happy with her accomplishment, and looked for her companion. His rhythmic movement had taken him several rows down the field.

Grace was now absolutely wet through. She did have a waxed hat but her hair had slipped out and was plastered to the side of her face. She had taken off her gloves so as to hold the paddle more securely and her hands were so cold and wet that they were painful. Still the rain went on. Still Esau worked methodically along the rows.

He's an old man, Grace told herself, must be all of sixty, and look at him. He's wetter than I am and not a complaint. And look at all the rows he's done and I'm only on my second.

She wiped her hand across her wet face – her handkerchief was soaked – and gripped her paddle.

'Grace, call it a day. Time for a hot cuppa.' Esau had stopped weeding and was making his way back towards her.

'I can't stop, Esau. I've barely begun.'

'You're wet through, girl, and you'll be no use to anyone if you're sick. Jessie'll have water ready for baths. It's near teatime. Come on.'

When she hesitated, Esau grabbed her hand and pulled her. 'Use your head, girl. There's no

70

one on this estate, from his lordship all the way down to me, as would expect you to work in this. We've already done a good day's work and you were milking too. Now run, the weeds and all their relatives'll be there tomorrow.'

They ran as best they could through mud that gripped at their boots, and arrived at the kitchen door looking as if they had been swimming through mud. Mrs Love met them and, to Grace's surprise, it was Esau she scolded. 'Get you to the fire to dry, Esau Youngman, you old fool. Always first out last in, and you, Grace, away and have a hot bath before I put the tea on the table.'

Grace turned to leave but Mrs Love stopped her. She looked ill at ease and hesitant but, eventually, she said, 'I spoke to Lady Alice about the chocolate. I'm sorry; sometimes my tongue gets away from me. I won't be so quick in future.'

'That's all right.' Grace had never had an apology from anyone before and was slightly embarrassed, unsure of what to say.

She was more embarrassed when she reached her room and found the latest copy of the popular magazine *Woman's Own* lying on her bed, and a sixpenny bar of Cadbury's Whole Nut chocolate lying on her pillow. Grace picked up the chocolate and smelled it. Lovely. It had to be from Mrs Love; a peace offering perhaps. She would insist that Mrs Love share it. Still sopping wet, she leafed through the magazine of stories, knitting patterns and handy hints, and vowed to read it as soon as tea was over.

She grabbed her towel, some dry clothes, and hurried off to the bathroom. She had it all to herself since no one else appeared to live in this part of the house, but surely that would change when other land girls arrived.

A notice on the wall above the huge bath with its great feet, not unlike those of a primeval monster, warned the bather to use only as much hot water as was absolutely necessary. Grace, who was beginning to thaw, thought that to lie in this enormous bath with hot water covering her all the way to her chin, would be the ultimate luxury, but having no idea of who might need a bath – what if Lady Alice herself hoped to soak? – abandoned all her dreams of hedonism and resolved to measure the water she allowed to flow into the bathtub. It was so large and so deep that after several minutes of flowing from the taps, the depth of water measured scarcely what the law allowed.

Grace undressed and sat down in the water, admiring the bruises on her legs. *What will my poor legs look like by Sunday?* Sitting in hot water was delightful, but the air around her shoulders was cold. She allowed the water to flow again and then, luxury of luxuries, lay down and found that the hot water, limited as it was, did indeed cover much of her. She lay there lazily until the water began to grow cold and then she sat up abruptly and began to scrub herself with her face cloth and the tiny square of carbolic soap she found on the soap tray. The smell reminded her of something and she shivered.

A bath somewhere else and I didn't like it – because of the soap? Grace put the fragment of soap back on the tray that was stretched across the bath, and stood up. As she rubbed herself dry, she thought of many things. There was so much of her early life that she did not know and she determined to find out as much as she could. She would ask Megan. 'Damn.' Again she spoke out loud; she had not written to Megan either. Not, she felt sure, that Megan was at all concerned, but Grace had to write to friends first.

She dressed, but not in uniform as she was off-duty. Her green-and-white-striped short-sleeved dress was one she had bought just before she left Dartford. She had thought it perfect for any social occasion at the training centre: the attractive matching bow that filled the neckline could be removed, leaving a small area of exposed skin.

Quite daring, she had decided at the time. She did not remove the tie now, however, as she felt tea was not really a social occasion.

She had expected to see the farm workers in the kitchen, but only Esau, Harry and Jack were there. Jack stood up as she entered.

What a surprise. She had seen men stand up when a woman entered a room but no one had ever stood up for Grace Paterson. She was thrilled and smiled at him as she sat down.

'Did you have a nice bath, Grace?' It was Mrs Love. She put a plate, with two large baked potatoes and a heap of grated cheese in front of Grace and smiled somewhat nervously.

Grace realised that what she said and did next was important. It was possible that she might be asked to remain on this farm for the duration of the war. Life would be unpleasant if she and the cook could not get on with each other.

'It was super, Mrs Love, the biggest bath I've

ever seen in my life. And a *friend*–' she stressed the word and hesitated for a moment before continuing – 'a *friend* gave me a bar of chocolate.' She looked at the hungry men sitting waiting patiently at the table. 'It's big enough for us to have a piece each with our cuppa.'

Mrs Love smiled and looked as if she was about to speak, but Harry spoke first. 'I thought I saw the postman's bike. So you've got a sweetheart somewhere, young Grace. Happen he'd like you to eat all of it, thinking of him with every delicious morsel. Young Jack here read something the other day about introducing sweet rationing. Being talked about, isn't it, lad?'

Jack did not answer and it was Esau who broke the silence: 'Can't have a bit of her chocolate before I have my tea. Was them venison sausages I saw coming out of the freezer, Jessie? That'll be a right nice treat and good for us an' all, my late wife always said. Scotch, she was, an' that's where venison comes from. Ever had it afore, lad?' he asked Jack, but carried on talking without waiting for an answer. 'His lordship has a place in Scotland. That'll be where this comes from.'

Mrs Love had been filling plates that she put down in front of each of them. She had served them at dinnertime, too. She did not sit down to eat with them but stayed near the great range, fussing with the fire and the enormous blackened kettle that sat on a hotplate. 'I do have venison sausages for tomorrow's dinner, Esau, and, yes, a friend of his lordship brought a box down for the house. Last year's culling, of course, but they're better, having been fed on grass all year. They're

74

like cows and sheep: need a hand from farmers during the winter.'

Perhaps the short lecture on animal husbandry was too much for the hungry workers gathered around the table because, for a time, the scraping of a knife on a plate or an occasional cough were the only sounds that disturbed the silence.

Mrs Love turned to Grace and Jack. 'Were you thinking it odd that we keep meat in a freezer and yet much of this great estate is still not on the National Grid? We have several generators and, believe you me, the earl is as anxious as anybody to get rid of them. His lordship has offered to house refugees. He – and Lady Alice, naturally – are aware that there are many unused rooms in this magnificent old house. The displaced of Europe will be made welcome, and with freezers, they hope to be able to feed them adequately.'

'The others not eating with us, Mrs Love?' Grace's voice sounded loud in the large room.

'The others go home at teatime, Grace. Esau eats his main meals here, but you do your own porridge of a morning, don't you, Esau?' Mrs Love turned to the older man.

'I could do my own tea, too. Not so well as you cook, Jessie, but I was learned to make a good barley soup.'

Silence fell again.

At last, when the atmosphere was becoming oppressive, Harry spoke: 'Saw you in the corn-field today, Grace. Weeding's a never-ending job.'

Grace smiled. 'Like ditching.'

'I like it better than the buses. Good fresh air, no difficult passengers, and young Jack here to explain things; nothin' this lad don't know.'

Jack was clearly embarrassed. 'Don't know a thing about buses.'

'Can you drive, Jack?' Grace had remembered her early-morning conversation with Lady Alice.

Again he seemed ill at ease. Could he be embarrassed by his obvious advantages?

'Sorry, Jack, I don't mean to be nosy; it's just that Lady Alice needs someone to help her drive the milk lorry.'

'If you've all finished eating, pass the plates down to the end of the table. The tea is ready and there's a box of biscuits. It's Jacob's 1940 Assorted but it's never been opened; two each.'

The question of Jack's driving ability was shelved. Grace drank her tea and took one digestive biscuit when the tin was passed to her. Mrs Love was correct. Even though the biscuits had been in the box for some time, they were still crisp.

Esau drank two cups of tea and ate his allotted biscuits very quickly and then stood up, wiping his mouth with his hand. 'I'm off home and I'll see you all tomorrow. Weeding the corn, Jessie?'

Mrs Love nodded but got up and walked him to the door.

Grace stood up, said, 'Good night' to the two men, who were still drinking tea. She was not expected to wash dishes and so intended to go to her room, write at least two letters, and then fall into an exhausted sleep.

'I've put a pig in your bed, Grace.' Mrs Love was in the hall.

For a moment, Grace was puzzled. A pig? And then, realising, she started to laugh. 'Thank you,

Mrs Love. It's not really cold but that was very kind of you.'

'We don't want you catching cold on your first day with us,' said the cook, and disappeared into the scullery.

Grace hurried up the uncarpeted backstairs and then along a linoleum-covered corridor to where the carpeting started – the dividing line between the servant areas of the great house, she thought, and the family part. That meant that she, Grace Paterson, land girl, was in the family quarters. Would that change when the several other land girls they were expecting arrived? As she opened the unlocked door of her room, she wondered idly where Jack and Harry slept and then rapidly pushed all such thoughts out of her mind.

First, she looked for her pig. She laughed when she saw its outline under the covers. What a woman of contrasts Mrs Love was: touching kindness one minute and grouchy martinet the next. Grace pulled back the covers to see the pig, the fat earthenware bottle that, filled with hot water, was used to warm cold sheets, or feet.

Megan didn't use pigs, certainly not for me. I don't remember one in the house at all.

Once again, she was beset with the annoying feeling that a distant memory was hovering just out of reach. 'Who did give me a pig?'

Unable to drag up the memory, Grace hurried to undress and, then, once she was washed and ready for bed, she took a new writing pad, which she had bought at the station, and climbed into bed. Yes, buying Basildon Bond paper and envelopes had been the right thing to do. She wrote her new address and the date and then sat back to think about how to write the letter. She could make Mrs Petrie smile by telling her that she had been given a hot-water pig. 'Imagine,' she could almost hear Mrs Petrie say, 'it's so cold where Grace is, she needs a hot-water bottle.'

At last, Grace was really ready and the words flowed across the lovely blue paper:

Dear Mrs Petrie,

I am so sorry that I did not tell you that I had joined the Women's Land Army. I wanted to do more for the war effort than file pieces of paper but it was wrong not to tell you and Mrs Brewer who have always been so good to me. Why the Land Army? I don't know exactly but I just felt that it was the right place for me. Megan never told me anything about our family but sometimes I seem to remember being in a field and being happy. Silly, I suppose. As you can see, I'm in Bedfordshire. I was sent to a training place in Kent, not really so far from you.

She stopped writing, wondering how to tell Mrs Petrie about Miss Ryland and poor Olive, and decided to skim over the training experience.

The four-week course is over and here I am, the only land girl on this farm. More are coming and there are some real farm workers and two other men. There's a cook, Mrs Love, and there's Lady Alice, whose father owns the place. She helps with the milking, would you believe? Even drives the lorry and would Sally ever be jealous of her beautiful fingernails!! Please tell Daisy and Rose where I am. I hope they are both well and

*that the boys are safe and sound. I'll stop now to write
to Mrs Brewer. Thank you for everything.*

She signed it and put the sheet in an envelope,
which she addressed quickly, as if afraid that if she
did not do it at once, she might not do it at all. Her
letter to Mrs Brewer was almost an exact copy and
that too was quickly put in an envelope and sealed.
She would worry about stamps in the morning.

Feeling as if an enormous weight had been
lifted from her shoulders, Grace turned off the
small bedside oil lamp that had been put in her
room at sometime during the day, lay down and,
within a few minutes, was fast asleep.

FOUR

A loud ringing woke Grace and, for a moment,
she could not remember where she was. Then she
threw back her covers and got out of bed. A quick
glance at the clock, which had stopped ringing,
told her that she had better hurry, or 'scarper', as
Mr Petrie used to say.

She *scarpered* and, less than fifteen minutes
later was in the kitchen, hoping for a hot cup of
tea. There was no sign of Mrs Love, but Jack
Williams appeared through the scullery door.

'Tea's ready, Grace, and I'll be going along with
you on the milk run this morning. Have to learn
the route.'

'So you do drive.'

'I don't very often, but I can.'

She turned away from him in annoyance. Had he just corrected her grammar, pompous oaf?

'I've made you angry and I didn't mean to. My father's an English teacher, and my sister and I used to try to be one-up all the time. Wasn't your family like that?'

'No,' she answered shortly, and made to push past him.

'Miss Paterson, I apologise. Please allow me to pour you a cup of tea.'

Grace walked back towards the range. 'I can pour it for myself, thank you.'

'Actually, you can't. Sorry, Grace, I've just made it and it's heavy, even for me.'

She nodded and mumbled her thanks. Jack carried the large teapot over to the table and filled two cups. 'Going to be a lovely spring day. Harry's sure there'll be blossom on the apple trees in a few days.'

'Cows wait for no man.' Mrs Love had come in. 'You hear Jack's going along this morning, Grace? Her ladyship will pick him up and let's hope he's got that trench dug or there'll be flood water all over the side lawn.'

Jack gulped his tea and set his cup down. 'Thank you,' he said to Mrs Love, although he had both made the tea and poured it. 'Later,' was directed at Grace as he left.

'My Tom wants to learn to drive.'

'I'm sure he will.'

'But that coward got all the chances, didn't he?'

Grace really did not want to become involved. Besides, what did she know about either conscientious objectors or Jack Williams, who had a sister and whose father taught English? 'I really don't think conscientious objectors are cowards, Mrs Love.'

'Then why isn't he in the Forces like my Tom?'

So they were discussing Jack Williams and not conscientious objectors. 'They don't believe in killing people.'

'Neither does my Tom,' said Mrs Love, 'except Germans, of course. He wants to kill lots of them.'

Grace felt very, very cold. She put down her cup. 'Golly,' she said, as if she had just realised the time. 'I'm due in the milking parlour. Sorry, Mrs Love; I have to dash.'

She was glad to be out in the lovely cool spring air and ran all the way to the milking parlour, dashing through the door just after Walter Green.

'Dammit, woman, don't scare my milkers.'

'Sorry.'

'Scrub your hands and then the udders.'

Grace hurried to obey. Carbolic soap again. When the war was over, she would never use anything but the finest, perfumed soap. Lady Alice had not arrived and, after she had milked three cows, Grace began to worry that she might have to milk the entire herd – *I'll never get the milk delivered if I'm on my own* – but then she saw that Walter was milking the cows on the other side. She relaxed and it seemed that so too did the cows. Not even the feisty ones gave her any trouble but stood patiently while they were being milked and made no attempt to kick either Grace or her pails.

'We'll take them down to the buttercup meadow and then we can have breakfast.'

A meadow full of buttercups sounded lovely and Grace looked forward to seeing it as she walked along with Walter, helping him guide the lumbering cows.

They reached a vast field, where several enormous trees grew. A thick hedge on which there were already signs of blossom divided the buttercup meadow from its neighbour but, to Grace's disappointment, there was not a spot of golden buttercup anywhere.

'You don't know much about the country, girl,' said Walter, after he had explained the life cycle of several wild flowers. 'This time next year, you'll be amazed by what you know.'

'I hope so,' said Grace, and they walked up to the house to join the others in the kitchen.

With the exception of Esau, everyone was present. But no, on looking round, Grace saw that Jack was missing, too. She wondered where he was and found herself hoping that he would get some breakfast, but then she reminded herself that whether or not Jack Williams had breakfast was none of her business.

She sat down between Walter and Harry. Mrs Love carried over a large iron pot that she put on a heavy brass trivet. She lifted off the lid to reveal thick, creamy porridge. It was so hot that little bubbles kept popping up on the surface.

'Porridge with cream this morning. That'll set you all up till dinnertime.'

Grace stirred the pot of porridge, watching until tiny bubbles broke the surface. She could hear Megan moving about upstairs.

82

'Come on, come on,' she badgered the contents of the pot, for a hot steaming bowl of porridge must be on the table when Megan came down for breakfast.

The teapot? Had she poured boiling water in to warm it? The generous spoonful of fragrant tea leaves was ready beside the teapot. Megan liked a good strong cup of tea and never seemed to run short. To give her credit, her older sister was perfectly happy for Grace to enjoy the tea, too.

Not for the first time, Grace wondered why her sister had given her a home in the first place.

'You all right, Grace? You've gone all funny.' Mrs Love was standing with a deep white bowl of porridge in her hand, waiting for Grace, who seemed to be in a daze of some kind, to take it. 'Didn't I tell you yesterday...'

Mrs Love did not finish whatever it was she was about to say because Jack had arrived and, seeing the commotion, had gone to Grace's side and was holding her wrist in his slim brown fingers while he looked at his watch.

At his touch, Grace started up, saw Jack holding her hand, and blushed furiously. She tried to pull her hand away but he tightened his grip so that she winced.

'I'm taking your pulse, Grace; you're fine. Probably, she just needs to eat, Mrs Love.'

Without another word, he moved away to sit beside Harry. Mrs Love continued to serve porridge. 'She went all funny,' she said, angrily, as she practically slammed a bowl down in front of Jack.

'I'll be with her on the milk run this morning

and I'll keep an eye on her. Nothing to worry about.'

Grace felt like bursting into tears. She had no idea what had happened, just that she had remembered something that had already swum away from her; something about porridge – but what? She felt stupid and was so embarrassed to find the others looking at her with concern. They quickly turned back to their breakfast bowls, when she looked at them and, for a time, there was no sound but the clinking of spoons and the pouring of tea.

Grace was first to finish.

'You should tell her ladyship you've had a turn,' said Mrs Love. 'If she's got him with her–' she jerked her head in Jack's direction – 'she might get by without you this morning.'

Grace tried to smile. 'It's nothing, really, Mrs Love. I'm so sorry to have been a nuisance.'

She picked up Lady Alice's coat and walked off towards the milking parlour.

Jack caught up with her before she had gone less than halfway. 'Feeling better?'

'Yes, thank you.'

'Good. Lady Alice terrifies me.'

Grace stopped in mid-stride. 'Why? She's working as hard as we are and she loaned me this coat.'

'Perhaps that's why I'm petrified. She's destroying all my preconceived ideas.'

They walked on and, just before they reached the milk lorry, Grace laughed. 'I don't know what you're talking about.'

'Nice laugh,' said Jack, and Grace felt herself blushing again, but this time, in the nicest possible way.

'You drive, Jack, and I'll give directions. 'Fraid that means you'll have to squeeze in behind, Grace.'

Grace, who had feared being stuck in the lorry with the heavy milk churns, was quite happy to squeeze into the back of the cab. Nothing could fall on her in this tight space.

Her worry that Jack would say something about her behaviour at the table was unfounded. On the way to the village Lady Alice told them that the next day they would also be expected to collect the milk money.

'It's quite simple: four pence halfpenny per pint multiplied by number, and two pence farthing the half-pint. Most of the villagers have it ready with the jugs. Usually, they're honest, but do a quick check.'

For the first time, Grace was thankful that she had spent so much time in offices. She could add, subtract, multiply and divide with the best of them.

'Any difficulty with that, Grace?'

'No, Lady Alice.'

'Ten times four pence halfpenny?'

'Three and nine pence.'

'Bravo. I won't insult you by asking you to divide farthings.'

'I liked arithmetic. We had a dragon for a teacher and, every Friday morning, she used to write a circle of numbers on the board and then she'd yell questions at us, and in no order so you couldn't work it out ahead, if you know what I mean. Some of us were pretty thick but we all learned to count.'

'Fascinating.'

The tone with which the word was uttered made Grace want to curl up. Instead, she closed her eyes, knowing perfectly well that if they turned round, the two in the front could still see her even if she could not see them. She made a rather childish vow never to speak to Lady Alice again.

The only sounds in the lorry before they arrived in the village were rather distressing noises from the engine and the occasional clunk as churns brushed against one another. The lorry drew to a halt. Grace and Jack got out and walked around to the tailgate, so as to reach the milk. For a slender man, Jack was surprisingly strong. It took two men to lift the churns on as a rule and, although Jack asked for Grace's help with the largest churn, he appeared to lift the smallest one easily.

'Which side, Grace?'

Grace shrugged and filled her jug. She sniffed and moved quickly away to the first house.

Jack was waiting for her as she finished.

'Are you all right, Grace? I can easily do the round if you're not feeling well.'

Grace was determined to pull herself together. 'I'm fine, Jack. I just feel stupid.' She looked in the jug, to make sure she had enough milk, and went off next door. When she came out, Jack was beside the lorry and Grace could see Lady Alice in the cab, looking at a piece of paper.

'Let me fill that for you.' Jack moved as if to take Grace's jug and she pulled it back, and somehow it fell, smashing into several pieces.

'Blast.'

Grace shouted so loudly that Lady Alice opened the door and looked out.

'It's only an old jug, Grace. Pick up the bits without cutting yourself and get another one. There should be several in the back.'

'Yes, Lady Alice.' Grace bent down, picked up the pieces and put them in a small heap beside the tailgate.

'Brush up the tiny bits, girl; there are barefoot children in this village.'

'Yes, Lady Alice.' Grace found the broom and the shovel in the lorry and did as she had been told, then took a larger jug and filled it with milk.

'Yes, Lady Alice, yes, Lady Alice,' Grace muttered to herself. 'Damn it, I wasn't going to speak to her again.' She realised immediately that she was being rather silly and felt even sillier when she heard Jack trying to stifle laughter as he filled his jug. She did her next deliveries efficiently and returned to the lorry to refill the jug, handing over the milk money given to her by one of the customers who would not be at home on the next morning. 'One and three pence halfpenny from Miss Shield. She's short a farthing...'

'...but will pay next week,' Lady Alice finished for her. 'If I had all the farthings out of which that seemingly charming old woman has diddled my family, I would be spending the winter months in the Bahamas, Grace. The winters after the war, of course.'

The deliveries completed, Jack drove the lorry back to the estate. Lady Alice sat in the passenger seat and Grace, once again, was squeezed in behind.

'Are you fearfully uncomfortable?' asked Lady Alice, who did not wait for an answer but carried on: 'It's perfect that you're not too tall, isn't it? I had a dear chum at school, taller than my father, poor girl. She could never have squashed down like you.'

The words 'I had a very tall friend at school, too' popped onto the tip of Grace's tongue and she felt so proud because she managed to swallow them. Lady Alice would have no interest in the Rose Petries of this world. There, of course, she wronged Lady Alice.

'Back to ditches for you, I'm afraid, Jack,' said Lady Alice when she had pulled up outside the front door of the main house, 'but it's going to be so useful to have another driver about the place. If you do Mondays and Saturdays from now on, and the occasional extra day when I have to be in two places at once, then I can manage the other mornings. Reasonable?'

'Absolutely, m'lady.'

Lady Alice jumped down lightly from the driver's seat and began to walk towards the door. Before she reached it, she turned. 'No harm in teaching Grace either; just make sure she doesn't crash.'

Grace and Jack watched Lady Alice until the door closed behind her.

'She didn't mean that?'

'Of course she did,' said Jack. 'If it makes you feel better, think of it as another task the upper classes can inflict on you. If you can drive, she won't have to hire a driver.' He looked into her face. 'What a bundle of doubts you are, pretty little

Grace. She's a decent human being. Look at the way she treats Harry and me.'

'This morning, you said she terrifies you,' Grace said, and was pleased that he looked uncertain. 'Besides,' she went on, 'you're almost a doctor and you can drive.'

'Yes, and she wonders why I'm not driving ambulances at the front instead of digging ditches in Bedfordshire. Come on, we'd best get this back and the churns cleaned before we start the day's work.'

Without waiting for Grace to say anything else, Jack started the lorry and drove down the back driveway to the dairy. There, they unloaded the churns, not nearly so heavy now that they were empty, and carried them into the dairy, where Walter was waiting to help them scrub them clean.

'Maybe you should teach Walter to drive, Jack,' Grace teased.

As she had expected, Walter looked horrified at the thought. 'Not me, lad, I'm a horseman. Always was, always will be.'

He told them how he had done the milk deliveries for years with a horse and cart. 'And he gave us good manure into the bargain. Can your engine beat that, Jack, lad?'

'Horses win hands down, Walter.'

In better spirits, Jack and Grace left the dairy. Grace's mind was still full of his description of her: 'pretty little Grace'. I'm not little, she thought, and Mrs Petrie always said I was pretty if too thin, but what Jack said about my 'bundle of doubts' – I don't like that much. Do I doubt people? Am I not too ready to think the best of them? Yes, I am, she answered herself, and then I find I'm wrong. Honesty then demanded that she add: but not all the time.

'Jack, why does Lady Alice wonder why you aren't driving ambulances at the front ... if I can ask you, that is?'

'Of course, you may ask anything you want, Grace. Asking questions is a really good way to learn. It's like this: I just cannot bring myself to believe that it's right to take another person's life. I know that I could not possibly shoot another human being.'

'Not even if he was a German.'

'Not even. Grace, I think we would find that lots of the German people don't want to be at war, don't want to shoot at us, bomb our towns. There must be objectors among them, too. Maybe their government says, "Right, you don't want to kill people, but we have to have someone driving ambulances."'

Grace was not sure that she completely understood, but she nodded as if she did. 'And should our government have asked you if you'd like to drive an ambulance?'

'They could have told me and I would have been perfectly happy. I don't want to die and so, yes, you can say I'd be frightened but I'd do my duty.'

Grace was surprised to see Jack blush as wildly as she had ever done. A strange feeling stole over her. Not even her adored Sam had ever made her feel quite like this. *What on earth's happening to me?*

Jack was talking and she'd missed his first words. '...if you are honestly interested. I can explain my feelings and my actions. It's quite simple. You see,

90

it's all in the Bible. God said, "Thou shalt not kill." So, therefore, it is morally wrong to go to war. There has to be a better way to deal with difficulties. And besides, I can't remember a time when I didn't want to be a doctor. Don't know why. Doctors maintain life; they save life. How could anyone expect me to do otherwise? It just doesn't make sense. Warfare is morally indefensible.'

Grace was painfully aware that she had had very little education or experiences that could be compared to Jack's. Obviously, he knew more and bigger words than she did and could quote poets and politicians. But the argument that God had said, 'Thou shalt not kill,' worried her. If God had said that, did he mean that it was never right to kill or did he mean that it was wrong to go out and murder someone? She remembered reading a newspaper article about her friend Daisy, who had seen a German pilot deliberately strafe a woman and child on Dartford Heath. Could that be called an act of warfare or should it be called murder? Oh, she could not bear to go on with this train of thought, especially since she had seen the newspaper long after the ghastly event and even then had not written to Daisy.

Jack was looking at her rather strangely. 'Grace, does it make it easier for you if I say truthfully that I would be perfectly happy to go into any area of warfare, helping qualified doctors as much as I can with my fairly limited training? But to put on a silly little uniform and allow myself to be encouraged to shoot at my fellow man – I simply can't do that.'

Grace felt unbearably sad. He believed so much

91

in what he was saying that he was prepared to tolerate being bullied, even cruelly treated. 'Jack, how do you know – as an actual fact – that God spoke to some human being and used those exact words?'

His look was both fond and pitying. 'Poor dear Grace. Of course, it's a fact. It's in the Bible and the Holy Bible is the word of God.'

She could not let that pass: 'Who says? God didn't sit down himself and write it, did he?'

'No.' The tone in which that one small word was uttered told him how annoyed, with her and the debate, he was. For her, somehow, these great moral questions were simple, but Grace had never been a regular churchgoer. Far from encouraging her to go, Megan had actively discouraged, even forbidden her attendance. It was only when Grace had left school and started working in a factory office that she had managed to attend the Christmas Eve service with her friends. It had always been a joyful occasion, but part of her wondered, sadly, if it was the music, the lights, the candles, even the vestments worn by the clergymen, that appealed to something in her, rather than the doctrine itself.

Basically, Grace was practical. A teacher saying, 'But the story of history is told by those who won the battles, not the defeated,' had resonated with her. Perhaps the victors did not tell the whole truth, and perhaps the man or men, no matter how holy or how wise, who did transcribe God's words, did not do it word for word.

'Gosh, poor Walter is scrubbing the churns by himself. We'd better run,' she said.

FIVE

Grace had never experienced anything as miraculous as spring on a farm. The beauty that met her eyes in the following weeks amazed her. Tiny curled leaves that opened overnight to show their different shades of green, fat flower buds that unfurled to reveal beauty that almost made her weep. Massed primroses made way for daffodils, hyacinths and delightful wild flowers that she had never seen before. Blossom appeared on trees and in the hedges that separated the fields.

'See them hedges?' Hazel told her. 'Every species of plant you've got in there shows you a hundred years in the life of the hedge. Look, know what this is?' he asked, pointing to a slim branch.

'No.'

'Hazelnut, and that's...?' He pointed.

'Holly,' answered the delighted Grace. 'And what's the prickly one with the blossom, Hazel?'

'May, Grace. Hawthorn,' he added since she had looked so surprised. 'And don't ask me why it's called May. Esau'll know, probably; his wife knew a lot about flowers, but all I know is we called it May blossom.'

'I think it's because it comes out in May,' Jack told her as they drove back from their next milk delivery. 'By the way, Lady Alice told me there's

93

a dance in the next village on Saturday night. She says we can use the milk lorry if anyone wants to go.'

The air became heavy with expectancy.

'Well?' he asked. 'Does anyone want to go?'

Is he asking me to go? Grace wondered, and what should she say if he was? They were, by far, the two youngest people on the estate, although Lady Alice was scarcely ten years older. For a moment, Grace found herself wondering about her employer. She was very pretty. Still not too old and the only child of an earl: why was her ladyship still unmarried? Perhaps she had loved and lost, like Grace herself with Sam? Grace took control of her mind. You're beginning to act out stories like Sally, she berated herself.

'Where does Lady Alice eat, Jack?' Much more down-to-earth than, 'Does Lady Alice have a gorgeous boyfriend?'

Once or twice a week, Lady Alice joined the estate workers when they were gathered in the kitchen for a reviving cup of tea, but she did not join them for meals.

'What's that got to do with whether or not you want to go to the dance?'

'Of course I'd like to go to a dance but that means you'd have to drive.'

'Of course I'll drive, if you'd like to attend. For heaven's sake, woman, how many dates have you been on?'

Grace thought first of the mean little house in Dartford and then of her friends. 'We all went out together, I suppose, to the church hall and the pictures. My friend Sally's dad used to sneak

94

us in sometimes.'

'It's possible that, by the time of the next dance, if there is one, you will be able to drive, Grace, or, if it's in the summer, we might be able to get our hands on some bikes, but in the meantime, Miss Paterson, would you do me the honour of accompanying me, and anyone else who wants to come along, to the farm workers' dance at the village hall?'

Grace longed to accept. The first time a man in whom she was ... at all interested had asked her for a real date and she hesitated. How she longed to say, 'That'd be nice.' She smiled. It was definitely a real date, but what would he say if she told him, and she had to tell him for how embarrassing it would be when he found out in the middle of the village hall?

'Has anyone ever told you that you have the most beautiful eyes?'

Beautiful eyes? No, no one had told her but she knew that her eyes were – quite nice. 'Lady Alice?' she repeated, since she had no idea how to reply. 'We never see her eating?'

'You are supposed to say, "No, Jack, you're the first person," or, "Every sensible man in Kent, Jack." My dear Miss Paterson, you have to learn how to take a compliment. But, never mind, we have years for you to learn. Of course Lady Alice eats. Did you think the aristocracy didn't? There's another kitchen in the main wing of the house. That's where I was the day Lady Alice asked me if I could drive. The housekeeper gave me some coffee while I was waiting.'

Grace was fascinated. She had wondered often

95

about the condition of the beautiful house. There was a housekeeper. She had no real idea of just what a housekeeper did besides looking after the house, a bit like a housewife, she supposed. 'I thought Mrs Love was the housekeeper.'

'She looks after this wing. I think there are three servants in the main house: a housekeeper, and two housemaids. Most of the house has been mothballed for the duration.'

Grace's overactive imagination suddenly produced a picture of the lovely old building completely covered in round white balls and she stifled a laugh. The memory of his words 'My dear Miss Paterson' did not make her want to laugh. She wanted somehow to hug the words to herself.

'Are you in the ditches today, Jack?'

'Trimming hedges.' He sighed. 'I do admire men like Hazel and Maurice; they know everything there is to know about farming. I can manage the work that only asks for brute force, even though it's a strain, but the finer points... Sometimes I feel so unutterably stupid. They never lose patience when they're with me but I bet they laugh their heads off in the pub.'

'They wouldn't laugh cruelly, Jack, and besides, you can save lives and they can't.'

'I was in the middle of the third year and so I would have a jolly good try, but I'm a long way from being a doctor.'

They drove on in a contented silence until they reached the back gates to the estate.

'Up for a driving lesson, Grace?'

Grace's stomach seemed to turn a complete somersault. A date and now a driving lesson. 'I'd love it, Jack.'

'I think Saturday morning will be the best time but I might be able to ask her ladyship if it's fine if we try just after tea some evenings. Evenings are getting longer and it's easier to learn in daylight.'

Grace looked again at her favourite view of the splendid house. 'Jack, do you ever feel that there's been some mistake and there isn't a war on?'

He pulled the lorry up to the milking parlour before he answered. 'No, I know only too well that there's a war on. I listen to the wireless reports, and read the papers, but I think I know what you mean. Where are the battles, where are the German planes that were supposed to be bombing England into nothingness? Mind you, there are rumours that it'll hot up in the summer. There is some rationing but we're eating like kings, although Mrs Love did say things'll change when the others arrive. And then those fabulous sausages we had that day, they're from his lordship's personal supplies; he's augmenting our rations but that can't go on for ever. And bear in mind, Grace, if this war goes on and on, as I think it will, practically everything we eat will be rationed.'

'I didn't know that.' Grace remembered Lady Alice saying that, while living on this estate, she would learn more than how to poleaxe a pig. She fervently hoped that she would never be asked to poleaxe anything but she certainly was learning, not only about land management and animal husbandry but also about people. Valuable lessons.

'Cheer up, Grace; you look sad. I'm very much looking forward to dancing with you on Saturday. Are you going to wear that pretty frock?'

She felt herself blushing and not only because he remembered the dress. 'Yes, it's the only one I have.'

They sat looking at each other for a few quiet moments. Then Jack opened the driver's door. 'We'd best get these churns washed or Hazel will be after us and, believe you me, he's scarier than Lady Alice.' With that, he jumped out of the lorry.

'I can't dance,' she hissed after him.

He heard the hiss, stopped, turned round and laughed. 'Of course you can. Relax, Grace, dancing is a natural animal mode of expression.'

'An animal mode of expression. Thanks very much, Doctor.' At least she had told him.

'When my mother went into service, it took a regiment of servants to carry buckets of hot water upstairs for baths, Grace. People didn't have a bath every day. Hot water straight from a tap is wonderful, isn't it?'

Grace was on her way upstairs to take a bath before dressing for the dance. She certainly did not want to tell Mrs Love that there had been no running water at all in the house in which she grew up and so she merely agreed. To her surprise, Mrs Love kept beside her as they progressed up the stairs.

'Spending quite a bit of time with young Jack, Grace. Not sure her ladyship would think that a good idea. A girl has to think of her good name, you know.'

Grace stopped in the middle of the staircase. 'My good name. What do you mean?'

'No need to get uppity. I have a responsibility.

Until other girls arrive, you're the only woman in a houseful of men.'

'Harry and Jack hardly make up a houseful, Mrs Love. Besides, I never see them in the house, except at the table.'

'I know that and you know that, but you're going to a village dance tonight and the village doesn't know that. Just be careful.'

Her joyful anticipation of a pleasant evening somewhat spoiled, Grace hurried past her.

'I see you've had his wireless the past two days. That's nice.'

Grace longed to say that listening to the wireless was more interesting than listening to Mrs Love but she restrained herself. Jack had handed her the wireless in full view of the assembled farm workers. Seemingly, Bob Hazel had taken a larger wireless out of an uninhabited cottage a few days before and had put it in the men's dormitory. Jack had loaned his much smaller one to Grace; there was nothing more to it than that. Surely, Mrs Love knew that.

She switched on the radio when she reached her room. How cheering it was to hear music and the evening news, although she would not be hearing that this evening. She would be dancing. A recording by the great Joe Loss and his band was playing as she took out her frock – she'd removed the tie – a carefully reserved pair of stockings, not silk, and her sole pair of elegant shoes. In a few weeks, Grace, who had assiduously saved what remained of her pay after the amount for her food was taken off, intended to buy white sandals for the summer. For the first time in her life, she had a little money of her own and could buy whatever she wanted. So far, clothing was not rationed but probably would be, like everything except those foods classed as non-essentials. Clothes rationing was 'only a matter of time'. She went off to the bathroom, thinking how perfectly the white sandals she could see in her mind would look with the green frock. Perhaps Jack would ask her to walk out with him. She could see them, hand in hand, walking along beside one of the streams on the estate, her new sandals startling white against the green grass

No, Grace, don't rush, she told herself, and stepped into the lovely hot water.

To her surprise, and slight disappointment, Harry and Esau had both decided to go to the dance. Esau said that he looked forward to an evening of company with farm workers he knew from the area, and Harry, who assured Grace that he would not ask her to dance with him, was looking forward to live music.

'I were listening to that Joe Loss while I shaved. That'd be a turn-up for the books if bands like his was to play for us.'

'He won't be in the village hall tonight, Harry; you'll have to make do with an old joanna, a fiddle and a squeeze-box,' Esau said laughing.

Grace, who was more accustomed to records played in the church hall, thought that the three musicians that evening were superb. 'We had local bands in the church hall sometimes, Jack, but I don't think any of them were as good as this.'

The hall was absolutely packed with people of

all ages, even fairly young children, and a brave attempt had been made to decorate it with such spring flowers as were available. The three-piece band was playing lustily and, while the others found a table, Jack took Grace onto the floor to dance.

It was some time since Grace had even attempted to dance but, to her great surprise, she was delighted to find that she could move easily with Jack, who was obviously an experienced dancer.

Of course. Jack was a university student. Students probably went to dances, if not every night, at least on Fridays and Saturdays.

'At your university, Jack, were there dances every night?'

'Work hard, play hard, Grace. Dancing's a great way to relax, don't you think?'

'I haven't been to many dances,' she said.

'We'll have to remedy that. You just need more experience to become a good dancer; honestly, you have a great sense of rhythm.'

Great sense of rhythm. She had heard those words before. Who had said them? Sally. It was Sally Brewer and she had been talking about Sam. Grace closed her eyes and conjured up a picture of Sam, but the picture did not want to form. She was here in Bedfordshire with Jack Williams, who thought she was pretty. Without regret, she felt the dream of Sam float away.

Sam will always be special, she thought, but this is different. That morning, she had had her first short driving lesson with Jack, who was nothing like Sam. Jack was not quite so tall as Sam, and he was more slender, but she was delighted to find that, like Sam, he was kind. He seemed to know that she was nervous and spoke quietly and approvingly. She felt herself respond to him. Such joy not to be shouted at, not to be found wanting. For a second, sitting there beside him in the lorry, she had wanted to push his slightly too long dark hair out of his brown eyes but had managed to control her hand. She blushed now at the memory. How forward that would have been. What would he have thought?

He had noticed her blush. 'It is a bit hot,' he said, 'and Lady Alice says we're supposed to mingle with the locals. Besides, I can see lots of lads who want me to break a leg so that they can dance with the prettiest girl in the hall.'

Grace, aware only of Jack and the music, looked around the room. Yes, several men were looking in their direction. 'They want to be able to dance like you, Jack.'

He laughed. 'Believe me, that's not it. We'd best join the others.'

With a final flourish, he steered her across the room to the table where their friends were. There was beer and cider to drink, and plates of tiny sandwiches were on all the tables. The empty glasses on their table, the crumbs and a crust or two showed just what a good time was being had.

'Is this what's called height-of-sophistication party food, Jack, lad?' asked Harry, pointing to the few tiny sandwiches that were left.

'In wartime, yes.'

'You were right about the music, Grace,' said the very happy Harry, as he lurched to his feet.

'Anyone ready for another beer?'

He ambled off and was soon seen standing in a corner near the stage, drinking his second beer and tapping his foot to the music.

'Is he all right?'

'He's a responsible adult, Grace. Esau, are you sure you don't want to dance or join some of your old friends?'

'Benefit of age, lad; they've been over while you two were dancing.'

'Would you like to dance, Esau?' asked Grace, standing up again to go with him.

But the old man had no time to agree or disagree, for Grace was snatched by one of the local farmers and spun furiously around the hall. Their movements could never be interpreted as dancing and he did not let go of her when the music stopped.

'Thank you,' she said, and tried to pull herself free, but she could not break his grip.

She was frightened but tried to stay calm. After all, they were in the village hall. No harm could come to her with all the farmers and their wives and daughters looking on. 'Thank you for the dance,' she said again, 'but please let go of my hand; you're hurting me.'

'What's a decent girl doing with a conchie? We know what to do with cowards and traitors. Now, you come along with me and sit with village folk that's doing their bit for the country.'

'I'm happy to sit with the villagers but I came with my friends from the Court.'

He began to pull her along, and Grace looked back towards the table, hoping that one of the men could see her plight. They were not looking in her direction. She gave in and walked across the floor. 'But let go of my hand or I'll scream,' she said.

'Bitch,' he said quietly but with real venom as he released her hand, which was now quite white, so tight had been his hold. 'Get back to yer conchies.' He had raised his voice so loud that dancers were stopping to see what was going on. 'We don't want none of your lot here, do we, lads?' he signalled to several young men standing near the drinks table, but most turned their backs.

Grace, who was rather shaken, wished they might have shown their disapproval by rescuing her. Just then, help arrived from an unexpected source.

'Had a bit too much of your best cider, Arnold?'

Hazel and a middle-aged woman had joined them on the dance floor. 'You know we don't want problems, especially ones that will get back to his lordship, do we?' Hazel put his arm around the man's shoulder and steered him towards his friends. Mrs Hazel smiled at Grace and began to chat to her as if they knew each other well.

'He makes delicious cider, Grace, but does tend to sample a little too much of it. Now, I want you to come with me to meet some workers from other farms. Don't worry, no one will bother young Jack with Esau sitting there.'

Grace, still distressed – although she tried not to show it – walked with Hazel's wife and soon found herself being introduced to farmers and their wives, other farm workers and several other land girls. Everyone who spoke to her, especially the land girls, who shared both horrid and amusing stories with her, was very friendly and welcoming. She received genuine offers of help of all kinds. One farmer's wife was a hairdresser and offered to do her hair for any special occasion.

'And Jenny, over there talking to her land girls, worked for a really fancy dressmaker in London. Wedding dresses are her speciality.'

Grace laughed. 'I won't need a wedding dress any time soon.'

'You can't see the way your young friend is looking at you ... and he's not alone either.'

Grace blushed. 'It's been lovely to meet all of you but I really think I should get back to our table.' She looked over at Jack and Esau and, seeing how happily they were chatting, wondered if they would even notice if she stayed away.

Mrs Fairchild, the hairdresser, said that she'd walk over with Grace to say hello to Esau and to meet Jack. 'We hear his lordship's accepted conscientious objectors. You have to understand that some folk in the area don't understand. Most of us has sons and brothers somewhere in Europe and we hear tell things isn't going too well.'

'What don't people understand, Mrs Fairchild? Conscientious objectors or the earl hiring them?'

'The conchies, of course. It's a man's sacred duty to kill anyone as wants to harm his family.'

Grace stopped in the middle of the floor. For a moment, she thought she might be sick. Kill anyone who wanted to harm your family? Was the woman serious? And she called such an action a sacred duty? 'Please excuse me, Mrs Fairchild, but I think Mr Youngman might want to get home. We've been here longer than we intended.'

'He's getting on, is Esau, and he's not been the same since his wife passed away. Well, do let me know if you want your hair doing. You have nice thick hair. Needs a bit of tidying, though, and maybe a more modern look.'

Grace agreed with her but had decided that if her hair grew down to her feet, she would not let this woman touch it. There was just something about her predatory eyes. She looked across the floor and was concerned to see that, in the few minutes she had been talking to Mr Fairchild, Jack had gone. There was no sight of Harry and only Esau sat at their table. He looked worried.

'Had a nice chat, Grace?' he asked with a brave attempt at a smile. 'There's some right nice folk around here.'

When Grace did not rush to agree, he added, 'And some as isn't quite so nice.'

'Mrs Fairchild says as there's rumours, I think it was rumours, about bad news from the war. Where are they, Jack and Harry?'

'Young Jack's gone to find Harry just in case he's been a mite too free with the beer. Some of it's home-brewed and a city stomach won't be used to it.' He turned around on the uncomfortable wooden chair and surveyed the room, exchanging a smile now and again. 'There's many here as is the salt of the earth, pet. Don't let one or two spoil your time with us.' He tried to sound cheerier. 'Friendly, like, the other land girls?'

Grace, who wanted to find Harry and Jack so that they could drive home together, tried to look interested. She liked Esau and, at any other time, would have enjoyed being able to sit and chat with him. There was so much about the land that he could teach her. 'Yes, lovely,' she said. 'One even went to the same training farm as me, but I'm a little worried, Esau. The man who grabbed me was really frightening, and that woman is… I don't quite know how to describe her.'

He got to his feet. 'Time was, not a man in this hall would have crossed me. I'm older than I thought. Come along with me. Jack'll have taken Harry out to clear his head.'

Spots of blood on the doorstep were the first signs that something was wrong. Grace gasped.

'Steady, Grace, there's a hundred reasons for a bit of blood at a dance. Let's take a look outside.'

There were more blood spots on the path. Grace wanted to run, shouting the names Jack and Harry as loudly as she could, but when she looked questioningly at old Esau, he shook his head. 'Listen a minute.'

She stood quietly, and so still was the air that she became aware of the absolute perfection of the spring evening. Bright stars and a quarter-moon lit the sky and she smelled lilac on the evening air. But the scent and the sight were now spoiled by the sound of shouting and even blows, which came from behind a shed just a few yards away.

'You away back and fetch Bob Hazel and I'll deal with this.'

Grace hesitated. 'Dear Esau, you find Hazel,' she said, and then, shouting angrily and as loudly as she could, she ran towards the shed.

A cluster of men were milling around, almost as if they were engaged in some primitive dance.

Something lay on the ground and, as she saw a man pull himself free of whoever was holding him, she recognised Jack's shock of dark hair. He shouted something and dropped to his knees beside the body on the ground. That was when Grace screamed. It was Harry and his face was covered in blood.

For a second, there was a stunned silence and then the crowd dispersed as men ran in every direction, leaving Jack and Harry on the ground alone in the pale moonlight. The hall door opened and light and men and women spilled out together. A woman ran quickly towards them and kneeled down beside Jack.

'Iris Simpson.' Grace recognised Mrs Hazel's voice. 'She was a hospital nurse. What happened, lass?'

'It's Harry.'

'Let's get you out of here. Bob will stay, and Esau. The lad's a doctor, isn't he?'

'Medical student.'

'They'll manage between them. Someone's gone for the policeman.'

'I need to stay, Mrs Hazel. I need to help.'

'What can you do?'

'I can tell the truth.'

'So can others here, Grace. They're not all against conscientious objectors, you know. If the constable needs you, he knows where to find you.'

'I won't leave till I see Harry.' She turned to Bob Hazel. 'I'm sorry, Mr Hazel, but he's my friend and I can't just leave him lying there. Is he dead? Is that why you're bundling me away?'

He did not answer but, putting his strong right

arm around her shoulders, he forced her to go with him to the milk lorry, in which Jack had so happily driven them to the village such a few hours before. His wife walked along on her other side, making sympathetic noises.

Grace knew that it was no use to struggle and she could see that she might well be in the way. 'Please, Hazel, I can't go back to the Court without the men. And where's Mr Youngman?'

That question was answered very quickly as Esau was sitting in the passenger seat.

'Now, Grace, sit here in the driver's seat. Esau'll keep you company, and me and the missus will be back quick as we can. One of the farm lads has a motorbike and he's gone to tell her ladyship.'

'No. What happened to Harry? You have to tell me, Hazel. I will not get into the lorry until I know. And Jack? Don't let anything happen to Jack.'

'Damn it, girl, have you never learned to do as you're told? Harry got into a bit of a fight – he's had a bit too much to drink and he fell and hit his head. Heads bleed awful but Jack and Mrs Simpson are looking after him and–'

He stopped as the strident sound of an ambulance disturbed what had been a lovely spring evening. 'Go back to the Court, Grace. You weren't there when the fighting started and so can tell the police nothing. You'll no doubt pass her ladyship on the way. Now go.'

'I can't.'

Before he could start arguing with her again, she reminded him that she had had only one driving lesson.

'You can start it and you can stop it? The bit in

between will take care of itself. Now, go home,' he ordered, almost pushing her into the lorry, slamming the door and turning away to run in the direction of the hall.

SIX

Jack had shown Grace how to start the milk lorry, how to turn off the engine, and had quickly explained gear changes. There had been no time to do much more than allow her to guide the vehicle along a fairly straight part of the road. Faced, however, with the current situation, she started the engine with shaking hands and managed to grind into first gear. Unsure how to get into any higher gear, she had dashed away the tears that had begun to fall, sent Esau a tremulous smile, and concentrated on getting back to the Court.

Later, she was to think what a funny sight the lorry must have been as it crept stumblingly along. But right now, all she could think of was Harry. What had happened to him? Could any local farm worker hate so much that he would set out to injure or kill a man whose principles were different from his own?

A loud sob escaped her and old Esau reached out and patted her left hand, as she clutched the steering wheel as if her life depended on it. 'There, there, Grace. There's always a bit of a fight at a dance, but it's never serious.' Grace tried to smile at him but could not. Esau had not seen the slight, still form of Harry on the ground. Harry, a bus conductor, who loved his new job out in the fresh air, a man of little formal education who revelled in working every day with a university student, and in learning from him. Did he know that the others learned from *him*, too?

'Look out!' Esau's yell of pure fright startled Grace. She was horrified to see that she had wandered over to the middle of the narrow country road and in the path of a car travelling quickly and heading straight for her. The driver swerved and scraped past her. No, surely not. But, yes, the driver of the speeding car was Lady Alice.

Grace stole a quick look at Esau but his face gave nothing away.

Afraid that she would ruin the engine if she were to try to go faster, Grace steered the lorry over to the correct side of the road and carried on. At long last, they were driving through the open gates of Whitefields Court.

A few lights shone from the windows of the great house and Grace carried on to the kitchen door. By the time she had parked, Mrs Love was at the door.

'Are you all right, Grace?'

'Yes, thank you.'

'Sit down, the pair of you. I'll make tea.' She turned towards the stove and moved a pot of milk onto a hotplate. 'Esau, her ladyship says you're to stay here tonight, in case anyone should need to speak to you. I've put pyjamas in the big room where Harry and Jack are sleeping but you'll both need to stay up until her ladyship returns.'

Neither Grace nor Esau seemed capable of

saying a word but sat near the stove, as if they needed warmth, sipping the tea and staring into space.

'Maybe you should get off to bed, Esau.'

He shook his head.

'You should go, Mrs Love. You need to be up so early.' Grace had seen the cook stifling a yawn.

'Lady Alice will come here to tell me what is happening. If Mr McManus needs to take to his bed, it's me that will care for him.'

Grace sincerely hoped that all Harry would need was a few days of recuperation in the capable hands of Mrs Love but, when she closed her eyes, she saw that spreading pool of blood. 'Damn it, we're at war with Germany and we spend our time fighting one another. It's so stupid.'

'Take your bad temper out of my kitchen, Grace. We don't need a land girl losing control.'

Grace's mumbled apology was lost in the sound of a car's arrival.

A few minutes later, Lady Alice walked in, followed by Jack. 'Harry has a severe head injury and is in the local hospital, where he'll receive excellent care. You, Esau, and you, Grace, should be in your beds. The cows don't care if you get no sleep but I do. Go, now.'

Esau and Grace stood up but Grace looked over at Jack who, apart from a few bruises on his face, seemed to have no serious injury. She made as though to move towards him but Lady Alice had not finished speaking.

'Is there water for a hot bath, Jessie?'

Being pleased with the affirmative answer, she turned back to Jack. 'A hot bath and then bed,

112

Jack. Mrs Love will bring you hot cocoa. Jack needs rest, Grace. You can console him tomorrow. It's possible the police will want to talk to you; highly unlikely but one never knows. Now go to bed.'

Her voice was firm but kind. There was no anger in it, no evidence of dislike. For the first time since the trouble had started, Grace relaxed. She had no idea how to get out of the room. Was she supposed to just walk out or...?

Esau had walked slowly to the door. He turned. 'Thank you, Jessie. Good night, m'lady.'

'Sleep well, Esau.'

Grace muttered 'Good night' in the general direction of the few people still clustered near the table and, with head bent so as to not to meet anyone's eyes, she hurried out after Esau.

The police did not want to speak to Grace. They had spoken to several people present at the dance and had questioned Jack intensively. They had also taken two local farm workers into custody. Grace's testimony was not needed.

She had slept fitfully and was up before her alarm sounded. She washed and dressed and hurried downstairs. Mrs Love, Hazel, Walter, Esau and Jack were in the kitchen, drinking tea.

'Get yourself some tea, Grace,' said Walter Green, the head dairyman. 'Her ladyship's busy and so I'll help you with the milking, but her ladyship will drive.'

Grace glanced across at Jack. He too looked as if he hadn't slept and was so pale that the bruises on his face stood out like bright badges, but there was an air of suppressed excitement about him.

'Are you all right, Jack? We could visit Harry this afternoon.'

He looked round as if to see who might overhear him. 'I wish I could, Grace, but...' He stopped talking and lifted the heavy teapot to pour her some tea. 'His lordship's on his way up and I'm to make myself available, so I can't leave the estate.'

'But we're allowed Sunday afternoon, and what does the earl want? You've done nothing wrong. He can't want to get rid of you. You work hard; everybody likes you. I like you,' she finished, embarrassed by her confession.

He made a sound, almost a groan, but said nothing.

Walter spoke loudly: 'Hello, anyone here as knows how to milk a cow?'

'Sorry, Walter, I'm coming,' said Grace, swallowing as much of her tea as she could but, as she hurried to the milking parlour, all she could hear was her own voice echoing in her head: 'I like you.'

How could I? How could I? He probably thinks I'm fast.

She was thoroughly miserable by the time the cows had been milked and taken down to the pasture. For once, she saw no newly opened flowers, no fresh blossom. Two of her cows had kicked over their milk pails, sending the warm fresh milk running like a white river down the middle of the byre and out into the mud on the yard. Walter had been sympathetic over the first loss – after all, the particular cow was known to be troublesome – but the second spillage infuriated him.

'Would serve you right if they docked your

wages. Keep your mind on the work you're paid to do, and stop upsetting my cows.'

It was unjust and if she had been able to run to some quiet corner, she would have wept, but she managed to pull herself together and apologise.

'Ach, well, maybe it wasn't all your fault. Even Bluebell can be a right bugger if she sets her mind to it.'

They had been on better terms when they walked back to the house for breakfast, although Grace could manage to eat very little.

'Starving yourself is not doing Harry any good, Grace. At least eat some porridge. Half a bowl,' said Mrs Love, setting it down in front of her, 'or I'll tell her ladyship.'

Grace could see no conceivable reason for Lady Alice to care how much or how little she ate but she succeeded in finishing the porridge.

Lady Alice was waiting outside the byre and was talking to Walter. 'There you are, Grace. My God, girl, it was you who almost drove me off the road last night. Terrific timing, I must say.'

Grace said nothing but settled herself in the lorry.

'Remind me, Grace, you did say you could ride a bike?'

'Yes, Lady Alice.'

'Mrs Hazel will lend you hers for a week or two.' She smiled. 'You are so transparent, Grace. Colour came back into your cheeks. I'm glad you're so worried about Harry. I rang the hospital earlier – he's had a reasonable night – and they'll let you in for two minutes, possibly ten.'

'Thank you, Lady Alice.' She took her courage

and asked, 'They're not in trouble, Jack and Harry? Some of the village men were horrible; said they didn't want conscientious objectors here.'

'Drink talks loudly, Grace.'

'One of them, he meant it.'

'The one who manhandled you, Arnold Archer, is in custody, and he'll sweat his anger out, believe me. A few days in gaol will do him the world of good.'

'A few days–' began Grace angrily, but Lady Alice interrupted.

'No one is the least interested in what happened to you, Grace, since nothing happened. It's unlikely that he's the one who knocked down Harry, and so he'll be incarcerated for a few days and will then go back to his wife, feeling extremely sorry for himself. I suggest that you grow a thicker skin. It happens, in one way or another, to all of us. A brooch pin is the most useful thing to have in your bag. Now, let us deliver the milk.'

Two hours later, they were back at Whitefields Court. Lady Alice parked near the dairy and, leaving the keys of the lorry with Walter, walked back to the house with Grace.

'There's the bicycle. Looks rather large for you but perhaps you'll manage.' She looked questioningly at Grace.

'I learned on a big bike.'

'Good. Jessie will give you directions to the hospital and she'll find something for you to take to Harry. I sincerely hope he's well enough to enjoy it. I know you are entitled to the afternoon off but I'd like to see you in the main house around four. Can you be back by then?'

'Yes, Lady Alice.'

'Good, there's such a lot to discuss. Enjoy Sunday lunch.'

She walked off and Grace stood for a moment, looking after her before entering the house through the back door.

All the farm workers – except Harry, of course – were already gathered around the table. A blue vase full of brilliant-red tulips stood in the middle of the table. From the long flat pot on the stove came a mouth-watering smell that Grace did not recognise.

'Trout,' said Mrs Love. 'A gift, and we won't ask who from. There's new potatoes and fresh spring greens to go with.'

Grace sat down in her usual seat and tried, unsuccessfully, to avoid Jack's eyes.

'Ever had trout, Grace?' It was Jack who had asked.

She kept her eyes on the plate. 'No, cod sometimes, or haddock.'

'How'd the delivery go?'

'Same as every day,' Grace said, and applied herself to her portion of fish.

'Why are you angry?'

'I'm not.' She hesitated for a moment. 'Or perhaps I am – at this whole situation.'

Mrs Love was now getting angry. 'I'd be grateful if my hard work producing decent meals was appreciated, instead of seeing them left to grow cold while some of you chat. One of the local men has fishing rights on a stretch of river and he thought these might cheer us all up.'

'Delicious, Jessie.'

'Really tasty, Mrs Love.'

Compliments came from all sides and, somewhat mollified, Mrs Love returned to stirring her custard.

'I like you, too, Grace.' Jack's pleasant voice was too quiet for any of the others to hear.

She blushed, a delicate pink, and ate some of the trout. 'My new favourite fish.'

'Mine too.'

There was no more chatting until the custard, served with a spoonful of last year's strawberry jam, had been finished. The men, their tongues loosened by the tasty meal, began to discuss the happenings of the night before. Mrs Love had told them as much as she knew of Harry's condition and they were all concerned.

'Grace is cycling in to visit, this afternoon, aren't you, Grace?' she said. 'She'll have news for us at teatime. As soon as he's on the mend, we'll all have a chance of seeing him. And now, Hazel would like a word.'

Hazel drained his tea cup and then looked around at the assembled workers. 'I have to tell you, his lordship drove up this morning and he is not pleased. There will be changes made, no doubt but, I'm sure, if we all carry on doing our duty–'

Three voices interrupted him, each saying more or less the same thing.

'We're not responsible for last night.'

'Quiet, quiet.' Hazel spoke quietly but everyone stopped talking and looked at him. 'If anyone's responsible, it's me for not keeping a better eye on everyone. There's not an ounce of malice in Harry and so I'll tell his lordship.'

'I was sitting with him, Hazel. I shouldn't have let him go outside on his own,' Jack piped up.

'He's a grown man, lad, not a child. And Esau tells me he didn't have that much.'

Hearing that, Grace looked down at the table, fearful of being asked to speak. Had they not all said that Harry had been a little careless?

'Well, Dr Williams?' Hazel said to Jack.

'He drank two bottles of beer. I never saw him with a bottle or a glass in his hand the rest of the evening: he was interested in the music.'

'So them from the village that says he was drinking all evening is telling lies? Grace?'

'I honestly don't know. I'm sorry. I never saw him after that nasty Mr Archer hauled me on to the dance floor. *He* certainly wasn't sober – I could smell it; and he said the locals didn't want anything to do with conchies. And he was out there when Esau and I ran out.'

'You'd best get ready to visit the hospital, Grace; and, Jack, I'll be walking you to the estate office. His lordship wants a word with you.'

'Am I the only one getting time off?' asked Grace, as the others prepared to return to work.

'There's a war on, lass, and animals still need feeding,' Walter said, with a laugh. 'We're going to lie in bed all day when the new land girls come. Now away to see Harry. Jessie'll keep you some tea if you're late.'

Grace returned to her room, looked longingly at the bed, and then went to the bathroom to freshen up. How she hated confrontation and, more than that, she was heart sore that she had had no real chance to speak to Jack. She wished she had not

119

told him that she liked him. He was a university student. He was probably laughing at her.

She pinched her cheeks in the forlorn hope of putting some colour into them and ran down the wide staircase.

Jack was standing just inside the door. 'Mrs Love says you're to give this chocolate to Harry.'

'Thank you.'

They stood silently for a moment, until Jack turned to leave. 'Did you hear what I said, Miss Paterson?' he said, and then, to her great surprise, he kissed her. His lips landed half on her lips and half on her face.

'I'll do better next time,' he said, and hurried out.

SEVEN

Grace followed Mrs Love's directions and, with only a little help from a local policeman, found the hospital. She was delighted to dismount from the elderly bicycle that Mrs Love had found for her to ride. Not only had it the hardest seat she had ever encountered, but the efficiency of its brakes was definitely questionable.

Hoping to cheer up Harry, Grace had worn her prettiest blouse, pink, with its puff sleeves, Peter Pan collar and tiny pearl buttons, but instead of a skirt she had decided to wear her Land Army-issue breeches. It was warm enough to do without a coat and so she wore a pale grey cardigan. She found a parking place for the bicycle, fastened it with an old chain given to her by Mrs Love, and went into the hospital. She tidied her hair and went to the front desk to find out where Harry's ward was.

There were several long corridors with wards on either side and it took Grace some time to reach Harry's, only to find that she was a little too early. Doctors were making rounds and no visitors were allowed.

A nurse was sitting behind the desk and Grace asked her how Harry was.

'Are you family?'

'Not exactly; we both work at the Court.'

'I'll call that family. He has a skull fracture, but he's strong and fit, so should be fine.'

Grace had never heard of a skull fracture and, at the picture the two words conjured up, had gone a little pale.

'It's bone; it'll mend, but it will take some time. He won't be doing much ditch-digging for a while.' She looked up the corridor. 'Doctor's left. You can go in but don't excite him and don't stay long.'

Grace hurried along the corridor, pushed open the doors of the ward and walked in. A nun was standing just inside the door. A wave of joy swept over Grace. 'Sister,' she breathed, 'oh, Sister, it's so nice...' She stopped in confusion.

'I'm not Sister, pet, merely a nurse. Who are you visiting?'

Grace stared at her without speaking, her eyes huge in her white face.

'Here, pet, sit down, you've come over faint.

121

Were you looking for Sister Hart? I'm afraid, she's on a break.'

She had pushed Grace gently into a chair by the doors, and Grace, now feeling both confused and incredibly stupid, got to her feet.

'Sorry, it was just... I'm perfectly well, honestly, and I'd like to see my friend, Harry McManus.'

The nurse looked at her doubtfully. 'Very well,' she said after a moment or two, 'but don't you go passing out on him.'

Grace assured the nurse that she was perfectly well. 'Cycled here, a bit tired. Sorry.'

'Six down, left-hand side.'

With such simple instructions, Grace was able to locate Harry without staring at any of the other occupants. There was a chair beside the bed and she pulled it closer to his bandaged head. 'Harry, how are you?'

His eyes were closed and he made no reply.

Grace looked at him for some time, wincing a little at the ugly bruising on his face. Somehow, Harry, a spare man, looked even thinner after just one night in hospital. She wondered if he was unconscious or asleep, and if it was possible that he knew she was there and could hear her. 'Everyone sends their best, Harry: Jack and Hazel and all, and even Lady Alice. Mrs Love gave me a bar of chocolate for you. That was nice, wasn't it?' She did not add that it was on instructions from Lady Alice. 'His lordship is here, the earl, and I think Jack has to talk to him. He'll be telling him you did nothing wrong.' She waited but there was no response from the still figure on the bed. 'I'll get back to the Court, Harry, and maybe get a chance to see you during the week. Cheerio.'

She walked quickly back to the swing doors, turned for a moment, just in case he had moved, and then left. A different nurse was now at the desk.

'Mr McManus, my friend, he didn't move at all. Is that all right?'

'We don't want extra movement at this point. Try to visit later in the week but in the evening, after tea. Maybe he'll be on solid food by then. Has to be awake to eat, right?'

'Nurse, is this normal?'

'As night follows day, love. Your friend's doing well.'

Considerably relieved, Grace left the hospital, found the ancient bicycle and cycled back to Whitefields Court.

By the time she arrived back, Grace was exhausted. As she parked the bicycle, she wondered how long it would take for her to become accustomed to it. *Maybe I should put some hay on the seat like they told us to do with tractor seats, if we drove one, that is.* She was about to giggle at the amusing mind picture of her cycling through busy streets with hay sticking out all over the place when she remembered that she had been told to report to Lady Alice at four.

Ten past. Oh, God, she'll be furious.

Grace was hot and thirsty, and her legs, unused lately to cycling, felt as if they might buckle at any moment. She was also quite sure that her hair was an absolute mess. Would it be better to run – or crawl – upstairs to wash her face and brush her hair, or to go directly to the estate office?

Of course, she made the wrong decision.

'Good heavens, Grace, how dare you come into my home in such a mess? You look as if you've been ditch-digging all day. No,' she said, as Grace made to leave, 'now that you're here, we might as well get it over. Sit down before you fall down.'

She pointed to a chair and, when Grace was seated, she moved to sit behind the beautiful wooden desk that dominated the room. 'I take it you saw Harry. Is he improving?'

'I don't really know, Lady Alice. He ... he seemed to be unconscious but the nurse said that was normal. She said to come in the evening, sometime after his tea.'

Lady Alice made a sound that could have signified either agreement or disagreement. 'My father was here this afternoon,' she said after a pause. 'I'm sure Jack will tell you what the result of their discussion was, but in the meantime, I have to think about your future, Harry's and, more importantly, I have to consider what is best for this estate. Relationships with the village are extremely important and, quite frankly, they have suffered a blow–'

Grace interrupted. 'Harry is not to blame.'

'When you're quite finished.' For a moment, Lady Alice looked angry and then, she said, 'You really must learn to trust us to know what is best, Grace. Harry is going to need care for some time. We will arrange that. The man who knocked him down will undoubtedly go to prison for assault; that will not be accepted quietly by some. You see, it means that a woman with several children will be without her husband for who knows how

124

long. Work will have to be found for her, probably here. In light of some unsubstantiated threats, by the lowest element, against Jack and, I'm afraid, you, Grace, you will be moved.'

'No, please, you have to believe that we did nothing wrong for you to send us away. It's not right. I know I have a lot to learn but I'm learning and I work hard. I'll do better, I promise I will. And I can't believe you'd send Jack away. He's doubly punished because of his principles.'

Lady Alice stood up. She was white with anger but obviously determined to keep control of her emotions. She remained silent and motionless for a moment and then, she said, 'Did no one fight for you as you were growing up, Grace? Is that why you seem to have assumed the role of Lord Protector of everyone else? I suggest that you allow me to look after the people on this estate as I have been trained to do. Go to your room now and we'll talk when you have learned to control your tongue.'

Grace tried to walk proudly from the room, embarrassment and anger warring inside her. What had happened to her since she had made the decision to leave Dartford? It was as if she had left the quiet, docile Grace behind. At the training school she had fought with Miss Ryland. Here in this glorious part of England that she already loved, she had at first antagonised Mrs Love and now made an enemy of Lady Alice.

She tried to calm herself down before she reached the kitchen door. *I want to stay here. I want to plough and plant and watch things grow.* She bent her head. *I want to … be friends with Jack.*

'Don't be childish, Grace. You need to eat some-thing.' Mrs Love, carrying a tray, had climbed the back stairs to bring Grace an evening meal, and now saw that not so much as the cup of tea had been touched.

Grace looked at the food. 'I can't.'

'Can't. You will not or you are unable to eat?'

'Your father an English teacher like Jack's?'

Mrs Love took a noisy and deep breath, which she expelled before speaking. 'Her ladyship wants you fit for the milking at five in the morn-ing. Now, eat your tea, have a hot bath and listen to your elders and betters.'

'Elders, maybe. Betters? Explain. I haven't done anything wrong and I'm being sent away.'

'For your own good, you silly girl. There's talk in the village as how you led Archer on.' She saw that Grace was ready to erupt again, and went on: 'Yes, yes, everybody knows it's rubbish but it's better for now while we wait to see how Harry does and what the police say. Now, have your soup.'

Grace looked at Mrs Love quietly. Was there a look of dear Mrs Petrie about her? 'It stuck in my throat.'

'Tomato soup does have that annoying prop-erty. Come along, everyone else has gone and I'll warm this up for you.'

Mrs Love waited and, eventually, Grace stood up. 'I'm sorry.'

'I am, too, mostly about this ridiculous situ-ation; must have been something to bring his lordship up from London.'

'Did Jack say anything?'

'Not to me. Perhaps he'll say something in the morning. Business as usual for now.'

They continued down to the kitchen and were surprised to see Jack sitting in the inglenook.

For just a second, Grace wished she had tidied her hair and then, stoically, she decided that her hair didn't matter. 'Hello, Jack,' she said, just as Jack asked her about her visit to Harry.

'Sit down, the pair of you, and I'll make some cocoa. We have Bournville and Rowntree's.'

'Bournville, please,' said Grace, just as Jack called out Rowntree's.

'There, that's settled,' said Mrs Love, and took down a tin of Ovaltine.

Somehow, that little silliness relaxed the atmosphere and Jack moved to the table and pulled out the chair beside his, for Grace.

'Did you see him?'

'I sat beside his bed for quite a while, hoping he'd wake up.' She bent her head to hide the ready tears.

'A head injury.'

'The nurse said a fractured skull.'

Jack made no comment and his face was impossible to read.

'How did he look?'

'Thin.'

'Thin, Grace?' broke in Mrs Love. 'He's as skinny as a stick.'

Jack reached out and covered one of Grace's hands with his own. 'I know exactly what you mean. Don't worry; it sounds as though they're keeping him sedated. Give his skull a chance to mend.'

Mrs Love put cups in front of them. 'Don't know why I'm spoiling you two but that one's Bournville and that's Rowntree's.'

Jack smiled and switched the cups.

Mrs Love returned to reheating Grace's soup and, with her back to them, asked how long Harry was likely to remain in hospital.

'It's a serious injury; probably several weeks.'

'But when will he be well enough to get back to work?' Grace asked. 'Surely, he won't be ready for ditch-digging?'

'For goodness' sake, girl, you're not responsible for everyone. Drink your cocoa.' Mrs Love turned to Jack. 'What's her ladyship supposed to do with no workers? The land won't plough itself. When are you going, Jack?'

Jack stood up, took Grace's bowl of soup from the cook and ushered her over to the table. 'Bring your Ovaltine with you, Mrs Love, and I'll tell you as much as I can.' He waited until they were settled. 'Lord Whitefields is allowing me to stay here and work as best I can until he can find a better solution. This bit you know already, Mrs Love. Lady Alice is concerned for Grace, and his lordship feels strongly that she should be with women of her own age. He's gone back to London to talk to various bodies about rehoming refugees, hiring more land girls, getting me into some kind of medical role. We'll be informed when we're informed. In the meantime, Grace, we'll work with Hazel to the best of our ability.'

'I don't need to be with women of my own age.'

They ignored her. 'There's too much work for

me and a few old men. I can't do all the hedging and ditching on my own. Who knows, maybe the powers that be will send more...' He hesitated, as if he did not want to say the words 'conscientious objectors', but, eventually, he took refuge in, '...men like Harry and me. If that happens, you'll still be one very pretty young lady in a house full of men of all ages.'

Mrs Love bristled. 'I know how to run a household. They won't be nowhere near her.'

'Please, Mrs Love. We know that, but no one else does.' He stood up and hesitated, as he looked down at Grace. 'Got to get up early. Thanks for the cocoa, Mrs Love.'

And he was gone.

Grace finished her meal, her appetite reduced once more.

'Haven't you never met a lad before, Grace? You got too fond of Jack too quickly. Best put him out of your mind.'

'Thank you for...' Grace gestured towards the remains of the food on the plates. 'I'll have a breath of air, a bath and off to bed.'

'Best thing, lass. You'll get over this, you know; we all do.'

Grace left the kitchen and stood with her back against the ancient stones of the building. They comforted her somehow. What had they seen and endured in their hundreds of years of history? With all her might, she wished that no German bomber would find this lovely building. She would remember its strength, its resilience, wherever she was sent. She turned to go back inside, heard a sound and she jumped in fright.

'Didn't mean to startle you, Grace.' It was Jack. 'I came out for some air – just felt unable to breathe for a minute there.'

'Poor Grace,' he said, 'none of this is your fault and I'm so sorry you got involved in it.'

How sad he sounded. She felt an urge to put her arms around him. Did he not need reassurance as much as she did?

'Don't worry, Jack. I'm a qualified land girl,' she said proudly, 'I'll be fine.'

To her surprise, he moved even closer to her and, for a second, she froze. 'Jack...' she said.

'Let's not lose touch, Grace. Will you write to me? If you write here, I'm sure they'll forward it.'

He did not give her time to formulate an answer but, in the evening twilight, he leaned forward, touched her lips with his, turned and was gone.

'I'll write.' Her words disappeared in the twilight's lilac air and she did not know if he had heard.

But all their problems seemed suddenly very minor when they arrived for breakfast next morning.

'Shut up, all of you.' The shouted order was so unlike Mrs Love that everyone in the kitchen stopped what they were doing – eating, talking, moving – and looked at her in consternation. Mrs Love continued, ineffectually, to twiddle the dials on her wireless set.

'Give over, Jessie, what's up? Your Football Pools?' Hazel had gone over and gently moved her away from the wireless. 'I'll do it, Jess. This isn't like you. What station are you after?'

'Bob, I saw today's headline in her ladyship's paper when I were in the main house. All our troops, they're in France, and they're getting killed, all of them.'

At that, everyone in the room stood up, their eyes expressing all their fears, and looked at Bob Hazel.

'I've found the damned wavelength. Sit down and listen.'

They had missed most of the Home Service broadcast but, from the few sentences that summed up what had gone before, they learned that thousands of British troops were stranded on beaches in France, to which they had retreated, or been pushed, by the advancing might of the German army.

When nothing new could be learned, Hazel switched off the wireless. 'I want every man here – and girl,' he added, almost glaring at Grace, 'to eat their dinner and get back to work. We're a man short since last Saturday, in case you've already forgotten. Walter, you've a good strong back on you; give young Jack a hand. Our lads'll need feeding with good English food when we get them home, and we will have it ready for them.'

Grace tried but, although she drank tea, almost gulping it as if she were parched, she could force nothing solid across her lips. Sam Petrie was a soldier in Europe somewhere. Her heart broke with pity for her friends as they, no doubt, waited for news of him.

For several days, the workers on the Whitefields estate gathered in the kitchen at every moment they could spare from the fields or the barns. They

131

listened in fear and gradually dawning hope as the word Dunkirk was burned into their brains, and they cheered as they learned of the Armada of little ships that set out across the Channel in the most glorious of rescue missions. Lady Alice left the newspapers for them, so that they could read over what they had just heard on the wireless, and, encouraged and strengthened, they worked harder than ever. For each one, it seemed to Grace, somewhere over there, there was a Sam.

And then, one morning, even before the tales of courage from Dunkirk had finished, there was more news. Italy had declared war on Britain and France and the German army had taken Paris.

All Grace knew of Italy was that Italians made delicious ice cream.

'What happens to people from Italy who live here?' she asked. 'The ice-cream man where I grew up was Italian; really kind man, but if people don't like Jack and Harry, what will they feel about Italian people living here?'

'Shouldn't think anyone will worry, Grace,' said Hazel. Britain's a civilised country.'

'Course they will,' argued Walter. 'They'll be smashing chip-shop windows like them buggers do with the Jews in Germany.'

A few days later, Grace was put on a train to a village she had never heard of in Scotland.

'It's for the best, Grace,' said Lady Alice, as she handed her a rail warrant. 'You'll like the farm, and we have land girls there already. You'll make friends.'

EIGHT

Scotland, before Christmas 1940

Grace sat back against the pillow on her bed and pulled her feet up so that she could rest a book on her thighs while she read – bliss. Her ever-active conscience, however, would not allow her to lose herself in *Kidnapped*, an exciting book by Robert Louis Stevenson. She was both embarrassed and angry that until she had arrived at this farm, she had never read Mr Stevenson's work; why had no one told her about these exciting stories? There was a name written on the inside cover, Elsie Mc-Gregor. Had Elsie been a servant in this house? She was not among the land girls who now worked Newriggs Farm on the East Lothian estate of Lord Whitefields. Since she had arrived in Dartford thirteen years before, Grace had scarcely left the town, and yet now, here she was in another country, Scotland. She had laughed with pleasure on the cold train journey north when, after examining her rail warrant, the train guard had told her that the carriage she was in was half in Scotland and half in England. When he was gone, she had looked round quickly and then, childishly, she had stood, legs wide apart, one foot she hoped in Scotland, the other still in England. Grace had joined six other land girls: two Poles, three English and one Scot. Grace remembered saying that she

133

did not need other girls or women around her but she had to admit that it was stimulating to find herself one of so many. The Polish girls, Katia and Eva, fascinated her, for she had not been intimate with any foreign people before.

'Her ladyship expects you to look after the Polish lassies, Grace,' said Mrs Fleming, the farmer's wife. 'She knows you're a bit shy but they're not, they're very friendly, and God knows what they've been through for they haven't enough English to tell us. One sings all the time – can't make out a word, Polish probably – so they can't have been through too much, right? Only happy people sing.'

Grace wondered at the truth of that statement. Not that she could sing, but she did remember rocking and humming to herself whenever Megan had gone out after locking her in. Enough of that. She returned to the book. Had Elsie brought the book to remind her of home? But why would she need to be reminded of home if Scotland was home? Her random thoughts went on.

Am I Scottish? Paterson doesn't sound Scottish, does it? All the Scottish people I've met here have names beginning Mc or Mac. No, Fiona hasn't, and she is most definitely a Scot.

Oh, the longing to know where she came from, what her parents had been like, if they had loved her. She thought of the dream or memory that came to her, always when she deliberately did not seek it. She saw a field drying under a hot sun. There were rows of plants she now recognised as strawberries. A young woman with dark hair was kneeling between two rows, pulling off fat red berries and putting them in a trug held by a sunburned little girl in a patched cotton frock. This dream or memory had started the day Grace, and Ron and Phil, her friend Daisy's brothers, had started to dig a plot for vegetables in the wasteland of a garden behind the cottage in Dartford. Grace could almost feel the heat, smell the strawberries, savour the warmth of the dusty ground between her bare little toes. She started and looked down at her feet. She did not have bare little toes. She was a young woman, not a child. But could it possibly be that she was that little girl and, if so, who was the pretty young woman? Her mother? Megan?

Grace sat straight up on the bed. 'Grace Paterson, the things that go through your head,' she said loudly. 'Read the book or go to sleep. You have to be up before five.'

But still, thoughts came, and now they were memories of Jack, pushing aside the memories of Sam. No man had ever measured up to Sam, Daisy's brother; Sam was wonderful. Would Jack? But he could not, for they were now hundreds of miles apart; it was possible that they might not meet again. For the first time in the months since she had left the Court, Grace remembered her almost bizarre behaviour when she had gone to the hospital to visit Harry McManus. She had addressed a nurse as 'Sister', thinking the woman was a nun. A nurse did not resemble a nun. It must have been a trick of the light, or the way the nurse's uniform reminded her of a nun's wimple.

The nun. A nun. Which nun? A faint, fleeting memory showed a picture of a small girl – herself? – sitting beside a nun on a train. Try as she

135

might, nothing further was conjured up.

Her mind went back to those last weeks at the Court. Lord Whitefields had talked to someone in authority and a mere three weeks after his lordship's visit, Jack had gone. Now he was somewhere, who knew where, and was being taught how to drive an ambulance. Perhaps he was already actually working in war-torn Europe.

Grace felt a shudder run through her. Sam and Jack. No, she could not bear it. She would think of something pleasant. Christmas.

So far, no one on the farm had said a word about Christmas leave. If she was given leave, where would she go? Surely, she could no longer expect to spend Christmas Eve and Christmas Day with the parents of her school friend Sally Brewer. She smiled with remembered pleasure as she conjured up pictures of Sally and the twins, Rose and Daisy Petrie, and, of course, the Petrie boys, Ron, Phil and Sam. What fun they had had and how she had treasured being enveloped by the warmth of these families.

Grace stood up and straightened her spine. I need to write to Daisy and Sally, she thought.

The previous Christmas, her friends had delayed their celebrations to look for her. Grace almost cringed again with embarrassment as she recalled being so unhappy that she had hidden in that horrible Anderson shelter – she shuddered as she remembered the crawling earwigs – but they had found her, Sally, Daisy and Rose, and taken her to the Brewers' for Christmas dinner.

Why had Daisy never answered Grace's sad little letter she had written after leaving Dartford?

Neither had Mrs Petrie. Grace felt herself grow ice-cold. *I did write to them, didn't I?* She thought back and nodded in silent agreement with herself. Yes, she had written. There was, however, no memory of actually posting the letters.

Grace went to the window and looked out. She loved the view from it. Every day it was just a little different. Right now it was like the view on many Christmas cards: stark trees against a white landscape; in the distance an ancient stone build-ing with candlelight gleaming from a window. In the Christmas cards she had bought at the village shop, the ancient building was a church but it was a candle in a farmhouse window that shone today. It was still, technically, daylight but soon it would be dark and the light from that candle would be visible for miles, and certainly from German bombers flying above them.

Grace had reached for the blackout curtains when she was interrupted by a cheery voice.

'Gracie, can you away doon tae the office? Mrs Fleming wants a word.'

Grace looked up at Fiona Burns, another land girl, who had poked her head around the door to deliver the message. 'What can she want, Fiona? I'm sure I had this afternoon off.'

'I'm sure an'all, but I think she has a message for you. Jist think, it'll soon be Christmas, an' so it'll be an auld freen saying, Merry, Merry.'

'Thanks, I'll run.' Her spirits lifted. Jack. It could only be Jack, the only person, apart from Lady Alice, who knew where she was stationed. At last, he was going to tell her where he was and how he was doing. He could be anywhere in

Europe where there was fighting.

She stood outside the office door for a moment, taking slow, deep breaths, before knocking.

The door was opened. Mr Fleming, the farmer, stood there and, at the table, sat his wife. 'Sorry to interrupt your free time, Grace. Come on in and sit down.'

A few minutes later, Grace sat quietly, a cup of tea on the table in front of her, trying to come to terms with what she had just been told.

Mrs Fleming had said, rather bluntly, 'There's no easy way of saying this, Grace, but I'm afraid we have just had news that...' She had swallowed and was silent for a moment.

Grace looked at her. Someone had to be dead. Sam? She wanted to scream, 'Oh, no, please don't let it be Sam.'

Mrs Fleming had spoken again but Grace had heard nothing.

'Grace, are you listening? It's your sister, I'm afraid. There was a raid last night and, I am so sorry, Grace, but your sister is dead,' Mrs Fleming had said.

Now, Grace was trying to take in this unexpected and horrifying news. For the past four months, according to the news on the wireless, which all the girls, even the Polish ones, listened to as often as possible, Dartford had suffered almost continual bombing. Night after night, German bombers, on their way to London, or on their way back, dropped their bombs on the town. Apparently, the night before, a bomb had fallen on the High Street and Grace's sister had died in the destruction of her shop. Such appalling waste – of property, yes, but also of opportunity. If it was true. It could not be true. Grace had heard the words; she understood what they meant but she could not take it in.

'I'm sorry, but what was she doing there at night? She closes up at six. There must be some mistake. The shop got hit, but Megan wouldn't have been there at night. There's been a mistake.'

The farmer and his wife looked at each other. 'Poor Grace,' said Mrs Fleming. 'Her body was found this morning. Come on, lassie, will I get you a brandy? Such dreadful news.'

'It's not,' said Grace, and saw horror fighting the sympathetic expressions on their faces. How could she explain? Of course she was sorry that Megan had been killed. Had she suffered? She hoped not. But Megan had not loved her, had shown her little kindness. She had taken her in and, often, Grace had wondered why. A sense of duty? She would never know now. A blank feeling flooded over her and she felt alone, adrift. There was no one in the whole world who belonged to her or to whom she belonged. Where would she go when this job was over?

Mrs Fleming had refilled Grace's tea cup. 'I've put two sugars in, Grace. Sugar's good for shock. His lordship is arranging for you to get some leave. A Mr Petrie will meet you at the station and take you to a Mrs Brewer. You know these people?'

Grace nodded.

'That's nice. Now, until some arrangements have been made for transport ... and the ... burial an' all, we don't expect you to do any work. You just take what time you need to pack some things

139

and ... well, and get your mind straight. Awful time of the year to get such bad news but, if we're in luck, we should be able to get you on a train in a few days.' Mr Fleming, who obviously found the conversation difficult, tried to joke: 'An' I'm not wanting to have to look for you all over the farm, Grace. Canteens will be crowded and, don't ask me why, but you lassies aren't allowed to use the Naafi ones. Some idiot as doesn't know what you're doing for the country thought that one up, but the missus will make you some sandwiches. Some merry Christmas.'

Grace nodded in agreement and wiped her eyes. Megan was dead. Her sister – as far as she knew, her only living relative – was dead. 'There was so much I wanted her to tell me,' she said, and then realised that the Flemings did not know her circumstances. 'She's so much older, you see,' she said.

Was it because of Lady Alice that she was given six whole days' leave? Six days of not hearing the shriek of the alarm clock in its tin basin at four forty-five every morning. That was nice, but there was even more pleasure in store. Grace was going ... she wanted to say she was going 'home' for Christmas, but she had no home, not legally, that is, since Megan had died, and she, being both penniless and in the Women's Land Army, was to be evicted from the cottage.

'We regret this action, Miss Paterson,' the letter, received only two days after Megan's death, had said,

but our first duty is to our client, who wants the

cottage fully occupied. He understands that you will be returning to Dartford for Miss Megan Paterson's funeral and is happy for you to occupy the premises until 31 December – (the rent having been paid until that date). You do understand that, in light of the countless displaced and homeless people arriving in England each day, our client feels obligated to let the cottage to a family.

Grace read the heartless letter over and over on the long slow journey to Dartford. How she would have loved to yell at the man who had written it, telling him that he could, with her blessing, let it immediately, but she had not even acknowledged receipt. Surely, there had to be something, anything, somewhere in that little house that would tell her more about herself and her family. She had – that is, had had – a sister, so there must have been parents and, surely, Megan would have known them.

Fred Petrie and his daughter Rose met Grace at Dartford Station. As if knowing her inner turmoil, Rose enfolded Grace in her arms, and hugged her. 'We forwarded your card to Daisy, Grace; afraid she didn't get leave this Christmas.'

And that was the tone of the sad, happy visit. No recriminations, merely acceptance. Grace was brought up to date on everything that had happened to both families and, by the day of Megan's funeral, she felt as if she had never been away. It had been both pain and pleasure to sleep once more in that comfortable flat above the Petries' shop, to know that Sam, whom she now knew to

141

be in a prison camp somewhere in Europe, had slept in the room next door. Her dormant feelings for Sam had risen up like growling lions. How could she have thought of anyone else?

The wireless in the kitchen looked and sounded as if it had not been turned off since the last time she sat in this heart-warmingly familiar little room. Christmas carols and the new housewife's favourite selection of songs played constantly between news broadcasts and comedy programmes. Grace, who, with the other land girls, loved listening to the wireless when there was a break from the often unending procession of farm work, thoroughly enjoyed renewing old acquaintanceships, with programmes like *Music While You Work* and *ITMA*. Lately, like many of the hard-working land girls, she had fallen into an exhausted sleep while the programmes were playing. Here, in this unostentatious family home, she unconsciously learned the words of popular songs like 'South of the Border' and the Petrie family favourite, 'When You Wish Upon a Star'. Did they all hope that the song's promise, that they would receive everything they dreamed of, would come true? Grace was sure that the safe return of the Petrie brothers was on everyone's wish list.

'Wear your uniform to the church, Grace, dear. Doesn't hurt to let everyone know how you are spending the war,' Mrs Petrie said, as the family and friends gathered in the flat before setting out for church. 'There's been some talk, but we'll all be here beside you. I'm sure Megan was very nice, but you're not Megan and that uniform says that clearly.'

Dear Mrs Petrie. Grace understood what she was trying to say. Did she really think Megan had been 'nice', or was it that she could not, would not, speak ill of the dead? Or was it that rumour-mongers wanted to tar Grace with her sister's brush?

Mrs Brewer reached out and touched her arm. 'You all right, Grace? You've gone awfully white.'

'I'm fine, Mrs Brewer, just thinking of absent friends – isn't that the words people use?'

Later, she reminded herself that Sam was not the only Petrie to fight for her, and her heart sang with memories of her friends. *Daisy's still my friend, although she's making other friends, like that girl called Charlie. I'll tell her about Eva and Katia and the others in my next letter. She'll be pleased.*

Only once did she return to the small cottage where she had lived ever since some unknown person had brought her to Dartford and handed her over to the sister she thought she had never met before. Frightening to remember that she had been only seven years old. On the morning after Megan's funeral, Grace decided to go, alone, to her former home. Her whole being resisted under-standing why it was so important that she go back, but, apart from the knowledge that it was her duty to make the house as clean and neat as possible for incoming tenants, this was her one-and-only chance to unearth any personal documents that might be mouldering away in that miserable place. All she wanted was the simple information that everyone else seemed to take for granted. Who was she? Who were her parents? Why had she been in care of some kind? Who had put her there?

Megan? But Megan had been in Dartford. Her parents? Everyone in the entire world had parents, at least in the beginning. Where were hers and why had they not wanted her? What could a little girl have done that was so wrong?

Often, over the years, she had tried to force her mind to remember something, anything, but life seemed to have started the day Megan took her to the primary school in Dartford, and Sam Petrie and his sisters had become her champions, her heroes.

Since Mrs Petrie was busy in the shop, Mrs Brewer, who worked in the evenings, offered to go to the house with her. 'It's not pleasant, going through a house after a death, pet. Let me help you. It won't be hard for me because … it's not as if I'm affected. Don't think I've ever said much to Megan, certainly not what I really wanted to say, me and Flora.'

But although Grace was able to smile at the picture of these two lovely women castigating her sister, she refused her kind offer. 'I'll be fine and you have things to do to prepare for Christmas. I can't tell you how much I'm looking forward to being with everyone this year.' She patted her friend's shoulder gently and insisted, 'Don't worry, I'll be all right.'

'All right, dear. But, Grace, better not go down the High Street; won't help, seeing the destruction.'

Grace had not wept at the ill-attended funeral, although she had been sad, sad more for Megan, a casualty of the constant bombing of the town, than for herself. Neither did she weep in the

144

house, feeling more embarrassment at the untidiness and grime in the place than any other emotion. It had not been much of a home: no warm, cosy fire with two armchairs drawn up to it where the two sisters could chat and relive the events of the day.

She searched, however, and with mounting despair, for answers to her questions. Almost frantically, she struggled with drawers so full that they were difficult to open, but not one appeared to have been set aside to hold the legal documents that each person was supposed to have. Occasionally, her hopes were raised as a letter was unearthed on unusually fine quality stationery, and, even once, a parchment-like paper that had obviously been in its strict folds for many years. Her heart sank as she realised that her treasure trove consisted of letters to Megan from admirers and, to be fair, one or two from employers.

I must have had a birth certificate. I know my name and I know my date of birth. There must be papers somewhere. And Megan's birth certificate. Where is that?

Grace rifled through papers that she found in almost every drawer in the house that did not contain Megan's often-unwashed stockings and underwear. She slowed down and decided calmly that the best thing to do was to collect all letters and odd papers, vowing that, as soon as possible, she would study each one to see if they revealed any secrets of her own life before Dartford.

Another unpleasant task was somehow to get rid of the unwashed clothing. Grace wondered if she could bring herself to wash any of it. In her

145

work, she was often deep in mire, surrounded by dirt, but, surely, that was clean dirt, whereas soiled underwear was not.

'No one would want someone's used stockings, would they?' she asked herself. 'Am I wrong? Is it that my feelings about Megan are clouding my judgement? Displaced women are coming into England and they have nothing. Is it right to throw perfectly good things away simply because they need to be washed?'

She made no definite decision and, finding an empty shopping bag in the scullery, she pushed all the unwashed clothing that she had gathered into it. She would think about it later.

She took no long last look round; there was nothing she wanted to see. Stuffing the papers into her capacious WLA shoulder bag, she hurried out into the cold December air and back to the warm sympathetic welcome of the Brewers, whom she had promised to visit. As she hurried along, she remembered Mrs Brewer's argument as she had offered to accompany her. 'I do wish you'd let me help you, Grace, love. Flora Petrie agrees with me, clearing a house is no easy task.' Mrs Brewer had looked anxiously at her daughter's friend. Grace was pale, but then she had never had much colour. Working outdoors should have brought a healthier glow. 'At least come in for a cuppa when you've finished. The gas might have been turned off at the house, with the air raids and everything, so you'll get nothing there,' she had made Grace promise.

Now, as Grace reached Mrs Brewer's door, the woman greeted her: 'Stay and have a bite to eat.

146

It'll be lovely to have you all to ourselves. We do miss Sally so much and all those lovely Saturdays when Fred sneaked the four of you into the pictures. Weren't those days lots of fun?'

'Lovely fun, and we'll have them again when this is over; we agreed to that.'

'Can't be the same, pet. You're all growing up. My Sally on the stage, Daisy flying like a bird and she's got ever such a nice boyfriend besides. Quite posh, Rose says.'

Grace did not want boyfriends to feature in the conversation and she quickly brought it back to the immediate future. 'I've brought away all the documents that I could find, Mrs Brewer. I don't want anything else from the house. Maybe some family that's been bombed out could use the furniture, or the dishes and pots.'

'Are you sure, pet? There's certainly displaced families as could make use of them.'

'Her clothes, too, Mrs Brewer.'

'Everything, Grace? Are you really sure? She had a fur coat, you know, real rabbit. She's a bit taller than you, but just think how nice and warm it would keep you in the fields.' Mrs Brewer stopped. She had seen the girl shudder at the thought.

'Don't worry, love, me and Flora will get rid of everything. Now what you have to think about is enjoying Christmas Day. It'll be like old times, won't it? My Sally, if she can get here, and you and Rose; pity Daisy can't come. First, the Watchnight Service, then home for cocoa. Fingers crossed there's no air raid. But there won't be, will there? Germans like Christmas same as us, don't they?'

'Course they do, Mrs Brewer.' She would bring

up the subject of the unwashed clothes after Christmas.

But, of course, before Christmas was over, they were found by the renting agent and sorted, by the indefatigable Mrs Brewer, into wearable and not wearable. After disposing of the worthless clothes, Mrs Brewer washed the others and donated them to one of the many groups desperately looking for clothing for refugees.

For the first time in their long friendship, the Petrie and Brewer families, which included Grace, had Christmas dinner together. The long-legged boys who had taken up most of the space at the Petrie table were never again going to gather together around that table. Young Ron was dead, and although Sam would, hopefully, come back one day, no one actually knew where he and sailor Phil were. Daisy was on duty, as was Sally, who had come home to wish her parents – and the unexpected Grace – a Merry Christmas, before returning to London. Entertaining the troops was of vital importance to the war effort. Rose Petrie and Grace tried to be all the others for the two sets of parents and everyone pretended that everything was lovely, as they thought of those who were not there and relived memories of happier times.

A few days later, Grace was back at the farm-house in Scotland.

Her journey had been long, cold and tiring. She had returned no wiser about her background. Grace's frustration had grown, as it had been quite impossible to examine the papers while standing in a crowded train or even when seated, often squeezed against either the window or the door. If she moved her arm even a little, in the hope of pulling out an envelope, it was likely that her elbow would jar the person beside her, who was suffering the same discomfort. She had been unable to examine them at the Brewer house. Oh, Sally and her parents would have left her in peace to read but better to spend the little time she had enjoying the love and friendship of this family.

Since she had been unable to tell the Flemings when she was arriving back, there was no one at the station to meet her. It was a long, cold walk back to the farm at Newriggs, and she was pleased to be carrying so little. She had worn her lace-up boots with the woolly linings and was grateful that her feet were comfortable. She walked along, aware that she was alone and miles from the farmhouse, but she was more conscious of danger from the skies than on the road. There were raids in this area – after all, it was no great distance from Edinburgh and not far from RAF East Fortune, a ready target for the enemy.

She fantasised about a steaming hot bath, but this was not Whitefields and there was no running hot water. Water for baths had to be heated on the open fire and on the cumbersome old iron range – which had to be 'blackened' regularly. The land girls were almost certain that their duties did not include domestic service – after all, there were scarcely enough hours of daylight in which to do their farm work – but, in the interests of harmony, had decided to take it in turn.

As Grace plodded along, her spirits drooped lower and lower. It was bitingly cold but not what regular farm workers called 'too cold for snow', and she doubted that she would reach the farm before snow began to fall. Just then, she heard a noise that cheered her instantly: the tinkling of a bicycle bell. She stopped, looked behind her and saw the two Polish land girls, Katia and Eva.

'Grace, you are walking,' Eva pointed out. 'We have been in picture house for improve English. Why are you walk in cold?'

Grace was prepared to answer but the girls chattered to each other in Polish; their gestures told Grace that they were discussing her predicament.

'We have solve problem,' said Katia, thus disproving Mrs Fleming's assertion that she did not speak English. 'Bike of Eva is for man and has bar, so you will sit on bar and I will make go. Eva is not with strength of me and will make go this bicycle and carry also your bag,' she managed eventually.

Grace tried to protest but the girls were adamant and she found herself on the extremely uncomfortable bar, whizzing along the bumpy farm road. They sang together in Polish and, with Grace, in execrable English, and they laughed a lot, especially when Grace slipped off, as she did occasionally, but they did reach the shelter of the farmhouse much more quickly than she would have done on her own.

It was too late to boil enough water for a bath but there was a pot of a dish Mrs Fleming called stovies. Consisting mainly of potatoes – and in Mrs Fleming's case, a small amount of leftover beef, including the scrapings from the bottom of a roasting pan – the dish was a godsend for farmers' wives faced with the duty of feeding several

150

hungry young people, as potatoes, and, in fact, all vegetables, were not rationed. Mr Fleming, like most of the farmers in the area, grew potatoes on his farm. Throughout the rest of a long, cold winter, Grace was to become used to ingenious ways of serving potatoes, although her favourites remained Mrs Fleming's thick potato soup and the stovies. Eva and Katia complained that everything was sadly lacking in seasoning, and the more English – or Scottish – they learned, the more they were able to regale the other girls with mouthwatering tales of Polish food.

All the land girls liked the Polish girls. They knew little about them, apart from the fact that they were Catholics who'd escaped from their ravaged country some time before. Gently, but firmly, Eva and Katia refused to talk about the escape, saying only that very brave people were involved.

Grace, who worried that she felt too sorry for herself, admired the girls' courage. She watched them sometimes, wondering what it was that made them able to be so brave. Katia, the older girl, was tall and quite angular but with the most beautiful eyes – calm eyes that somehow told of great suffering. Her thick long dark brown hair was pulled back and tied firmly with a piece of coloured wool. Eva was like a fairy princess, with a rippling fall of pale gold silk, longer even than the taller Katia's, and braided into two plaits, which she curled on the top of her head like a small crown.

Grace would never forget their humour or kindness.

Now she was grateful to find that no allowance

was made for her bereavement. She could find no feelings at what was termed 'your sad loss' except some measure of annoyance that, even in death, Megan had told her nothing, and a nagging feeling of guilt that her sister had found her completely unlovable. She threw herself into her work, until she could think of nothing but discomfort, and mud and an aching back. The other girls, and especially the Poles, made friendly gestures, patting her on the shoulder if they passed behind her as they went to sit at the kitchen table, motioning to her to come closer to the fire. Occasionally, she found herself blessedly alone and she started looking at the papers she had thought might, just possibly, reveal something. Nothing. No birth or marriage certificates. No letters at all written in the twenties. Had there been letters that had been destroyed by Megan? But, if so, why? Had not one person been interested in the small Grace who had appeared in Dartford, possibly in the company of a nun, and had been taken in by the late Megan Paterson?

Oh, Grace Paterson, she chided herself, these poor girls from Poland don't even know if their families are still alive and they take time to comfort someone they think is in mourning. She yearned to say, 'I'm not, don't worry about me,' but she could not and determined instead to try to accept a situation she could not change.

Letters from Dartford arrived less than a week after her return, from Mrs Petrie, from Rose and from Sally. A few days after that, there was news from Daisy, bringing Grace up to date with her life. Joy and interest in the exciting things that were happening to Daisy carried Grace through the winter. She would have liked to write to Sam in the prison camp, via the Red Cross but, being too shy, asked Daisy to pass on her best wishes.

It was a time of hard and often unpleasant work not aided by the weather. If it was not raining, it was snowing, and, although countryside covered in pristine white snow was pleasing to the eye, it was not so much fun for the girls. Katia and Eva made light of the snow; in fact, they found the constant complaints of a few of the girls quite amazing. It was winter and in winter there was snow.

'And this is not snow much,' said Eva, who then raised her hand above her head to show the others how deep real snow got.

'And this we do well,' shouted Katia, and she caught up a handful of soft powdery snow and threw it at Fiona.

'Call that a snowball?' countered Jenny, a small, round and usually quiet girl. 'I'll show you a snowball,' and, for a few mad moments, all seven girls forgot the war and their worries and behaved like children.

For the next few gruelling months, there was little time for play as Bob Fleming and seven young women tried to get through the winter. The three jobs most loathed by the girls were clearing ditches, cleaning the byres and, the number one, universally hated – killing rats. Winter weather made the rodents even bolder as they tried to find food. Bob kept his few milk cattle indoors almost all winter and mucking out was an unending task. Standing thigh-high in filthy ice-cold water, shovelling out muck of all kinds, was both heart-breaking and backbreaking, even for the usually sunny Eva. Her pleasant soprano voice was heard all over the farm from morning till night but never when she was in a slurry drain.

'There's a grand cowboy picture on in the village, girls,' Bob Fleming said, hoping to cheer them up. 'I wish I had spare petrol so's I could take you, but the air base has promised to lend us some bikes.'

The land girls were unimpressed.

'Cowboys chase cows, Mr Fleming. That's farming. I for one have quite enough here without cycling in a blizzard to see more, no matter how scrumptious the cowboy,' pronounced Sheila, the English girl whose own home was just over the border. 'Now, if you promised me *Rebecca*...'

Even Eva and Katia had no interest. 'We have learn "yippee" and "pardner", so is all done.'

But an unexpected telephone call would soon take Grace into the rather uninspiring little grey village – *and* to the film.

NINE

'Jack, I can hardly believe it.'

'I'm very sorry about your sister.'

Mrs Fleming had been out of breath after climbing up two flights of stairs from the locked room that housed the telephone to the attic rooms where the land girls were billeted. She had shouted from the foot of the second staircase, hoping the girls would hear her, but they were all listening to Jenny's wireless and laughing uproariously. 'Sorry to interrupt the fun,' she'd puffed, 'but there's a Jack on the telephone for Grace.'

'Woo hoo,' teased the girls. 'Give 'im a kiss from us.' But Grace was already halfway down the stairs.

Five minutes later, her heart pounding, from running up and down all the stairs, she returned to the bedrooms. 'All right, all right,' she answered their clamours, 'Jack's a chap I met at Whitefields and he's coming up at the weekend – before he leaves for France.'

No matter how much pressure they tried to exert, she refused to say another word.

'Well, then, tell us what dead bodies are in the telephone room.'

'There's no bodies. I didn't really look at it, to be honest; it's very tidy. I expect they keep it locked, in case we try to telephone Clark Gable.'

'John Wayne.'

'James Stewart.'

'Roy Rogers.'

'And Trigger.' The names of favourite film stars, both two- and four-legged, made them forget the telephone call. Grace, naturally, went over and over in her head the few moments she had been able to share with Jack.

'What's it like in the wilds of Scotland?' Jack had asked.

'Not so comfortable as the wilds of Bedfordshire, but lovely; really nice girls, especially two refugees.'

'Whitefields is taking in refugees, too, not sure when they'll arrive. Got to go, just wanted to remind you we said we'd write. See you soon.'

'Yes, that'll be lovely.'

What an unexpected event. Jack. Why was he coming to Scotland and was he or was he not going into action? It was all very exciting.

Two days later, her hair washed and styled by Eva, and with whatever make-up could be spared by each of the other girls applied to her pale cheeks and to her lips, Grace waited at the farm gates for Jack. She was wearing the fur-lined coat, which Lady Alice had insisted that she take, even though the issue overcoat had arrived, and she thought that, apart from her boots, she looked quite nice.

Jack certainly thought so. His eyes shone with undisguised admiration as he looked at her, but he quickly noticed several pairs of female eyes watching them both and, pretending not to have seen them, helped Grace into the car, waved in the general direction of the hidden land girls and drove off.

'Actually, your friends made our meeting easier, Grace. I wasn't sure what you expected. I do know what I wanted to do.'

Grace blushed a very feminine shade of pink. 'It's nice to see you, Jack.'

'I should have written but her ladyship thought it might be better all round...' He did not finish, and Grace, who would have liked to know what it was that her ladyship thought, asked about Harry.

Jack looked relieved. 'How's Harry?' was obviously an easy question to answer. 'He's doing really well and the Whitefields have accepted responsibility for his care and treatment, which is absolutely splendid. The doctors say he should make a complete recovery, but his speech isn't what it was and he certainly isn't fit for manual labour.'

'Poor Harry. Does he have family?'

'No, no one. His wife died in childbirth over twenty years ago ... the baby didn't survive. He's in a sanatorium. Mrs Love visits him; somewhat ashamed of herself. But tell me all about you.'

'There's nothing to tell. Can you tell me why you're here and what you're doing?'

'Easy, I'm here to take you out for a meal and then we could go to the pictures if there's a picture house. I haven't seen a film in ages.'

Grace looked at his face as he drove. It was a very pleasant face but it looked like the face of a man who was avoiding the issue. 'And you just happened to drive here from wherever you are.'

'Sorry, Grace, I thought I had explained everything on the telephone. The earl got me into the ambulance drivers' programme. I've been working with them and now I'm ready to set off. My unit is leaving ... in a few days. In the meantime, we were given leave and Lady Alice told me I could go home to see my dad and my sister and, before I go south again, visit the Flemings, not to check up on you or the others – you will have regular visits from Land Army officials – but to pick up another delivery of venison. That's why I have the use of this car. My people were impressed, I can tell you. I had asked about you several times but Lady Alice didn't seem to want to tell me anything. No doubt, she thinks I'm a bad influence.' There was a moment of silence. 'She said ... well, she said I'm too driven, too one-dimensional, whatever that means, but when I was leaving, she told me you were here.'

A bubble of pleasure began to swell inside Grace until she felt that she and it might burst. As if he understood, Jack moved his hand from the steering wheel and squeezed her hands, which were clasped together tightly in her lap. Even her shoulders seemed to burn with some previously unknown fire. She turned to look at him again and he smiled at her.

'I want ... no, are you hungry? We might not be able to find anything exciting to eat.' He laughed and she laughed, too, spontaneously, joyfully. She felt she did not care if she never ate again – such a mundane thing to do, eating. She wanted, oh, what did she want? To sit in this car so close, so very close to Jack Williams and to drive on and on for ever.

But of course they did not. A minute or two later, they were in the village and looking for a tearoom.

'There's one opens jist afore Easter, laddie, but besides the pub, that's it. There's a hotel for the golf just fifteen, maybe twenty, miles that way.' The helpful passer-by they'd asked shrugged his shoulders and carried on.

'I can't take you to a pub, Grace, not in Scotland; it's not the same as an English public house. Your reputation wouldn't stand a chance if you were seen.'

They were both quiet, remembering the last time they had been together and worrying about reputations.

'Do you like cowboy films?'

'Love them; there's one on in the village.'

'Picture houses sell crisps and sweets. Miss Paterson, would you care to dine on potato crisps and fine chocolate while watching to see if Hollywood has managed to have a bad guy in a white hat being foiled by, wait for it, a good guy in a black hat.'

Grace smiled at him. 'Sorry, that just wouldn't do.'

The trailers for the next film to be shown in the village were running when, carrying their rather odd evening meal and still laughing, they found their seats in the one and threes, much grander seats than the ones Grace occupied when on her own.

Oklahoma Frontier, starring 'the one and only Johnny Mack Brown', was probably as exciting as any film of that type but, try as she might, Grace was aware only of the nearness of Jack Williams. Even through the thick sleeve of Lady Alice's coat, she was aware of his arm. Every nerve end in her body was tingling and she had no appetite for the sweets he had bought for her.

Could I even taste the finest steak if one was handed to me?

She sensed Jack move and, the next minute, his left arm was resting on her shoulders. She tensed, and he whispered, 'Is it all right? I just had to touch you.'

There was an extremely loud 'Shush' from

159

somewhere in the seats in front and they laughed with surprise at the sound. Others in the row laughed too for the command had been so much louder than Jack's quiet murmur and more like a sneeze than a word.

It was now impossible for Grace to concentrate on the film. She seemed unable to think of anything but Jack's arm; the men and horses galloping across the screen in front of her were no more than a blur. She heard shouts and shots but made no sense of them and was quite, quite sure that she had never been happier in her entire life, except that the weight of the masculine arm on her shoulder had reminded her of other masculine arms that had comforted the child Grace. *Like a brother. Sam.*

The film over, they stood up and followed the sizeable crowd outside. 'Don't think I would go to a crowded cinema in a big city, Grace. My mind would be on air raids throughout the evening. Not what I call fun.'

'You're right; we have been lucky, compared to my friends in Dartford. There were alerts while I was there at the beginning of the year, and here we have the occasional sortie over the Forth and one or two of the local farms have had bombs jettisoned in the middle of productive fields, but when we hear the planes we sit holding hands, and this lovely Polish girl sings.'

'Sounds nice, especially the holding-hands bit. But old Hitler's determined to get Mr Churchill and destroy London.'

'He'll never do it, Jack, not against forces like ours. My friend Daisy is a Waaf and her brothers are in the services. The oldest one is a prisoner of war in Germany,' she said sadly.

'I salute them, Grace, but I just couldn't do what they do.'

Was the lovely evening to be spoiled? Jack had sensed a change in mood too and made an obvious effort to cheer her up. 'I'd best get you back to the farm. Nice not to have to be up for milking, though.'

Grace laughed. 'Yes, Mrs Fleming milks her three cows but we're still up before five. There isn't a time on a farm when workers sleep late – apart from the day off, that is, but two of the girls, both from Cornwall, as it happens, have been on farms where the rule is: if you're not there for breakfast when it's served, you have to do without.'

'That's appalling. Land girls have the price of their meals taken out of their wages before the farmer hands on what's left. That is so dishonest. I hope they reported the farmer.'

'No idea. I certainly wouldn't have argued with Mrs Love.'

Jack laughed and held her close against his side. 'You fought with everyone.'

'But not for me, Jack; I don't think I'm good at fighting for myself. Daisy's brother, Sam, he looked after all the weaker ones.'

They had reached the car but, before unlocking the door, Jack pulled Grace round to face him. 'And you fell in love with big, strong Sam and want to be just like him. That's a lovely story, Grace. I hope he loves you, too.'

'Don't be silly, Jack, and besides, I think Sam's in love with another of my friends.'

161

Jack opened the car door and waited until Grace was sitting down before going round to the driver's side and getting in himself. He said nothing as he started the car and reversed it out of the space he'd found.

'Thank you for taking me to see the film, Jack, and for buying the sweets.'

He smiled at her, and her heart, which seemed to have sunk, lifted again. He really did have such a lovely smile.

'You're very welcome, Miss Paterson. The next time I have some leave, I'll try to do better than three-penny bars of stale chocolate.'

'It wasn't stale,' said Grace, but her brain was repeating 'the next time' over and over.

'You, miss, didn't eat any, so how would you know?'

Everything was normal again and they were able to talk about their work, the latest news, and even what they hoped to do when the war was over.

'I hope you're going to finish learning to be a doctor, Jack,' Grace said as she looked out at the countryside, illuminated by a bright moon and – shockingly to someone used to the complete blackouts of the south of England – an occasional lighted window.

'Those idiots seem to forget how close they are to Edinburgh. That's right, guide them on their way.' Jack fumed at the careless householders but had not answered her question.

'We have had a few bad moments. Aberdeen gets a pasting regularly and, of course, Glasgow and the docks. I suppose they'd like to knock out the Forth Bridge, and maybe some factories. But

162

don't worry about the lights. The wardens will spot them. Jack, I hope you're planning to go back to the university?'

'First, I have to survive, Grace.'

The words hit like a blow. Survive? He was going out to a war zone to drive ambulances through everything the enemy could throw at him. Her heart seemed to leap with terror. 'But you will, you must.'

He looked at her face in the limited light from the sky. 'Sweet, sweet Grace. You really care.'

'Of course I care.'

'I have to kiss you; I've wanted to all evening.' Jack pulled onto the rough grass verge and stopped the car. He did not wait for her to say anything but leaned over and kissed her passionately on her lips. He was indeed doing a better job than the first time.

Grace was surprised by the strength of the first kiss and more or less merely accepted it. Then Jack leaned over her again; he did not kiss her but looked into her eyes and then he traced the contours of her face, her cheeks, her forehead, her nose and, finally, delicately, her mouth. His touch set her on fire. He bent to kiss her again but connected with the brake lever and swore softly.

'Grace, I can't kiss you properly in the front seat of this car.' He stopped for a moment, as if thinking, and then continued. 'There's a lovely long seat in the back. Could we ... would you sit with me there for a few minutes? It's too cold now for kissing outside and perhaps the Flemings might not be happy to see one of their land girls being kissed good-night at their front door.'

She hesitated for a moment and he saw that and said, 'Don't be frightened. I want us to ... well, I want us to write as you promised and to see each other when I come back. Don't you want to write to me? I'm not a fearless soldier but I am going into battle. If you'd rather not, then that's all there is to it.'

'Of course I want to write, Jack, and to get letters from you. It's just that Mr Brewer always told my friend Sally not ever to get into the back seat.'

'A few kisses, Grace, for me to remember. Oh, God, that sounds so corny. In fact, it's just what some Lothario would say. I'm sorry, I shouldn't have asked.'

He sat up straight and reached out to turn the key, but Grace stopped him. 'A few minutes, just to say, till you come home safe, right?'

'Of course. Now, you mustn't feel pressured, Grace. I respect you and I still want us to write and to see each other.' She turned away from him, opened the car door, got out and let herself into the back of the car. Jack followed her.

They sat for a moment, quietly looking at each other. Grace could feel heat all over her body and her heart seemed to be beating so loudly that she thought he must be able to hear it. This then, this turbulence, was love. She had no more time to think as, with a sound like a strangled groan, Jack drew her into his arms and began to kiss her.

'What time, in the name of God, do you call this, Grace Paterson? We were worried sick. We're responsible for you, you know, and let me tell you–' Mrs Fleming pointed to the old grand-

164

mother clock in the hall – 'if you'd been two minutes later, I would have been telephoning Lady Alice in the morning. What have you been up to?'

Grace's already flushed face coloured deeply. She put up a shaking hand to try to tame her hair, which she just knew had to be untidy, and lowered it again. 'We went to the pictures, the cowboy one, and then we drove back.'

'And stopped to look at the view, I suppose.'

'We're walking out, Mrs Fleming, when Jack gets back, and we're writing to each other. I gave him my address.'

'I hope to heaven that that's all you gave him. Get upstairs, and don't wake any of the others.'

Spring came with its abundant beauty, as if nature were rewarding the seven land girls for tolerating the miseries of the past winter, but no letter arrived from Jack. Grace tried to hide her growing misery from the others but she could feel the questioning but caring eyes of Eva and Katia. Mrs Fleming's eyes were not so friendly.

One morning, she encountered Grace alone in the farmhouse vegetable plot. 'You're looking awful peeked these days, Grace; you're not coming down with something, are you?'

Grace glanced up from the carrots she was thinning and tried to smile. 'No, Mrs Fleming, I'm not.'

The farmer's wife looked her up and down, until Grace flushed at the scrutiny.

'If there's something you need to tell me, best to do it early.' Still she stared.

'I need to get on with my work, Mrs Fleming.'

165

Mrs Fleming made a sound not unlike that made by the farm collie when it sneezed, and stalked off. Grace bent once more to her task but her mind continued to work as furiously as her hands.

What if? What if...? It can't be anything else. Dear God, what will I do if I am? Where could I go? Why hasn't Jack written? He has no respect for me. No, perhaps he's hurt. Would Lady Alice tell me if...? Would she know?

She had been so used to finding solace when she worked directly with the soil but, today, no gentle peace caressed her. Her whole body was filled with memories of that time with Jack. Merely giving herself permission to think of it filled her with pleasure. Oh, they had not meant it to happen; Jack had assured her over and over again, but it had happened and it had been wonderful. Never had she been so close to another human being. The feeling of complete belonging, of loving and being loved, was something that she had never before experienced.

And just then it was as if the dream girl in the field was with her there in that orderly kitchen garden. She could see her smiling, bending closer: 'My precious little Grace, my own little lamb.'

My mother. Grace straightened up. She had had a mother; of course she had, and it was the pretty girl in the field.

'Her speaking voice is pleasant but is it her voice or am I imagining it? I have to find her, or to find out what happened to her and why I was...'

A huge wave of nausea rose up in Grace's stomach and she managed to turn quickly and vomit over the small dry-stone wall and into the field.

Trembling and sweating, she sat for a moment on the wall, until her stomach behaved itself.

'You all right?' It was Jane, another of the land girls. 'God, girl, you look bloody awful. First, you stand talking to yourself and then you barf for England. How are you going to tell the Flemings that you're up the spout?'

'Up the spout?' Grace had never heard the expression before.

'Preggers, you idiot.'

Pregnant? Oh, no. Grace was forced to face a dilemma she had been avoiding for weeks. She was, she had to be, and the other girls thought so, too. Did she have the courage... 'No, no, I had a turn, that's all. Please, Jane, don't say anything.'

'Won't need to if you behave like that again. I'm off to cut down a tree. I came looking for a helping hand but you won't be any good.'

'Yes, I will, Jane, and I've finished the carrots. Need to spend some time on the onions but I can do them after dinner. I've never cut down a tree before.'

'Neither have I, but that doesn't seem to bother the Ag. Committee. Come along, but the slightest hint of vomit and I'll tell the Flemings your secret.'

No point in trying to persuade her that there was no secret. All was not well but, if the power of prayer really existed, there would be no secret. If the power of prayer was real, a letter would come from Jack ... today, tomorrow, next week, next month.

She picked up her bag, which contained her

midday meal, and followed Jane out of the garden.

'Seemingly, the Ag. people are saying that every bit of land that can be ploughed and planted must be ploughed and planted, and the Flemings have one or two trees that have grown in the wrong place. So, down they come.' Jane saw the look of panic in Grace's eyes and laughed. 'They're not giant oaks that have been growing since the Roman invasion, Grace; they're fairly young saplings and shouldn't give us any problems. Ever used a saw?'

'Sorry, no.'

'Me, neither. For goodness' sake, girl, don't look so terrified. Together, according to the War Office, there is nothing we can't do.' She laughed at the puzzled expression on Grace's face. 'Tell yourself that every morning when you're cleaning your teeth with your bright, sparkling Kolynos dental cream, available at two shillings and two pence, or a handy portable size at one and three. Not got a wireless, Grace? They advertise like this in newspapers, too.' A moment later, she became very serious. 'Look, there they are.'

Two tall, slim beech trees were growing almost at the very edge of a ploughed field. Beside them, someone had left an axe and a double-handed saw.

'If I remember rightly, we have to decide which way is safest for them to fall. Frankly, I don't know if they told us which side to make the original cut – seemingly, that's quite important but they're not huge chestnut trees, are they? So let's not worry too much. Come on, Grace, think. Where should they fall?'

Grace looked and thought. 'I haven't the

slightest idea,' was what she wanted to say but decided that honesty was perhaps not always the best policy. 'Into the field,' she said after some deliberation. 'Any other direction and they will get caught in other trees. The field hasn't been sown yet; fewer problems. Do we have to cut them up, too?'

Jane agreed that that was probably part of the job. 'Right, I'm older and bigger. You don't look as if you could even lift the axe. Stand over there. I'll give it one or two whacks and I suppose there will be flying chips.'

'Wait, aren't we supposed to wear protective clothing? Eye shields or something like that?'

'No idea, and I don't think the Flemings have either.'

Jack and Harry had cut down trees. Had they had special equipment? Grace realised that she had never actually seen Jack working – once in a ditch, perhaps, but never cutting down trees. She looked again at the two trees they intended to fell, and shrugged. *They're not really that big.*

'I'm ready, Jane.'

Grace moved away from the first tree, as Jane lifted the axe and positioned herself so that she was facing the tree, but not in its path if it fell the way she hoped it would. Once, twice, three times, she hit it.

'I've got it started, Grace, yippee.'

Grace moved closer. Yes, there was a large gash in the trunk. 'Poor tree. I wonder if it hurts.'

Jane threw down the axe in disgust. 'Don't be stupid. It's a tree.'

'It's alive.'

'It won't be when we're finished with it. Come on, take your side of the saw.'

They had been given a long bendable saw that had a handle on either end. Grace picked up her end and together they approached the tree.

'I believe a steady rhythm is needed,' said the more experienced Jane. 'You stand that side and I'll stand this and we'll start. I'll pull and then you'll pull, evenly. I do remember Mr F saying pull, don't push. It should fall straight ahead if we get the cut right but, just in case, make sure you keep your eyes on it and listen. Maybe it will warn us. Probably, it'll groan sadly for you as its weight pulls it over.'

Grace ignored the teasing and they began. It did take some time to set a rhythm as, occasionally, because of the weight of even such young trees, the saw stuck and they had to start all over again.

'Is there anything lying around that looks like a wedge, Grace? There was something in the manual about using a wedge to keep the gash open.'

No wedge was spotted. 'Possibly smaller trunks don't use wedges,' suggested Grace after admitting that she had never read any manuals.

'Never mind, let's set up the rhythm again.'

They started once more, pull and pull, pull and pull, and eventually – at least to the two inexperienced land girls – their actions seemed totally professional and the gash in the trunk grew deeper.

They stepped back and jumped up and down with excitement as the tree did indeed begin to groan.

'It's going, it's going...'

Jane jumped over the fallen trunk and hugged Grace. 'We did it, we did it. Mr Fleming thought we were just "bits o' lasses", as he calls us. How are your hands? Mine are red-hot even with gloves.'

'Beginning of a blister. It's not too bad, though.'

'Let's have a break and eat our sandwiches.'

They spent very little time on their meal; cold water, one sandwich with a scraping of Marmite and another with slices of beetroot was hardly the most appetising picnic lunch, especially if you loathed Marmite, as Grace did.

'At least the bread's home-baked,' she tried to cheer them, 'although I do think I've eaten quite a lot of beetroot this summer.'

'Different grub from Whitefields, I expect,' said Jane, who had pulled apart what was left of a sandwich and was staring at the Marmite as if she hoped that it would turn miraculously into something else.

'Yes, but we were told that things would get tighter there, what with more rationing and no fruit coming in any more. I do miss fresh fruit.'

'This farm's got berries: rasps, strawberries and gooseberries. They're for the market, of course, but he does give us the bruised ones and any he can't sell.'

'I'll look forward to that,' said Grace, getting up from the clump of heather on which she had been sitting.

'August earliest, unless there's a heat wave.'

'Never mind; it's nice to look forward. Now for the second tree.'

At the idea of herself as a feller of trees, Grace

started to laugh and Jane joined her.

'I think it was imagining a strawberry, which no doubt we'll be planting, fertilising, weeding, picking and packing, side by side with a tree,' said Grace. 'Is there anything we won't be able to do when the war's over?'

They were both silent. Although the county was on the flight path of many of the enemy planes that droned overhead – sometimes by day and night – in the sky above them, so far the farm had not experienced a direct air raid. It would be so easy for some of the workers on this rather remote farm to forget sometimes that battles were being fought on the land, on the sea and in the air, and that lives were being torn apart all over Europe. Grace realised that her new Polish friends lived every waking moment with this awareness, as she herself thought of Sam Petrie and Daisy, and her other friends in action somewhere, especially Jack. Where was he? Why had he not answered any of her letters?

'I have a friend in the WAAF, Jane; she's got a boyfriend who's teaching her to fly.'

Both decided that flying a plane was more exciting than spreading muck all over fields or even cutting down trees. They chatted about various wartime occupations as they went back to the second tree and threw down their bags again.

'No, Grace, every war job is vital and your friend Daisy wouldn't be much use without the food you and me is growing, so let's get on with it and cut down this bloody tree,' Jane said solemnly.

What went wrong? Were they too sure of themselves? They had successfully cut down one tree. Had they believed they now knew everything there was to know about the art of felling?

Asked about this later, they said they had done everything exactly as they had done the first time.

Jane made the initial gouge in the tree bark and she and Grace then each took a handle of the great saw, stood with legs apart to help their balance and began the back-and-forth movement of the teeth. Everything was exactly as it had been before but, somehow, the direction in which the tree was falling changed. How could that have happened? They watched in disbelief and, as they listened, they felt their hearts begin to pound. The tree groaned. Even its groan of pain or anger sounded different from the other one as it veered off course and fell – swiftly and noisily – towards Jane.

'Jump, Jane,' yelled Grace, but Jane, as if rooted to the ground, stood gazing in terror at the falling tree. It crashed through the tops of the trees in its path, slicing through the new green leaves so that they fell as if blown by the autumn's first storm.

It was Grace who jumped, her arms outstretched to push Jane over; there came a muffled thud and then silence.

Initially, Grace was surprised to find that she could not move. Every bone in her body ached. She tried opening her eyes and was terrified to realise that they were already open and yet, she could see nothing. The realisation that she was lying half-on, half-off a soft, warm body, her face squashed into the ground – which, no doubt, accounted for the unbelievable pain in her neck – came swiftly and, with it, memory. Jane ... the tree.

173

She tried to move but was held down. Of course she was. The branches – thank God, not the trunk – of the felled tree were holding her down, and beneath her, Jane.

'Jane?' Her voice was no more than a whisper. 'Talk to me, Jane.'

The answering whisper was quiet but coherent. 'Get off me. I can't breathe.'

Jane was alive. Thank God, thank God. 'Jane, Jane, are you hurt?'

'Get off me,' Jane begged again. 'You're crushing me.'

Grace tried to move but only a rustle of leaves showed that her efforts were useless.

She still hurt but knew that somehow she had to get off Jane, who might be hurt very badly. 'The tree's on top of us, but we've been lucky. Honestly, we've been very lucky because it's the top branches and they're slender.'

'I'm going to die,' Jane whimpered. 'Help me, please. I don't want to die.'

'You're not dying, Jane, believe me, and Mr Fleming will come soon. Listen to me, please listen. I'm going to try to push myself off you. If I can get one hand on either side, I'll try to push myself up but I'm worried that...' No, she could not tell Jane that she was worried that if the other land girl had sustained some serious chest injury, her own movements might cause further damage.

Grace felt decidedly sick and knew that a cold sweat had broken out on her brow. She had to get off poor Jane before ... before she herself was sick. Her stomach was heaving and the old cramps, with which she was so familiar, were crunching

174

her stomach. For days, she had prayed for it to start – how she would have welcomed the pain – but now, she had to look after the smaller girl and not worry about herself.

Praying that every slight move she made would not hurt Jane, Grace managed to get her hands free and she slid her right hand onto the ground beside the left side of Jane's chest and the other hand down onto the right. 'I'm going to try to push myself up and off your poor chest. I'll try really hard not to hurt you.'

Jane said nothing.

For a moment, Grace lay still, trying to calculate how many branches were on top of them. 'It's not the trunk. We're really, really lucky, it's only branches and not the big thick ones,' she said again.

Still nothing from Jane, but Grace could feel her breathing.

'My friend Daisy, or her twin sister, could push themselves off and the dratted tree, too, Jane; really good athletes, runners especially.'

'Just do it, Grace,' came a feeble voice.

Grace summoned up every reserve of strength, planted her hands firmly into the ground on either side of the inert body, took a deep breath and pushed. The light, leafy branches on her back did move. Her arms began to tremble with strain. 'I mustn't drop on her. Oh, please don't let me drop on her,' she whispered, and tried to straighten her exhausted arms. She felt herself weaken and the pressure on her already tired and sore body was unbearable – almost. With a supreme effort, Grace managed to hold the branches off while she tried to swing herself gently to one side.

Realisation struck. *Oh, God, if I do that, the branches will fall on her face.* She could not hold much longer; she moved her left leg and felt it touch the ground beside Jane. Then, still bearing the weight of the branches on her back, she managed to slip off onto the ground. Her right arm was now lying on Jane's chest and thus took the weight of the released branches.

And at last, there was a gasp of relief from beside her. 'Thank you, Grace, thank you.'

'Actually, I think I should sue for damages or even have her arrested for assault.' Jane, one arm in plaster and her face covered in bruises and pieces of sticking plaster, lay comfortably in her bed, surrounded by the other land girls who had been avidly listening, over and over, to what could have been a tragedy and was now becoming an exciting story.

The two girls had been expected back in the mid-afternoon but, when they had not arrived, no one had seen anything strange. Neither land girl had ever sawn down a tree and so, naturally, they would take longer than an experienced feller.

'It's taken them a bit longer to get the hang of it,' Mrs Fleming had echoed the suggestion. 'They'll be back soon lookin' for a nice hot cuppa.'

But when they had not, the farmer, not sure whether to be angry or worried, had taken the tractor and driven over to the field, where he had experienced the worst fright of his life. The two land girls lay motionless, side by side, under the top half of a tree. 'My God, they're killed,' he yelled in shock as he jumped from the tractor.

'No, we're not,' muttered a feeble voice. 'I think Jane's hurt but she can talk and move one arm. I'm all right, just can't move any further and my arm's given up trying to keep branches from smothering her.'

In seconds, the farmer was beside them. He assessed the situation quickly. 'Can you crawl out, Grace, if I lift the branches?'

'I think so.'

'Good lassie.' He grasped several thin branches in his strong hands and pulled.

Grace was now aware of pain all over her body. She had been so conscious of the need to help Jane that she had striven to ignore it, but now it seemed to intensify. Her shoulders, arms and legs ached from her attempt to push Jane backwards out of the projected path of the tree. The lashing of the branches across her thin shirt added to that but the knifing pain in her stomach now eclipsed everything and she stifled a yelp of pain.

Mr Fleming, all the muscles in his arms standing out like cords, strove to keep the tree from falling back on Jane as, painfully aware that he was unable to help her, he watched her struggle. 'Check the lassie, if you can, Grace.'

'I'm all right,' came a feeble voice, 'but I don't seem able to turn over.'

'I'll help, Mr Fleming. What should I do? I could help you drag it.'

'A skinny thing like you. Best run to the house an' get the missus, if you can. Your face is a mess, lassie.'

'Probably dirt,' said Grace, trying to wipe some

of the dirt from her hair and eyes.

Grace moved over beside the farmer and grasped the branches. 'We can try, please.'

He looked at her. 'One two three, pull,' he said after a somewhat intensive scrutiny.

Grace somehow summoned up reserves of strength and pulled with the much taller and stronger man. The tree moved.

'Well done, Grace. Again.'

Jane was free.

'Should we get a doctor before she moves, Mr Fleming?'

The farmer kneeled down beside Jane, who was now moving her legs tentatively. 'My head hurts, and my arm,' she told him.

'Maybe we should–' began Grace, who was desperately trying to remember everything she had learned when she and Daisy had attended first-aid classes in Dartford. They had had a booklet entitled *Emergency Street First Aid for Air Raid Casualties*. Surely, there had been something about possible head injuries.

'A nice hot cup of tea and a lie-down and you'll be fine, won't you, Jane?' Mr Fleming interrupted her.

Jane agreed, and gingerly, with help from both Grace and Mr Fleming, she got somewhat unsteadily to her feet.

They looked at the tractor. 'Can you pull yourself up with your good arm, Jane?'

'I'll push you from behind, very carefully. Good job it wasn't your right arm.'

Jane held onto the tractor and pulled while Grace pushed her up and, with some strangled whimpering, poor Jane managed to get herself into the cab. 'I've never been inside a tractor before,' she managed bravely.

Mr Fleming climbed in beside her. 'Jump on the trailer, Grace,' he called.

Although Grace was completely incapable of jumping, she did manage to scramble onto the trailer, and in a few minutes they were making their way, as steadily as possible, back to the farmhouse where Mrs Fleming was becoming more and more agitated.

'What happened? Are they all right?' she called.

The relief on her face when she saw that both girls were able to walk indoors, mainly under their own steam, was palpable.

'She needs to see a doctor,' said Grace. 'I'm sure her arm's broken.'

'It'll be a bad sprain. I've some lentil soup keeping warm in the oven. A plate of that will set you both up grand.'

'Look at her; she can hardly stand up. I took a first-aid course at the beginning of the war, Mrs Fleming. That arm isn't sprained.' Just then, Grace gasped and doubled over in pain.

'God in heaven, what's up with you? Two hurt, Bob; we'll have the Committee here and be closed down.' Mrs Fleming was frantic.

Grace straightened up. 'I'm sorry,' she said. 'It's nothing, just a pain. Excuse me,' and without another word, she ran from the room and outside to the lavatory.

When she returned several minutes later, she still had a stomach cramp but her spirits were lighter. She had wept as she sat in the cold outhouse, but they had been tears of relief. She had prayed that her monthly cycle was simply late and now she knew that she had not miscarried and she was grateful. The guilt she felt because of her conduct was painful but Grace wondered how she could have borne the guilt that would accompany miscarrying a child.

She was pleased that the kitchen was empty – her face had to be a real mess with tears and mud mixed. A note on the waxed cloth that covered the table said, 'Grace, taken Jane to local infirmary. Have some soup and make yourself some tea.'

Grace had no appetite for lentil soup, no matter how tasty. She went upstairs to the room she shared with two of the other girls, where she tidied herself before returning to the kitchen. A cup of tea was now exactly what she wanted.

Around five thirty, the remaining land girls made their way back to the farmhouse for the evening meal and were surprised to see Grace putting out teacups. Quickly, she filled them in on the events of the day. 'And so I've made some tea, good and strong, but I have no idea what to do about food–'

'When did they go?' Eva interrupted her.

'I'm not exactly sure but it was mid-afternoon; we'd had our picnic.'

'I once waited five hours in an emergency room,' Sheila Smith informed them gloomily, 'but it was in Carlisle and cities are bound to be busier.'

Almost everyone had a tale of woe to share and they were so busy talking that they did not hear the Flemings' ancient car as it bumped its way up the farm road.

'Sorry we're late, girls,' were the first words they heard as a very pale Jane was ushered into the kitchen. 'Poor Jane had a bit of an accident, silly girl, but she's fine. Aren't you, Jane?'

Jane said nothing and Mrs Fleming continued: 'I'll take Jane upstairs and put her to bed. She's not going to be much use for a day or two.' She looked around at the girls. 'Glad you made yourselves some tea. Now, I've a lovely cottage pie in the larder and if one of you could pop it into the oven and someone else cut bread – am I not after baking some lovely loaves just this morning – supper will be ready in no time. Come away, Jane, dear, slowly does it. Put the wireless on, girls. Maybe there's something funny on as will cheer us all up.'

The girls assured her that they would take care of everything and they began to do what she had asked. But, as soon as they heard the slow-progress party reach far enough up the stairs to be out of earshot they put down whatever they were holding, turned up the wireless and sat down.

'That arm's in a plaster,' two of the girls said, stating the obvious.

'And her face is a mess and you're not much better, Grace. That big bruise must hurt like hell,' said Sheila. 'What does Mrs Fleming say?'

'Not much. I think there must be forms to fill in if one of us gets hurt, even if it's our own fault.'

'Was it fault of Jane?' Katia asked.

Grace's eyes filled with tears. She was so tired and longed to go to bed but she was very hungry. 'I don't know. We did what we did the first time and that was perfect. I have lots of little scratches, from twigs and that's what Jane has.' She did not say that her body had protected Jane from the full impact of the tree's fall. Neither had she any intention of telling them that her arms and her back were also covered in bruises.

'We are in England where it is allowed to ask questions,' said Eva. 'We will ask.'

Not even Fiona bothered to remind her she was in Scotland. 'Let's talk to Jane, first,' she suggested, 'and, depending on what she tells us, we can deal with it.'

The decision made, they finished preparing the evening meal and sat down to wait for the Flemings.

'Not worry, Mrs Fleming,' said Katia, later. 'Is late and we are all going in bed. I take plate to Jane and help her eat.'

Mrs Fleming looked at them, indecision in her eyes. 'If you're sure, girls; it's been quite a day and you working girls need a good night's sleep.'

'I'd be glad to help with the milking, Mrs Fleming,' offered Grace. 'You've had quite a day, too.'

Her offer was refused. Mrs Fleming loved her cows and enjoyed working with them but, somehow, Grace's offer had completely restored harmony between the girls and their employer. They did not go immediately to their rooms but went to the one shared by Jane and the Polish girls, where they found the invalid propped up on her pillows. She ate a little of the food but was more thirsty than hungry.

'Now, Jane, tell us what happened at the hospital.'

'I was in a bit of a state; it really was painful. Mr Fleming said he'd take care of all the details and I was trundled off to have my arm looked at. Quite a bad break, the doctor said, and it hurt like hell having it set, I can tell you, almost as bad as when I fell on it, or was thrown on to it by our commando-in-training here.'

Grace, unaware that Jane was teasing, looked distressed, and kind-hearted Sheila stepped in. 'She's only teasing, Grace. We won't let her sue you. She knows – don't you, Jane? – that you might have been killed if our Grace hadn't pushed you out of its direct path.'

'I was teasing,' admitted Jane, 'but, to tell the truth, I hadn't actually thought about it because, one minute, I was cutting down the blasted thing, the next minute it was falling towards me.' She looked at Grace, at her pale scratched cheeks. 'Gosh, Grace, it landed on you really. You should have gone to the hospital too.'

Grace attempted a smile. 'Don't worry, girls, got some scratches, that's all. After all, it was the leafy branches that hit us...'

'Because you pushed me backwards. You're a heroine.'

'A war heroine,' added Fiona.

'Nonsense. Katia, what was it you wanted to ask?' Grace had rarely had so much attention and she did not relish it.

'Jane has already answer. She did not speak with doctor, to tell him she has no proper training. Mr Fleming has do all talking, which is interesting because if he has speak five words in a row since I am coming in this farm, it is miracle.'

183

'Maybe someone will come to question Grace, someone from the Ag. Committee or the landgirls' office,' said Sheila, 'because he'll have to report the accident.' She stood up, her fingers to her lips. 'Ssh,' she whispered, 'someone's on the stairs. That really was the best cottage pie, wasn't it, Jane?' she continued more loudly. 'Delighted you're not badly hurt, and now we really had better get off to bed.'

The girls chorused, 'Good night,' and the four who shared the second bedroom trooped out.

They saw no one, but they believed Sheila. One of the Flemings had been on the stairs.

'Fiona, is that you?'

They were startled to hear Mrs Fleming's voice. She stood, with a lighted candle, at the foot of the stairs. 'I just minded on the day's post. There's two for Grace, one for you and a postcard for Katia.'

Fiona pushed past Grace and ran downstairs and, having picked up the post, handed over Grace's letters and went off to deliver Katia's postcard.

Grace, her heart thumping wildly, did not even thank her but went to their shared room and sat down on her bed. At last, at last. She recognised Daisy's handwriting, and the other one, which was a Forces Mail envelope, was from ... oh, please, oh, please...

Dear Grace,

If I told you where I was they would cut it out but I am where I want to be. The work is endless but the knowledge that I am doing what both God and my

184

father want me to do makes my load light. I will not tell you of the sights I see but all I will say is that war has to be the ultimate stupidity. Surely, after countless years of civilisation, it is not beyond the brains of man to find some other way of settling a disagreement.

Dear, sweet Grace, I cannot tell you how much our time together meant to me. Memories fill my mind when horrors fill my eyes. I pray that all is well with you. Should you need help of any kind, please contact my father. He will not fail you.

I have one letter from you which I keep in my pocket but from things you say I know that it is not the first letter you have written and one day, possibly, the others will arrive. I live in hope as do we all.

Take care of yourself, dear, sweet Grace, and write telling me how you are.

Jack

Grace read the letter over and over. She noted Jack's father's name and his address in York. She would not need his help.

'You'll wear the paper out reading that one, Grace. From Jack?'

Grace smiled weakly up at Sheila. 'Yes, took ages.' She did not add that she had looked in vain for one single word of love. 'This one's from my old school friend Daisy, the one in the WAAF. It should be interesting.' Sheila moved away and Grace opened Daisy's letter.

Dear Grace,

Life really stinks at the moment. I'd been staying with my friend Charlie in London. Such a lovely house. Charlie's dad took us to a play and then out to

185

supper at a posh hotel. It was one of the loveliest evenings I have ever had. I stayed at their house and had a super time. But they're dead now, Grace. Just a few days after I got home, Charlie, her dad, who was just as nice as mine, and two of their staff. It was a bomb. Charlie's mum had stayed in the country but I can't begin to think of how she must feel. I hope you're all right on your farm. I think about you a lot.
Please write.
Daisy

Jack alive and Daisy's friend Charlie dead. 'It's chance,' whispered Grace, 'nothing more than chance. Oh, I wish this bloody war was over.'

'Come on, Grace, you've had a ghastly day and now bad news from your friend. Let's get you off to bed.' Sheila was trying so hard to cheer her up. 'Be positive. You and Jane are all right and so is your Jack.'

Grace undressed, put her clothes ready for the morning and got into bed as quickly and as quietly as she could. Her heart was heavy and, although she now knew that her worry of the last month was groundless, she had a stomach cramp twice as bad as her usual monthly one. Serves me right, she thought as she climbed into her bed. Now that there had been time really to think about the events of the day, she realised just how serious the tree-felling incident could have been.

Are Jane and I lucky to be alive? Yes and no. Because I propelled Jane and myself backwards, the trunk did not hit us and so we were not really in grave danger. The Flemings did worry and they did come looking. And did the shock bring on my

186

monthly or would it have happened anyway? I don't know, but I won't go through that again.

Her last thought before she fell into a deep sleep was not of Jack somewhere in Europe, driving his ambulance through who knew what danger, but of Daisy, her school friend.

I'm going to save every penny, never mind summer sandals, and, if I get any leave, I'll go home, home to Dartford.

TEN

A few weeks later, Mrs Drummond-Hay, the inspector from the Women's Land Army, came to see the conditions in which the girls were living and could find no glaring fault. Yes, it was not the most modern of farms, having a limited supply of electricity. Farms were not on the National Grid and so generators were used. There was no running hot water but the house was comfortable, the beds basic but warm and clean, and the meals were adequate and often seasonally supplemented by small treats from the farm's own gardens.

'The wife feeds the land girls the same as we have ourselves. There's fruit and vegetables all year, bottled fruit in the winter months, but as many strawberries and rasps as they can eat in the summer. We don't stint our workers and we all eat together in the evenings. The land girls have the use of my wireless when they want to listen to *ITMA* or dance music, girl things. They have good bicycles, loaned to us by the air base, and the village is scarce three miles from the front door, which they can use as easy as me.'

'Why wasn't I informed of the accident?'

'Bring you out here for a broken arm? I left the farm to manage itself while I spent hours at the infirmary with the girl. Her wellbeing was my first concern. They examined her, fixed her up and sent her home. She was fine.'

'And, for the past three weeks, has been taking a wage she has not been earning.'

'Who says? Look at her. She's out there now, weeding the turnips; she feeds the pigs, the Polish lassies clean them out for her, and she scours the milk churns. She frees up my wife for heavier chores. All right, maybe she's not doing as much as the others, but you can't say she's not doing her bit and earning her wages.'

If Katia believed that the farmer had difficulty in stringing words together to make sentences, she would have been amazed at how eloquent he could be when cornered.

Mrs Drummond-Hay looked at him until he quailed under her gaze. 'I am prepared to make allowances, but an injured land girl must be sent home. We are not running a charity. Jane is underage and is her parents' responsibility.'

'Your notes should tell you that my home is now at the bottom of a very large hole and the one remaining member of my family is, I believe, somewhere in Europe.' Jane, her left arm still in plaster, had come in while they were talking and had certainly heard the conversation of the last few minutes.

Mrs Drummond-Hay spluttered. 'Believe me, if I were to spend hours reading notes, young lady, I would have no time to do the work that is necessary, even vital. I'm sure we are all extremely sorry about your sad loss but I must remind you that we are at war and hundreds if not thousands are in–'

She got no further, for Jane had walked out, saying, 'I'll be with the nicer pigs if I'm needed, Mr Fleming.'

The two people left in the kitchen looked at each other.

'Intolerable rudeness. The war makes strange bedfellows but I suppose I must make allowances,' said Mrs Drummond-Hay as she gathered up her gloves and her papers. 'I did intend to talk to the other one, Grace something-or-other.' She looked at him sternly. 'You are sure that everything had been done that should have been done to make sure your land girls were adequately trained?'

'Absolutely. They've all been at one of the schools and I train them myself.'

Mrs Drummond-Hay emitted another rather strange noise, possibly of disbelief, and put a tick on one of the papers.

'I have several farms and hostels in the area to oversee, Fleming. No doubt you will be open to a spur-of-the-moment visit.'

He merely nodded as Mrs Drummond-Hay took her departure. 'I wonder what her ladyship would think of a lady like that madam?' he muttered to himself. 'And should I tell Jane that calling her a pig wasn't too clever?' He was smiling as he headed out to the pigpen.

Later, all the girls gathered in the larger bedroom to listen to the wireless. They danced together, pretending they were debutantes at the Ritz and, when they tired of that, they discussed the visit.

'She's not a bad old cow,' said Sheila. 'Believe me, I've had a dragon and a saint, and Mrs Double-barrel fits somewhere in between. After all, she did come out to check that you were all right, Jane.'

'Yes, but didn't exert herself enough to talk to Grace.'

'What could I have said?' asked Grace in some alarm.

'You are the only person who knows what actually happened.' Jenny surprised them by speaking up. 'You were there the entire time and Jane was either unconscious or stunned.'

'Mr Fleming did his best and so did we,' Grace said, nodding towards Jane.

Grace did not want to leave Newriggs Farm, unless it was to return to Whitefields Court, where she now realised she had been happier than at any stage of her life. She had liked all the old farm workers, especially Hazel and Esau, and, she would admit to herself and no one else, Lady Alice fascinated her. A woman of birth and privilege, and yet there she was doing manual labour. She could have kept Jack on the estate for the duration of the war but, knowing that his skills were needed more elsewhere, she, and her father, had gone out of their way to have him transferred.

It was fun to live with so many girls, especially foreign ones; it reminded her of her life in Dartford, her close friendship with Daisy, Rose and

Sally, the kindness of their parents.

'I've never seen prettier trees than the ones on this farm,' she said suddenly, and the others laughed.

'What on earth brought that on, Grace?' asked Sheila, while Katia and Eva tried to find enough English words to describe how much more beautiful Polish trees were.

'What nonsense is this?' The door had been thrown open and Mrs Fleming, wearing a rather past-its-best dressing gown and with her hair in curlers, stood on the threshold, a lamp in her hand. 'The oil in that lamp has to last you till Sunday and there's no spare candles. Anyone late in the mornin' and I'll have Mrs Drummond-Hay back here to deal with you. There's a farm in the valley needs land girls an' there's no running water at all. Think on that.' And she was gone.

They would laugh about the formidable sight of Mrs Fleming in her nightwear in a day or two but, in the meantime, the girls fled to their beds and almost everyone was soon fast asleep.

Grace tried to sleep but her mind went round and round, going over the evening's conversation. The friendship that was growing between all the land girls reminded her again that she had not answered the letter from either Jack or Daisy and, although she had not heard from Sally, she knew how busy Sally's exciting new life was. One day, she promised herself, she would see Sally on the stage.

No gossiping tomorrow, if I can stay awake after supper, Grace resolved. Instead, I'll come up here or, I know, I'll sit on that lovely stone dyke and write to everyone, including Jack. He's on the front line, like Sam, and so I shouldn't mope when his letters don't arrive. We're walking out. He meant that and that's special. First chance I get, I'll cycle into the village and post them.

She had offered to strip the branches from the felled tree trunks, knowing that her spirit relished hours of solitude in the open air. Newriggs Farm had few modern facilities or appliances, but, in its slightly old-fashioned way, it was quite lovely and Grace always felt better after merely looking closely at plants and flowers. She fell asleep, crossing her fingers that Mr Fleming would grant her request.

The job he had for her, however, was as far from communing with nature in all its beauty as it was possible to get.

'I'll handle the tree work, Grace, but there's rats needs killing.'

So far, she had managed to avoid this unpleasant but necessary task. She had never before been told to do it, and Eva had even refused. 'I not kill nothing.'

'Bloody hell.' Mr Fleming had looked at Eva as if he could not quite believe his ears. 'A Polish conchie on my farm,' but he had said no more. Now, it was Grace's turn.

'Now, you know what to look for – scratch marks on walls are a good indicator. You'll maybe see tracks on dusty floors. It's not likely you'll see an actual rat until we bring in the grain – then you'll see plenty – but you'll hear them if you stay quiet; they're grand climbers and they're in the lofts. Be careful when you're up there, for I've traps set and one accident is more than enough. We've barn cats, too, and they do their best but there's too many vermin; it has to be poison.' He pointed at the foot of the door of the old stable. 'See them scratches?'

Grace shivered a little as she agreed that she did.

'Rats chew constantly; if they can't get food – and they'll eat anything – they chew fence posts, skirting boards, you name it. Their teeth never stop growing; can you imagine that?'

'Poor things, why don't the teeth grow through their skulls and kill them?'

'Because they chew and chew and chew, built-in survival. Right, now another thing to remember is that they're creatures of habit. If they find a source of regular food, they return to it, over and over, and that helps the rat-catcher.'

'I'm to put food, mixed with poison, out for them?' Grace asked doubtfully.

He looked at her. 'Did they not teach you anything at that farming school? If you weren't such a good worker, Grace, you'd be out.'

She tensed a little. 'I wasn't told how to kill a rat.'

'Right, listen and learn. First, find your infestations. Do that by finding their tracks in the dust. If you can't see tracks then get some flour from the missus or some of that smelly white powder women put on after a bath and make a trail from where you see a lot of scratches. If rats are there, they'll make recognisable tracks. You follow the tracks and put down some food. Just food, no poison. Get them used to a free feed. You might have to do that in different bits of the barns and sheds – until two or three days have passed and every morning the food is gone. That's the day you lace it. All you have to do after that is pick up the dead ones. I'll find somewhere to store them until we have enough to make a trip to the incinerator worthwhile.'

The incinerator? To Grace, rat-killing was sounding more and more horrid, but she was a land girl and there was a war on. 'Yes, Mr Fleming.'

'That shouldn't take too long, Grace; a bit of looking around the farm, deciding where to lay powder. That should take you maybe until dinner time; this afternoon, you'd best work in the beet field.'

Back-breaking work, thought Grace, but at least she would be out in the fresh air. 'Yes, Mr Fleming,' she said again.

'Good, and now away and find some powder. And mind and make a note for me of where the big infestations are. Every barn or shed where you put poison or find a dead rat will need to be well cleaned, but one job at a time, right?'

He walked off before she could parrot, 'Yes, Mr Fleming,' back to the farmhouse. Since she possessed none of the bath powder the farmer had suggested, she asked Mrs Fleming for a bowl of flour.

'Why do you need flour?'

'To lay a trap for rats, Mrs Fleming.'

'Horrible creatures, Grace; ever seen one?'

'Scurrying across the yard, I think.'

Mrs Fleming poured out some bread flour for

her. 'Dirty job, but at least it's your turn for a hot bath before tea. Be back here just on half-past five and I'll have water boiled for you.'

A hot bath. So exciting. There had been hot water on tap at Whitefields but here it had to be boiled and carried upstairs in buckets. If the farmer was at home, he helped but, on days when he was unavailable, the girls helped one another.

Grace was quite cheery when, carrying a large flashlight, she got back to the largest barn and pushed open the heavy, creaking door. The floor was a mass of dirt and dust, pieces of hay and unrecognisable droppings, but her sturdy leather shoes protected her feet.

She closed the door behind her so as to fool the rat population into thinking it was night-time, but, as she stood in the semi-darkness listening for scratching, she felt fear creeping, and then rushing up her backbone. 'I'll get you, rats,' she shouted, and then, thoroughly ashamed of herself, she hurried out into the lovely sunshine and walked quickly to the old stables. Most of the farm's horses had been sold as mechanisation came in but the two most loved by the Flemings now spent most of the warmer months grazing in an almost idyllic meadow, complete with tall shady trees and even a stream. Their stables, by contrast, were as dismal as the barn. With her newly acquired knowledge, Grace soon found evidence of infestation. The wood separating the stalls was scratched and chewed, as was the bottom of the doors. Old straw or hay and possibly a few elderly oats lay in the bottoms of the mangers and Grace decided that her first task would be to empty them. Dust flew up, causing her to sneeze but, doggedly, she carried on. Apart from the chill and the clouds of dust that were rising everywhere and settling on her hair and her clothes, Grace enjoyed being in the stable. Rising above all the unpleasantness was the smell of hay and of horses.

Grace had little experience of horses. There had been two large working horses on a farm she used to visit just outside Dartford. The farmer had allowed Grace and her friend Daisy to perch on their broad backs, but that was as much as she knew of horses. Yet she loved them, considering them the most beautiful of all animals. Grace was deep in thought as she walked from one stall to the next, digging her hands deep into the dry hay that still lined the manger. The next moment, she screamed in fright as something rustled under her fingers and jumped towards her face. Her scare inadvertently caused her to move backwards just as an extremely large rat leaped at her from the depth of the manger. Grace seemed frozen to the stone floor; she could not even scream as, in that split second, the rat flew through the air. The breath stopped in her throat and somehow her hands rose as if to stop its path to her face but, instead of clawing at her face, it landed on her shoulder. She felt its claws dig into her flesh as it fought to maintain its grip but somehow strength came from some unknown well; her vocal chords unfroze, she screamed again and the rat released its grip, slid down her back and landed on the stone floor behind her. She waited in terror, unable to move, to turn, expecting that at any moment the rat would sink its teeth into her flesh,

196

but she heard a scurrying and when she did turn, the rat had disappeared.

Her heart, which had been beating so quickly that it was in danger of jumping right out of her body, slowed its beat and she wiped the cold sweat from her brow. 'Pull yourself together, Grace,' she said, 'and just hope no one heard that scream.'

She stopped shaking, decided that only a fool would have put bare hands deep into a nest of hay and made her way outside, where she leaned against the badly whitewashed wall and took a few breaths of farm air.

She looked at the door. This was it. There was at least one rat in the stable and her job was to kill it. For a moment, it occurred to her that she might have frightened the rat more than it had frightened her but, on reflection, decided that that was highly unlikely. She swallowed the bile that was rising in her throat and went back inside.

Deliberately, she forced herself to walk to the manger that she had been cleaning and looked up. Above her was a loft, no doubt a comfortable home to hundreds of rodents. She had to go up there but, when she reached the ladder that led to the loft, she stood for a moment, listening. Nothing. No little creature with horrible ever-growing teeth was crouching up there, ready to pounce. She climbed slowly and, as soon as her head approached the loft floor, she switched on the torch. No beady little eyes. She finished the climb and stood up, stretching her spine. Evidence of the presence of small animals was everywhere.

Little prints crisscrossed the dusty floor; there was evidence of gnawing on every plank of wood and she shuddered in distaste as she found sausage-shaped droppings. Rats, rats and more rats.

I'm standing in their WC.

Grace closed her eyes for a moment, shook her head as if to banish all nasty thoughts and opened her eyes again. No need to pour Mrs Fleming's flour on the floor. She was surrounded by prints.

She went back down into the stable much more quickly than she had climbed up and, once on the floor, looked around to see where it would be best to leave some food. The stable door creaked open a little and a cat walked in. It looked at Grace as if annoyed to find a human being in its favourite dinner hall.

'You're not doing a great job, cat: this place is alive with rats.'

The cat sidled up to her and attempted to wrap himself around her leg. Grace shuddered; she was unfamiliar with cats and hated the fact that the few cats with which she had had contact, seemed to want to ... to what, be too close too soon, perhaps. Gently, she pushed the animal away, deciding that, no matter how warm summer became, she would wear Wellingtons, not shoes in the barns.

Since she was at work in the farm buildings, she returned to the farmhouse for dinner, a hearty bowl of vegetable-and-lentil soup and a slice of home-baked bread.

'If there was enough water boiled, Grace, I'd suggest a bath right now. You're a right picture.' Mrs Fleming laughed but it was not unkind laughter. 'Are you done for now in the farm buildings?'

'Yes, I'm going to the beet fields.'

'Glad we didn't waste hot water on you then,' said Mrs Fleming with another laugh. 'Best carry some water with you; it's going to be a hot afternoon.'

How did the others manage to take an afternoon break? Grace drank water as she worked. The hard work and the hot sun made her very thirsty. After an hour, she felt that she would never again be able to straighten her spine, but somehow she did. She looked out across the beet field and there in the next field was Eva. The Polish land girl was sitting against the trunk of a tall mountain ash, a beautiful tree that Fiona, the Scot, called a rowan. Curls of white smoke rose from her cigarette into the graceful branches of the tree. Eva's work would be done and done well, and yet she had time to rest. How does she do it? Grace thought, as she returned to hacking away at the persistent weeds that grew among the beets.

She was quite exhausted and absolutely filthy when she heard Eva calling, 'Come on, Grace, you are having bath and water is colding.'

'You look as cool as when you went out,' said Grace in envy. Eva was dusty but she had worn a turban round her bright hair and now she removed it and shook her head. Her dungarees were uncrushed. Grace looked down at her own and decided that she looked as if she had slept in them.

'Is nothing, Grace; maybe dirt not likes persons with yellow hair.'

'Very possible.'

To her surprise, Eva linked arms with her and together they walked and skipped back to the farmhouse, where Grace was escorted upstairs by bucket-carrying land girls.

'Wash your hair first or you won't have clean water to rinse it,' Fiona said. 'Do you want me to rinse your hair for you?'

Never had Grace sat naked in a bath while other girls milled around, helping. She could not begin now. 'No, thanks, don't want to make any of you late,' and with that, they trooped back downstairs, leaving Grace alone.

She did wash her hair first, wrapped her head in her towel and stepped into the water. Bliss. She sat down, wishing she had all the time in the world just to lie in hot water feeling the aches and pains slowly dissolve. She remembered in time that she must, in no circumstances, be late for supper.

Bob Fleming had shot two rabbits and so the delicious smell of stew met her on the stairs and immediately she felt far hungrier than she had been for some time. Rabbit stew, containing lots of onions, carrots, leeks, potatoes and whatever else Mrs Fleming had in her larder or kitchen garden, was a treat much appreciated by the usually very hungry and hard-working girls. A round, crusty loaf of Mrs Fleming's baked bread sat on the wooden bread board and there was a large glass of fresh milk beside each plate.

'Oh, and there's something else,' said Mrs Fleming as she began to serve large portions. 'Sheila, reach up above my china dog and fetch out the post. Sorry, girls, there was only Grace here at dinner time and I forgot all about them.'

Sheila distributed the letters and cards and, as always, only a few of the girls received anything.

200

'Wow, quite a fat letter for Katia, I think,' said Sheila, and handed over a large envelope, which Katia looked at and then pressed to her heart. 'Is from sister of my father. She is escaped from Warsaw before war. I will read after.'

'One for Jane and one for Fiona.' These letters were handed over, looked, at and stuffed into overall pockets to be read later.

Sheila looked very carefully at the last letter. She glanced at Mrs Fleming, who nodded and then handed the letter to Grace. 'For you, Grace, awfully official-looking.'

Grace took the letter and looked at the envelope. 'Oh, dear,' she said, 'it's from solicitors. That's lawyers, isn't it? What would solicitors want with me?'

'It's not always bad news, Grace. Maybe there's something due you because your sister died. Do you want to read it now or will we eat our tea?'

It was obvious that Grace wanted to read the letter and that the others wanted to know what was in it. She put the envelope face down on the table so that she could not see the solicitor's name. 'Shameful to let such a lovely tea go to waste, Mrs Fleming. Shouldn't think there's something now for there never was anything before. It'll keep.'

During the meal, which everyone ate very quickly, Grace tried to chat as easily as the others but her mind was going over and over all manner of scenarios. To her the meal seemed endless but she tried to be patient. 'I don't see why the girls can't read their letters over a piece of my marmalade cake and a nice cup of tea, Bob.'

'I'll away to the office for a while to let them get

201

on,' said Mr Fleming, and he pushed back his chair, nodded and strode off.

Mrs Fleming cut generous slices of cake. 'There's fresh eggs in this,' she told them. 'In a month or two, I'll put raspberries in – better than marmalade in the summer.'

Sheila passed the plates of cake and Mrs Fleming began to pour tea. 'He's a bit nervous of private things; wouldn't want to hear things as is too personal. I'll slip away too if you'd like.'

Katia started to giggle. Mrs Fleming was large and probably incapable of slipping anywhere. The awareness that Katia too could see the funny side of the words spoken by the farmer's wife relaxed the other girls.

'Nothing personal in mine,' said Jane. 'Anyone's welcome to read it.'

'Mine too,' said Fiona. 'A raid on Edinburgh, not too ghastly; it's in the papers and on the wireless. Can't think why we didn't hear that; we're no' a million miles away.'

'Sorry,' began Grace, standing up. 'Sorry, it's just … sorry.' She got to her feet and ran from the room, leaving the others looking after her in mingled interest and dismay.

Mrs Fleming stood up. 'Help yourselves, girls. I'm away to see if she needs anything. Who's close to her?'

'We all like very much Grace,' said Eva whose language skills were growing every day.

'I'm glad of that, girls. I'll see what I can do but if you wouldn't mind not going to bed yet, girls. Maybe a good play on the wireless.'

Grace was sitting on her bed. To Mrs Fleming's surprise, there was no sign at all of tears.

'Is everything all right, Grace?'

'Yes, Mrs Fleming. It's just a surprise, getting a letter from a solicitor.'

'A nice surprise, I hope.'

Grace made no reply.

'Have you come into money, Grace?'

'Nothing like that. It's just, well, it won't mean anything to anyone but me. Seems the firm that owned the building ... the place where my sister died, have found a box that belonged to her, has her name and address on it, and they want me to collect it.'

'And where is this firm? Dartford, I suppose.'

Grace nodded, too upset to speak.

'Ask them to send it to you in the post.'

Grace shook her head. 'The solicitor says ... because it was in the property ... they want to open it but they won't do it until I'm there.'

'Sounds peculiar. Never heard of such a thing. I'll talk to Mr Fleming, but we'll be harvesting in a few weeks. Now, if you're not upset, do you want to come down and drink your tea?'

Grace shook her head. 'I can't, Mrs Fleming. I need to think.'

Mrs Fleming assured Grace that she would help her in any way she could. 'We were a bit concerned about you after that lad was here, Grace. Lady Alice said maybe she'd made a big mistake telling him where you was. I'm saying no more, but in future, tell me when anything is wrong.'

Grace promised and, when Mrs Fleming left, she undressed and curled up in bed, hoping that none of the others would come up early. She relived the first weeks at Newriggs and her despair then that there was no word from Jack. And then she felt the anguish of the terrible weeks after her ... what could she call it, date with Jack? But rising above everything was this news from the solicitors. There had been an inventory and some items of possible value were unaccounted for. Had they been destroyed in the fury that had taken the lives of Megan and some unnamed Canadian or were they in the box?

Open it, open it, Grace cried in silent agony. I hope Megan wasn't a thief. But they'll just take any stuff back. They can't blame me. Maybe there's something about me in the box, some information that will explain why I was handed over to my sister, and by whom. She pushed her face into the pillow. Why won't these dreams I have show me more? Is there somewhere someone who thinks about me, worries about me? She turned over again and lay quietly, picturing a cosy kitchen like the Petrie kitchen; two comfortable if slightly battered chairs near the fire. *And a cat, a nice cat ... no, a dog, I would be happy with a dog. And two people, two...*

But no picture of the second person drew itself in her mind.

Letters? Once more, she had forgotten. Angry with herself, Grace threw back the cover and, after getting out of bed and finding her notepaper with matching envelopes, returned to the sanctuary of her bed and began to write.

For once, words poured out, to the grieving Daisy, Mrs Brewer, Sally, Mrs Petrie, Rose, to

Jack. She talked of her work, her distaste for rat-killing, the beauty of the land, the pleasure of living with girls from different countries and of learning from them. To everyone but Jack, she wrote of the worry over the solicitor's letter and she finished each, 'Hoping to see you soon. Love, Grace.'

Her letter to Jack was almost abrupt. It was obvious from his letter that he had worried that she might be pregnant, although he had never used the actual words. But although he had said that his father would have helped her, he said nothing of how he felt about the possible situation and nothing at all about any feelings he had for Grace.

Dear Jack,

You will be glad to know that I do not need any help from anyone. I am fine and enjoying the work on the farm, except for the rat-catching. We have two refugees, Polish girls, who are trained land girls but they don't talk much about the war. They tell us a bit about their country, especially the food, and one has a lovely singing voice but it's all in Polish. I hope no one is shooting at you,

Grace

Was the last sentence a bit silly? He's in the war, she reminded herself, but she could not possibly write what she wanted to write. She wanted to ask him if he still cared for her, if he had ever cared for her, but ... she could not write, 'You held me and I felt loved. But you did not love me.'

Another face shimmered before her inward eye.

Sam. Sam, who had never let her down. He would never let anyone down and, her heart lifted as she realised that, even when she had grown too old to be held, Sam had always made her feel safe.

Grace put the letters in envelopes; she would post them when she cycled into the village with the other girls.

She lay down and, when the others crept in, they were sure that she was sound asleep.

ELEVEN

The crops grew tall in the fields, the rats were killed, collected and incinerated, and were somehow replaced by other rats. Summer fruits – raspberries, strawberries, gooseberries – swelled and ripened, and currants of many colours danced like jewels on their branches. Farmers all over Britain, asked to do the impossible, did it with some muttering and the help of the Women's Land Army, squads of conscientious objectors and even prisoners of war. There was no such thing on a farm as a five-day week or an eight-hour day. Lamps were hung from trees and on hedges so that harvesting could go on. The Nation had to be fed.

Letters from 'foreign fields' were few and far between, and too often the news that did come was unwelcome, but still Grace and her fellow land girls at Newriggs Farm wrote and posted their little notes, hoping that they would reach their loved ones. All the girls, and the Flemings, too, worried about Eva and Katia, their Polish land girls. They knew little about them, only that each had fled to Britain before the fall of Poland, leaving parents and grandparents behind. When news seemed to travel too slowly between the south of England and that little farm in the south of Scotland, the English girls would look at their Polish friends, noting how bravely and efficiently they went about their work, and would stiffen their backbones.

'Tomorrow, we'll hear tomorrow,' were the words spoken in hope all over the country.

Grace had given up thinking of the pleasure of a few days' leave in order to return to Dartford to see the solicitor about her sister's locked and mysterious box. She had written to the firm, explaining the situation, and had given them written authority to open the box and to examine the contents. Mrs Petrie was to be her represent-ative at the opening. Grace knew that anything of importance that was found in the box would be safe with Mrs Petrie and so decided to try not to think of it.

That, of course, was when Mrs Fleming told her that she had been given a forty-eight-hour pass and a travel warrant. Mr Fleming drove her to the railway station and promised to telephone the solicitor's office to give them her approximate time of arrival. They, in turn, would alert the Petries.

The train was only thirty-five minutes late on departure and there were no long and unexplained delays, and so she arrived in Newcastle in plenty of time to catch the London train – if the London train would come. It did – seven hours after it was due to arrive. While she waited, Grace finished the Walter Scott novel she had borrowed from the farmhouse and ate her sandwich. Mrs Fleming, obviously aware of the difficulties of travel, had spread an egg salad between two slices of her home-made bread. She had filled a small glass jar with fat red raspberries and each one had remained uncrushed. Her delicious picnic cheered Grace as she waited and waited. With so short a leave, every hour's delay made it less likely that she would be able to visit the solicitor.

As always, Mrs Petrie would be making something special for her to eat; she would have whisked through the twins' bedroom, making sure that Daisy's bed – which is where Grace would sleep – was immaculately tidy, clean and comfortable.

'And I'm not going to get there,' she groaned.

She looked around the station: soldiers, sailors, airmen, Waafs, nurses, and all seemingly waiting for the train to London. Were they going to new bases, or home on leave, or heading abroad?

Sam. A tall, slim soldier with sun-streaked fair hair was standing, his head bowed as if he were grabbing a moment's rest. Everything about his size and his posture shouted Sam to her. How wonderful. Sam had been set free and was returning home. She did not think it unlikely that a POW returning from France or Germany to England would arrive in Newcastle. She ran forward and touched his arm. 'Sam,' she began, 'Oh, Sam, I'm so...'

'Name's Lawrence, love, but if you want me to be Sam, I'm happy to oblige.'

Lawrence was nothing at all like Sam. Grace found herself blushing furiously and wishing that the ground would open and swallow her up. It did not. 'How stupid,' she said. 'From the back ... sorry, you just...' She wanted to weep and could say no more.

'Looked like Sam from the back,' Lawrence finished for her, 'and you hoped and hoped. Sorry. One of these days, he'll come back. I would if you were waiting for me.'

The train service saved her from further embarrassment. Above all the noise of a busy station, a voice patiently tried to alert passengers to the expected arrival of the very late London train. Grace apologised to the soldier again and walked swiftly down the platform, pushing her way through the crowds. She needed to get on the train and to be as far from Lawrence as it was possible to be.

The train was crowded before it even got into the station: many people, hungry, tired and extremely disgruntled, had boarded at Edinburgh and almost six hours later found themselves approaching Newcastle when they might have expected to be very close to London. Grace, too small and too polite to push, found herself pressed between two large soldiers who argued with each other over her head. The men, however, were past masters at finding ways of being as comfortable as possible and, for part of the journey south, they allowed Grace to sit quite comfortably on their kitbags while they continued their argument above her head. At the first stop, where several people left the train, they *innocently* blocked the door to a carriage until

Grace had managed to squeeze herself into a seat inside, and all this without a single word to her.

Two hours later, the train stopped again. Since there was nothing on the platform to indicate the name of the station, the passengers had no idea where they were in relation to their final destination.

'Where are we?' the voices echoed.

'Haven't a clue, mate. York, Darlington, who knows? But I do believe we're in *merrie olde England.*'

Not much help; but humorous.

An hour or so later, Grace managed to persuade a poorly dressed elderly man to take her seat. His age and his unusual accent reminded her of the Petries' customer, Mr Fischer. At Christmas, Rose had told her as much of Mr Fischer's story as Daisy had confided in the family and, for a moment, Grace wondered if this old man might be a brilliant refugee who was travelling incognito, but she soon abandoned her theory. Surely, someone working for the Government should not smell quite so badly. She returned to the corridor, where she found that her knights in not-so-shining armour had given her place on the kitbags to two middle-aged women.

'Rather have you sitting at my feet, love,' said one, with a pleasant smile.

Those were the last words he was ever to speak as, just at that moment, there was a massive explosion.

Grace woke to screams and cries, the unbelievable noise of metal grating on metal, and smells, horrid smells of smoke and burning – and death. She was crushed beneath a heavy weight and yet her mouth, her eyes, her nose seemed plugged full of this sickening odour. She could feel that her face was wet but the source of the water, if water it was, was hidden from her. She tried pushing at what was holding her down but there was no room to push. Was it groaning, the weight? Was it not a suitcase or kitbag but a person?

Oh, God, someone's lying on me.

The heaviest hailstones she had ever heard beat down along the length of what was left of the roof of the carriage. Snow in summer? No. The staccato sound accompanied more screams, groans and then silence.

Enemy planes, their pilots determined to finish the job the bombers had begun, were strafing them.

'Have you not done enough evil, you imps of Satan?' an old voice screeched from somewhere beside her. 'They're dead, the soldiers,' went on the voice. 'They saved you, girl, threw themselves on you, but if help doesn't come soon, we'll die too and their sacrifice will have been for nothing.'

That was when Grace realised that it was not water running down her face but blood, a brave soldier's blood. 'Speak to me,' she whispered, 'please speak to me, please be alive,' but everything was silent.

'Am I dead, too?' Grace asked, and, although no one answered, she was surprised to find that the idea did not frighten her. It certainly was uncomfortable and so difficult to function with this weight upon her and her face pressed to the metal floor of the carriage, but the pain was bearable, and such air as was reasonably clear was certainly at floor level. Thick smoke hung over them and where there had been screams there was now deathly silence.

Powerless. She was powerless, a feeling that she knew well. 'Please, is someone still there?' she asked. 'Please, if you talked to me, please say something.'

No one spoke but, a few moments later, she heard metal screeching as if it were being ripped apart and the place she was in filled with light and voices.

'Utter carnage, no one survived this,' said an authoritative voice from high above Grace's head.

Grace summoned up all her energy. 'Help,' she called.

It was a feeble noise but someone heard it. 'Careful, lads, there's someone under all this.'

Grace lay listening to voices, to noises, none of which she could recognise, and then, at last, some words she understood. 'This poor lad's the last one, I think. Lift him carefully, God rest his soul. I did think I heard a woman's voice a moment ago. One, two, three, gently now, gently.'

The crushing weight was gone.

'Damnation, there be a land girl here. Careful, careful, must be her as I heard.'

The next few hours passed in a complete blur. Grace was lifted onto a stretcher and carried to an ambulance, where she was examined by the oldest doctor she had ever seen. He smiled at her. 'Do I look more like Father Christmas than your friendly physician? Still *compos mentis,* I assure you, my dear, and skilled enough to tell you that you're a very lucky young lady. Some bad scratches, one of which I've sewn up, and you're bruised from head to toe. A night in hospital, where we can keep an eye on you – observation, just to make sure – and you can continue. The soldier who fell on you saved your life, you know. Amazing luck.'

The tears began then; at first, trickling down her blood-streaked face and then gushing as she sobbed as if she would never stop. 'It wasn't luck,' she managed at last. 'He threw himself on me deliberately. I'd been sitting on his kitbag earlier.' She tried to sit up, to look around. 'Where's his friend? He was with another soldier.'

'God and modern medicine willing, the other chap will make it. He's on his way to surgery. Nurse,' he called, 'can we get this young lady a blanket and a cup of tea with sugar?'

Grace tried to say that she was all right and that she needed to get to London, but if anyone listened – and perhaps they were all far too busy dealing with real casualties to listen – no one paid the slightest attention.

Aware and grateful that she was not a priority, Grace sat quietly, enjoying the warmth of the tea provided by the ladies of the Women's Voluntary Service, and the comfort of the blanket. She began to recover from the shock and offered to help but was rejected.

'You are aware that the enemy took great pleasure in blowing up your train, and most of its passengers, to bits, girl? We want you in the hospital overnight, recuperating, not working. The WVS will talk to you, to see if they can contact your family or your unit, and so do your best to enjoy the rest; harvest-time everywhere, isn't it? You'll want to conserve your strength for that.'

A lady from the WVS did not speak to Grace until much later that evening, some hours after she had arrived at the hospital. To Grace's acute embarrassment, she had been washed and put into a hospital nightgown.

'You should have tried the soup, my dear,' the immaculately dressed woman said as she looked at the unfinished meal on Grace's bedside table. 'Your poor system received a dreadful shock and a nice bowl of soup would have done wonders for it.' She smiled, as if to say, 'And now we'll move on.' She pointed to Grace's Land Army-issue handbag. 'Apparently, you were still holding that when they found you. We had to look inside to find your name and address, Grace, but the people who live in that house in Dartford say they have no idea who you are.'

Everything came flooding back: the ghastly little house, Megan's death, the letter from the estate agent's allowing her a few days to bury her sister, searching in Megan's untidy drawers for anything, any clue as to her family, for a family must have existed. 'My older sister was the tenant; she was killed in a raid before Christmas ... at her place of work.'

'Beastly, I'm so sorry. Are there no other relatives – a parent, an aunt, anyone?'

'I had an appointment tomorrow morning with a solicitor. I had hoped he would know more than I do and I planned to stay with friends. You'll find a letter from the solicitor in my bag and the address of my friends.'

'Thank you, Grace. And the farm where you work?'

'Fleming, Newriggs Farm, East Lothian. The full address is in my notebook.'

The WVS woman got to her feet and pushed her chair to the wall. 'You're not going to make that appointment, I'm afraid. Don't worry, I'll get a message both to the solicitor and to your friends.'

'Don't let Mrs Petrie worry, please.'

'I won't. Sleep well, Grace. You're a very brave girl.'

Next morning, Grace was quite sure that she hadn't slept at all. Even people who are trying to move quietly often make a great deal of noise. Her soup bowl was gone and she had not been aware of anyone removing it.

'Feeling better?' said a voice, as a cool hand grasped her wrist and took her pulse. 'Well, we are doing better this morning. A nice bowl of porridge and a cup of tea, and then we'll see what Doctor has to say.'

'How far are we from London, Nurse?'

The nurse, who had turned to go off to her next patient, stopped. 'Not the slightest idea, love. Has to be at least a hundred miles, maybe more. Does it matter?'

'I need to get there and back to Scotland by tonight.'

'Not going to happen, pet. Just say prayers of gratitude to be alive. If the doctor lets you leave and if, and it's a very big if, there's a train, you

215

might get back tonight, but Jerry really made a picnic of the line. Fixing it'll be a priority but there's priorities all over the shop. Now eat your porridge when it comes – give you a better chance of getting out.'

Grace struggled to sit up. The very thought of porridge made her feel ill but she had to get out of the hospital immediately. So many questions chased one another around in her agitated mind. Had the solicitor been notified, and Mrs Petrie, and the Flemings, and how, from a hospital bed, could she find out if it was possible to get back to Newriggs Farm before her forty-eight hours were up?

The trolley arrived with bowls of the most un-appetising porridge she had ever seen, but she took one, determined to swallow every morsel, somehow. 'I'll be back in a jiff with tea. Would you like a nice piece of toast? Nurse said you'd be hungry, since you had nothing yesterday.'

'Thank you. That would be lovely.'

And it was. Even better was the arrival of a second WVS volunteer. 'Miss Paterson? You may not have a family, my dear, but you certainly have friends: a Mrs Petrie, a Mrs Brewer, a Miss Partridge and a vicar, a Mr Tiverton.'

Grace had no idea how to answer. She had met Mr Tiverton occasionally but had never attended his church. She would have to think. 'The lady managed to get a message to Mrs Petrie?'

'Indeed. Via Miss Partridge from Dartford, who joined the Women's Voluntary Service six months ago. She is invaluable. Mrs Petrie and Mrs Brewer asked us to remind you that you will always have a home with them. Mr Tiverton, dear man, will accompany Mrs Petrie to your solicitor's office when a new appointment has been arranged. Your priority right now is getting well and returning to front-line duty, for that's what your work is, Grace, front line.'

'Can I get up now?'

'Don't be in such a hurry. Doctor has to check you over and we're trying to rustle up some transport.'

'A Spitfire?' Grace said it with a wry grin. Where was Daisy? What fun it would be if Daisy could hide her in a plane and fly her back to Scotland.

The WVS lady was not amused. 'Just rest for the moment. God knows when you'll next get a chance.'

'A lorry?' Grace, passed for duty by the doctor, and now washed and dressed in her uniform, had been sitting in the front hall of the hospital for nearly three hours, waiting for news of a possible train.

'Best they can do. Come on, love, buck up. There's nurses in this hospital would give their eyeteeth to travel a few hundred miles with thirty-eight soldiers, all of them healthy and in one piece.'

The orderly picked up Grace's bag and escorted her outside, where an enormous military vehicle was parked. Cheery faces of all ages and sizes peered out from the canvas covers at the back.

'What a reward for bein' a good boy,' yelled one of the soldiers as he leaped down lightly from the lorry. 'Here we are, love, all ready to take you home.'

'I think not, Private Adams,' said a more authoritative voice. 'All of you stop gawping and get back inside.' The boy – for to Grace he looked extremely young – turned to her. 'Miss Paterson, Lieutenant Gilroy,' said the older man. Grace almost expected him to salute but he merely nodded. 'We are your escort back to Scotland and I do think you'll be more comfortable up front with us: the driver, Sergeant Ives, and myself. There isn't a great deal of room but it's marginally more comfortable than in the back. If I may take your bag?'

Grace managed to mumble a thank-you while she wondered how she was to get into the front. She was delighted to be wearing breeches when she saw what an enormous step-up she would have to take.

Lieutenant Gilroy stowed her bag behind the seat and then jumped in beside her. He introduced her to a much older man in uniform, who merely smiled at her, and then they were off.

The great green lorry trundled its heavy way north and Grace and the young officer managed to carry on a conversation most of the way, Sergeant Ives interrupting every now and again with a pertinent observation. The soldiers were 'going into the field' and Grace understood at once that all the friendly young men sitting cramped in the back of the lorry and the two in front were going into action. She thought of Sam; Sam who had once more become so real to her.

'I have an old friend in Europe,' she said during a break in the conversation. 'He was captured at Dunkirk.'

'POW? Hear from him much?'

'His parents hear. It's difficult. The Red Cross in Geneva...' She stopped. What was she doing? Careless talk.

She saw the soldiers smile at each other. 'We know all about the Red Cross, Miss Paterson. We are on your side.'

Grace felt very foolish.

'They do have a good track record; letters do seem to turn up eventually. I hope you hear from him soon.'

Grace felt herself blushing, but, if Lieutenant Gilroy noticed he said nothing.

They were quiet for a while as the sergeant concentrated on his driving. 'The depot, sir?' he said, after they had been quiet for some time.

'Jolly good, Sergeant. We're going to stop for re-fuelling of men and machine, Miss Paterson. In this instance, men means ladies too. There's an officers' mess where you'll be welcome to freshen up.'

Grace, who had been concerned about the long hours of travel, relaxed. 'Thank you, Lieutenant. Are there women in the army?'

'Good Lord, yes: drivers, nurses, secretarial staff, observers, cooks and cleaners – can't think how many positions. It's a brave new world.'

'Another friend is hoping to join the Auxiliary Transport Service. She hopes to drive Mr Churchill.'

'If that's what she wants then bully for her. I'd

be scared to death myself. What about you, Sergeant?'

The sergeant knew his lieutenant well enough not to answer.

They pulled in at what seemed to be a remote army camp and, less than an hour later were on their way again. Grace found her head nodding – after all, she had been awake most of the night – and she was soon fast asleep.

'I think that's your Farmer Fleming waiting over there,' was the next thing she heard.

Her first thought on hearing the lieutenant's pleasant young voice was, please don't let my mouth have been hanging open. She shook her head. 'I am so sorry, that was rude.' She hoped she had not been snoring? Did she snore? No one had so far told her of it.

'Delighted you felt safe enough to rest, Miss Paterson. Grown men have been known to weep when they hear old Ives here is driving.'

Lieutenant Gilroy opened the door, jumped down and reached up a hand to help Grace down.

'Thank you, Lieutenant. Thank you, Sergeant.'

'An absolute pleasure,' said Lieutenant Gilroy, and the sergeant smiled and nodded.

Bob Fleming was there, a large dark mass among many dark masses. 'What a time you've had, Grace, but the army to the rescue. You'll have to tell us all about it the morning.'

Eva was in the kitchen when they arrived at the farm. 'Poor Grace, you have fearful time. How we are pleased to see you.'

'I'll away to my bed, if you can manage things,

Eva. The missus needs to get her sleep, Grace; the cows don't care that you near got killed. They still needs milking.'

'I have heat up some soup and make cocoa, Grace. You must be with much hungry?'

Grace wasn't sure if she was with hungry or not. She felt utterly exhausted and longed to go to bed but Eva had obviously stayed up to look after her. 'You go off to bed, Eva. I'll drink the cocoa and come right up.'

'Is good. We are having sleep till six and half.'

Grace looked at the wag-at-the-wall clock. It said 'two and a half'.

'Very nice, Eva,' she said, and together they sat quietly at the table while Grace discovered that she did have an appetite and finished the soup. 'Pea and ham, lovely.'

'Many peas and some sausages, but sausages, ham, is all from pig.'

They laughed, drank the cocoa, washed up and crept upstairs to bed. In no time at all, they were both sound asleep.

TWELVE

Next day, Grace found herself assigned to very light work, weeding and watering the farm's kitchen garden, and collecting various summer fruits.

'We know all about the dreadful time you've gone through, Grace, and there's been a report sent up to the local district nurse just so's she's aware of what happened. You know, my heart seems to stop beating every time I think of you on that train, so you're not to strain yourself in any way and you'll tell me if there's anything, won't you? You take things easy. Should be lovely picking raspberries and maybe I'll show you how to make a gooseberry fool, if you find some nice ripe ones. They can be sour, can't they?'

Grace, who, as far as she could remember, had never eaten a gooseberry, agreed wholeheartedly with Mrs Fleming. It seemed the best thing to do.

Onto her head she stuck the very floppy pre-war sunhat Mrs Fleming had unearthed and went out into the garden, followed by the farmer's wife's voice. 'You be sure and keep that hat on, Grace. Doctor said as how you was concussed. Don't like the sound of that word.'

Me neither, thought Grace, but kept her opinions to herself. She decided to weed first as she felt that the taste of the picked fruits would be better if they stayed on their stalks as long as possible – but she did pop a raspberry or two into her mouth as she passed them. The flavour was incredible. How she pitied all the people in the world who had never eaten a raspberry straight off the bush.

She forced herself to attend to the weeds. Standing was easier but, having decapitated two carrots, she decided to kneel down – less chance of damaging the plants.

The sun rose higher in the sky as Grace worked on. At one point mid-morning, Mrs Fleming brought her out some tea.

'Everything all right, Grace. You haven't got a headache?'

'No, Mrs Fleming; this is lovely tea.'

'Others are all in the fields and have their sandwiches. I'll give you a shout when Mr Fleming comes in for his dinner and you can eat with us.'

'I'm all right out here.'

'Not with a concussion.'

That appeared to be the end of the argument and so Grace continued with the weeding. The postman cycled past, calling, 'Given the boss the post. He's in the old office.'

The old office. Grace had never heard of a new office, let alone an old one but, after all, there were several buildings around the farm that seemed to have no use now. Possibly the great change that the demands the war was making on the running of this farm had made some buildings obsolete. Mrs Fleming had talked of converting one or two former barns into dormitories for city children to live in at harvest-time. Volunteering to spend a few weeks helping out on a farm during the summer holidays was a new government initiative.

Jack and Sam insinuated themselves into Grace's mind as she thought of the harvest. She had tried so hard to think of neither man. Jack had answered a few of her letters but there was no communication from Sam. She could see them now in her mind's eye, tall blond Sam, even thinner now, for surely there would be little food in a prison camp, and the shorter, darker Jack, with his beautiful hands, hands that had made her sing. She shook her head and stamped her booted feet in the dusty soil to rid herself of the memory. Something caught in her throat and she felt tears stinging her eyes. *Don't remember. Don't think.*

But the intense memory rose and she almost cried out. *I am like Megan. I've been with Jack.* No matter how hard she tried to push the thought away, it would not go. *They call Megan a slut. Am I a slut? But it was different, wasn't it? Jack was going off to war. I had to: it was the right thing to do.*

Standing there among the rows of raspberry bushes, she faced the truth. *No, Grace, you wanted to.*

For some time, she picked furiously, filling basket after basket. At one point, Mrs Fleming stuck her head out of the open window of the scullery. 'Slow down, Grace. You'll overheat and you're not taking enough care with them rasps.'

'Sorry, lovely berries.'

Harvest-time; such a beautiful time of the farming year. She found herself wondering if there were land girls and conscientious objectors helping farmers in the fields of France, or was fertile land now being destroyed by the pounding of bombs and the heavy boots of countless soldiers? *Destroyed.* The word hit an echo in her brain. Something she had heard a long time ago, at school. Sally ... it was Sally in some play about wars and kings. Words came to her: '...fertile France ... wasting ruin...' Try as she might, nothing else came. She would ask Sally sometime. Thinking of Sally reminded her of Sam. Did Sam know anything of farming? Did Jack? No, Jack would be driving his ambulance wherever it needed to be, for Jack had courage. Somehow she knew that he would not think twice about answering every plea for help. She was not used to praying but she heard a voice saying, 'God keep them safe,' and realised that the voice was hers.

Another voice was calling. 'Dinner's on the table, Grace. Wash your hands and come now.'

She hurried inside with her baskets, washed her hands in cold water in the scullery and then carried the baskets into the large kitchen. Mr Fleming was already seated and making inroads into a plate of food that seemed to be mainly mashed potatoes, peas and runner beans.

Mrs Fleming saw her quick glance. 'We'll have some meat at tea-time when the others are back.'

The farmer said nothing as he ate. He stood up when the plate was empty. 'I've some work in the old office. I'll be in for a cuppa about four.' He took a handful of Grace's raspberries, nodded and walked off.

'Got a lot on his mind, not just the farm; they're constantly bothering him, never-ending it is.'

'Must be,' said Grace, trying to sound sympathetic when she wanted to ask if there were any letters. Seeing none on the mantelpiece, she decided that if they had gone to the old office, they were still there.

'Don't work too long. Berries will keep another day and we want to make fools. These will do for dessert at tea-time, maybe some jam,' Mrs Fleming added rather dubiously. 'I think the stock of sugar I put in before the rationing is about gone, but maybe you could get one more basket. Raw rasps and straws don't need sugar, do they?'

'No,' was the short answer as Grace went out.

'And the gooseberries,' Mrs Fleming called after her.

With no one to talk to, Grace found her mind wandering as she picked. She thought of her aborted visit to the solicitor and wondered why she had not been told of the box when she had attended the funeral. She decided that it was unlikely that the shop had been searched and cleaned up for some weeks after the bombing. After all, the bodies had been found and removed and that was – the important action. She decided to relax and wait.

'Better not go down the High Street.' Again she heard Mrs Brewer's voice.

Destruction. The shop had been destroyed, like the fields of France. Jack surely was in France. Where else were there battles? Was Sam a prisoner in France? If so, where might he be?

Her mind roved as she strolled among the bushes. When Mrs Fleming called her in to help make a gooseberry fool and some raspberry jam, Grace was both hot and quite exhausted.

'You're no use to me at all, Grace. Away and lie down.'

That evening, after they had eaten a delicious meal of mutton stew, followed by the refreshing gooseberry fool that Mrs Fleming had prepared – without Grace's help – Grace asked if she could have a word with her.

'Of course, Grace. I'll help with any problem, if I can.'

Grace looked at the round, work-marked face, at the smiling, although tired, eyes. Yes, she could trust Mrs Fleming. 'It's not exactly a problem. I wanted to ask if I could borrow an atlas.' She did not expect the reaction she got to what she thought was a very simple question.

'An atlas?' There was a complete change in the tone of voice. 'What would a land girl on a farm in Scotland want with an atlas?'

Grace found herself wishing that she had waited until she was able to cycle into the village to the small library, which would be certain to have at least one atlas. To refuse to answer would only lead to deeper suspicion. How quickly we have learned to distrust one another, thought Grace sadly. 'To look at a map of Europe,' she said in as normal a voice as possible.

'Europe? Whatever for?'

The question shot at her like a bullet from a gun. Grace was more than slightly surprised by the note of suspicion in her employer's voice – and eyes. She tried to understand it in the light of the flood of warnings the Government was sending out these days. CARELESS TALK COSTS LIVES appeared on many humorous posters.

Propaganda posters sprang up like mushrooms. There was one with huge red letters: KEEP CALM AND CARRY ON; and a series of posters aimed specifically at women. JUST A GOOD AFTERNOON'S WORK posters wanted women up and down the land to know that even a few hours of war work each week would help to defeat the might of Germany.

Now Grace stood in the comfortable farmhouse kitchen and answered truthfully: 'When you very kindly arranged for me to attend my sister's funeral, I learned that my friend Daisy's

227

brother, an army sergeant, is a prisoner of war. All they really know is that Sam's somewhere in Europe, wherever the Germans have their camps. If they make prisoners work just like we do, I wondered what kind of countryside, crops and things he might see; just a sort of interest, Mrs Fleming. I haven't looked at a map since I was about fourteen.'

Mrs Fleming stood, her arms folded across her waist, just under her less-than-generous bosom. 'I'll need to ask Mr Fleming. There's things we're not encouraged to do; keeping in mind we have foreigners here. If he says it's not a problem then I'll look it out for you.'

Grace thanked her and left, wondering why she had even bothered. Mrs Fleming obviously saw spies everywhere.

'Stupid to share anything private,' Grace muttered to herself. That was a lesson she had learned a long time ago. If no one knew your secrets then they were safe. On her next time off, she would cycle or walk into the village library.

She climbed the creaking wooden stairs to the large attic that she shared with three others. Jenny and Fiona were writing letters and Sheila – judging by the lurid cover – was deep in a torrid tale of intrigue and romance. Grace went to the window, sat down in the comfortable elderly chair and looked out across the farm. A few years before, horses, cattle and sheep would have grazed there. Because of the desperate need for a commodity as basic as bread, wheat, oats and barley now waved in the light late summer breeze.

Perhaps Sam was working on a French or

German farm at this very moment, and, who knows, perhaps he was shooing inquisitive animals out of his way, or had large farm animals been slaughtered to save food? So much she did not know. When Sam came home and she talked to him... No, she would never talk to Sam again. She was grown up and did not need a champion. Besides, how could she speak to Sam after being so intimate with Jack? In all the months since, there had been only two letters from Jack and neither satisfactory. Even in those most wonderful moments in the car, he had never used the word 'love'. *Of course he's bound to think me no better than Megan.* Grace felt worse when the thought came to her that, no doubt, Sam would think the same.

Still, she tried to remain positive and to repeat over and over that Europe was one large field of battle and letters were bound to get lost, but how tired she was. She leaned her feverish head against the glass. *I am no better than Megan, no better.*

The other girls jumped from their beds as, without a sound, Grace slid down the window onto the floor.

'They let her out of the hospital too early and we've had her working out in the hot sun and she's not fit.' Mrs Fleming, fetched by Sheila, was almost wringing her hands in desperation.

'Let's get her up and into her bed; it's probably just shock from the bombing of her train, not to mention waking up to find a dead soldier bleeding all over her.'

'That's enough, Sheila. You're no' very sympathetic, are you?'

'I'm realistic, Mrs Fleming, and I've read about shock coming even weeks after something nasty has happened.'

Jane, who had heard the commotion and come to see if she could help, was more positive. As she bent down to help lift Grace, she saw the girl's eyelashes fluttering. 'There, see, she fainted, working in the hot sun all day.'

'We have all worked in hot sun all day,' Fiona pointed out.

'But none of us survived being bombed by a German plane, kept in hospital overnight and then sent hundreds of miles squeezed into a military transport vehicle.'

Sheila laughed. 'Some girls have all the luck. Well, you are a sucker for punishment, Grace.'

'You can't send her home, Mrs Fleming: she's another one who doesn't have one,' said Jane boldly. 'We'll take care of her, won't we, girls?'

'We will help, too, I and Eva,' said Katia, who had also come in after hearing the raised voices.

'I'll have to talk to Lady Alice. I need to mention something else to her anyway. Katia, come downstairs and make Grace some tea. Put some honey in it.' Mrs Fleming walked to the door and then turned and looked back at Grace's slight figure on the bed. 'You're not in any pain, are you, Grace?'

Grace tried to sit up but was pushed back by Jane and Katia. 'I'm perfectly well, Mrs Fleming. I'm sorry to be such a nuisance.'

'Aye, well, we'll see just how much of a nuisance you have been.'

'What on earth did she mean by that?' Sheila

remained standing, looking questioningly at the door that had shut behind Mrs Fleming and Katia.

'She thinks I'm a spy,' said Grace, so softly that they had to bend down to hear.

'Good Lord, why?' The girls were now perched on the edge of Grace's bed.

'I asked her if I could see an atlas.'

'And why would that make her think you were a spy?'

'Because they look for spies everywhere,' Sheila interjected. 'Haven't you noticed the times he disappears? "I'm away to my office." There's a radio in one of the unused sheds. I saw it when I was rat-catching and he was absolutely furious that I was in there.'

'What is problem about radio? He like to listen when he works; this is not strange.' Eva had joined them, having heard Mrs Fleming and Katia walking downstairs.

'It's not a wireless, Eva; it's a radio for sending messages. Check if Mrs F is downstairs before I tell you.'

Eva left the room, was gone for a few minutes and returned. 'This is with excite. Tell.'

'Believe it or not, there is a government organisation that's a sort of civil defence. It's called "Something" Observer Corps – possibly Royal, I can't remember. The people as join have to sign, wait for it, the Official Secrets Act. They're asked, "Can you kill a man in cold blood?"'

'That's dreadful. And you think the Flemings are in it?'

'Absolutely. Once, when I was in the telephone

231

room, I saw this little booklet, and it had a Special Duties Section about sabotaging and killing and stuff.'

'Oh, Sheila, you're exaggerating.' Grace could not believe what she was hearing.

'I haven't seen the booklet since, so there. People as can't join the services because of their work or even illness of some kinds, they join it to observe everything around them. Farmers are their favourites because they're out in the country, and isn't that where a plane might drop a spy? Farmers and fishermen, out and about, seeing everything that goes on, and usually covering miles every time they leave their own front door. They can see; they can hear. They watch for enemy planes; it's actually quite hard because some of them are ancient and yet they stay out all night looking for planes or spies on boats. A woman at my last place said someone even went out lighting fires as decoys. Not sure how that works but, seemingly, Jerry thinks he's hitting something important and he's wiped out a couple of old haystacks. These observers see something a little bit strange or someone says something in the pub and so they radio their...' Sheila wasn't quite sure who 'they' would radio.

'Their supervisor,' suggested Jane.

'That's a good enough title, but who would be the tiniest bit interested in Newriggs Farm?'

'Hitler. And it's not the farm, it's all the miles of open country round it for hiding in. Think about it. The Scottish capital isn't very far away and there's docks there, and just over that hill–' she pointed somewhat vaguely towards the

232

window – 'is RAF East Fortune. Katia says she's heard from friends that there's rumours about upcoming Polish manoeuvres down here. The Poles are wonderful; many qualified pilots who managed to escape from Poland are flying with our air force and they certainly want to have an army, or at least some Polish companies, to do their bit for Britain and for Poland, too. Lots of European men are here and wanting to help the war effort. Maybe they couldn't get back home when war was declared – students at universities, for instance. This county is a perfect place for training. You could hide a tank in the gully near the orchard. Now, what if a German spy came in on a small boat, maybe a fishing boat, and he's disguised as a fisherman but he pinches an old bike and cycles around here, or he gets dropped on the next raid over Edinburgh, sees some manoeuvres and radios his controller to send bombers? Terrible. But our defence is this network of supposedly simple folk who go about their business but see and hear everything.'

'And Bob Fleming is one of them, the saviour of his nation?'

'Why not? Mrs F, too. Grace asked for the atlas. That shrieks "spy".'

'Doesn't shriek. It very quietly says, Grace P wants to look at a map of Europe. I should imagine Mr Hitler might be worried – but Mr Churchill? No. If she suddenly became interested in a map of England, its ports, railway lines, sea defences, et cetera, then someone might worry. Why do you want to see the map, by the way, Grace?'

'The family I stayed with when I went to my sister's funeral – their son is a POW. I just thought he might be working on the harvest and I wondered where the countryside was. Stupid, really.'

'No, it's not,' began Sheila, who then uttered a loud 'Shoosh' as footsteps were heard on the stairs.

'Time to be thinking about bed, girls,' Mrs Fleming said as she entered the room. 'How are you feeling now, Grace?' The farmer's wife, looking rather flustered, was peering down at the invalid.

Grace was becoming rather tired of this question. 'Ready and able, thank you.'

'Good, Mr Fleming says you're very welcome to look at his atlas.' She still looked a little ill at ease. 'We had to report the incident to Lady Alice, I'm afraid, and she will ring you here tomorrow when she's done with the milk round.'

When she had gone, all the girls, except Grace, started to laugh. 'Who's Lady Alice?' asked Jane. '"When she's done with the milk round." Is she the horse? That is so funny.'

'It won't be if she hears you,' said Sheila. 'Her father's an earl and they own this farm, so better be on your best behaviour in case she decides to come and see our little spy for herself.'

The excitement over, they separated and then got themselves into bed.

'For such a harmless little person, you do get yourself into some scrapes, our Grace,' said Jenny. 'Now we'll all be agog to hear what the aristocracy want with you.'

'They're going to chop off her head,' said Sheila.

'We'll not let them,' said Fiona. 'But we'd better get to sleep, or am I the only person in this room who has to be up at the back of four?'

There was a communal massive groan as everyone settled. Grace lay for some time wondering about the prospective telephone call and then she too fell asleep.

Lady Alice rang while they were all at breakfast and Grace hurried to the tidy little room where she had received the call from Jack all those months ago.

Lady Alice began by commiserating with her over the train disaster and asked her how she was.

'I'm very well, Lady Alice. Thank you.'

'Good, but I don't think you can be too well with everything that's happened to you. I do wish you had told me about this solicitor in Dartford. That should have been cleared up months ago. Now, tell me truthfully, are you happy there?'

Grace thought for a moment before answering. 'Yes, Lady Alice, there are nice girls here and we all get along; there are two Polish land girls – I'm learning a lot from them.'

'For heaven's sake, don't tell Mrs F. She will certainly report that. Were you tracing Jack – in the atlas, that is?'

'No.'

'Too abrupt, Grace, but I'll put that aside. Does he write?'

'I've had two letters but he doesn't say much.'

'That's about all I've had. He's doing a job, the one he wanted to do. You haven't asked about

235

Harry. He's back here, asks about you. He'll stay with us. Hazel keeps him busy but not stressed.'

'Thank you for telling me, Lady Alice; I do worry about Harry.'

'Eventually, he should make a full recovery. At least, we all hope so, but he's old and we're all he has. One more mouth to feed here won't make much difference. By the way, finally heard that several new land girls are being assigned. Hazel, Esau and I wondered if you might not want to come and help us break them in. Think about it.'

The line went dead. Grace listened for a second or two just in case it was a line fault and then hung up.

Deep in thought, she remained beside the extremely tidy desk. To go back to Whitefields Court? Her first thought was of hot running water, her second; do I want to leave here? The farmhouse was fairly primitive but the farm itself was quite beautiful. The Flemings were all right; in fact, Mrs Fleming was probably easier to deal with than Mrs Love, but Mrs Love was a better cook and – at least in the time Grace had worked there – had better ingredients. On the plus side for Newriggs, the different girls were interesting and the few she was getting to know better were very pleasant. If she left, she would really miss Eva and Katia, Sheila, Jane – in fact, all of them.

She left the office, still thinking. Is this what life is? Meeting people, loving them, leaving them or having them leave. If only there was a way to have all of them all the time. Is that, she wondered, what a real family is?

'Going to stand there all day, Grace, while

everyone else does your work for you?'

She had not seen the farmer standing in the kitchen doorway. 'Sorry, Mr Fleming.'

'Her ladyship want anything in particular?'

'Talked about the people I knew at Whitefields and my health, just this and that.' She hoped she was not lying. Lady Alice hadn't exactly asked her to go back, had she?

'Well, there's berries needs picking. Wear the wife's hat, take water and come in at twelve for your dinner. Got a watch?'

'Yes, Mr Fleming.'

'Get on with it, then.'

Another reason for going back to Whitefields. Hazel was much nicer than Mr Fleming. Grace's honesty rallied again and reminded her that the farmer had driven to a military base in the middle of the night to pick her up.

She resolved to put everything but her work out of her head and went to collect the hat and some water.

'Oh, there you are, Grace. With everything that's gone on lately, I've forgotten the post. You had two letters and they're on the kitchen window-sill.'

Two letters. How exciting. Grace thanked Mrs Fleming and hurried through to pick up the letters. She took them with her out into the raspberry field, anxious to rip them open and read them. One was from the solicitor and the other ... at long last, from Jack.

She stood between two long rows of laden bushes, the scents of dry earth leaves and ripe and overripe berries filling the still air around her head. Left hand, right-hand? What Jack has to

237

say? What the solicitor has to say?

Dear Miss Paterson,

On the morning of the twentieth past, in the presence of Lady Alice Whitefields, Mrs Flora Petrie, the Reverend K. L. Tiverton and Mr Garrick Thomas, partner in the firm of Thomas, Crawford, Shortcross and Thomas, and myself, Mr Leslie Crawford, senior partner in the same firm, a metal box found in the ruins of 11a High Street, Dartford, and belonging to the late Miss Megan Paterson, formerly manageress of the said property, was opened and the contents examined.

I am delighted to inform you that no object belonging to the owners of 11a High Street, Dartford, was found in the box and therefore the contents of the box, consisting of one gold half-hunter, beautifully engraved, several personal letters (which we hope will be of interest), a quantity of photographs, one birth certificate, two marriage licences, and one notarised will, now belong to you and will be couriered to you at your present address as soon as possible.

We would also like to assure you of our willingness to help you deal further with this matter.

With kindest regards,

It was signed with a flourish, 'Leslie Crawford'.

Grace read it several times. Her first thoughts were, how did Lady Alice get there? What has this to do with her? But realising that she was hardly likely to learn the answer unless Lady Alice told her, she turned over the letter to look at the back, although she was perfectly aware that there was nothing written there. She looked into the opened envelope, for what she did not know, but there was nothing there.

Photographs. How wonderful, but were they pictures of Megan and her friends or – she felt her heart leap as she thought of it – could at least one be of her parents?

Megan had kept letters. Please, please could just one say something about me?

Birth certificate. Her own or Megan's, surely.

A will. She had always known her family were poor. Megan had really enjoyed telling her how she had arrived in Dartford with the clothes on her back and a nightgown. Therefore, the will in the metal box could be of no real value; historical perhaps, and that would be interesting and might tell her about yet another member of her family. So exciting. How she wished there was someone with whom she could share this. Mrs Petrie knew. She would write to her, but, first, she would tell Daisy and Rose, and Sally and Sally's parents.

As for a half-hunter – she had no idea what that was. Lady Alice spoke of hunters but they were horses, and a horse, whether gold or flesh and blood, could not get into a small box. She was laughing now, giddy with surprise and delight.

'You've not moved much, Grace. Are you ill?' a voice called.

Oh, heavens, Mr Fleming was in the same field. 'No, I'm all right, Mr Fleming, getting to it right now,' she called. 'Beautiful fruit.'

She worked diligently for almost two hours without a break, sipping, every so often, from her jar of water, her mind busy with the contents of the solicitor's letter. She had folded up the slim letter from Jack and thrust it into the breast pocket of her land girl-issue blouse, and was startlingly aware of how close to her heart it lay. What of Sam? Had she forgotten him again so easily? Sam, who had only ever been kind to her? She ached to read the letter. Perhaps the contents of Jack's letter would help her to think straight.

She had picked carefully, slightly overripe fruit in one basket and raspberries at the peak of perfection in the other. The Flemings hoped to sell all the perfect berries to local shops; they were proud of their reputation: no underripe or overripe fruit in a Fleming basket. Grace glanced at her watch and was surprised to see that it was already noon and she was at least ten minutes from the farmhouse.

'You're on your own, Grace. Mr Fleming's at the corn. We want to harvest just before it's fully ripe and it will ripen and dry beautifully in the fields if this weather lasts.' Mrs Fleming, a turban wrapped around her head, was on her way out. 'There's a salad for you on the cold shelf in the pantry. When you've had a rest, go back to the berries and pick some strawberries if you're feeling up to it.'

'Thank you, Mrs Fleming, but I'm sure I'm all right. Don't you need me at the corn?'

'With Lady Alice maybe coming in and that Mrs Drummond-Hay snooping in the area, you're better among the bushes; there's some shelter. Don't rush your salad. In fact, peel a pot of potatoes for me – that'll keep you safe indoors for a while.'

Lady Alice? Mrs Drummond-Hay? Were they interested in her, in her need for an atlas, or what?

Grace practically stamped her way to the larder

to pick up her salad. How inviting it looked: fresh lettuce leaves from the garden, fresh peas, spring onions, thin slices of fresh white turnip, a not overly generous slice of tinned Spam – for which she was delighted – and a sliced boiled egg with the yolk just perfect, not hard and crumbly and not too soft. It was dressed with some kind of vinegar, a little oil and some fresh herbs from the garden. 'And all the others are out in the fields with sandwiches.' She looked again at her plate. Yes, not even the tiniest sliver of beetroot.

She picked up an egg slice with the fork, raised it to her mouth and was hit by a terrible thought. Was this salad prepared for her or might such a lovely salad have been prepared for Lady Alice? Grace practically ran to the larder. No, no other plate was on the cold shelf. Relieved, she returned to the kitchen, where she ate every bite, a slice of farm bread with a scraping of butter, and three strawberries from a bowl beside the sink.

Food, together with solitude and privacy, had made her forget her letter. Grace gasped. What did such forgetfulness tell her about herself? Grace took the pitifully thin and wrinkled letter from the pocket over her heart and began to read.

Dear Grace,
Only my father's letters are getting through to me but seldom. We have a code, and each letter, since I left for the front, has been numbered and so if ten arrives before I have seen number six, then I have some idea of time. I number mine to Father in the same way and he tells me that once four letters, and all out of order, fell on the mat at the front door on the very same day.

241

I have to confess that I did not write to either of you for some weeks: sometimes I am too tired to hold a pencil. The work is never-ending and we stop only to sleep a little and to eat when we can. I will not tell you what I see or what I hear but the noise is continuous, sometimes all day and on into the night. And, at other times, a silence falls, a silence so profound that, once, I thought the world, and not just the war, had ended and then it started louder than ever and, oh, my dear Grace, noise is so exhausting.

My first letter to you was not one of which I am proud. You gave me everything, Grace, or I took it and when I thought about it, I was terrified. Not for me, you must believe that. My father would be angry but he would never reject me, and, as I hope you under-stood, neither would he reject you. No, I did not tell him that a lovely young woman might arrive at his door, because I was ashamed, not of you, but of myself. We did not have time to fall properly in love, but, if you do not hate me, perhaps we can, as we planned, walk out when this insanity is passed. I would like to walk with you up the pathway through the lilacs to the door of my father's house. I superimpose that picture on the sights I see here, and thus keep my sanity.

I think about you in the fields and hope you do not have to work too hard. I remember Harry and worry about him, but I'm sure the Whitefields will look after him. He has, I think, one of the sweetest natures of any man I have ever met. And Hazel and Esau and the others, splendid fellows. Are you learning Polish? I think I would try if I were in that company. I could learn German here and also improve the French I learned at school. One hears these languages con-stantly.

242

Across the bottom corner of the page was his name, 'Jack'. The letter had quite filled both sides of the page. It was the longest letter Grace had ever had from anyone. Had Mrs Fleming read this letter? If she had, she would know exactly what had happened when Jack took Grace to see the film. But she had said nothing.

THIRTEEN

All seven land girls saw Grace's box arrive, although none of them knew that the rather splendid car that drove up to the farmhouse door carried it. Grace alone recognised Lady Alice.

'What a lovely frock,' said Jane as she eyed the slim figure approaching the gate.

'All right for some.' Sheila too thought that the charming cotton frock with its light brown background splashed with exuberant yellow daisies was definitely the last word, but she was only too well aware that she was not one of the 'some'.

'And her shoes and gloves,' breathed Katia, who then expressed her admiration more volubly in Polish.

'Why is she not with bag? Is possible new land girl with smart car?' Eva looked and sounded very doubtful.

'It's Lady Alice,' said Grace.

The girls stood, some admiring the vision of summer perfection, the others wondering what had brought the vision north. They were not left long in ignorance.

'Come along, girls, don't dawdle. Grace, bring the girls into the kitchen before they get sunstroke.'

In the farmhouse kitchen, Mrs Fleming was on the point of serving the Sunday midday meal, usually the only time the girls ate their 'dinner' together with their employers. Despite having been pre-warned of Lady Alice's visit, she was startled. 'Lady Alice, how very nice to see you.'

'I didn't mean to disturb lunch, Mrs Fleming, but I'm afraid I need to talk to Grace – the office will do. Send one of the others along with some tea and I'll be out of your way as quickly as possible. Save Grace's meal.' She nodded to the other girls, who were still admiring her clothes, said, 'Come along, Grace,' and left the kitchen, not through the door that led to the dark corridor where the office was, but out through the garden door.

'Your box, such as it is, is in my bag, and I thoughtlessly left that in the car, which, incidentally belongs to friends in Edinburgh who are sacrificing their petrol for you; you can assure the others that I came up by train and will return in the same uncomfortable manner.' She reached into the little car and brought out a white leather handbag with a gold clasp and gold piping around the handle. 'Let's go in and sit down; there really is rather a lot I have to tell you. I suppose what right I had to stick my nose into your affairs is really the first thing you want to know.'

Speechlessly, Grace followed her back into the kitchen, where Lady Alice called out, 'Excuse us,' as they passed the table. Grace smiled as she saw the envious glances directed towards the elegant bag. She knew she would have several questions to answer about it later. Her heart, which had calmed a little, began to race as they walked down the corridor.

'Electricity will do wonders for this house, Grace; shouldn't be long before it's on the National Grid.'

In the office, Lady Alice sat down on a chair that badly needed new upholstery and directed Grace to the leather chair at the desk. 'Perhaps you'll need to lay things out on the desk, Grace. Startlingly tidy, isn't it? I do wonder if it's ever used.'

It was obvious that she was not awaiting a comment, as she lifted a badly dented metal box out of the beautiful bag. 'Got rather a bashing in the bombing; funny things, bombs. It blew the shop apart but didn't open the box.'

The box, unopened, sat in front of Grace, who felt as if somehow her tongue was sticking to the roof of her mouth. Photographs, letters. How badly she wanted to see them.

'Would you prefer that I left?' asked Lady Alice quietly, as a knock on the door heralded the arrival of the tea.

Grace had somehow lost the gift of speech and she shook her head as Lady Alice poured tea, put in milk and sugar, and placed a cup and saucer beside Grace's right hand.

The box lay open, its contents visible. First, was a small leather box, which Grace removed and put on the table; whatever it was, it was not a letter and she would look at it later. Next, was an old, rather brittle official document. With hands that shook, Grace lifted it from the box. It was a marriage certificate stating that a marriage had taken place in 6 April 1895 between one Alexander Hardy, gentleman, and Abigail Smythe, spinster of this parish. She was confused. She had never heard either of these names before and what, if anything, did they have to do with her?

She laid it carefully aside and took out the next document, a birth certificate. That told her that a girl, Margaret Hardy, had been born to Abigail and Alexander Hardy in September 1898.

Deeply distressed, Grace pushed the box aside and stood up. 'There must be some mistake, Lady Alice. These names mean nothing; I've never heard of these people. They can't be important to me.'

'Sit down again, Grace, and listen to me.' Lady Alice waited until, grudgingly, Grace had obeyed her. 'I took it upon myself to be there when the box was opened. You were sent to me as a land girl and I feel responsible – *am* responsible – for your welfare. My father rang the solicitors, explaining the difficulties you were experiencing and they allowed me, with Mrs Petrie, who really is a very caring human being, and Mr Tiverton, to oversee the opening of your sister's box.'

Grace was still rather angry; she had told the solicitor that Mrs Petrie would represent her. They had no need of Lady Alice. But then she thought for a moment and realised that the world being what it was, having a titled lady in her corner could only be positive.

'Thank you,' she said quietly. 'Mrs Petrie has always been kind to me.'

It was obvious that Lady Alice understood all the thoughts that were flying around in her head. 'Mrs Petrie, Mr Tiverton and I sat down over a very good cup of tea – Mrs Petrie knows her teas – in fact, she has persuaded Thomas, Crawford, Short-cross and Thomas to become a customer of Petrie's fine teas. Quite frankly, they were de-lighted. Superb service and cheaper than London.'

Grace smiled at the idea of Mrs Petrie soliciting custom. She had to admit that she probably had told the posh solicitors that their tea was of inferior quality. Well done, Mrs Petrie, she said to herself.

'She did say she wanted to write to you. Have you heard from her?'

'No, she's too busy. Probably about this box.'

'Of course, but perhaps you should look at the will, Grace. Indirectly, it refers to you.'

'Me? Lady Alice, these people are from long before I was born.'

'The second marriage licence should help.'

Grace looked at the papers in the box and closed her eyes for a moment against the enormity of all that was happening. She had wanted to see the papers and now that they were in her hands she was afraid of what they might tell her.

'Grace, Mrs Petrie, Mr Tiverton and I took it upon ourselves to study the birth certificate, the marriage licences and the will, so that, if it was necessary, we could help you deal with their contents. There are surprises for you here, and most of them are pleasant. We have not looked at the letters or photographs; they are there for you to read when and if you want to read them. The

247

legal documents are important. May I?' Lady Alice did not wait for the small nod from Grace but reached in and withdrew a second aged paper, then handed it to her.

As if it was made of the finest, most delicate substance, Grace took the paper and opened it with great care.

It was the will of Abigail Smythe Hardy and was very simple. Abigail left her gold half-hunter and the sum of five hundred pounds to her daughter, Margaret Hardy, or to any heir of the body of the said Margaret Hardy or Paterson.

'I don't know what it means, Lady Alice.'

Lady Alice picked up the small box, opened it, and showed Grace the contents. 'This is called a half-hunter, Grace. It's a watch and this one is rather lovely – gold, of course, and, if you turn it over ... see, beautifully engraved initials. A. S.: Abigail Smythe, your grandmother.'

'My grandmother?' Tentatively, Grace reached out and, with the tip of her index finger, touched the gold watch, which lay on the inside cushion.

'It's yours, Grace; pick it up, or perhaps you'd prefer to read the second marriage certificate. Here, read it, and believe it.'

The second marriage licence announced to the world the marriage of Margaret Hardy and John Paterson on 26 June 1919.

Grace, her face glowing with hope, looked up. 'Do you mean ... is this, are these...?'

'Your parents, Grace, yes.'

'I think I was born in 1921.' Grace thought she might weep with happiness, but she closed her eyes tightly for a moment and, feeling again in control, smiled happily at her employer.

'Mr Crawford is perfectly willing to represent you in this, Grace. I suppose five hundred pounds is not a fortune, but we need to discover where it is. If, for instance, and highly unlikely, your grandmamma kept it in a box under her bed, then no doubt it is still worth five hundred pounds ... probably less, but, if the money is in a bank or has been invested, then who knows how much it has accumulated by? All depends on when Mrs Hardy died.'

Grace could not even begin to think of what the possession of hundreds of pounds might mean. To her, ten pounds was a magnificent sum. She could not take in the thought of owning five hundred. Her thoughts were firmly focused on her mother and her grandmother. 'Margaret. Abigail,' she said and smiled. At last. Her family, her very own family.

'But, Lady Alice, she is my grandmother, a relative, someone apart from Megan who might...' She could not continue. Lady Alice could not possibly understand what it had been like to grow up unloved by any family. 'If she's still alive, even if she's old, maybe she would still want to see me, or know about me.'

'I'm absolutely certain that she would have wanted to know you, Grace, but, unfortunately, the presence of this lovely watch tells us that she is dead. I am sorry, but somehow Megan got her hands on the watch – which you say you have never seen – and that tells us it stayed, for whatever reason, in this box. She did not wear it where it might be recognised. Solicitors don't hand over legacies willy-nilly, you know, but they do hand them over to the person named in the will and that person is your mother, Margaret Hardy Paterson. If she too was dead at the time of Mrs Abigail Hardy's death then–'

'They gave it to Megan.'

'She was your half-sister, was she not?'

'Yes.'

'But she is not an heir of Margaret Hardy Paterson's body, Grace. You are. Now, I think I've left you with enough to do for the next few weeks and I must get back to Edinburgh in the hope that I will find a train south tomorrow at the latest. Cows don't milk themselves, unfortunately.'

'What should I do now, Lady Alice?'

'Read the letters, look at the photographs, be happy. I hope you will meet some lovely relatives, and enjoy Granny Abigail's watch. I'll ring you if I learn anything more. Come along, your dinner is still waiting.'

The kitchen was empty except for Mrs Fleming, who was plucking a hen, rather an old one if it were one of those that pecked around the farmhouse.

'There's sausages, mashed potatoes, peas, carrots and early turnip on the stove, keeping warm. Hope it's not too dry. I'm sorry I read your letter from Jack, Grace, but it's my job and it's your own fault for asking about maps.' The words shattered the warm air like a thunderclap.

'Our postman in Dartford said it was against the law to interfere with the Royal Mail. You had no right to read someone else's post, and I have every right to look at an atlas. The library has several.'

'But we're in the Observers; it's our job; we have even signed papers about it. What do they want from us? As if the farm wasn't enough. Mr Fleming read it and was worried about all the foreign-language stuff and so I read it and gave it to her ladyship, and she said not to worry about it; nothing that really needed reporting.'

'Then why did you report it and why did you read it in the first place?' Grace was furiously angry.

'I told you, it's our duty. We worried about you when you got sent up here. What had you done to get turfed out of Whitefields Court? Interest in maps is frowned on, speaking foreign languages is bad, too. There have been spies so good at speaking like us that we didn't know they were spies.'

Grace's mind was a jumble of fury and excitement, hope and despair. She knew that she could not sit down in the room with this woman and eat anything, not right now, anyway. 'As it happens, I never had time to look at a map. I'm going out to pick currants. First, I shall take this box upstairs, and I really would prefer that you not look in it. Since Lady Alice already has, you don't need to, do you?'

She moved to run past Mrs Fleming but was stopped.

'Grace, no one is going to say anything about personal stuff; we read it because we was worried.'

Grace hurried upstairs and put the precious box in her drawer. She would have to tell the other girls about its contents and was happy knowing that they would be pleased. The watch was beautiful, five hundred pounds was an absolute fortune, but knowing for the first time in years that her mother's name was Margaret – such a lovely name – and her father's was John – a manly name – was quite wonderful. Mrs Petrie? Would she have told the twins and the Brewers? Grace decided that she had better write to everyone with all the exciting news. Somehow she felt more like a real person. She had parents, Margaret and John, and a grand-mother, Abigail – another lovely name – and a grandfather, Alexander, surely a name fit for a hero.

She ran back downstairs and through the kitchen and out into the garden without stopping or looking around. She picked up baskets and ran to the currants.

'Stop running in the hot sun, Grace. You'll make yourself ill.' Jane's voice – or was it Sheila's? – flew across to her from a strawberry field.

She waved in acknowledgment and slowed down to walk quite sedately, as surely befitted a young lady who owned a watch of pure shining gold.

The redcurrants hung on their slender stalks like glamorous earrings or bright red jewels. Grace ate one or two but their taste did not match their beauty and she laughed. Sorrow and disillusionment had been forced out of the way by sheer joy. 'My mother's name was Margaret Hardy,' she carried on a make-believe conver-sation. 'Grandfather Hardy called her Maggie but my grandmother, Abigail, spinster of this parish, would not allow it. And neither will I.'

Her silliness burned off and she was sad again.

When did my mother die? Where? Did she love me? Did my father, John? Oh, how she ached to be free to return to the box, to the letters and photographs.

The basket was full of redcurrants. Carrying the full basket in one hand and the empty one in the other, she moved to long rows of tall blackcurrant bushes. She regretted her grand gesture of refusing to eat her dinner. Apart from two or three redcurrants, she had had nothing but a bowl of porridge since four thirty that morning and her empty stomach groaned and complained.

She heard rustling. Someone else was among the currants, or perhaps a farm dog or cat was looking for an edible snack. Grace looked along the row where she stood and then was surprised when Mrs Fleming pushed her way between two bushes. 'Would serve you right if I let you cut off your nose to spite your face. Sit down there on the warm ground and eat some cheese, and here's a bottle of tea. Now, don't tell the others, for running after you lot is not what I'm supposed to be doing.'

She gave Grace no time to thank her but pushed her little basket into Grace's hands, picked up the full basket of plump redcurrants and walked off down the row of bushes.

'To spite my face!' Grace laughed. 'I suppose I know what that means and she's right, of course.' She was hungry and opened the box, her second metal box of the day. Pieces of cheese, radishes, a pickled onion and a large buttered oatcake. A feast.

Dungarees were perfect for sitting down almost

253

anywhere, and so Grace sat down, leaning her back against one of the stakes that carried the wires for the bushes, ate a radish – obviously freshly pulled – a piece of cheese and part of the oatcake. Then she drank some of the tea, which was very refreshing, and carried on until there was only a crumb of oatcake lying on the bottom of the tin. Grace wet her index finger and scooped up that final delicious crumb. She finished the tea and remained for a few minutes, enjoying being warm, surprisingly comfortable and well fed.

By the time one or two of the others called to her as they made their way back to the farm-house, she had filled the basket. A good feeling. Work well done.

'Tell us all.' Sheila was the first to speak. 'You are the long-lost daughter of an Italian prince; he longs to take you home to your castle but wants you to stay here until the war is over because he thinks you're safer here. He is planning a party and we are all welcome.'

'If you already knew, Sheila, why did you ask?' Grace teased her friend, thinking that Sally Brewer would probably have reacted in the same way.

'You are rich now, Grace, and will leave us.'

'No, Sheila was being silly. I think that's a film she saw. I have found out a little about my family and the best bit is I did have parents.'

'Big deal. Wasps have parents,' said Jane, wildly swinging at one that persisted in buzzing around her head.

Even Eva and Katia laughed and Grace promised to tell them everything she had discovered after tea. With that they had to be content.

For the more romantic of the land girls, the hours until tea was finished and they were free to go to their rooms crawled slowly past. For Grace, the time flashed past. Her mind seemed to be spinning with all she had learned and all she still had to find out.

When they were finally in the larger of the two rooms and everyone washed and in their night-clothes, she took the box from the drawer, telling them everything that Lady Alice had discovered and passing the gold watch among them, beseeching them to take care.

'Is wonderful, Grace,' said Katia. 'Is most beautiful watch I have see ever. Please this lady person will find your much money.'

Grace wanted the 'much money' to be found, too, but, more than that, she wanted desperately to read the letters and look at the photographs. 'There are old photographs and some letters here, girls. But I need to read them to see if there's any information. I promise that if there's anything about me or if there's a photograph of my mother or father, I'll show you.'

With that, they went off to their separate beds. Grace sat up in hers and took out the envelope that contained the photographs. Megan outside the shop, Megan and two people Grace did not know on the pier at Brighton. Megan, Megan, Megan. But just when Grace was about to give up for the night, there was a picture of two fashion-ably dressed women standing near a lake on which two swans were swimming. The dresses and the hairstyles were very old-fashioned, rather like pictures in the history books at school, and then,

255

her breath almost stopping in excitement, Grace looked more closely at the bodice of the older woman's satin gown. The watch. Pinned to the older lady's bodice was the gold half-hunter. Grace turned over the picture. 'Abby with Mags near the Serpentine.'

For a moment, her breath actually seemed to stop. Abby had to be Abigail and Mags was surely, Margaret. She had the almost overwhelming desire to put the photograph on her heart. 'My mother,' she said, 'and my grandmother.' For the first time that she could remember there were two people – besides Megan – who were part of her life. Totally overcome, Grace lay down and closed her eyes.

She heard someone else stirring and quickly pulled herself together.

'Can I help you, Grace?' It was Jane.

Quickly, Grace rubbed her face with the sheet. 'No, Jane, thanks. I'm sorry if I disturbed you. It's … it's just that I've found a picture of my mother; first time I've ever seen a likeness; it made me so happy. Tomorrow, I'll show it to everyone.'

Jane patted her shoulder and went back to her own bed but it was a long time before Grace fell asleep.

Grace's papers and photographs were of vital importance – to her. For Farmer Fleming nothing was more important than getting in the harvest while the good weather lasted. Night after night for weeks, the land girls at Newriggs Farm fell into exhausted sleep. Grace's precious box remained unopened in the drawer, although, at times, she felt as if the box was calling her, teasing her with all the information about her family that it contained, but she was too busy and much too tired. Occasionally, she tried, took the box out, found a letter and sat at the window to read it, if possible by natural light. She would begin but, before she had read a few lines, her head was nodding and the words were swimming around, unrecognised, on the page. Accepting defeat, she would slip off the window-seat and creep into her bed.

For weeks, harvesting went on long into the night. 'What did I tell you?' laughed Sheila. 'Government initiative: Plough by Night. Bet this is an official secret.'

Although conscious of the possibility of an air raid, lamps were lit and hung in the hedges to guide the harvesters as they worked tirelessly. No time to look up at the beautiful moon to remember nights of wandering hand in hand with someone very special under just such a moon. After stumbling home over the stubble, the land girls – pleased as always that they had done it and would do it again tomorrow and the next day until the nation's food bins were full – could barely find the strength to remove their clothes, struggle into nightwear and fall into bed. Many mornings found them fast asleep on top of the rough army-issue blankets. Even had she been awake enough to look at a letter, experience told Grace that she would make no sense of it. Her family would have to wait. She had her mother's picture: for Grace, at that moment, it was enough.

The poster announcing a dance in the village hall, price two shillings and sixpence to include live music, the ubiquitous stovies, and beer –

heavily watered down and adulterated with potato instead of barley – was looked at once with longing and then ignored.

'I think I have forget what man looks like,' complained Katia. 'And what is living music. This, Eva and I are not understanding.'

'Just means there'll be living musicians there, not records, and, oh, joy, just think, if they've got the band from the air base, they'll all be men,' said Fiona, adding meaningfully, 'real ones,' when Mr Fleming passed.

The girls laughed and then decided that Fiona had been too unkind. 'It's not his fault,' said Jane. 'That's what marriage does to you.'

'It's what dealing with you lot does to me,' the farmer said over his shoulder.

'Well, pigs might fly – he's got a sense of humour.'

A few days later, Grace was delighted to receive a letter from Sally. She opened it with increasing excitement and the very act reminded her that she had not yet found the courage to write to Jack. She had to write to him, as a friend. But first, she had to read this very welcome letter. What wonderful thing could have happened to her lately? A part, even tiny, in a West End play? A part in a film? How exciting that would be? Sally Brewer from Dartford up there on the big screen. Grace would insist that all the land girls come with her to see the film. The single sheet of paper fell from her hands. *Daisy, oh, dear, dear Daisy.* She closed her eyes to shut out the sight but it would not go.

'What's happened, Grace? One minute you're over the moon finding out about your family and

258

the next you look like you've lost everyone you ever loved.'

Jane, Eva and Sheila gathered round her.

'You are unhappy, Grace?' asked Eva.

Grace sniffed hard. 'Sorry, girls, it's not me. A friend, a very, very special friend, her chap's just been shot down. He's ... he was a Spitfire pilot.'

'Oh, this is much sad. He is boy who teach her to fly.'

'Yes, he did, and now he's dead and all I can do is kill rats.'

'We could ask the Flemings to let you go to see her,' suggested Sheila.

Grace blew her nose hard and swallowed. 'No. The WAAF won't even let her go; they're not engaged or anything, not official, and she has work to do. So do we, so let's get on with it.'

Even the prospect of finding happy things in her box of photographs and letters could not comfort Grace that night. This was the reality of war. People were dying every day and those who loved them wept for them but carried on. And those who loved those who wept wrote letters giving what little comfort they could.

Grace wrote a short note to Daisy. What could she say about Adair even though she remembered Daisy's excitement as she talked about seeing a real aeroplane in the old stables at Old Manor Farm? In the end, all she said was that she was sorry and that she sent Daisy her love. She hoped that would comfort Daisy a little.

While she had her notepaper out of the drawer, she answered Jack's letter. She told him that she had received one letter from him in which he mentioned their last meeting and his hopes of taking her to meet his father.

I would like to walk under lilac trees, Jack, something so very peaceful and English about that. Sometimes I think the world will be at war for ever but if it ends and we meet again, that will be nice.
  Your friend, Grace

Not, 'love Grace', for she no longer knew whether or not she loved Jack or even if she loved Sam. Of course she loved Sam – she had loved him since she was a little girl – but perhaps her feelings were only those of a girl for a big brother. Would she have felt those overpowering feelings that had swamped her will, her judgement, if she had been with Sam on that night and in that car? Her mind was confused. Too much was happening. Should she have told Jack that she had been given a picture of her mother? She would certainly have told Sam if she had been writing to him. For a fraction of a second, she felt like taking her letter to Jack and tearing it into little pieces.

Another good thing about being on a farm. If there was a stamp on the letter, the postman was perfectly happy to take it to the post office. From there it was a matter of chance.

FOURTEEN

Late Autumn 1941

'We are going to have a white Christmas.' Grace was sitting in a window-seat, looking out over Whitefields home farm.

'And this is surprise you, Grace?' Eva looked out, made a disparaging noise and went back to sit on her bed where she was working in an English exercise book. 'I will write English are with surprise to see snow. It always is snow in Poland for Christmas.'

'The English are surprised to see snow,' said Katia very slowly. 'In Poland, there is always snow for Christmas. Write that, Eva.' She turned to Grace and laughed. 'And she can add, and before and after Christmas, too.'

Grace, Katia and Eva had been at Whitefields since the end of the harvest at Newriggs. One day, they had been working on one farm and, the next, they were told by Mrs Drummond-Hay that they were being sent south to Whitefields.

Grace had challenged Mrs Fleming. 'Why, Mrs Fleming? What did any of us do wrong? I know I asked for an atlas but Katia and Eva – they have done nothing.'

'We're being sent some men for the winter, POWs, I think, and maybe some conscientious objectors. We want two barns redoing as dormi-

261

tories, so next summer we can have some city children for working holidays. Men are needed for the heavy work and we can manage the farm with four land girls till the turn of the year. And who knows, Grace, maybe her ladyship thinks she can keep a better eye on you in England? Eva and Katia: possibly she just wants them to have more experience of travelling and language but I didn't ask Mrs Drummond-Hay to spell it out.'

Grace thought about it and was sorry for the Flemings. They had worked their farm for three generations and then the war had come and the Agricultural Committee in some far away city seemed to have taken over, telling them what to plant and how much, and which animals to keep. Perhaps when the war was over – and surely it had to end soon – the farmers might feel in charge again, keeping changes that they agreed were for the better, bringing back some treasured ways. She remembered a very poignant moment when Mr Fleming had been shown the new machine that was going to make ploughing and harrowing so much easier and efficient for him. He had looked across his field. 'A good horse and a good ploughman together, prettiest sight in the world, don't you agree?'

Not yet twenty-one years old, Grace, who agreed with him, had thought that the day of the great horses was over but had said nothing.

Grace, Katia and Eva had arrived at Whitefields Court in late September, a few days before the new land girls. Soon, they were all settled in. Meeting all her old friends again had been a joy for Grace, and even Mrs Love had seemed pleased to see her back. She had proudly and happily told Grace that she had heard from her son who had been promoted to leading seaman.

'Next thing you hear, your Tom will be a petty officer,' said Grace, her heart skipping a beat as she remembered young Phil Petrie.

Mrs Love, overcome that Grace had remembered her son's name, astonished both of them by hugging Grace warmly.

Surprisingly, just the day after they arrived, Lady Alice had offered Grace a way of legally earning a little more money. She had also suggested that Grace could open the opportunity to Katia and Eva. The money-making scheme was to do with rosehips, the fat orangey-red seed container that formed on wild rose bushes as the fragile flowers withered.

'We haven't the delicious imported fruits we got used to before this ghastly war,' explained Lady Alice, 'but here on this farm and, in fact, all over this beautiful island of ours, we have rosehips. The briar rose delights us in the summer with its delicate beauty and then, in autumn, look, rosehips, every single one a great source of vitamin C. I know it's asking a lot, Grace, as you land girls work so hard all day, but if you can manage to gather rosehips in your free time, I'll give you two pence per pound for your pocket. Mrs Love makes delicious syrup and we can sell that, too. Does that appeal? Do feel able to say if you prefer to read a book or go to the pictures.'

'Two pence for every pound sounds great, Lady Alice. We can start saving for Christmas.'

'All the local children will be picking like mad;

they're not supposed to come on to the estate, but don't chase them off, and, besides, there are places you can reach that they can't. Ask Esau where the best ones are. Might be fun for Eva and Katia. Gathering rosehips is so English, I think, and they might enjoy themselves.' She stopped in thought. 'Probably wild roses in Poland, too, Grace, but even so, the girls might relax and have fun, and there is a little spending money to be earned.'

'I'll certainly ask them, Lady Alice. And if they were used to gathering rosehips in Poland, they might feel quite at home.'

Grace found Katia in their shared room when she went upstairs to wash before their evening meal.

'You mean that if we are pick the roses hips after our working is finished, we will earn money extra?'

'Yes, Katia. Lady Alice wants some rosehips to sell to the companies who produce syrup. They're full of vitamin C, which is terribly important since we can't get our usual sources: oranges and fruits like that. I'm going to do it; don't you think it would be nice?'

'We are spend all our time out the doors. In free time, Eva and me is enjoy reading and rest.'

'Me, too, Katia, but we're not paid all that much and I thought a little extra would come in handy. There are lots of them growing all over the estate; I think we could make a little money quite quickly.'

'Is good to have little money and I think Eva will say yes, too, but are all girls doing this? We are with gratitude to be safe in this land and do not want...' She stopped as she tried to translate, from Polish, the words in her head.

'Special treatment, something like that? I don't know, Katia, if everyone has been asked, but I think they will be. Lady Alice is allowing the village children to gather rosehips for their schools and I feel that she thought it might be something that we would enjoy doing. I certainly would.'

'Good, we will pick after the work. Thank you.'

'It's Lady Alice's idea, Katia; it's business. I'm almost sure anyone who's not too tired to do extra work will be able to join us.'

And so it proved. In pleasant late summer or early autumn evenings, the land girls, carrying old gardening baskets that Mrs Love found in one of her spacious cupboards, went off to the areas suggested by the men who knew every inch of the estate, and returned as twilight deepened into darkness, their baskets full. Each basket was put down on a bench, where Lady Alice had left labels with each land girl's name. Mrs Love weighed the rosehips and kept a running total of poundage.

Katia and Eva seemed to enjoy the evenings even more than the others. It was, in a way, merely a continuation of their everyday work, but they were relaxed and shouts of laughter, Eva's delightful voice and the voices of the others rose and fell until, baskets full and very tired, the girls returned to the house where Mrs Love had a late supper ready for them.

Shortly after her return to Whitefields, Grace visited Harry at work in Hazel's garden and, almost immediately, wondered if Lady Alice was correct and the lovely old man would fully recover from his head injury. His memory was impaired. He had little recollection of the incident in which he had been injured but he remembered Jack and Grace, something that touched her very much. It seemed that, if he had not looked after poultry before, he had discovered a talent for looking after hens and so Lady Alice had increased Hazel's flock and Harry looked after them devotedly.

'Hear from young Jack, lass?' he asked every day, and, every day, Grace said, 'No, Harry, but he won't know I'm back here yet.' There had been no reply to her earlier letter. Had he written?

Just stop thinking about him, Grace.

While she was settling, in and getting to know the new girls, Grace had put the unread letters at the very back of a drawer out of temptation. She had kept the photographs in their envelope in the pocket of her dungarees and she looked at them whenever she had a spare minute. When Grace had taken those of Megan with various people out of the envelope for the first time, her impulse had been to throw them into the waste basket. She needed no reminders of her half-sister. But then she had a further thought. She would, she decided, examine each one carefully and if she recognised the people in them as being people she had seen with Megan, she would throw them away. It was unlikely that Megan's friends would ask questions about her much younger half-sister.

'What happened to Megan's mother? Poor Megan, did her mother die young, too?' No older woman had ever visited while Grace and Megan had lived together, and no parents or other relatives were ever mentioned. Grace sighed. It was the first time she had ever felt any sympathy for Megan and she decided that she was growing up, becoming more mature and capable.

Late one evening, when the others were asleep, Grace took out the letters and held them and their secrets tightly for a moment. And then, methodically, she looked at the postmark on each envelope and began to put them in chronological order. Better and more sensible to read them in order, if there was any sequence, for the writing was not always the same. She warned herself against getting her hopes up. It was possible that none of the letters referred to her or her parents at all. Immediately, doubt jumped in. But if they are not important, why were they kept? *Oh, please don't let them be sad little love letters – unless of course, they're my parents' letters.*

She was far too stimulated to sleep and so, perfectly aware that she would regret it in the morning, she selected the earliest of the letters and read it.

Dear Gert,

Seems he took the London train last Saturday fortnight. Fred and Jim saw him as they was crossing the High Street. Looked a right spiv, shiniest black and white shoes you ever seen, slicked back hair and a jaunty hat like the men in the pictures wear. Fred ran after him hoping to get back the ten bob he loaned John but he'd already got on the London train. The ticket seller wouldn't tell Fred where John was going so he could be anywhere between Glasgow and London.

I wouldn't cry over him, Gert, love, as we all thinks as you and Megs are better off without him. Fred

wants that ten shillings back and says he'll go to the
berries to put a few bob by for the winter. Your favourite
bad penny does the berries some weekends and bad
pennies, as our Fred is fond of saying, always turn up.
  Give Megs a big kiss from us.
  Aunty Fran

Grace folded the sheet of paper, feeling as if her hands were dirty after reading it. It was such a personal letter. Was the man, the bad penny who owed someone ten shillings, her father, John Paterson? If so, he was the man Gert and Megs would be better off without. Megs had to be Megan, her sister, and so Gert was Megan's mother, and John Paterson was her husband and Megan's father. Grace looked at the envelope. The envelope was of inferior quality and the postmark was blurred but she thought she could make out the word 'Stirling' and a date: '2.6.14'. That was seven years before her own birth but, more importantly, the year of the beginning of the Great War.

She had had enough of prying and probing. She shoved the letter back into the box, turned off her lamp and snuggled down to sleep.

The morning brought order and routine. Grace was delighted to follow her schedule, milking, cleaning out the milking parlour or, at least, supervising three of the newly qualified land girls, keeping warm as the winter was already making its presence felt.

One morning in early December, Lady Alice stopped her as she was returning to the kitchen.

'You girls have a wireless? Heard the news?'

When they had free time and were not too tired to stay awake, the girls tended to listen to music or to comedy programmes, and there had been no time for reading newspapers. She did not answer quickly enough for the concerned Lady Alice.

'Good God, girl, yes or no doesn't need major thought. The Japanese air force has practically destroyed the American navy at their base, Pearl Harbor, which is in the Hawaiian Islands.'

'The entire navy?'

'And too many of the sailors, Grace. What a damn merry Christmas, but one good thing is, it has brought the Yanks into the war. They have been helping us in many ways but now we'll get their forces, too, thank God. Tell the girls.'

Do I want to? Grace asked herself as she continued into the house. Such appalling destruction of ships and men could hardly cheer Katia and Eva. As it happened, the news of the bombing and the British disaster that followed it had been deemed so important that a *Forces Favourites* programme had been interrupted.

The girls were huddled around a small wireless on the kitchen table and, for once, Mrs Love was not complaining about where they put their elbows. 'Sit down, Grace, and I'll serve. There's been terrible news. Two of our biggest and best ships, the *Prince of Wales* and *Repulse* have been sunk by the Japanese, not long after they destroyed all the American ships somewhere in the Pacific Ocean.'

'The ships in Hawaiian Islands, in Pacific Ocean,' said Katia, with tears in her eyes. 'In Krakow, in our country, we have seen me and

Eva, a film of Hawaii. Is much lovely.' The shock of the news had affected Katia's always improving English.

Grace hugged her. 'Have some breakfast, Katia, girls. Come on, not eating before a long, hard day of physical labour won't improve things. It might make it worse, if we can't do our bit, the way all those poor sailors did theirs.'

All the land girls who were still seated at the table did try to finish breakfast but, all in all, it was a very bad day.

Lady Alice waited for Grace after milking a few mornings later. 'Good morning, Grace. What do you say to a few days Christmas leave? Last year wasn't much fun and, if you left here a day or two early, you could see your solicitors.'

Grace was very hungry but somehow her appetite disappeared at the word 'solicitors'. 'My solicitors?'

'Don't repeat everything I say, Grace. Thomas, Crawford, Shortcross and Thomas, your solicitors. They have found your five hundred pounds and you'll be glad to hear it's been very cleverly increasing and multiplying. Mind you, they'll sting you for searching for it but you'll still be ahead. Say you leave here the twentieth; it's a Saturday, ghastly day to travel but every day is these days, and at least one or two of your chums might not be working. Train back Boxing Day? Almost a week, best we can do.'

Too much was happening and too many thoughts were chasing one another around in Grace's head. How foolish she had been not to sit

270

down when she was given the box and to devour every word of every letter. Why had she been so reticent? Some evenings, I was too tired, she excused herself, and then immediately argued that if she had not been, for some inexplicable reason, afraid to read the letters...

Yes, admit it, Grace. You are afraid.

'I have found my own family. Incredible. I know my mother and my grandmother. I will never be afraid again.'

Christmas, a proper Christmas, with carols and the midnight service, holly and decorations. The Brewers and the Petries always had Christmas trees – oh, it would be wonderful.

Lady Alice had found whatever she had been looking for in her bag and was looking rather strangely at Grace. 'Hello?' she said. 'You are with me? Good. I'd let Eva or Katia go, but it's a tad difficult to travel to Poland this winter. I'll take them into the main house. They'll have to be content with singing around my Christmas tree. You say Eva has a lovely voice. That will be pleasant.'

'Sorry, Lady Alice, I'm very grateful and I'll write to Mrs Brewer to see if it's convenient.'

'When will you understand that there's never an inconvenient time with decent people like them. Now, for heaven's sake, go and get some breakfast before Mrs Love has apoplexy.'

Grace's journey from Biggleswade down to Dartford was not too inconvenient as wartime travel went. There had been a raid in the London area, which had mangled several lines, and so it took almost as long to get through the suburbs to an undamaged platform as it had taken to stutter across England. Grace was delighted to see that she had only twenty minutes to wait for a connection and her sagging Christmas spirit rose as she saw a WVS stand quite near her platform. She tried to pay for a cup of tea but the women called out, 'Happy Christmas, love,' as they handed her a mug of tea and a small finger roll filled with fish paste.

'Merry Christmas, ladies,' said Grace, and she stood enjoying the snack while watching the women dispensing not only tea and sandwiches but happy smiles and Christmas greetings. Two other land girls stopped but mostly the customers were men in uniform, men from all the services and from several different countries. It struck her that many of those on the platform were thousands of miles from home and, silently, she wished them all a safe return to their loved ones.

She was so involved watching that she had, in the end, to run for her train, but she caught it and, Christmas spirit in the ascendancy, was given a seat by a young airman. The gesture reminded her of other kindnesses and there were tears in her eyes as she thanked him and sat down.

No one was at the station to meet her but she had not expected there to be and she merely stood for a moment, basking in the knowledge that she was actually going to see all her friends at Christmas, before setting off, in complete darkness, towards the Brewers' home. She had forgotten the reality of the blackout. Yes, there was a blackout in rural areas but houses were few and far between. The Whitefields seemed to manage

272

blackout security on their own. The moon and the stars had illuminated England's countryside before the war, were doing so now, and no doubt their beautiful light would still shine when the war was over. Here, in the town, all was changed: nothing, to Grace, was familiar. She was both delighted and relieved when she finally found herself at the Brewers' house. She knocked.

The door was opened almost at once, and there stood Sally.

The girls, not usually demonstrative, hugged each other.

'Sally Brewer, I can't believe how gorgeous you are: like a real film star, prettier even.'

Sally, as always, took the compliment in her elegant stride. 'Well, Grace Paterson, thank you and, if you don't mind my saying, this has to be the ugliest hat I have ever seen.' She snatched Grace's WLA hat off her head and stuck it on the already overloaded hallstand. 'And let it stay there,' she said. 'Come on, Mum's in the kitchen, Rose did a shift this morning and will be here soon, absolutely dying to see you.'

'Daisy?'

'Not yet.' She saw the disappointment on Grace's face. 'But she is coming. For at least one whole day, the four of us will be together. Oh, and I meant to ask you, what do you think about Sam?'

Grace's heart jumped. 'Sam? He's all right, isn't he?'

'Oh, I can't believe you don't know. Mrs Petrie said she was going to write to you but then, she was rather overexcited in the spring; seemingly, Miss Pritchard practically ran the shop.'

'Excited? Tell me, Sally.'

Sally looked at her, as if wondering how a director might suggest she deliver the line. 'He escaped,' she said simply. 'God alone knows where he is. No one's heard but we're all being really positive.'

'And he hasn't written to his family or you?'

'Don't be daft, Grace, escaped British prisoners can't just walk into a post office and say, "Please may I send this letter to my mum?"' She said nothing about a letter to Sally Brewer.

They heard the front doorbell. 'We'll get it, Mum,' she called through to the kitchen. 'Come on, Grace, go and open it; it'll be Rose.'

Grace smiled and hurried to the door, and so began a very happy Christmas holiday.

That first night found Grace and Sally still awake after midnight. Loath to part with Rose, they had walked her back to the Petries' shop and Grace had listened avidly to tales of the orphaned boy, George, whom, initially, Daisy seemed to have adopted or sponsored but who was now almost a member of the family and a firm favourite with everyone.

Since neither Grace nor Sally had to get up early next morning, they sat up in bed talking: sadly, about Daisy's loss, and, positively, about Sam's escape. It was obvious to Grace that Sally loved Sam very much, so determined was she that he was not dead but somehow making his way across Europe.

'What a great film it would make, Grace.'

Earlier, Rose had confirmed that an appointment had been made with the solicitors for Monday morning, at eleven o'clock. Unlike Grace, Sally found the idea of hidden documents, missing money and beautiful gold watches extremely exciting. 'It's like a play, Grace, and you're the heroine, although I'm afraid, in that ghastly nightgown, you don't look much like a heroine. I am definitely heroine material, although perhaps, to be fair, like Rose, you would be better; although Vivien Leigh's dark and she was stunning in *Gone with the Wind.*'

It was obvious that Sally was prepared to talk all night, and Grace had a sinking feeling that she would still hear the Whitefields alarm clock in her head at four thirty next morning.

She did wake early, from habit rather than from long-distance alarm sounds, and lay in bed, telling herself that resting was almost as good as sleeping, and going over and over in her head the questions she hoped to ask the solicitor, Mr Crawford.

On Monday, in the solicitors' office, she found that Mr Crawford provided her with answers before she had even asked the questions, and the answers were sometimes to questions that it would never have occurred to her to ask.

The good news – that Margaret Hardy Paterson had inherited the legacy and had safely tied up the inheritance until her daughter, Grace Hardy Paterson, came of age – was both exciting and confusing. Grace had never had a bank account. Money was needed to start an account and Grace had never, in her life, had any money. While she had worked in Dartford, Megan had taken everything, except for a few shillings per week, for

Grace's board and keep, and since Grace had joined the Women's Land Army, any money left at the end of each week had simply stayed in her purse. Now she found herself a woman with a sizeable bank account – and a gold watch.

There was other news, too, news that Grace found difficult to understand. Mrs Petrie held her hand as Mr Crawford told her that the marriage ceremony enacted in 1919 between Margaret Hardy and John Paterson appeared, to all intents and purposes, to have been bigamous.

'Bigamous?' Grace could not or did not want to believe this.

'A bigamous marriage–' began Mr Crawford.

Grace cut in, coldly, 'I know what bigamous means.' She added, 'Thank you,' more quietly.

'There appears to be no record of divorce proceedings between this John Paterson and his first wife, Gertrude Monroe Paterson. At least, so far, all our research has drawn a blank.'

An almost embarrassed silence fell for a moment, while Grace tried to understand the importance of everything she had heard. Realisation hit her like a lightning bolt. 'I'm illegitimate,' she said, so quietly that Flora Petrie hardly heard. 'No wonder they threw me away. They didn't want a...' She could not say the word.

'No one threw you away, Grace, dear. Your grandmother mentions you in her will.'

No, she doesn't. If she knew I existed when she wrote the will, she would have mentioned my name. I must read those letters thoroughly. No more excuses, Grace, about being scared to find out. What could be worse than this?

'One of our clerks is researching Scottish registers of deaths. If Gertrude Paterson, née Monroe, died before 1919, then there would have been no need for a divorce.'

Grace's spirits rose. 'Gertrude isn't too common, is it, Mr Crawford?'

'Quite popular, Grace. The difficulty is that we need to search in several counties. We know where they lived with their daughter, Megan, but – I don't know if you knew this – but Mr Paterson seems to be a member of a large family of travellers.'

Travellers. The men with large suitcases, which they insisted on opening on the doorstep so that the lady of the house could see the exceptional quality of their sheets and towels. 'Good for nothing but dusters,' Mrs Petrie used to say. The war seemed to have put a stop to them.

'What did he sell?' Grace asked, as she wondered whether it was possible that she had opened the door of the Dartford house to her own father.

Mr Crawford looked at her in surprise and then he laughed. 'Quite different type of traveller, Grace; part of the history of our delightful island. Travellers follow the crops, fruit mostly. A travelling family might spend the winter in a town, but in the summer they pick fruits, returning to the same farms year after year; they're usually well known to the farmers and welcomed.'

The picture imprinted itself on her mind again. A field; a young woman with a child, their bare feet dusty in the warm dry soil. Raspberries.

'Was Margaret Hardy a traveller, Mr Crawford?'

'Certainly not before 1919, Grace. Her father was a bookkeeper in a large insurance firm.' He rifled through the papers in front of him. 'Kent, if I remember rightly, somewhere in Kent. Canterbury, that's it, Canterbury. How could I have forgotten that? Not a million miles from Dartford, now that I come to think of it.'

Mr Crawford ordered tea for them. 'I think you'll be quite pleased with this cup, Mrs Petrie,' he said with a smile and she agreed with him.

He turned to Grace. 'Now, Miss Paterson, I think we've gone as far as we can until the New Year. Do be assured that if we uncover any more details about your parents, we will let you know as soon as possible.'

'Grace has still to go through some of the papers, Mr Crawford,' Mrs Petrie broke in. 'It's been hard for her, hasn't it, dear? But isn't it likely that answers will be in them?'

The solicitor agreed with her, they wished one another Merry Christmas, and then Grace and Mrs Petrie left and began to walk through the town towards the Petries' shop.

Grace started to laugh. 'You're amazing, Mrs Petrie. I was so impressed with how you talk so easily to a head lawyer.'

'It's all thanks to Miss Partridge, Grace. She told me to make sure that we do everything we can because the lawyers charge for everything they do – have to, I suppose, to pay wages and such – but your nan thought forward and so should we. You might even have as much as a thousand pounds behind you and we want it to grow, not be eaten up by legal bills.'

Grace was somewhat overwhelmed. 'But they have to be paid, Mrs Petrie. I'd never have found out all this without them.'

Mrs Petrie adjusted the faux-fur scarf on her best coat before she spoke again. '"The labourer is worthy of his hire," Grace, but we don't want him labouring over something we can do ourselves, do we? Especially not at Christmas?'

Someone else had quoted that bit about labourers. It was so familiar. Probably a vicar, thought Grace, as she agreed with Mrs Petrie. 'I asked Mrs Love to put the box in the estate safe while I was down here, but I did bring a few of the letters with me, just in case there was time and ... actually, I carried one or two pictures to look at. One is of my mother, Margaret, and one of my grandmother, Abigail. Isn't that the loveliest name? Wish they'd called me Abigail instead of Grace. Anyway, I'll show them to everyone.'

'When you're ready, love; and, Grace, your own name is a proper ladylike name.'

The rest of the day was spent doing the hundred and one things that families need to do at Christmas, including shopping for a dress for Grace for Christmas Day. She had never actually thought of buying new clothes; the last thing she had considered buying had been white sandals and now it was winter and the sandals had never been bought. She refused to remember why. But on a cold fresh winter day in Dartford she walked through the second-hand stalls in the market with Mrs Petrie, who hoped to find a dress that could, with a little work, be made absolutely perfect for Grace.

'You should see the gorgeous dresses Mrs Roban made over for Daisy, Grace, love. Doubt we'll find that quality but you never know. Oh, look, isn't that green wool pretty, and green is lovely for Christmas.'

'Sorry, Mrs Petrie, not green. Almost everything I wear is green.'

'Red's perfect for Christmas and would look good on you.'

Grace looked at the high-necked long-sleeved woollen dress. 'Sorry,' she said, wondering where the courage had come from that caused her to argue with someone who had always been kind to her. 'I'd look like a ripe cherry.'

That comment made them both laugh but Mrs Petrie would not be put off. 'Nonsense, pet, you're a lovely young woman and red would look ever so good on you with your lovely brown hair, but, if you find solid red too much, we can always find a nice collar, maybe even cuffs. I could put them on and we wouldn't even need to ask Mrs Roban for help.'

'That's extra work, Mrs Petrie. Let's look a bit more for our Christmas shopping, and, if we find nothing, we can always go to Horrell and Goff, or Potts and Sons.' Agreed, they wandered around the stands. Grace found a pretty box of soap, not a whiff of carbolic about it, and a pair of woollen gloves that Mrs Petrie assured her would be perfect for young George, the orphan who was now living with the Petries and helping out in the shop.

'We've got him some magazines, boys' ones: *Rover, Boy's Own* and *Triumph* – being a lad, he'll be happier with them than with his new winter boots. But let's have a look over there, Grace, love.'

Grace wanted a dress, but then: 'Wow, Mrs Petrie, look, isn't that a genuine Fair Isle?'

Almost hidden among a line of jumpers and cardigans, Grace saw a light beige hand-knitted cardigan. She slipped it off the stand and held it up to look at it. It was the image of a cardigan she had once seen in a knitting feature in the *Land Girl*, the WLA magazine: buttoned up to the neck, long sleeves and, across the top of both the back and the front, the most exquisite band of the age-old and very complicated pattern.

'Check inside, Grace. The backs of real Fair Isles are almost as complicated as the front.'

Grace turned the buttoned-up cardigan inside out and, yes, there were the telltale ends of the various colours of wool – blue, pink, yellow, green, white – all sewn in.

'Absolutely beautiful, pet. Any flaws or darns anywhere?'

'To be honest, I don't think I care; it's so beautiful. Must have taken weeks to knit.'

'And it'll cost a fortune, maybe as much as two or three guineas. God knows what they cost new.'

I can't possibly spend that on a second-hand cardigan, no matter how lovely it is, Grace thought, while Mr Crawford's voice saying 'five hundred pounds' seemed to go round and round in her head. 'Look at the price for me, Mrs Petrie. I think I've got thirty-five shillings left.'

'You in the Forces, pet?' asked a voice behind her, and Grace turned to see a short and very thin woman wearing a turban and with a wrapa-round apron covering her clothes. 'That'd look lovely on you; all the girls is wanting them, wear 'em over frocks, with a nice blouse; speaks for itself that cardy does.'

'You're right; it is lovely but I probably can't afford it.'

'Funny thing, I just reduced it, seeing as it's Christmas but I'd like it to go to someone wot's doing her bit for us.'

'Grace is a land girl,' Mrs Petrie broke in.

'Thought so. You do 'ave the ugliest hats, don't you? Think it's my duty to 'elp you out. A guinea for the next minute then it goes up again.'

'A guinea? Do you mean it?'

'Merry Christmas, pet.'

Hardly daring to believe her luck, Grace handed over the money, wished the stall keeper 'Merry Christmas' in turn and walked off with Mrs Petrie. She was stunned. 'I can't believe I actually own this.'

'About time nice things happened to you, love. More than a nice frock would have cost you, though.'

'I love it, and she's right, they're very fashionable. Wonder what Rose'll say?'

'Probably that you was robbed, over a pound for an old cardy,' said Mrs Petrie, with a laugh to show that she was teasing.

She was wrong. Rose looked at the cardigan, examining the age-old pattern carefully. 'It's gorgeous, Grace, and I've got a skirt'll be great with it.' She smiled at the confused look on Grace's face. 'Mum, remember that mustard wool we bought, thinking I could let it down a bit? It's been hanging in the wardrobe over a year and I've never done anything with it. We can turn it up for Grace and her waist isn't that much smaller than mine – a belt will hold it up.'

Grace was, once again, feeling somewhat overwhelmed by the kindnesses she was receiving. She thanked them but reminded her friends that she had a perfectly respectable dark green skirt to wear with the cardigan, and no more was said on the subject.

In the evening, almost like old times, Grace, Sally and Rose went to the cinema. When the film – *49th Parallel* – was over, they went up to the projectionist's booth and helped Sally's father to close up.

'Be still, my beating heart.' Sally pretended to swoon. 'Honestly, Daddy, if I can't marry Leslie Howard, I will never marry.'

'What happened to Jimmy Stewart?' teased Rose.

Sally pretended to glare at her. 'Why is life so difficult?'

'What about a man who isn't just a pretty face?' Grace felt that she should join in the fun.

'Just? Just?' Sally and Rose were stunned.

'Fourteen again, are you, ladies?' teased Mr Brewer. 'Come on, we'd best walk Rose home.'

Rose argued with him but he was adamant. 'Don't know who's out and about in this blackout, and, besides, what if you was to trip over something?'

To that there was no reasonable answer.

Back at the Brewers, Grace took out the envelope into which she had put some of the letters, and went into the kitchen where Sally's mum was making cocoa, to ask if she could sit there for a while and study them.

'Of course, love, but don't stay up too late,' said Mrs Brewer, as she poured the cocoa, before shooing Sally off to bed. 'Don't worry about waking our Sally; she's slept through bombings.'

Once she was alone, Grace opened the envelope, took out another letter, and began to read. The writing was so strange in comparison with that in modern letters and whole words had faded or disappeared altogether through age. At first, she felt strange and somewhat guilty for reading another person's private past. She realised, however, that it was likely that the letter writer, this Aunt Fran – as well as the recipient, Megan – was dead.

She apologised silently for reading the letter, which had been written in 1916.

Dear Megs,

Thank you for ... birthday card. What a sweet little girl you are. It's your dad's ... not seeing you. God knows where he is ... maybe even in the army. Uncle Fred says they're so ... for soldiers they'll take anybody, even a good-for-nothing like your pa. Even prisoners. There's a thought. If your dad was banged up he coulda joined up. That means your mum's entitled to a few bob a week from the government. Haven't a clue how she'd find out but tell her I'll take the bus in Sunday to see her. That'll be nice.

See you about dinner time,
Aunty Fran

Megan had been 'a sweet little girl' when the letter was written. Grace thought about her sister.

She would have been about eleven years old and was obviously unhappy because she did not know where her father was.

From the content, she had guessed at the missing words and hoped she was correct.

He doesn't sound like a very nice person, she decided, and nothing at all like the sort of man a lovely girl like Margaret Hardy would have married. It's as if there were two men called John Paterson.

She snatched up the letter, which she wished she had never read, and stuffed it into the envelope. She decided that she would never read another one. But she did.

Instead of slipping into the bedroom she was sharing with Sally, Grace stayed in the kitchen at the table. In order to save electricity, she lit a candle and, by its light, read the letter at the bottom of the few she had brought. Because it made clearer a little of her life story, she was pleased that she had seen it, but its information still left huge gaping holes in her history; holes, she felt, that would never properly be filled in.

The letter, beautifully written in black ink, was dated 19 August 1927, and the writer was the matron of an orphanage in a town near Glasgow. It became painfully obvious that she and Megan had communicated before.

Dear Miss Paterson,
We are delighted that you agreed so readily to give your orphaned half-sister a home. Living with a loving relative is always better for a child than the best institution.

I have enclosed the valuable watch your late step-mother was wearing when she was hospitalised. Grace is, at present, much too young to be entrusted with it but I am sure you will guard it safely for her until she is old enough to wear it. The monies left to her through her maternal grandmother's will are, of course, safely invested, and when Grace attains her twenty-fifth birthday – as is stipulated in Mrs Abigail Hardy's will – a tidy sum should have accumulated to ease her future.

We are very lucky to find that a Sister Anthony from the local Nazareth House is travelling to London on 1 September. Permission has been given for her to accompany Grace to London and also to take her from London to Dartford. There, she will hand the little one into your loving sisterly care. I cannot tell you how I wish all our little ones had the same good fortune.

It was signed, 'Mhairi McPhail, Matron'.

Grace picked up her letters and, taking the candle with her, crept into Sally's bedroom. There, she undressed quickly, pulled her nightgown over her head, slid into the little bed Mr Brewer had set up for her, and blew out the candle. There was a muffled grunting sound from Sally. Grace held her breath for a moment, afraid that she had disturbed her friend's sleep. But all was well: Sally slept on.

It was Grace who lay awake, trying to digest everything that she had read. Her mother had been in a hospital where – sadly – it was obvious that she had died. The question of how Megan came to have the gold watch in her possession had been answered so simply and she, Grace, had once been with a nun, this Sister Anthony. Her dream of a nun had, in fact, been a memory.

Grace curled up into as tight a little ball as she could manage. No more, she thought. I don't think I can bear to know any more. My mother died and it looks as if she had me with her when she went into a hospital in Glasgow. But what was she doing there? I need to know everything I can about her but, oh, how I hate having to read the rest of the letters. I'd love to set fire to them.

Finally, she fell asleep, thinking of questions she did want answered.

Of course, she had had no intention of burning the letters. She took the photograph of her mother and grandmother on the beach and slipped it into her wallet. That accomplished, she set herself to enjoying a Christmas holiday with her oldest and dearest friends.

Christmas Day itself, even with home-grown, home-cooked ham to eat, presents – including a cleverly, and rather speedily altered mustard skirt for Grace – for everyone in both families, was almost an anti-climax, so exciting had Christmas Eve been. Flora and Fred Petrie had been delighted to receive a letter from their sailor son, Phil, a few days before Christmas. Phil's letters were as rare as letters from Sam and the family tried hard to be patient; after all, how easy could it be to post a letter on a ship? They discussed the problem often but had never really discovered how a letter from a ship, possibly in the middle of one of the world's great oceans, arrived safely to a house thousands of miles away. They accepted it as they accepted many of the new wonders of medicine and science. They waited nervously for

Daisy to come home and to hear all about the friend with whom she was having dinner in a Dartford Hotel. Flora wanted desperately to meet this man who meant so much to her daughter for, not only was he older than Daisy, he was also a foreigner. Flora was angry with herself because she had not readily held out a welcoming hand to either the dashing young aristocrat, Adair Maxwell, whom Daisy had loved and lost, or to this Czechoslovakian pilot, Tomas Sapenak, with whom her daughter was now sharing Christmas Eve. She wanted to make him welcome but had so little experience of dealing with people outside her own little world. Daisy's sister and their friends, on the other hand, were disappointed that Daisy was keeping her friend to herself.

They had forgiven her, though, and went to meet her as they all made their way to the midnight service.

'Here,' Sally Brewer called as she held out a lovely red cashmere beret to Grace. 'You can't wear that ugly WLA hat on Christmas Eve. Come on, Grace, I'll feel really warm and happy seeing that bright red hat on your little head.'

Grace smiled and took the beret that did indeed look very pretty on her dark hair and, yes, it was warm. Two years earlier, she would have argued and refused, and Sally would have said, crossly, 'Come on, Grace, don't be so stupid,' but now she was gentler.

We have all changed in two years, Grace realised as, arm in arm, the girls walked through the dark streets to the little church. No bells were ringing, golden light did not stream from ancient windows, and almost everyone spoke in whispers as they made their way to the service. How wonderful it would be when the bells rang out again and light and glorious music streamed from the church.

An excited shout broke the wartime-induced silence. 'Grace, oh, Grace, how wonderful to see you.' It was Daisy, not changed at all, even though she was now a proud member of the Air Transport Auxiliary.

The two girls flew into each other's arms like homing pigeons, and hugged and cried and drew back to look at each other and then hugged again.

'Well, Sally,' said Rose, pretending to be hurt, 'we might as well go off by ourselves, since we're not wanted here.'

And then, of course, came more hugs, chattering and yet another excited showing of the photograph of Grace's mother and grandmother.

Daisy handed it back to Grace. 'They're beautiful, Grace, and you are the absolute spitting image of your nan.'

Grace hugged Daisy again, looked quickly at the photograph, looking for similarities, before teasing Daisy that, since they were said to be more like twins than the real twins, Daisy too must look like the lovely Abigail.

Next, she joined her friends in their questioning of Daisy.

'Did you have a fab dinner?'

'Where is Tomas spending Christmas? I suppose he's Catholic and won't attend a Church of England service?'

'When do we get to see him?'

'I already have. I ambushed the poor man last

Christmas,' confessed Rose. 'He's tall, very distinguished-looking and has the most gorgeous accent, doesn't he, Daisy?'

Daisy refused to be drawn on anything other than the matter of where Tomas had gone. She explained that he was spending Christmas with their local farmer friends, the Humbles, and, since Alf and Nancy would be awake very early, he did not want to disturb them late at night.

In a tight line of four, the old friends walked into the ancient church, smelling the incense, the candles, the freshly cut fir and holly branches. The church was by no means as well lit as it used to be but, for a moment, the girls stood in the candle-lit vestibule and looked at one another. Then, tears of happiness in their eyes, they entered the church and prepared to share in the Christmas service.

Grace and Sally did not return with the Brewer parents to their home after the service. Instead, they joined Daisy and Rose Petrie at their large flat above the family's small shop, Petrie's Groceries and Fine Teas. Before the war, the flat had always been crowded with young people, friends of the family, for the twins had had three older brothers. Now, Ron was dead, Phil, according to his letter, was 'somewhere at sea' and Sam, an escaped POW, was – who knew where? The girls stood for a moment in the doorway as the apparent emptiness seemed to strike each one.

'I never realised how big this living room is,' said Sally, and then coloured with embarrassment.

Daisy hurried to her aid. 'I know exactly what you mean, Sally. The boys certainly filled the chairs, didn't they?'

'And they were never alone. Seems we couldn't walk across this floor without falling over a long pair of legs.' Rose, almost as tall as her brothers, smiled at her friends and took a Christmas card from the mantel above the empty fireplace – another difference the war had made. 'Ta-ra. Look at this, girls. A priest – yes, a real priest – a Father Petrungero, an Italian who works in Dartford, brought it this morning, and how Mum managed to keep both quiet and still breathing is a Christmas miracle.'

Sally read the card and squealed with excitement. 'I don't believe it. How wonderful. Grace, look, it's from Sam.'

Grace, her face almost white in the firelight, took the card with a hand that trembled. 'See you soon.' It was Sam's handwriting. She had seen it before – the last time on a note to his mother. He had sent good wishes to Sally in that note. 'Thank God,' she said with simple sincerity. 'It's fabulous. Sam is coming home, safe at last. What wonderful news to get at Christmas. I suppose you have no idea when.'

'Not a word. We're just so...' Rose Petrie's eyes filled with tears but she managed to control herself. 'Girls, let's make paper chains, the way we used to. Dad's got some of that silvered paper that lines tea chests.'

'Ugh,' said Daisy with a smile, 'they'll smell of tea.'

'When has this flat ever smelled of anything else? Come on, Daisy, scissors, the glue pot. Grace, make us all cocoa. Sally, help me get all this breakfast stuff off the table.'

They were fourteen again.

Rose and Sally, the tallest, spread the paper over the table and began to cut it into long strips. When all the strips were made, Rose handed a large handful to each of them with her instructions. 'Right, cut them into three-inch pieces, and then glue them into links and a long chain. Pity they'll all be silver.'

'No, Rose, silver's ever so elegant. I bet everyone in Bloomsbury has silver chains. Shoosh,' she said suddenly, 'this is your mum's favourite.'

They stopped working and listened as a programme of songs and Christmas carols, chosen by serving men and women was playing. 'Listen, "We'll Meet Again". Oh, I love this one, too,' said Sally, singing along with Vera Lynn.

The pasting and chaining went on, carols in the background, and, in the foreground, repeated cries of, 'Oh, do you remember...?' Before the girls stopped for the night, an enormous chain of silvered links covered every available surface.

It was one of the happiest evenings they had ever spent together but, at last, Sally and Grace crept quietly down the stairs and returned to the Brewers'.

Sally was asleep at once but Grace lay for some time, unable to sleep, thinking about the precious gift of friendship, of the things she was learning about her family, but, on this special night, wondering where Sam was, and how he really was, and whether or not he ever thought of her.

Oh, to have been born into the Petrie family. She contrasted how the Petrie parents spoke to their children with how Megan had spoken to her.

There had been sharp words occasionally in that cosy flat above the shop, but they were immediate. 'Don't tease your sisters,' and the scolding was over. Words of comfort came next. 'That's a good boy; big boys must look out for little girls, and for smaller boys. That's how little boys become good men.'

Grace tried to remember one tender word from Megan but all she remembered was unkindness.

'Why did I have to put up with you? No use to anyone, you are, and not a soul wanted you. Where was your ma's family when you needed a home? Nowhere. They begged your pa's legal daughter to take you in.'

And then, one cold, winter night, just after Grace had started work in the factory, Megan had added, 'If it wasn't for that nun talking about money coming, I'd have drowned you long ago.'

Not for a moment, at twenty-one years old, did Grace believe her sister would have drowned her, but as an eight-year-old, she had believed every word.

FIFTEEN

March 1942

'I don't believe I'm hearing this, Grace.' Lady Alice was angry and Grace felt slightly queasy; she hated disappointing her employer, who had been, she knew, incredibly kind to her. 'I don't

293

want to add up all the favourable treatment you have received in this house – but I will. Christmas leave for your sister's funeral, Christmas leave last year... Shall I go on?'

'I know I've been treated very well, Lady Alice, and I'm grateful, but all I'm asking for is one day, even just a twelve-hour pass. I could get to Dartford and back if–'

'There was a prevailing wind and no German raids,' broke in Lady Alice. 'What is so important that you find yourself brave enough to ask for leave months before you are due any?'

'I'm sorry, I shouldn't have said anything.'

Lady Alice smiled. 'Oh, Grace, don't you know I'm perfectly well aware how hard it was for you to ask. Something very special has happened. Tell me.'

Grace was aware that Lady Alice knew she found it difficult to ask favours. She certainly was a good employer. 'Sam,' she said. 'Daisy wrote to me. Sorry, my friend Daisy Petrie wrote to tell me that her brother has just turned up.'

Lady Alice sat down at her desk and sighed. 'Take your time and start at the beginning, and do try to make sense.'

Grace took a deep breath. 'Sam Petrie was a prisoner of war in Germany,' she began her explanation. 'He escaped last year and managed to get to the north of Italy where he worked – on a farm, as it happens – but now the partisans, or whatever they call them in Italy, have got him into France. A British plane picked him up – with some others – and flew them home.'

'And why should you be given special leave to

go to see him? You have an understanding, a relationship with this Sam?'

How could she possibly explain Sam? 'No, Lady Alice.'

'Then do go back to work, Grace. You're ploughing today, are you not?'

'Yes.'

'Then, we'll see you at lunchtime.' She waited until Grace reached the door. 'From my limited experience, Grace,' she said, and her tone was gentle, 'your Sam won't want to see anyone at this point, no one. Trust me, he needs time.'

'Yes, Lady Alice,' said Grace, without looking round as she walked out.

Grace went over the plans for ploughing with Hazel, who had been delighted to welcome her back to Whitefields Court. 'Couple of the new girls have very little experience, Grace. We'll need to start from scratch with them; ploughing's maybe a step too far at the moment and I think I'll ask Esau to bring them along, gentle, like. Liz was at a farm in Devon for a few weeks till she got ill and was sent home. Think the poor little thing had nothing but porridge, sandwiches without proper filling and bottles of cold tea. Her gran wrote a strong letter, saying as how it shouldn't be allowed, some farmers working land girls like dogs for a few bob, outside lavatories, a bath once a week in an outhouse, if they was lucky. Taking advantage of the war, like the black marketeers. You try to get her to relax a bit; she's terrified of her ladyship; hides if she sees her coming.'

'We're all scared of her at the start, Hazel. Liz'll be fine. Is she any good at milking?'

295

'Absolutely, loves animals and, funny thing, terrified of Lady Alice but not worried about great heavy beasts as could crush her like a fly on a windowpane. Lovely thing is, they seem to take to her an'all. Even that cantankerous old bitch Molly stays quiet with her.'

'No kicking over pails?'

Hazel laughed and shook his head. 'She's got a gift.'

'And won't the Ag. Committee be surprised at how much more milk we're sending them? Liz, the secret weapon.'

Grace enjoyed being alone in the field. She felt so in control. The little tractor was a joy to guide and, for Grace, there was not much that could compare with seeing a long straight line of beautifully turned soil. Pigeons and, on occasion, seabirds followed her and her splendid metal horse. It was exhausting work, especially when the plough did not slice cleanly through the earth. Hardened mud, stones and even thick roots tried her patience and the sharpness of the plough. Stones could cripple a plough and she had to be alert constantly.

She worked conscientiously for a few hours and then, hot, thirsty and tired, she stopped for a few minutes' rest.

'Grace, you are wishing a cup of tea?'

Grace laughed as she wiped the sweat from her forehead. When would Katia's command of English make a sizeable improvement? 'Yes, Katia, I want a cup of tea,' she called out.

The Polish girl climbed over the fence and walked down the length of the field, a basket in her hand. 'We are having tea, and a ... one of these things, delicious.'

'Scones.'

'Look, Grace, is blossoms already.'

The girls were sitting on a hummock at the side of the field, their backs against the stone dyke. Mrs Love had sent the tea in a Thermos flask. It was hot, and the scones, thickly spread with farm-fresh butter, were, as Katia had said, delicious. Grace looked at the trees at which her Polish friend was pointing. 'I think those are two really old apple trees, Katia. This field used to be an orchard.'

'In Poland, we have orchard with many trees. Blossoms are very beautiful.'

'Are you happy here?'

'Happy? This is strange word. If you are meaning, can I forget for one second that I am not know where my family is disappeared, then, no, I am not happy. If happy means, can I look at pink and white blossom on a tree and ... like this blossom, then, yes, Grace, for this time, I am happy.'

Grace felt dreadful. How could she have been so crass, so unthinking? 'I am so very sorry, Katia.'

Katia smiled. 'I know you are, and, yes, I like to be on this beautiful field and to live in beautiful house. I like you and I like Eva and especial to hear Eva sing. This Hitler stops her going in...' she thought for a moment, '...you know what is conservatoire?'

'I think so: a music school.'

Katia said nothing but wiped a crumb off her breeches before standing up. 'When war is over.'

Grace, who found herself wanting to howl in despair at the cruelties of war, said instead,

'Absolutely, Katia, when this war is over.'

Katia walked back towards the house, the much lighter basket swinging from her hand, and Grace returned to her ploughing. Her joy in it had gone, though, and she continued through duty not pleasure. Admonishing thoughts ran through her head. Sam is home and he is safe and I am moping because I cannot go to welcome him, while Eva, who has lost everything, still sings as she works ... and Katia mourns for her friend's lost chances.

She ploughed on and, eventually, felt a little better. Lady Alice had brought the Polish girls to Whitefields Court. Why? Newriggs was primitive in comparison to the house in which they were now living but the Flemings had done their best by the land girls, and, compared with the farm where poor Liz had spent a few miserable weeks, Newriggs was palatial.

Grace caught up with the new land girls as they walked back in the sweetly smelling air to the house for lunch. 'Have a good morning, girls?'

They were all chatty. Hazel, Esau and Walter had worked with them and Liz had been particularly impressed by Walter, the head dairyman.

'He was ever so helpful, Grace, and he actually said I had a gift for cows.'

'That's terrific, Liz. Are you going to go out on deliveries?'

Liz hung her head but said nothing.

'She will when I'm driving.' Connie Smart answered for her. 'I'll drive and lift the churns, and Lizzie here can run in and out of the houses. By the way, her ladyship says as how you started driving lessons, Gracie. Get very far?'

Grace looked up at the much taller and heavier land girl and knew that for some inexplicable reason she had made an enemy. But she was no longer the timid little girl who had been sent to this farm almost two years before. 'No, Connie, but I'm delighted that there is another driver.' She turned to Liz. 'Hazel says that Walter knows everything there is to know about cows. If he says you have a gift, he means it.'

'And here's her ladyship's little pet telling you, too, Liz, so now you really know.'

Grace was taken aback, so strident was the note of dislike in Connie's voice. She decided to ignore the remark about 'little pet' and to continue doing as she had been told, which was to make all the girls feel welcome.

'When I first came to Whitefields, I found Hazel, Esau and Walter always willing to explain things I didn't understand. They'll be the same with all of you.'

'And some of us more than others,' said Connie. 'They even had time for them conchies, even the dafty who feeds the chickens, though maybe our head girl here will tell us all about him.' She stopped deliberately and looked challengingly at Grace. 'It was something about getting blind drunk and trying to kill someone from the village, wasn't it?'

Grace was so shocked that she stopped walking and, with the exception of Connie, the others automatically stopped beside her.

Aware that she was now walking on alone, Connie halted and looked back. She stared at Grace, as if daring her to say anything.

Grace hated confrontation but she could not allow Harry to be maligned. Yes, he was taking time to recover from the injury, and his memory was not what it had been, but he was not, as Connie so crudely put it, daft. 'Not a good idea to mouth off about things you know absolutely nothing about, Connie; that could get you into a great deal of trouble. It's not just the other local farm workers who are loyal to one another; there are men with principles on this estate. And, by the way, it's Grace. Not Gracie.'

'I know all about it, Gracie. You don't catch me staying here, sucking up to the aristocracy in my five minutes' free time. I cycle into the village every spare minute I get. There's some people there only too willing to spill the dirt on this place.'

How much to say, if anything? Grace gave herself a mental shake. 'There was a spot of trouble at a dance, girls, and I'm afraid a farm labourer from the village actually went to gaol for injuring Harry McManus, a decent man, a conscientious objector, who worked hard on this estate and who is slowly recovering from a serious head injury. I've already warned you, Connie, but Hazel and the other men on this farm would not be pleased if they heard you talking like this.'

The bigger girl pushed her face closer to Grace's. 'And you're going to run to tell your friend, Alice in Wonderland, I suppose. Mrs Love did say you two is tight.'

An exasperated voice shouted from the back door of the great house. 'You lot want your dinner? Then move. If not, we'll share it. You got till a count of ten. One, two...' Without waiting to

300

see their reaction, Hazel turned and walked into the house, slamming the heavy door behind him.

Two of the new land girls started to run. 'He doesn't mean it,' Grace called after them. 'Mrs Love cooks more than enough for everyone.'

'Even squirts like this one,' said Connie, giving the much smaller Liz a vicious push in the back, which sent her sprawling to the ground. Grace moved to intervene but Liz had already picked herself up. She turned on Connie.

'You don't scare me. I been dealing with fat bullies all my life. Now, keep outa my way or I'll set the bull on you.'

Grace realised that it was she who was supposed to be in charge here. 'Dinner first, girls, and then I think Hazel said there's harrowing needs doing.'

Grace was amazed by Liz's reaction. The girl had worked on a farm where she had received little food and absolutely no kindness and had only told her sad story after she had been taken ill. Now, here she was challenging a much taller and heavier bully. Was Liz able to stand up for herself because she had a loving family behind her? They walked together into the kitchen. As the others chorused, 'Sorry, Mrs Love,' Liz hung back just inside the door with Grace. 'She's scared of the cows, Grace.'

'And you're not. What about the bull?'

'Walter says he's gentle. Treat him nice and that's the way you'll be treated.' Liz looked at Grace out of eyes that had seen a great deal of misery. 'You have to be sorry for Connie; she doesn't know how to be gentle. Maybe no one was ever been gentle with her.'

Grace, who had been afraid of many people in her life – her sister, bigger girls and boys at school, Miss Ryland in a bad mood, even Connie, because she recognised the malice in her – felt an affinity to the younger girl. 'Tell me if she gives you any trouble.'

Liz smiled. 'I'll be all right. She won't come near the dairy, if she can help it. Can I say something, Grace, even though you're in charge?'

'Of course, Liz. That's why I'm here.'

'Connie's looking for trouble; it's all she understands. When she sees no one's out to get her, she'll calm down. And don't worry so much. I came up hard. I can handle myself – and the Connies of this world.'

In a happier frame of mind, Grace and Liz moved into the kitchen. Mrs Love had made chicken soup, using the bones of the chicken they had had roasted for dinner the day before. Since it was still too early for leeks, she had used onions, garlic and parsley – which always seemed to be available – to flavour the stock and the rice. 'Another month...' she said to the newcomers, 'give me another month and you won't believe what the kitchen garden will produce.'

The meal over, the girls dispersed to the various jobs Hazel had arranged for them. Harrowing could not begin on Grace's field as the ploughing was unfinished, so Grace returned alone to the field and began to work. There was a chill breeze blowing and she was glad of the hard physical work, which kept her warm. She carried on until darkness began to fall. Utterly exhausted from the full day of backbreaking work, Grace wondered if she could stay awake long enough to join the others for tea. Perhaps there would be time for a bath; soaking in a lovely hot water would be refreshing.

'There's tea in the pot, if you want a cup, Grace. Two or three of the others fancy a lie-down before tea. Don't think some of the younger ones are used to a full day's hard work.' Mrs Love was kneading dough on the scrubbed table. She laughed. 'Maurice took two of them to meet mangles and Dave was showing nettles to some of the city ones.'

'Everyone knows what a nettle looks like, Mrs Love.'

'Maybe, if it's two feet tall and growing right in front of you, but they're sprouting up all over the place at this time of year. Maurice was laughing with Hazel about one of the city girls mixing up nettles and blackberries. She certainly won't mix them up if they get growing, will she?'

Grace agreed that a mix-up was unlikely. 'Shame to have to cut back all the blackberries. I love them.'

'The prettiest flower is a weed if it's in the wrong place, and, with the Agricultural Committees coming in snooping every time you turn round, Hazel needs to make sure food crops are growing everywhere they can put down a root; and if that's in a nettle bed or a blackberry patch, then nettles and blackberries has got to go.'

Grace agreed with her in principle, especially about getting rid of the nettles; after all, nettle soup was the only edible item she had ever heard was produced from the plant, and just how much of that could a nation swallow? But blackberries were different. Yes, they had to be destroyed if they were growing among food crops but, what if cuttings were taken and new plants grown somewhere else, over a wall perhaps? She would talk to Hazel.

In the meantime, she went upstairs, just imagining how the lovely hot water would ease her aching muscles.

In her room, her eyes immediately sought the chest of drawers where she kept her box of treasures. Aware that there were still letters to read, she took out the box and then an unread letter. Nothing of any interest. It had taken only a few moments. Surely, there was time for one more.

Eventually, she remembered that she had come up to indulge in a nice, hot bath. She almost sprang from the bed. Too late. She had lost her turn and ... for what? The letters she had read had obviously been kept for sentiment only. She hurried down to the kitchen.

It was Eva who first said something about Grace's obvious preoccupation. 'Hello?' she called across the table. 'Are you ill, Grace, with tiring, with bored?'

Grace tried to smile. 'Of course not.' She sought to change the subject. 'These rissoles are delicious, Mrs Love. What's in them?'

'Minced Spam, bits of grated cheese, parsley and one of Harry's eggs. Amazing what an egg and a bit of parsley does to a meal. You do seem a bit preoccupied, Grace, and I never heard the bathwater. Are you sure you're all right?'

'Maybe she got a letter today from somebody special,' Connie said, laughing and continued eating.

'No post today, or not so far, and it's a bit late now,' said Mrs Love, who was still looking at Grace. 'By the way, girls, one of the men says as there was a bit of arguing and shoving earlier.' She looked at Connie as she spoke and noticed how Connie averted her eyes. 'Lady Alice won't tolerate any nonsense in this house, which is, in fact, his lordship's main residence and has always been a happy family home. Did anything happen today, Grace? I know you're not the oldest but you are supposed to be the senior land girl.'

Grace looked directly at Connie who again found her Spam rissoles fascinating. 'No, I don't think anything happened that Lady Alice needs to know about, Mrs Love.'

'Oh, but Liz–' began Katia.

'...was telling us how she has absolutely no fear of the bull,' Grace broke in. 'We take our lovely little hats off to her, don't we, girls?'

The others, including Connie, agreed, and the meal went on quietly.

Mrs Love stopped Grace on the way upstairs after the evening meal. 'A word, please, Grace.'

Grace had no option but to return to the kitchen with her. Once there, Mrs Love lost no time in coming to the point: 'What's bothering you, Grace? And don't say "nothing" because I can see stress in every line of your body.'

'I really am all right. It's kind of you to worry.'

'It's my job.'

'And it's mine to help the new land girls, and

305

that's what I'm doing.'

'Connie's a bit rough and ready.'

'She does her fair share.'

'Old Esau saw her push Liz down.'

'Liz is a match for her, Mrs Love.'

'What bothered you when you went upstairs? And do stop lying to me, or fibbing, if you think that's a better word.'

Unable to meet her eyes, Grace looked down. 'I was really silly, stupid, in fact. I sat down and read two letters. I haven't yet made time to read everything.'

'Why don't you give your box to Lady Alice to keep in the safe for you? Oh, by the way, she had a telephone message from Jack Williams. He hasn't contacted you, has he?'

'Why would he contact me?' Grace knew she was flushed and could almost hear her heart beat. Jack, after all this time. 'He didn't telephone from over there, did he?'

'Oh, no. What would that cost, if it even works from abroad? He got some leave and wanted to know about Harry.'

He cares about Harry and he was a medical student; he would be interested in Harry's recovery.

'That sounds like Jack. Harry really liked him, you know. He loved listening to Jack talking as they worked.'

Mrs Love took off her flowered wraparound apron and hung it on a peg near the sink. In doing so, she revealed a very beautiful blouse.

'Wow, Mrs Love, that is pretty. Is it real silk? I don't think I ever saw a blouse of real silk.'

Pleased, Mrs Love preened and then twirled so

that Grace could see every detail of the pale pink, pure silk blouse. She pointed out the generous floppy bow at the neck, the small pearl buttons and the exquisite hand-stitching of the button-holes. 'Christmas,' she said with a proud smile. 'From my lad, my Tom, all the way from the Far East, wherever that is... They had a pass for a day and he spent all his wages on it.'

'I can imagine. It's really lovely and you look very nice in it.'

'It's for best, but sometimes I just have to wear it for an hour or two. Makes me feel wonderful. If your hands are clean, you can touch the bow.'

Knowing it would please her, Grace looked at her hands, and then gently touched the blouse. 'Softest material I ever touched, Mrs Love. He must love you very much.'

'Well, that's as may be,' said Mrs Love, trying to hide just how much she appreciated Grace's reaction, 'but I want you to know that her lady-ship won't allow no bullying, so you tell me if it happens again.'

'Good night, Mrs Love,' said Grace quietly as she left the room.

SIXTEEN

The news that Jack had been in England took Grace's mind off her suspicions for a day or so. Lady Alice would have told him where she was – if he had asked, of course. There had been no

307

letter for such a long time that it was almost as if Jack thought what had happened between them was something that had happened to another person in another place. Grace, who had been physically tired, having spent over eight hours ploughing and who should have immediately fallen into a deep and restoring sleep, lay in bed – it seemed for hours – listening to gentle snores and murmurs, and wondering about Jack. Could she ask Lady Alice if he had visited or planned to visit Harry? She decided that she could not.

She was surprised, too, to find that her body remembered Jack. Oh, how sweet their loving had been. She turned over to hide her face in the pillow as tears coursed down her cheeks. For Jack, it had not been loving; it had been... No, she could not bear to name what it had been. She tried to drive all memory of him from her mind and surely then her body would forget, too.

She forced her mind to focus on the contents of her box. Was it not enough to know the names of her parents and her grandparents? At last, after all the sad years of being made to feel worthless by her sister, she knew, not only the name of her mother but what she looked like; she could hold in her hand a watch that had belonged to her mother and to her grandmother before that. Margaret Hardy went through a legal marriage ceremony with John Paterson. Even Margaret's parents, righteous upstanding people that they were, thought the marriage valid.

But Grace had gone to a school where illegitimate children were mocked by their peers, where any child in an unusual situation was judged to be, in some way, wanting. At least that slur had rarely been cast on her in Dartford, for Sam had dealt with it on the rare occasions when it had. If anyone had been unpleasant, it had been Megan. Megan, who, for all those miserable years, had held on to the beautiful watch and, more importantly, the papers, and who had never once mentioned them to a little girl desperate for some stability.

No, she could not sleep. She had to look at some of the old photographs and perhaps read a letter or two.

She slipped out of bed, listened for a moment to the other soft sounds of exhausted sleep, then crept across the occasionally creaking wooden floor to retrieve her precious box from the drawer. It was much too late to think that natural light might allow her to read the letters, and so she crept as quietly as she could to the door, praying that it would open silently. Once out of the bedroom, Grace tiptoed to the bathroom, opened the door as quietly as possible and slipped inside. Praying silently but fervently that none of the land girls would need to visit this surprisingly modern room, she closed the door and turned on the recently installed electric light.

Did it cost the Whitefields an absolute fortune to run? She did not know, but decided that it probably did and, therefore, she would read only a few letters. She sat on the solid oak lavatory seat and looked through the photographs, hoping to see a small Grace, but there were no pictures of children. She decided that the photographs were mostly of Megan and her family and, therefore, would be of no interest or importance to her.

309

'But we have the same father.' The realisation came to her that relatives on the Paterson side were her relatives too and so decided to study the photographs later.

Letters. Letters could hold clues. She looked at one or two and wondered why they had been kept, for there was nothing of any importance in them. None, so far, had shed any light on Grace's personal story.

As the cold seeped into her bones, Grace wondered what on earth she was doing, sitting on a lavatory seat instead of sleeping in her bed. She had almost decided to return to the land-girls' room when she picked up a letter and saw several words pop out at her.

'She's had a bairn, Gert, a lass. Well, much good he'll do either of them. He's following crops in England. Somerset, Kent, anywhere there's a crop, and she goes with him. He's that stupid, he doesn't realise that cousins of ours...'

That was all there was on that piece of fragile paper, but it was more than enough to destroy any hope Grace had had of blessed sleep that night.

'I'm the child,' Grace said to herself, 'and Gert, who was obviously still alive, is Megan's mother.' She felt sick and closed the box with a crash that could have wakened a light sleeper. She realised that she was very, very cold; but what was from the temperature of the room and what from what she had read? She did not know. *No records of a divorce. That makes me illegitimate.* Like a very old and stiff woman, Grace stood up, turned off the light and went back to the large bedroom. The relaxed comforting sounds that her friends made assured

Grace that they were sound asleep. Quietly, she put the box away before seeking the comfort of her own bed. As she lay there, it was not of herself that she was thinking but of her mother. How she must have loved John Paterson to give up so much to follow him all over the country.

Her last coherent thought before sleep finally claimed her was: if Megan had lived, would she ever have told me?

That thought was still in her head next morning when she threw cold water on her face in an attempt to feel awake and refreshed.

She looked out and was surprised to see a light covering of snow all around the house. Her first feeling was that it was so lovely. Her little world was white and pure, not a print of bird, or animal or even barn cat spoiled the snowy blanket. More awake, she found herself annoyed, for it was almost April and she wanted to look out at flowers in the garden and blossoms promising autumn fruits on the trees.

The others were awake, and grumpy and sleepy in equal measure. They washed and dressed as quickly as they could, grabbed Wellington boots and coats and hurried down to the large, heated kitchen for their first refreshing cup of tea. There was no conversation, only a flutter of subdued thanks to Mrs Love as they hurried out to their various chores.

They were still quiet when they returned for the generous breakfast that Mrs Love had ready for them, but, as their healthy young appetites were appeased, the chattering began.

'Eva is learn new song,' announced Katia.

The land girls had quickly realised that Eva's voice was something more than merely pleasant; that it was, in fact, something out of the ordinary. She sang in Polish as she worked, and sometimes in Italian, a language she did not speak but which she had begun to study before the war. They also knew that, had there been no invasion of Poland, she would have been studying music at a very famous conservatoire in Krakow. Even Connie listened to her, although, unlike the rest of the household, she did not congratulate her.

'Which English songs, Eva?' Grace asked. 'Folk songs, opera, love songs like "Don't Sit Under the Apple Tree"?'

'Much more important,' said Katia sternly. 'She is not learned all words yet, but it is song of Potato Pete.'

Even Mrs Love laughed. 'Well done, Eva; you are very patriotic. I shall choose something from the Potato Pete cookbook for supper when you have learned the words.'

Since home-grown carrots and potatoes were in plentiful supply, Potato Pete and Dr Carrot had been introduced to encourage the British house-wife to use them in different ways. Mrs Love had already tried 'curried carrots' as a change from plain boiled carrots but with mixed success.

'Don't cook carrots or potatoes for breakfast, Mrs Love, please,' begged Liz. 'Your porridge is just perfect.'

'There's a recipe for carrot jam, Liz. How about porridge with a big spoon of that?'

'Time for work, girls,' said Grace. 'Mrs Love is teasing, Liz. Aren't you, Mrs Love?'

'Maybe, maybe not.'

As Grace walked out with the others to see what Hazel would say about the unexpected late snowfall, she reflected on how much easier her own relationship was with Mrs Love. Tension that seemed to have dogged them in Grace's early days at Whitefields had melted away as easily as some of this light snowfall. Whatever had caused either thaw, she was glad of it.

Since Grace, Liz, Susie and Katia were working in overgrown meadows far from the house, they carried sandwiches, fruit and water, to sustain them during the day, and so did not return to the house until the early evening, when darkness was already beginning to fall.

'With any luck, the bathroom will be free,' said Grace. 'Liz is smallest, Katia. Shall we let her have the first hot bath?'

'I'd kill for a cup of tea,' said Liz, and was taken aback by the shocked gasp from Katia.

'She doesn't mean it literally, Katia,' said Susie with a laugh. 'What would you call it, Grace?'

'Don't know if it has a special name, Susie. An expression, I suppose. It's just an expression, Katia.'

Katia relaxed and began to laugh. 'Oh, we have expressions too in Polish but, since you are not knowing my language, I can't tell them. Come on, I am like Liz, killing for a cup of tea.'

They were the last workers back to the house and the first pot of tea had been emptied, but Mrs Love was in the process of brewing another one.

'And there's a nice moist slice of cake there for anyone who wants it. And, Liz, there's a letter for

313

you, a postcard for Susie and Beth–' she looked round at the assembled girls – 'when she gets here. Nothing for you, I'm afraid, Katia. Grace, you have two letters, and a postcard – lovely picture of a cottage in the Lake District.'

'Sorry, Katia,' said Grace, as she picked up her post. Liz was already reading her letter with evident pleasure.

Two letters, and she recognised the writing. In an effort to calm her heart rate, she looked at the postcard, which was indeed of a very lovely thatched cottage. She turned it over.

Dear Grace,

Thank you for writing. No, I'm not here but wouldn't it be nice? One day.

Hope you're well,

Love, Daisy

Despite the unpleasant knowledge that was constantly invading her thoughts, Grace smiled. Daisy had remembered that they had often spoken of having a walking holiday when they were older. Now they were older and the opportunity had passed.

She looked at the letters. They were from Jack but there was no number to tell her which had been written first. 'I'll take these upstairs, if you don't mind, Mrs Love?'

'Best take a cup of tea with you and a bit of this cake.'

'I'll be back in a tick,' she promised, as she did as she was bid.

Once in her room, she made a guess, based on

314

the condition of the envelope, and opened one. It had been written more than five months before.

Dear Grace,

Today was a good day. I received two letters from you, written weeks apart. I suppose they follow me all over the country and I try not to be bad-tempered because making sure that letters do eventually arrive must be very close to the bottom of a long list of 'urgent things to do'. Of course, those of us who wait for the letters want our needs to be at the top of the list. I don't think you can quite understand the joy that even a few lines of communication bring but it really is like being with [there was a large blot of ink there, as if Jack had thought hard about what he wanted to say before he had written] a friend.

I hope that I may be given a week's leave soon. I haven't celebrated Christmas at home since before the war. It's full-on here though and every journey I make is 'really' necessary and that is rewarding in itself. If you see him, or if you write to Harry, give him my love and tell him I will try to see him if I am given leave. If he's strong enough to travel, I'll ask him to come home with me.

Jack

Grace read it through again, realising that she should have assured Jack that she did, as often as possible, see Harry. She reread it. Once more, she was disappointed. The beginning was promising. Receiving letters from her had made it 'a good day'. That was nice. But the content of her letter had certainly not made this 'a good day' for her. Perhaps, if she was used to receiving lots of letters, she might have some idea of what Jack was actually feeling. She recalled the letters in her box. Each one was written by someone completely at ease. That was it. There was a definite tenseness about Jack's writing. She wondered if he even wanted to write to her. Surely, he did not feel that, because of what had happened between them, he was obliged to write to her? That really would be impossible to bear.

Gently, she opened the second letter. It had been written less than a week after the first one.

My dear Grace,

Today I have witnessed hell. Believe me, it is impossible to overestimate or accept what brutality man is capable of inflicting on his fellow man and I find it absolutely impossible to understand. Your smiling face swims before me and I focus on your lovely eyes, your nose – such a sweet little nose, Grace – and your soft red kissable lips. Sometimes you are so real that I put out my hand to hold you and the image dissolves, melts away. Your image is all that is beautiful here in this madness but, every minute of every day, I am glad that I have had the strength to follow the only path that is right for me. I cause none of this: I try, with every fibre of my being, to alleviate suffering, but, obviously, if I were fully trained, I could help more. The doctors are more than human as they operate in conditions I could never have imagined before coming here. How any injured man comes out alive, I do not know, but each one is a testament to their dedication. I will get through this war and I will finish my studies.

Too late for lilacs, Grace. Maybe next spring,
Jack

If he was able to see her face then his last letter had certainly made it possible for her to see, not his face, but the appalling scenes he was witnessing. The work on this huge estate was hard, the hours were long, but Lady Alice and Mrs Love made sure that home life – and it had become their home – was safe and secure with every physical need fulfilled.

She became aware of the water gurgling out of the huge, claw-footed bath in the cavernous bathroom next door and wondered, for a moment, if Liz had remembered how little water they were allowed to use these days. She wondered how Jack, and the men like him, washed. Surely, for the medical teams, cleanliness was especially important.

She looked up from the letters, having decided not to dwell on their contents, and into her head jumped the recently read letter that proved, once and for all, that she was illegitimate. If the 'bairn' in the letter to Gert was herself, then the letter had been written sometime in 1921, and Gert Paterson, Megan's mother and her father's first or only legal wife, had been very much alive.

'It doesn't matter, it doesn't matter,' said Grace to herself. She shook her head, closed her eyes, opened them again and looked straight ahead. 'I can live with this,' she said. 'My lovely mother did not know that the man she loved was already married. There is no shame attached.'

She straightened her spine and went back downstairs.

'Grace, we are just kill for cup of tea and nice

cake from Mrs Love. Is with carrots and Eva was singing Potato Pete song.'

'What a lot of nonsense.' Connie had obviously returned to the house after Grace and the others and was now sitting with them, a half-eaten slice of a moist, dark-brown cake on a plate in front of her.

Grace moved to the window and looked out. She saw the vast back lawns that had been transformed into vegetable plots, the summer houses, closed for the duration, the tennis courts that had received the same brutal if necessary treatment as the lawns.

The great estate was spread out as far as the eye could see. Its magnificent gardens were gone, replaced by mile after mile of crops. She straightened her back and smiled. What was it Katia had said when she arrived?

'Look, Eva, this is England. Thanks God.'

'You're so right, Katia, this is England, thanks God.'

SEVENTEEN

Late spring 1942

The train seemed to crawl across England. Grace tried not to fret, tried reading her book, but, today, Sir Walter Scott failed to capture her attention.

'Keep moving, keep moving,' she begged, as, once again, with a gentle hiss of steam and a slight shuddering, the train coasted to a halt. Like the majority of the passengers, Grace turned again to the window. Nothing. A field, beyond which lay another field. The view from the other side, somewhat restricted by the number of people in the packed corridor, seemed to be exactly the same. The great monster of a train, now more lamb than lion, had stopped miles from anywhere.

Passengers, inured to the difficulties of wartime travel, grumbled to themselves, sat down – those who had seats – and prepared to wait.

'Hope it's not ruddy Jerry,' said the thin woman across the carriage from Grace. 'Won't bomb us in daylight, will he?'

Personally, she doubted if she would ever again enter a train without reliving the raid that had killed the friendly soldiers who had saved her life by throwing themselves on top of her. What should she say? 'There haven't been so many daylight raids recently'? Or, 'No', 'Yes', 'Maybe'? Or, 'We would hear a plane, so don't worry'? Grace imagined that she heard strafing planes almost every time she looked up into the sky. That would go away, eventually.

'Perhaps it's out of coal,' she said at last.

She sincerely hoped this last was unlikely, although coal, mined in Britain for hundreds of years, seemed to be in short supply. Or was it the men to mine it who were hard to find?

She smiled, and said, 'Probably something on the line,' as if she knew what she was talking about. 'Cows do wander. I'm in the Land Army and the stories I could tell you about where even pigs get to.'

At long last, the train hissed its way into a station; they were in London and, if her luck held, there would be a train to Dartford soon.

Seventeen minutes, time to find a cup of tea at a canteen. Mrs Brewer would have a nice tea ready for her, she always did, but since Grace had had nothing since her bowl of porridge at seven that morning, she was both hungry and thirsty.

The canteen was packed with tired travellers and a dense fog of cigarette smoke hung over everything. To someone who spent hours each day alone or with only one or two people, the noise of so many voices calling orders or greetings to friends was deafening. Grace struggled towards the counter, hearing different accents and even different languages before she was finally able to say, 'A mug of tea, please, no sugar.'

The tea was hot and strong – and *sweet*. Had the overburdened woman on the other side of the counter not heard, or did railway tea always come complete with sugar?

No matter. Grace drank it and was revived. She looked at her watch. This time tomorrow, she would have seen Sam Petrie for the first time since before the war.

She was thrilled, of course, and so grateful that Lady Alice had changed her mind. One day, she was furious because Grace had asked for leave and, the next, or so it seemed, she was saying that Grace must go and see her friend's brother. Really, sometimes it was simply impossible to read Lady Alice. *Give her credit,* decided Grace, she is so good to Katia and Eva and she's impressed by Eva's voice. 'Waste of talent,' she had said when she heard Eva singing. She had obviously felt much the same about Jack.

Grace had a small dream herself, where Eva was concerned. Somewhere, there was £500 growing every year. Grace had never dreamed of having so much money, but Eva... Could £500 be of use to her? When she was brave enough, Grace thought she could talk to Lady Alice and possibly even the rather frightening solicitor.

But, thanks to her ladyship, Grace was now in Dartford and going to see Sam.

He was sitting at the window, reading a newspaper but he stood up when his mother said, 'Sam, love, look who's here. It's Grace. You remember Grace, Daisy's best friend?'

Grace, her stomach churning with barely suppressed excitement, walked into the comfortable front room, which had been used so rarely before the war: Christmas and New Year's Day, birthdays and when the vicar visited. Now, it appeared to be where Sam spent most of his days, as he tried to adjust to being a free man or, being on leave, as he preferred to call it.

Grace's first thought was, how changed he was and, yet, how much the same. She had read stories in which the heroine's tongue had stuck to her teeth or the roof of her mouth, and never actually believed that a tongue could behave like that – until now. Her mouth was as dry as the topsoil of a field as it waited for rain. Had she made some terrible mistake by coming? Was Lady Alice correct in saying that the returned prisoner of war would want only his close family around him, and certainly not some old friend of his sisters?

321

'Welcome home, Sam,' she said. 'It's great to see you.' She hoped that he could not see how her hands trembled, or sense her astonishment at the waves of emotion coursing through her veins.

'You, an' all,' he answered, easily enough. 'You've grown up. In the Land Army, they tell me. That must be hard work.'

'That must be hard work?' Did that remark sound like the old Sam? But he was not the old Sam. He was a war veteran who had fought in one of the bloodiest battles of this beastly war, who had been injured, captured and imprisoned. He had escaped; and would they ever know the whole story of how that was done? Somehow, he had made his way across Europe and found sanctuary in Italy, working with the partisans. She could not begin to think of how he had found his way back to England. She realised, of course, that he could not have returned to his family without a great deal of help.

Grace believed that in that moment she felt her heart swell with pride and, yes, love. She refused to think about that love for, if she did, she would certainly weep, and no returning hero deserved to have to deal with that.

Mrs Petrie, without realising it, helped Grace through the next few minutes. 'Why don't you two sit down in here and be comfy, while I fetch some tea?'

'No, Mum, we can have it in the kitchen like we always do.'

'Grace has come a long way, special to see you, Sam Petrie. The least we can do–'

Grace interrupted, 'I'm happy in the kitchen,

Mrs Petrie, just like old times, old friends to-gether.' The last three words almost stuck in her throat.

Flora looked at the young people and gave in. 'Sit in here then, while I take a cup down to your dad. Tell Grace about your walk across Europe, Sam. The things he's seen, Grace. You wouldn't believe it. Grapes growing in fields, would you believe? Mountains covered in snow all year round. Tell Grace about the Alps, Sam.'

Flora disappeared through the kitchen door and Grace and Sam were left looking at each other. Both were embarrassed. Sam spoke first.

'Sorry, Grace, I didn't mean ... what I mean is... Grapes and Alps, poor Mum.'

He stopped and the thoroughly nervous Grace took charge. This was Sam. Sam, her flesh-and-blood hero, who had protected her from bullies, made sure she had a turn at playing the cowboy in the white hat, instead of always being the bad guy in the black hat who invariably came to a bad end. She felt sick as she remembered that she had come to a bad end. She felt hysteria rising. He had not been there to save her and so she did, after all, deserve the black hat.

She looked at him, really seeing him this time. He was bronzed by sun and wind, thinner per-haps, for the skin seemed stretched tightly across his nose and cheekbones, but harder and stronger. His blond Petrie hair was bleached almost white.

'Does the sun always shine where you were, Sam?'

He laughed naturally and she liked the sound; how long since she had heard it?

'No, the summers were hot, hotter than anything I can remember here, but the winters? Seems like it was either snowing or raining; never seen such snow, and, yes, the sun sometimes was shining in the winter. Sunshine on snow, Grace: it's like the earth is covered in millions of tiny sparkling stones, diamonds maybe. But tell me about you. Mum told me about your sister. I'm right sorry.' The words were light but his tone was not. It was as if each word struggled to form itself.

How she wished that she had arranged to stay with the Brewers. Sally's mother would certainly take her in for the night and she could return to Whitefields immediately in the morning. What would Sam think of her if she were to say, 'I feel very little difference, and certainly I am not unhappy or very sad,' which was true but might sound unfeeling? She regretted the manner of Megan's death but it was not as if she and Megan had ever loved or even really known each other.

To her surprise, Sam sniffed, like a dog scenting the air. When they were children, he had made them all laugh by doing that.

He smiled at her, as if he sensed her discomfort, and it was the old Sam again. 'Smell them scones, Grace. Come and help me eat them; big as I am, I can't keep up with Mum's baking.'

'She wants to make up for lost time, to cook you all the things you have missed.'

Once again, he managed to smile at her, the way the before-the-war Sam – the Sam who was the eldest brother and who felt it was his responsibility to look after the others – used to smile. 'I know,' he said, 'but does it have to all be on the same day and on the same plate?'

In the kitchen, Flora had finished piling hot buttered scones onto a large plate. Three cups and saucers – showing Grace that she had now become a guest rather than an old friend – were lined up on the floral waxed cloth. Or, lovely thought, perhaps the cups had been taken out to show Sam how special he was, how absolutely delighted his family was to have him home safe? In the middle of the table near the scones sat a round ceramic jar.

Flora pointed at it with pride. 'Saved for a special occasion. Guess what's in there at two shillings and sixpence the pound,' she finished, awe in her voice at the enormity of the cost. Grace had been on farms in different parts of the country, from the south of England to the south of Scotland, and so had a fairly good idea of the nature of the treat, but she said, 'Good heavens, don't tell me you've gone and bought something at Fortnum's, in London,' simply to please Flora.

'Fortnum and Mason? Not likely, although I do believe the teas we buy and sell are every bit as good as theirs.'

'Course they are, Mum. Now tell us what you've got hidden in your jar.' Sam pretended to think for a moment. 'It's never blackcurrant jam.'

Flora, delighted with the reaction, shook her head. 'Well, it's not jam since you can't see through. Right? And it's never honey for the same reason. Isn't that right, Grace?' To Grace, it was obvious that Mrs Petrie was enjoying teasing her son. 'Honey comes in clear jars, doesn't it?'

'Absolutely correct, Mrs Petrie, although one

325

of the girls I work with told me she bought a *tin* of honey for her grandmother last Christmas in Fortnum and Mason's – lovely shop, she said. I believe the honey came all the way from Canada.'

'A tin? Imagine. But it can't be as good as ours, Grace, not coming all the way from Canada and in a tin. Has to be in a jar, honey does.'

Sam looked over at Grace, with the look that said 'we're conspirators' warming her. 'Come on, Mum, we can't stand the suspense. If that's English honey you're hiding in that jar I, for one, would like to taste it. Just to compare it, mind, with the honey we had in Tuscany; honey from flower-filled meadows that stretch for miles.'

'Miles of flowers, our Sam? You're joking.'

'Miles, Mum, and every colour under the sun.'

Sam had been to Tuscany. Grace tried hard to remember if she had ever heard of the place. The girls had told her that he'd been in Italy and so this Tuscany with all the flowers must be there. How much there was to learn about his experiences. Grace tried not to feel frustrated. He had had experiences that were bound to have changed him. Or had they? She remembered Jack's last letter with something approaching horror. He too had seen things and experienced things that had changed him. And so Sam, this tall, strong man, could not possibly be the same Sam who had marched so boldly away. I'm not the same as I was when Sam and I last met, and he has suffered as I have not.

'Sam, were you frightened?' Where had those words come from? 'Oh, I'm so sorry, what a stupid thing to say, to ask. I shouldn't have said anything.

I'm so sorry, Sam.'

Sam rose to his feet. 'Grace, don't worry. Of course I was frightened; we all were. It's the noise really. I can't think when there's noise.'

But Flora too had jumped to her feet, her face suffused with anger. For a fraction of a second, Grace thought Sam's mother might hit her, but she did not. She turned away from her towards her son. 'Sam Petrie, you've never been afraid of anything in your life. What were you thinking of to ask a question like that, Grace?'

Grace was angry with herself, and embarrassed. She had spoiled the treat that Sam's mother had prepared for him and, by doing so, had hurt Mrs Petrie. Mrs Petrie, who, with five children of her own, had always opened her door to a neglected child from who knows where, had knitted cardigans for her, fed her when Megan had left nothing for her to eat, always made sure that there was a birthday present and a Christmas present. Oh, how could she have been so crass? She swallowed the tears that threatened – and Sam was there as he had been so often in her childhood.

'Poor little girl.' He smiled. 'Think that's what I said to you all those years ago at school. It's all right, Grace, don't upset yourself. Haven't there been enough tears in this family already?'

She was in his arms, held against his chest; she could feel his heart beating. 'I feel stupid,' she said, pulling herself away.

'Nothing to feel stupid about; old friends like you and me. Now, are you going to show us what's in that fancy jar, Mum, before your lovely scones get too cold.'

Mrs Petrie stood back, frozen, her feelings and instincts warring with one another, and then she, too, put her arms around Grace. 'Sorry, Grace. You'll have to forgive me for snapping. I'm that relieved to have him back in one piece, I can't think straight – even when there's no noise; so there, our Sam. Now, I'll just put these scones in a tin and fetch warm ones from the oven.'

Sam waited till his mother had turned her back on them and then he winked at Grace, showing her that they were united in appreciating his mother's loving nature. 'Didn't I tell you she's baking for Montgomery's army?'

Somehow, Flora managed to laugh. 'I'm baking for my family, Sam, never mind General Montgomery; although I dare say the poor man would like my scones. Come on, Grace, dear – aren't you one of this family? – you can open the jar.'

They were too good. Grace could not understand why they cared for her the way they did. Her sister had not cared. As far as Grace was aware, Megan had never questioned Grace's sudden disappearance, never worried, never felt the slightest guilt. She had kept the box and the connections to Grace's history that lay inside. What had she hoped to gain? If Megan had cared anything at all for her, Grace would have given her the beautiful gold watch, the money, anything. She looked now at the Petries. 'You're the loveliest people in the whole world,' she said and, feeling herself forgiven for any error, picked up the ceramic jar and tried to open it. The top defeated her and Sam took it from her and opened it easily. Inside, the summer's honey gleamed like liquid gold.

'You first, Grace, love. Ladies before gentlemen in this house. Right, Sam?'

'You're right, Mum. It looks great. I suppose it's from the Humbles up at the farm.'

Flora unwound her floral wraparound apron, folded it and hung it over her chair before sitting down with them. 'The Humbles' honey is lovely but it's not theirs. I'll save them some. What do you think, Grace?'

'It's the cost, Mrs Petrie. I never saw honey as cost two bob plus sixpence for one pound and that jar's bigger than a pound.'

Flora was beginning to enjoy herself and to relax. 'So?'

'I was wrong. I think you're having us on and this honey has to be Fortnum's, definitely. I never saw anything from Fortnum's before, but they do say as everything is packaged lovely and that jar is beautiful. Am I right?'

Flora was almost dancing. 'You're right, Grace. When it's empty, I'll put roses in it – if we ever get roses again. Don't you think it'll look ever so lovely on the shop counter, cheer customers up on a rainy day?'

'It'll take more than that to cheer me up if I don't get to taste it,' teased Sam, and the difficult moments were over as each took some of the honey on a teaspoon, tasted it, and swore that they would never again accept honey – home-produced or Canadian – from any other outlet.

Grace slept that first night in the room that the Petrie twins had shared until Daisy had joined the WAAF. The evening meal had waited until daughter Rose, who worked in the local Vickers munitions factory, arrived home. The family never knew when to expect her as all munitions factories worked extra hours and even weekends. Rose was exhausted, and felt and looked dirty from all the dust that flew around her during her working hours.

She had been thrilled to see Grace again so soon after the last visit. 'I won't hug you, Grace, for then there'd be two of us dirty. Give me fifteen minutes to let the dirt soak off and I'll be back. Good day, Sam?'

'Great,' he answered. 'First there's the return of Grace Paterson, and, after that, scones with honey from a posh ceramic jar. We know how to live in Dartford.'

The bath revived Rose long enough for her to pick at the meal over which her mother had taken so much trouble. Mr Petrie, with George in tow, came up from the shop long enough to welcome Grace with a big hug, change into his uniform, and pick up the packed supper Flora had prepared for him.

'Dad's on fire watch tonight, Grace: Jerry's up to his old tricks again.'

'Air raids? I don't think I could handle any more air raids.'

'Don't fret, pet,' said Mr Petrie. 'Everything will be all right. I'm afraid I'll have to off and leave you; duty before pleasure. I'm glad you're here and I'll have time to catch up tomorrow. What do you think of our George? Grown a foot since Christmas, he has. Haven't you, you rascal?' After ruffling George's hair affectionately, Fred went off to his fire-watching duties.

Grace had met young George Preston at Christmas, when he had moved between the Petries and Miss Partridge. Now, besides working for the Petries, on Sundays, George was working at Manor Farm for Alf Humble.

'Mum's sure she'll lose George one of these days,' Rose said. 'Oh, he'll come home often to see us and Miss Partridge, of course – he's right fond of her – but he does love farm life. You two should have a lot in common. Just tell him all about something fun like rat-catching. Seriously, though, I pray this war's over afore he's old enough to go but, if not, happens farming is a reserved occupation and he'll stay here safe.'

Grace looked at the boy, whom the Petries wanted to keep safe, and saw the way he looked at Sam. The boy was obviously developing hero worship for the returned soldier.

Doubt entered Grace's mind again. Am I like George? she wondered. Did I follow Sam's every movement, think everything he said or did absolutely wonderful? Is that all this is, hero worship?

'At least our George doesn't disappear and get up to mischief these days. Do you, George, love? A reformed character, Grace, and we really don't know what we'd have done without him this past year,' said Mrs Petrie, smiling lovingly as George's face turned fiery red at the praise. 'Our Sam's going to teach him to drive soon as he feels like going out. Aren't you, Sam?'

'Right now, I'm going to clobber him at snakes and ladders. You lot are welcome to join us.'

Rose, and Grace, who claimed to be tired from her journey, went off to bed as soon as the dishes

331

were washed and put away. Sam, his mother and George returned to the front room to play board games.

Close your eyes, Grace said to herself, and it's like before the war.

Rose climbed into her bed and pulled up her blankets. 'Remember at Christmas, we talked about that awful Anderson shelter you had in the garden?'

Grace nodded, although Rose could not see her. She remembered talking about an unhappy experience but, of course, she had never told her friends about the many times she had been alone in the shelter and very frightened. 'I hate earwigs,' was all she said, and was answered by a soft snore.

Grace had intended to ask Rose the result of her application to the Auxiliary Transport Service. Several times, Rose, and even Daisy, had put off their applications because of worry over their mother, who had, naturally, taken the news of the capture of her eldest son and the death in action of her youngest very badly; but Flora seemed to be much happier now with Sam home and young George to look after. Grace looked across at the sleeping Rose. Perhaps she should wait and let Rose tell her when she wanted to do so.

So there were rumours that Jerry wanted to renew his bombing campaign. She had forgotten where the Petries went during air raids, or perhaps she never had known. For a moment, Grace wondered how she would behave in an air raid. She hoped she would not disgrace herself.

She lay down. She had been so tired and now she felt wide awake. She listened to the family sounds in the flat around her, an occasional frustrated cry from young George, 'Cheat, cheat,' as Sam was obviously winning, and short welcome bursts of laughter from Sam. It was all so very different from living at Whitefields with her new friends, but very much like sun-filled days before the war. She relived the moments when Sam had held her close to him. She had longed to relax against him, to feel his strong arms about her, keeping her safe from all harm. For a moment, she had felt that, at last, she was really where she belonged, not in this flat, but with Sam – for wherever he was she should be too.

There was no need to visit the solicitors' office on this quick visit. Mr Crawford had assured both Mrs Petrie and Lady Alice that they – and Grace – would be alerted if any more information relating to Grace's life or her family was uncovered.

'You can keep my Sam company for me, Grace. I need to get down to the shop and give Miss Partridge time off. She's been doing so many extra hours and, you know, she's a lady, not with a title like Lady Alice but she wasn't brought up to serve in a grocer's shop.'

'She loves it, Mrs Petrie. What else would she do all day?'

Mrs Petrie nodded as she stuck the ends of her turban in at the top. 'Still and all, we won't take advantage. As it is, she's an absolute godsend with young George. She says he's a clever lad. Never was in school long enough to learn to read and write proper, but you should just see his writing these days, and he's reading ever such thick books, Dickens and that.'

'Sounds fabulous. Well, if you're sure, I'll see if I can help Sam with anything.'

'If you could get him out of the house, that'd be nice.'

'He never leaves?' Grace could scarcely believe it. Sam, like all the Petries, was or had been an athlete. He had played football for a local team before he joined the army and as a soldier he had played for his regiment.

'Says he's had enough fresh air in the last two years to last him a lifetime. He's avoiding people, Grace. You're the first person he's spent any time with – apart from family, that is. I suppose he thinks of you as another sister and so he's relaxed.'

The words that seemed to cheer Mrs Petrie struck Grace like hammer blows. Sam thought of her as another sister. She wanted to curl up into a tight little ball and cry her eyes out. But she could not do that in Sam's own home. 'That's lovely, Mrs Petrie. Probably, I've always thought of him as a big brother.'

'Then I'll get off to the shop. If you can persuade him to go for a walk, the park would be nice, but if not, would you be a good girl and make us a nice pot of tea around ten? There's scones and carrot cake in the tins. Lovely and moist, it is.'

Grace assured her that she would carry out her wishes. She waited until Sam's mother had descended the stairs before going to the front room. It was empty, only the snakes and ladders box on the card table near the fireplace showing that there had been recent occupancy. He had to be in his bedroom and she could not follow him there.

She remained near the window, enjoying looking

out at the street below, seeing herself, Daisy and Rose and the fourth member of their tight little group, Sally Brewer, walking, skipping or running down that street, and always four abreast. The past few years had put tremendous strain on their friendship, for how can a friendship survive when the friends rarely see one another? We're managing, thought Grace. We don't see one another for months but when we meet it's as if we've never been apart. Fourteen years now, the four of us have been friends, and the twins and Sally at least three years before that.

'Why so pensive?'

Startled, she jumped; she had not heard Sam come in. 'Silly, but I was watching your sisters and Sally and me walking down the street. How many years have the twins and Sally been friends?'

He came over to stand beside her. 'Anybody looking up would think we're an odd couple, Grace. You're so tiny and I swear I grew even taller in Italy. But the answer to your question is, forever, I suppose. They were in the same first infants' class and I think Mum took the twins to a...' he thought for a minute, '...tiny-tots dance class or Tiny Teddies before that. Yes, I think it was teddy bears. Even then, Sally was the star. Did you ever take dancing lessons?'

Grace was about to say, 'Never.' Then an image appeared in her mind. She was the same age as she appeared in the dreams of the little girl and the young woman, whom she now knew to be her mother, and she was dressed as a fairy in a pretty pale blue dress of some type of soft floaty material. A pale blue ribbon was threaded through her hair and she had a pair of sparkling wings attached to her back. In her hand was a tall stick with a star on the top.

'They're giving you a very special job, my darling. You are the fairy guard who needs to stand at the door of the palace so that the bad fairies are unable to enter.'

Grace laughed ruefully and answered Sam's question. 'A few, I suppose,' she said. 'Problem was that I had two left feet and, instead of dancing around in a circle with the other fairies, the poor teacher invented a special dance for me. It was called standing still, and I was told to dance it through the entire performance.'

Sam laughed. 'I bet you were a wonderful little soldier.'

'I don't remember. I don't really remember anything, Sam, but I do know I still have two left feet.'

'Bet you don't.' He looked down at her only pair of civilian shoes. 'In fact, your little feet look absolutely perfect. I bet you're a grand dancer.'

'No. I have rarely tried.' The damped-down memories of that ghastly night when dear Harry had been attacked came flashing back and she struggled to banish them. She tried to laugh as Sam was looking at her, a question on his face. 'Deep down I must have remembered not even being good enough even to skip around in a circle.'

'Poor Grace. I haven't danced in years either. Come on, we'll give it a try together.' Before she could do or say anything, he clasped her right hand with his left, raising them towards his shoulder: her left hand instinctively rested on his right shoulder and she almost winced as his right hand went around her waist, guiding her gently against his body. The heat from it seemed to burn right through both her Fair Isle cardigan and her WLA Aertex shirt. So intense were the strange feelings that she feared she might faint. This was not the brotherly hug of their earlier meeting or even the fevered action in the back seat of Jack's car.

Sam looked down at her but appeared not to notice anything odd. 'Dancing's easy. All you need to do is listen to the music. The rhythm will tell you what to do. Now, I learned a really lovely tune when I was in Germany. It's called "The Blue Danube" waltz, though that's not what the Germans say. They call it *"An der schönen blauen Donau"*. One of the guards either played it on his record machine or whistled it all day and some-times all night. I was humming it on the way back home and the pilot told me its name in English. I'll hum it now and you count. Ready?'

Speechlessly, she nodded and he began to hum. It really was a pretty tune, Grace agreed, but, although she started at one, she had no idea where to stop as he half guided, half carried her around the room.

'Looks like I'll have to hum and count at the same time,' he said with a gentle smile, the smile that had plagued her dreams for years. 'One, two, three, one, two three,' he sang as he danced, Grace desperately trying to put her feet in the right place at the right time.

'You're not humming,' she protested.

'In my head, I am,' he said and, picking her up, he waltzed around his parents' front room, Grace in his arms.

At the end of the dance to no music, Sam stopped, but he did not release Grace. 'Well, who'd have thought it?' he asked of no one in particular. 'I was right. Grace, how about a little turn around the town?'

Grace thought her heart might stop beating, so filled with joy was she. She tried to be casual. 'Sounds lovely, Sam. I bet there's spring flowers out in the park.'

'Can you keep up with me, Grace? Remember, I walked across Europe.'

How was she to answer? Did he know his mother had wanted her to coax him outside the family flat? Was he angry? With his mother? With Grace?

'Sorry, Sam, no snow-covered peaks in Dartford, no great rivers carving their way to the sea.'

'You'll need a coat,' was all he said.

EIGHTEEN

He was standing on the platform. He stood out, not because of his height, which was in no way unusual, or his looks, which were pleasant and attractive although not particularly noteworthy, but because, among all the many men milling around in that few feet of ground, he was the only one not wearing a uniform. Although other men stood near, chatting, smoking, occasionally laughing, he was not part of them.

Grace lifted her hand to wave, but was unsure as to whether or not she had his attention. It was possible that he did not see her or, perhaps, he chose to ignore her and, drawing back as if she feared a slap, Grace let her hand drop to her side. There was some relief as the train drew her away more and more quickly each time the sweating stoker threw yet another shovelful of coal into the furnace. She felt chilled, not merely because the train was not well heated – it was, after all, still only spring – but because she felt that he wanted to make it quite obvious that he preferred not to acknowledge their acquaintance. But was that true? She was on a train; he was on the platform. Perhaps he had not seen her. After all, why should he think she might be on that train?

But she refused to be comforted. Jack ... her body seemed to sob his name. You made love to me and now will not even say hello.

Grace pulled her coat – WLA issue – around her for warmth – and possibly for comfort. Obviously, she thought, he has had leave and yet made no effort to contact me. But she had been in Dartford. The Petries were not teachers with telephones, but grocers; had he wanted, he could not have contacted them. *Does he find me unattractive? Or is it that he finds me quite below his notice?*

It was the lack of respect that she found so difficult to bear. I gave him what he wanted but lost his respect. She relived the few moments as the train had drawn in. I did not catch his eyes. Angry and humiliated, Grace lay back in the crowded compartment and faced the truth. Impossible to say for sure if he had seen her. She must put it out of her mind and think of her long walks with Sam.

For the first slow hour of her journey from London to Biggleswade, her mind had been filled with images and recent memories of Sam. Now, she sat looking through the windows as the English countryside flew past, and saw nothing. Two faces swam in her thoughts: Jack's, dark, lean, sharp-featured and, as she had been shocked to see in that quick glance, almost skeletal; and Sam's, equally thin and drawn but open and trusting. For the past two days, Sam and Sam alone had filled her thoughts.

For almost three years, she had missed Sam, and worried about him as he moved from his army base in Aldershot to 'somewhere in Europe', from battlefield to hospital, to prisoner-of-war camp, and then she had heard of his escape. In her imagination, she had pictured Sam, but she had not seen the tall, lanky, fair-haired Sam with the happiest smile, but, instead, a furtive figure in a dirty and torn uniform, running across ploughed fields in search of food and shelter in old barns and deserted houses – for was that not what Europe had become? There had, he told her quietly, been abandoned farmhouses, bombed-out hamlets, but there had been scenes of incredible beauty and majesty, and humbling courage and generosity.

For almost the whole of that three years, she had put a great deal of hard work into convincing herself that she thought of Sam only as the twins' oldest brother, a strong influence in her life as she grew up and, more importantly, as the man who loved the beautiful and talented Sally Brewer. That conviction had helped her deal with her relationship with Jack Williams, a relationship that had taken so much from her and seemed to offer little in return. Too late to wish it had never happened. Her first experience of intimacy had been powerful but she was sure that for the rest of her life she would regret that it had happened. She felt bruised but was glad that the bruises did not show, as she felt her relationship with Sam change and develop.

The past two days in his company had changed her perceptions of Sam and of herself. Once again, memories of his kindnesses and dreams of him had followed her and stayed with her. They had walked through Dartford, hand in hand, anonymous even to those who thought: surely that big laddie has to be one of Fred Petrie's boys? Or, that land girl, did she not live with that Megan Paterson, her as was found to be no better than she should be? Her daughter, was she? Or sister, some say. But apart from a few old and close friends who stopped for a moment to wish Sam well, no one bothered them, and Sam and Grace wandered through the town of which they were both fond. Sam exclaimed in pleasure when he saw a church or ancient house or structure standing untouched by enemy bombing and prepared to stand another thousand years.

'The destruction I saw in Europe, Grace... A lifetime isn't long enough to repair it.'

Hearing the note of tension in his voice, Grace steered them into the lovely gardens of the park. Daffodils and tulips enchanted them both, and

Sam refused to compare them with the Alpine flowers he had seen, but spoke instead of how happy he was to be safe at home, to see his parents and one of his sisters every day, to get to know the boy, George, who had turned up at the right time to fill the gap left by young Ron – not that it could ever be filled completely, but George would carve out his own place in the family and be loved for himself. The same with this girl at his side, no longer the child he had championed but an attractive young woman, taking control of her life, showing courage in leaving an unhappy situation about which she had never complained.

'Can you believe I thought of you a lot over there, Grace? What a scrawny little creature you were, the first day I saw you, bloodied little knees from being pushed down in the playground, tears in your eyes you wouldn't let fall? I see eyes before I see the whole face somehow, and you're like Daisy, really lovely eyes, and sometimes it would be your big eyes, dark eyes, but neither blue nor grey, a mixture somehow, but still I would see you smiling at me, scared-looking sometimes, like a puppy that's not sure if it's in for a slap or a treat. And the daft thing is, somehow you're more like Daisy than her twin sister.'

She said nothing, her heart beating faster with delight. He had thought about her. He thought she had lovely eyes.

'My dad's annoyed he never spoke to Megan,' he said quietly, not looking at her.

She had looked up at him then, her eyes bright and happy. 'No one spoke to Megan, Sam. Why should they? She kept a roof over my head, fed me, clothed me–'

He had not allowed her to continue. 'Mum told me she had kept papers about your parents, and photographs from you. That was wicked, Grace. And your inheritance? Why did she never tell you about that?'

Grace had wondered about that too but had tried not to think about it. It was in the past and best left there. 'I was twenty-one a few days ago, Sam. She was probably going to tell me then.'

'Twenty-one. And no party.' He grabbed her hand and pulled her round. 'We need to have a party, Grace, for you and for me. Have you any idea what this walk with you has done for Sergeant Sam Petrie? No?' There were other people in the park but he put his arms around her and held her close to him. 'He relaxed. I swear he actually felt stress fall off his shoulders and slide down his back, like snow off the roof in the winter. One minute, it's piled up there and, the next, whoosh, it's on the ground. Well, Sam Petrie's built-up snow has gone, he's himself again, and feeling a million tons lighter. Look.' He picked her up and swung her round so that the red bonnet Sally had given her on Christmas Eve fell off and landed among the daffodils.

He put her down and stretched over into the flowerbed for the hat. Then he put it on her head and pulled it down over her ears. 'Lovely hat, lovely eyes, lovely face,' and to Grace's surprise, he bent down and kissed her very gently on the lips. 'Lovely Grace,' he said, and kissed her again.

He still held her and she was glad, for her knees seemed to have melted like butter in the sunshine and she could not feel her legs at all. He was looking down into her eyes, as if searching for something: a message, a question, an answer?

'Should I say sorry?'

She shook her head. She was glad the kisses had been tender, for the moment would remain lovely; nothing in his kiss had made her think of Jack. 'Sally gave me the hat.' What possessed her to bring the beautiful, talented Sally into the conversation?

'Nice girl, Sally.' He still had hold of her hand, as if it was natural for them to walk like this, hand in hand.

She looked up at him, looking into the eyes that she remembered as always smiling with kindness and sheer love of humanity. 'Nice, Sam, is that all? I always thought you were in love with her; we all did. You even wrote a special message for her when we had the party. Surely you love her, you've always loved...'

He put his hands on her shoulders, as if to hold her down. 'Love, Sally? I like her; she is my sisters' friend, loads of talent and lots of fun. But love her? Don't ever tell her, Grace, but wee Sally and her constant posing bored me witless. She was forever trying to impress and, sorry, but it had the opposite effect.'

Grace closed her eyes and thought for a moment. Sally had bored Sam Petrie and yet she had been convinced that he loved her. Why? How foolish to realise that it was only because Sam had sent Sally good wishes because she got a place at the drama school, the first person any of them had ever known who was capable of going on to further education. Will I ever learn how to read people? she asked herself.

She opened her eyes and smiled, totally unaware of how enticing was that look. 'Bored? How could you? Sally's going to be famous.'

He laughed and what a happy sound that was. 'If there was snow on the ground, I'd rub your cheeky face in it, Grace Paterson. I meant she bored me when I was about sixteen, all that prancing around being this actress or that actress. You girls have no idea the consternation you cause. Now, forget Sally and think about a birthday party.' He bent down and kissed her again. 'Sweetheart, I can't face a big party, even for you. One day, the biggest party ever, but today, just you and the family, maybe Miss Partridge.'

'Sweetheart.' Was that the loveliest word in the English language?

'A pot of tea and some of your mum's scones will be more than enough, Sam.'

Feeling contentment such as she had never known, Grace walked with him, and he shortened his stride so that she did not have to struggle to keep pace. They chattered on. Weren't perceptions funny things? Wasn't the seemingly prim and proper Miss Partridge the funniest, kindest and cleverest woman in Dartford? And who would ever have thought that the old German refugee they now knew as Dr Fischer was a very famous scientist, with a long line of letters after his name?

'Courteous, Grace, that's what he was. I think we learned a lot about dealing with other people by just being around him.'

'I don't think I ever spoke to him, Sam.'

'Daisy says as he'll come back to us when the war is over. You'll like him; he's a gentle man.'

Long before she had boarded the train to London, the first stage of her journey back to Whitefields, Grace admitted to herself, though not to Sam, that she loved him. Surely she had never stopped loving him. Yet she had been with Jack, whom she did not love, and what would Sam say if or when she told him? Doubts assailed her, spoiling her bubbling happiness. What, after all, did she know of love? In her mind's eye, she had always been able to see the tall, slim Sam Petrie dusting her down that first ghastly day at her new school. Had she fallen in love then? If so, it was the love of a child for an older boy. Had it grown into the love of a woman for a man? Did she want to experience with Sam what she had experienced with Jack? Yes, very much.

And then, just a few hours later, she had seen Jack Williams waiting for the train that would take him, once again, out of her life, and her heart had seemed to turn over in her chest.

What a quivering jelly I am, she decided. She had loved him, of course she had, dreaming of a very different life when this war was over, because, although taken by surprise, she had welcomed his loving and she could not have done so had she not loved him.

And he would not even wave goodbye.

Is it possible to love two men at the same time? If I'd had a mother, would I know the answer?

Grace could have succumbed into pitying herself in her misery but, instead, she fought to pull herself together. *I am in the Women's Land Army. I will not sit and cry because I think I may have made a complete mess of my life. I need to think of Jack, too. Perhaps he didn't see me. So much is going on in his mind and I must not rush to judge.*

Sam had taken her to the station to wait for the train. 'I started a letter to you, Grace, and it's not finished, but I'll give it to you if you promise to read it when you get back to this grand place you're living in and not before.'

Of course she had promised and had kept the promise. Was she not good at avoiding reading letters?

Once back in the large room at Whitefields, listening to the soft sounds made by her friends – yes, how lovely, by her friends – as they slept, she read the unfinished letter.

Dear Grace,

Seems a bit daft writing to you after all the years you spent running in and out of our place. It was grand seeing you, made life a bit normal because you were just you and let me be just me, not some freak. Wee Grace Paterson, sitting there like she used to when she were a little lass.

Can't get my head around losing our Ron. Did you know Mum is making over his clothes for George? Dad is well pleased; she's stopped sleeping on Ron's bed at last. Mothers of the world has a harsh deal, Grace.

Anyway, it were grand to see you and I were delighted to hear all the good news about family and all.

Grace, I hope as there's a future for us but I have to tell you I want, I need, to return to my regiment. My wounds is long healed, thanks to French nuns and

347

Italian farmers. Those poor sods is on the wrong side now, Grace, but I owe them, decent folk.

The letter finished there but Grace held the words 'a future for us' in her heart.

A few weeks after her short visit to Dartford, Grace and Eva were walking back to Whitefields Court, enjoying the pleasant air, when they heard an aircraft approaching from the south. This was not a common event in the area but, as Grace and Eva listened, they assured each other that it was a friendly plane. Grace was determined to be certain that the sound they heard was that made by a Merlin engine and therefore they were in no danger.

'I'm quite sure it's a Spitfire, Eva, and therefore British. I grew up in Dartford and, believe you me, everyone soon learned the different sounds the various engines make.'

This was not exactly true, as Grace had joined the Women's Land Army early in 1940 and had, in fact, never been in her home town during one of its many major air raids. She wanted, however, to reassure her Polish friend, who had already experienced more than her fair share of warfare.

'Look,' she yelled in excitement, 'it's a Spitfire, trust me.'

Happy now and excited, both girls waved enthusiastically as the low-flying plane seemed to hover like a hawk in the sky directly above them. Later, they were unable to remember if they had heard anything. If they had heard a noise, the memory did not register, for the plane simply disappeared. One moment it had been there and the next the blue sky was filled with black debris that drifted down, spiralling, floating, like a nightmare of autumn leaves.

Eva had begun to shake. She looked at Grace for help. 'What is happen?'

'I don't know, Eva,' Grace began, but then she started shouting. 'See, Eva, look, a parachute, the pilot has escaped.'

The two land girls stood transfixed by the sight of a parachute drifting down slowly, pieces of what they thought had to be the Spitfire plunging earthwards in the air around him. Soon he was gone, carried by air currents or the spring breeze, across the fields and over a small rise in the seemingly endless flat land of this area of England.

Grace thought quickly. 'Eva, run to the house for help. Tell anyone you see and bring them: Hazel, Walter, the other men, Lady Alice. He's probably hurt. I'll run...'

Grace had no idea how she could help. She had a vague and not particularly happy memory of attending one or two first-aid classes with her friend Daisy Petrie at the beginning of the war. Had she learned anything? I have no idea, she thought, but I can run to him and I can shout.

She stopped and watched Eva, who had obviously understood, racing back towards the house. Perhaps Eva would find several of the farm workers. Grace hoped so, and, as she ran in the opposite direction, she could not help but remember that scarcely a year before, Jack, who could certainly have been of help to the downed man, would have been there.

There was a stitch in her side – she had never been much of an athlete – but she kept going, worrying in case the falling pilot would land with a horrid thump, perhaps causing further injury or even becoming tangled in the branches of one of the trees. It depended on the wind. She thought she could hear voices in the distance but could not be sure. *Please, please, let there be other people in the fields who can help him.*

The pain in her side was excruciating and, for a moment, she stopped, bent over in an attempt to ease it. She started off again immediately, happier that as she had stood easing her breathing she had distinctly heard shouting. Rescue was at hand.

Ahead was a steepish incline. Grace persevered and climbed to the top. Shouts and yells were coming from below. She could see dark smoke and flames shooting into the air from various patches of the field spread out before her. But it was, however, the sounds of the shouts that frightened her, for the voices were not filled with concern but with angry venom.

For a moment, the smoke cleared and she saw the dazed pilot standing, burning wreckage spread around him and littered in all directions as far as the eye could see. The Spitfire must have disintegrated. But men were racing towards him and Grace screamed in horror as the man who was wielding a hoe brought it down heavily on the head of the already stunned survivor, who crumpled in a heap on top of pieces of his wrecked plane.

'Stop,' she yelled as loudly as the men below

350

and, propelled both by anger and gravity, she sped down the incline, praying that she would retain a foothold, until she reached the bottom, where she almost fell into one of the smoking piles of debris. She became aware of strong, acrid, even pungent smells of leaked fuel, of smoke, of scorched metal, which made her eyes sting.

She had landed right beside the pilot and was astonished to see him struggling to his feet and holding out his hand to help her up while, at the same time, with his other hand, which appeared to be bloodied, he seemed to be desperately trying to open his flying suit and to get out of his harness.

'Jestem Polskim pilotem R A F,' he said several times.

'He's a bloody German,' shouted one of the young men. 'Can't even talk proper, doesn't understand a bloody word we say. We've had too many bloody Jerries dropping their bloody bombs on us – we're going to lynch him, aren't we lads?'

'Shut up,' yelled Grace. 'Do you understand a word he says?' She held the downed airman's arm tightly. *'Polskim?'* she attempted to copy his words. 'Polish?'

He nodded his head but he was swaying as he still fought with the fastenings of his suit.

'Someone give me a hand,' said Grace, as she tried to encourage the injured man to sit down before he fell down. 'I think his arm is broken and he needs to get rid of this harness. Lean on me,' she said hoping that he understood her meaning if not the actual words. 'Sit down and I'll help.' Why had she not learned some Polish from Eva and Katia? She pointed to herself and again said, 'I'll help.'

He understood the tone and, with Grace's help, sank slowly back down onto the ground, wincing with pain as he did so. She pulled out her handkerchief, glad that it was reasonably clean, and began, as gently as possible, to wipe the blood and accumulated dirt from his face. She was sure that the blood was from the blow rather than from the accident as there were signs of dried blood in his hair. 'I intend to tell everyone exactly what happened to this man.'

'Shove her out of the way, lads: it's that no-good slut as was with the bloody conchie; I'll get her too this time.'

Grace felt sick as she recognised the voice; it was the farm worker who had injured Harry. Here he was, out of gaol and preparing to hurt another man and threatening her. Without thinking, she slapped him as hard as she could. 'Stop it, all of you,' she said, thankful that it was already obvious that the others wanted nothing to do with their friend or his plan. 'I've sent for Lady Alice and Mr Hazel–,' again she stretched the truth a little – 'and no one is lynching anyone while I'm here.'

Another of the local farm workers approached her and was obviously both embarrassed and ashamed. 'I'll help.' He faced the pilot, an open knife now in his hand. For a second, wariness looked out of the airman's eyes and then he relaxed. 'I'll have to cut you out of this,' the farm worker continued. 'Quite a weight to drag behind you.'

Again, the pilot winced with pain as he was finally freed from both the harness and the flying suit. He spoke again. *'Mam na imie, Mateusz Jackowski. Jestem Polskim pilotem.'*

Grace had listened to Eva and Katia chattering often enough to know that, even without his saying so, the language was not German.

'Bloody foreigner.' The belligerent farm worker was determined to cause trouble.

'He's Polish, you fool,' said Grace.

'For the love of God, shut up, Arnold. You're making a damned fool of yourself. Look at him. He's on our side.' The other workers were now both annoyed and embarrassed by their colleague, especially since it was now quite obvious that the downed and injured pilot was wearing an RAF uniform with Polish insignia on the shoulder.

Luckily, it was his left arm that was injured, as each of the other farm workers shook hands vigorously with the rescued pilot and, speaking very slowly, loudly and distinctly, tried to tell him how sorry they were and how delightful it was to welcome a brave ally.

At that very moment, a rather battered car, driven by Lady Alice, hiccuped to a halt beside them. Out spilled Hazel, Esau, Walter and Eva. They were closely followed by Lady Alice, who took charge immediately. Under her direction, and with a great deal of help from a truly excited Eva, the Whitefields men tried to assess the rescued pilot's condition.

'For pity's sake, Eva, haven't you learned any English at all?' an exasperated Lady Alice asked as Eva chattered on.

'He speaks no English, Lady Alice, but he does look happier talking to Eva.' Grace hoped she was right to intervene.

Lady Alice grabbed Eva's arm in order to get her attention. 'Listen, Eva, we do not have time to find Katia and so you will have to come with us – God help us all – to translate. Do you understand?'

Eva replied in fluent Polish.

'Try to calm her down, Grace.'

Grace stared fixedly at Eva. 'Please stop talking.' To everyone's surprise, both Eva and her compatriot stopped talking immediately.

Eva remained silent while Hazel and Walter manoeuvred the injured man, as gently as they could, into the back seat of the old car.

'Pilot is from Poland, very fine, very brave,' she informed them when he was successfully seated. 'He is having hurt in arm and hurt in ears.'

'I'm sure he is,' muttered Lady Alice.

Eva managed, 'He is think from much noise.'

Lady Alice started the engine and called to Eva to get in beside her. She started to drive off and then rolled down the window. 'Hazel, I see an old friend is with us.' Her tone was full of sarcasm. 'Please talk to all the men from the village and get their stories. Grace, I'll hope to talk to you this evening, but did you see the crash?'

'No, but I think the plane exploded in the air.'

'Thanks. Much noise,' said Lady Alice, and drove off.

Back at the farmhouse there was a great deal of excitement. Some of the workers had seen both the plane and the parachuting pilot, others one or the other. Those who had seen nothing at all wanted to hear every detail.

'You can't mean it, Grace. Our Eva is translating for her ladyship, the doctors and the pilot?' said Connie, who, thankfully, was losing some of her aggression and being much friendlier with the other girls.

Even Katia smiled at the thought. 'This is large hospital, yes? There will be, maybe, a Polish person, a doctor even, but Eva will be good; she will work hard to make easy for them.'

'Should you not cycle down there, Katia?' Mrs Love had finished peeling a pile of the estate's own potatoes and had joined the group.

'No, I am not think so. This is good for Eva and language is not necessary for doctors. They look at injured pilot and say he has broken head. Is very simple, yes?'

'I hope he hasn't. Got a broken head, I mean,' said Grace. 'He was hit hard on the head by one of the men, though, and possibly he was injured as he fell out or whatever it is they do.'

There was a stunned silence. Then the girls began to talk at once.

Mrs Love got their undivided attention by banging two heavy iron pots together. 'Enough,' she said. 'I can't hear myself think.'

'None of us can hear anything, Mrs Love, after that clang. My poor ear drums.' Liz held her head between her hands and rocked her head up and down. 'The pilot tries to fall or jump out, Grace, but, for goodness' sake, don't ask me how. Someone told me once that they try to turn the plane over, release their harnesses and fall out, but if his plane exploded, possibly he was thrown out. Seems an absolute miracle.'

Again, Mrs Love took over. 'Grace was there and can tell us the whole story. First one to interrupt can do without pudding tonight.'

Connie raised her hand but said nothing.

'No questions, Connie, and you've interrupted.'

'Then I'll ask my question. Was he gorgeous, Grace?'

Everyone, including Grace, laughed. 'I don't know; poor chap was covered in dirt and mostly dried blood. Nicely tall, a real gentleman, quite slender. Apart from the knock on the head, I think one arm is broken because he had the dickens of a job pulling off his flying suit.'

'Naughty pilot. Why'd he take his clothes off?'

'To show his–' began Grace, but was interrupted by shrieks of raucous laughter. 'RAF uniform, you horrible lot.' Blushing furiously, she tried to speak calmly to tell them how frightening the scene had been. 'He needed to prove he wasn't German. One of the farm workers actually said they planned to lynch him.'

That silenced everyone and Katia was seen to make the sign of the cross.

'Thank goodness you and Eva were there, Grace.'

'I didn't do anything,' Grace began, and then remembered that she had slapped the farm worker, Arnold, hard across the face. He would not be best pleased. 'Lady Alice and Hazel were there very quickly and took charge.'

Mrs Love pushed herself up from the table. 'The whole world's gone mad,' she said. 'You lot have a full day's hard work ahead of you tomorrow. I'll have something on the table before long, chips maybe, and I've got some tins of sardines; good day to use them up.'

There were several disgruntled faces, including Grace's, at this announcement. She loathed sardines and especially tinned ones – all that oil, she thought – but she said nothing.

Connie did. 'Can we put the wireless on, Mrs Love, get some music, Benny Goodman maybe, or Joe Loss, have a little dance around the kitchen?'

'Stay away from the range with your jitterbugs.'

Grace smiled, remembering being in Sam's strong arms as he tried to teach her to waltz. 'Find a waltz, Connie; one, two, three, one, two, three,' and she held up her arms and danced to the other side of the table.

'Think the bloke hit her on the head and all,' laughed Connie. 'La-di-da waltz, indeed.'

'Polka,' demanded Katia, holding out her arms to Liz. 'I teach everyone polka. Is good, happy dance.'

For the next fifteen minutes, Mrs Love stood half-turned to her rapidly frying chipped potatoes and watched joyful mayhem as the usually quiet, exhausted girls, tried to learn how to waltz, polka, or jitterbug to whatever music they could find on the little wireless. She saw smiles and even tears as the girls remembered happier days and perhaps dreamed of fun-filled days to come. She did not want to bring their silly, girlish behaviour to a halt but they needed to be fed. Luckily, Eva and perfectly fried chips arrived together.

Realising it would probably save time in the long run, the girls gave Eva time to relate the whole tale, in Polish, to Katia while Mrs Love coaxed them to sit down and have their supper.

'You can talk while you're eating; sorry, it's not what I meant to make tonight but the chips is lovely and, if you don't like sardines, there's Crosse and Blackwell's Essence of Anchovies, a little of that on the side for dipping might be nice, or there's always good old HP. My Tom loves his HP.'

Grace wondered if she was the only one who found this new talkative Mrs Love rather strange. She knew too that she and Connie had never got on together but, lately, there had been a distinct thawing of the fairly icy relationship and she welcomed that. Life would be so much more pleasant for everyone if they pulled together.

'Gone to sleep, Grace?' Connie was banging the large sauce bottle up and down.

'Sorry, just had a silly thought, nothing important.'

'Katia is ready to tell us what happened. For goodness' sake, Liz, we can pour and drink tea while we're listening. Sit down ... please,' Connie added as Liz looked tearful. 'I'm bigger and I'll do it.'

'There is not much to tell. The pilot's name is Mateusz Jackowski, and he is in England since 1940. On return journey from ... war, his plane began make strange noise, engine make stutter, stutter noise and he thinks, I must get out, but he is looking down and seeing workers in fields. He tries to make plane go away from fields and then he hears loud explode and nothing more until he is feeling wind on his face and then he is on the ground and people are running and shouting, very angry voices. Girl is shout, something hits his head. He tries to say, I am Polish because obvious they think he is German. Then he thinks he is dead for angels come.' Katia laughed then, a delightful sound. 'He thinks one angel speak English but one angel is definite Polish angel.'

Everyone laughed at that and there was some teasing, until Connie loudly called them to order. 'And is the poor chap all right? And what about the idiot who wanted to lynch him? I can't believe an Englishman would try to lynch anyone, even a German.'

'He certainly did, and what's worse, at the very beginning, one or two of the others were right there with him,' Grace told them. 'I think he owes his life to his lovely Polish angel.'

Grace waited until the land girls had stopped cheering Eva, who seemed to be rather embarrassed, and then asked if Lady Alice had said anything about the downed pilot's condition or his treatment.

'Is miracle, Grace. He is having only two breaked bones, and bad cuts on head and other places. They are want to examine inside of him and make stitches in him. Tomorrow, they will tell more. Lady Alice is come tomorrow, when we are having early cup of tea and she will ask many questions.'

Mrs Love stood up. 'That's wonderful, girls. Now, I'll wash up and you girls get away to your beds. Katia's exhausted and Grace and Eva must be, too.'

'Sorry, Mrs Love, just one more question.'

'What on earth, Connie–' began Mrs Love,

who was also very tired, but Connie didn't wait.

'Katia, is he handsome?'

Katia and Eva looked at each other, spoke for a minute and then smiled. 'Mateusz is very pretty.'

'Woo hoo, we'll draw lots to visit,' said Liz, as the girls hurried upstairs.

'Without chances, Liz,' said Eva. 'Matt is with no English and already he has see two, no, three angels in uniform.'

NINETEEN

How did she do it?

Lady Alice knocked on Grace's door before the shrieking of the alarm clock shattered the night's silence next morning. She shattered the night's sleep, too, but the girls groaned, muttered silent oaths and wearily climbed out of bed. 'Seems we've been here before, Grace. Can you haul on some clothes and meet me in the kitchen? I'll make some tea.'

Grace, asking herself how her employer could possibly look so refreshed so early in the morning, mumbled some sort of reply, which must have been coherent as Lady Alice went off downstairs.

Grace joined her as quickly as she could and accepted a large mug of strong, hot tea from Mrs Love.

'One can't put someone in prison for threatening to kill, Grace; at least, I think it might be a

360

tad difficult to prove that Arnold was serious. He is known to be quite a bag of wind, you know.'

There was silence as Grace tried to think of what to say. If she told Lady Alice that Arnold had also threatened her and had, in fact, ordered the others to 'shove her out of the way', would that be classed as a criminal offence? The first time she had had dealings with this particular farm worker she had eventually been sent away for 'her own good'. She did not want to be sent away again. Whitefields Court was so much closer to dear, old Dartford – and, for the present, at least, Sam – than Newriggs Farm.

'Has anyone ever warned you *not* to seek to join any of the Secret Services, Grace? Everything going through that pretty little head of yours is written loudly and clearly on your face. Don't worry. We'll make quite sure he never sets foot on this land.'

Grace lowered her eyes as she thought of what Katia had told them, of what the pilot had said about Grace and Eva. He had called them angels in uniform. She would not let the ghastly Arnold do any more harm. No matter what the cost to herself, she had to speak. 'That awful little man lifted a hoe and smashed it down on the head of a defenceless man, a pilot, fighting with our air force to keep people like Arnold alive. I was standing right beside him. The pilot, I mean, and I had no time to react, to do anything.'

'So that's how it happened. The doctors wondered if some part of the plane had hit him as it fell past him. I can't think why he wasn't killed, Grace; a guardian angel perhaps. Thank heavens his flying helmet stayed on his poor head.'

'If that's all, Lady Alice...'

'No, it isn't. Have you learned to drive yet?'

'No, Lady Alice.'

'Pity. Connie will have to do today. I plan to give Eva and Katia a few hours off, to go in to chat with Flying Officer Jackowski – if the doctor gives permission. Afraid that puts a lot of extra work and responsibility on you. Can you take charge of the three o'clock milking?' She did not wait for an answer but continued, 'Soon the evenings will be much longer and we can let crops take care of themselves for an hour or two while Connie gives you driving lessons. Such a shame Jack didn't complete your lessons.' She stood quietly for a moment, while Grace was wondering if she should stay or go to the early milking. 'He's had a particularly bloody time of it,' Lady Alice continued after a while. 'You're not still writing to him, are you?'

'I have been, Lady Alice, as a friend.'

'Thank God that's all he is. Nice chap, I don't deny that, and if he gets through he'll make a splendid doctor, but, quite frankly, I think he'd be hell to live with.'

'Can I ask what you mean by bloody time of it, Lady Alice?'

'I'm afraid his principles don't appeal to everyone.'

'But because of these principles and beliefs, he is doing incredibly difficult and dangerous work, and no, he has never actually told me anything, but I listen to the wireless when I can, and read the newspapers when I see them, and so I know that there are bullies in the army as well as everywhere else.'

'We did suggest that we try to get him out, Grace, but he was quite angry, stupid boy. Still, I'm glad you're not emotionally involved. You're the sort that bends too much, and Jack's one of those who refuse to bend at all; an impossible collaboration.' Lady Alice made as if to head towards the door but then she turned back to Grace. 'How was your old friend's brother, by the way? Haven't had a second to ask you.'

'He was ... very well, thank you,' said Grace, annoyed to find that for some absolutely stupid reason, she was blushing furiously.

'Like that, is it?' said Lady Alice, this time definitely on her way to the door. 'Leaves the way nice and clear for our Polish girls, and our *Polskim pilotem's* bound to have chums, isn't he?'

Grace stood watching the heavy door close behind her. If I live to be a hundred, she thought, I'll never be able to read people. Every time I think one way, something happens and I have to think the opposite. Thank God for cows. Feed them, milk them, let them graze in a nice green field, and they're happy.

No one else was downstairs and so she fetched her coat – which was hanging with several others on the outside of the kitchen door – put on her outdoor shoes and walked up to the dairy. The cows were there already and so was Walter Green, the head dairyman.

'Well, hello, this is a nice surprise; I were expecting them Polish lasses, Grace. I hear that pilot lad is all right.'

'His left arm is broken, and there's another

363

break, not sure where, and cuts and general bruising.'

'And a clunk on his head, I hear tell.'

'Yes,' said Grace shortly.

Walter smiled at her understandingly. 'You want Arnold locked up. Don't fret, Grace, it'll depend on what the doctors say. The Whitefields won't let him get away with it. Now we need to start milking or these ladies'll be a hell of a lot angrier than Arnold and, believe me, they're stronger.'

Walter, of course, was the most experienced dairyman, and Grace knew that he would work down one side of the dairy much more quickly than she would. But she began at the beginning of her line of mature dairy cows, determined to do her best and to work as efficiently and professionally as she could. Half an hour or so later, Connie and Liz joined them, Liz working with Walter, and Connie, with a friendly smile, joining Grace. Knowing that Connie was not too fond of cows, Grace was surprised to see her, but she smiled encouragingly and continued milking.

At last, the milking was finished and the cows ready to be taken out to the field by Liz and Grace. Now the milk had to be delivered and the dairy washed down, a hard and usually cold job.

'Who's delivering with you, Connie?' asked Walter as he looked round the dairy, but he was reassured when he heard that Liz would join her as soon as they had closed the gate on the herd. 'And who's cleaning this place?'

'No idea where everyone's gone this morning. Probably the Polish girls are delivering with me

364

because they're getting time off this afternoon to visit the lad that got rescued yesterday. Have Susie and Beth been on cleaning detail lately?'

'Wouldn't know half the new girls if I was to fall over them, and I hear tell we might get some prisoners of war for the harvest.'

'Hear that, Grace, prisoners-of-war for the harvest,' Connie said as Grace returned, Susie and a rather older land girl whose name was Holly accompanying her. 'Fancy an Italian myself, very romantic language, Italian.'

'You'd know,' said Liz, with a grin, 'but what I heard yesterday was that there's Yanks a few miles away.'

'Real, live Americans. And you didn't tell us?' Connie was stunned.

'I forgot. Somehow, a pilot baling out of a burning plane practically onto my head, sort of got in the way.'

'Let's have no more nonsense with your Italians and Polish pilots and Americans,' said Walter, who was now as grumpy as the placid Walter ever got. 'What I want to know is, who is cleaning this dairy?'

'We are, Mr Green,' chimed Holly and Susie.

'Good, and it's just Walter. Get your aprons on and get started, for they're out there making more milk for this afternoon.'

Grace was smiling as she left the dairy. Somehow, Connie was not nearly so abrasive these days, and she and Liz, totally at odds with each other just a few months before, now seemed to get along well. 'Human beings are extremely complex,' Grace informed one of the large pigs scratching her back on a stone wall. The pig grunted and moved away.

'Now where am I supposed to be?' Grace asked Mrs Love as she returned to the kitchen.

'The list's on the board where it always is. Sit down and eat your breakfast, since you're here. I've got some bacon, potato scones and some nice tinned beans.'

The smell of bacon frying had enticed Grace all the way from the garden gate but, with so many new mouths to feed, what one could smell was not always what was left for late arrivals. Since she was ravenously hungry, she sat down, filled a large mug with strong, hot tea and settled to enjoying her breakfast. She had barely started when Holly returned.

'Sorry, Grace, but the missus wants to see you. She says if you're eating, she can wait but come round to the front as soon as you can.'

Mrs Love railed at Holly for referring to Lady Alice as 'the missus' before Grace could say anything.

'Sorry, Missus, but this is my fifth farm and I called the farmer's wife "Missus" on every farm. I never been in the same place with a Lady anything before.'

'Tell her, Grace, while I find some decent cabbages.'

'Did you call Lady Alice "Missus", Holly?'

Holly nodded. 'Yes, I did.'

'And what did she say?'

'"How droll", whatever that means?'

'Address her, speak to her, as "Lady Alice", not "Missus". She is not the farmer's wife. She is, in fact, the farmer, and a very hard-working one, too.'

Mrs Love returned with three late cabbages. 'Glad you're seeding today, Grace. I'm that tired of old vegetables and, honest, I like sprouts, I really do, especially fried with bacon and chestnuts, delicious, but if anyone brings me in another bag of sprouts thinking they're doing me a favour ... I don't know what I'll say. Just think, another month or so and we can have radishes, lettuce, fresh garden peas ... mouth-watering, and, by July, new potatoes.'

But Grace was not listening. She had eaten Brussels sprouts every winter of the war, and had either enjoyed or not enjoyed the experience but, for some reason, when Mrs Love had started to speak, her mind had gone blank and had then filled with images of the ghastly frozen cabbages and sprouts from the unbelievable winter of January 1940. They had picked the vegetables, she and Daisy, and Daisy had said her mum would make soup – 'waste not want not' – and Mrs Petrie had indeed used the vegetables that Grace had worked so hard to grow.

'You all right, Grace? You went all funny for a moment.'

'I'm fine, Mrs Love, just remembering that first winter of the war. I had a little plot in the back yard. Two of my friend's brothers helped us dig it. It was like digging through concrete; I don't know how they did it but they got a plot long enough and deep enough for me to plant things, with some help from the girls. We shared fresh vegetables for a whole summer. Best peas I ever

367

tasted. Sorry, think what you said took me back there.'

'Well, you better get back here and go and see the missus.' Mrs Love laughed. She glared at Holly, who was looking confused. 'Don't do as I do, Holly, do as I say. See you later, Grace.'

Leaving her unfinished breakfast on the table, Grace ran round to the front of the ancient building. She saw it so seldom that it took her breath away anew to look at it. It wasn't just the size; it was the sublime artistry. No plain functional wall of newly fired bricks with bleak rectangular windows placed every so often, but great stones hauled from quarries in the region and then carved and decorated by some master's hand. Who was he or they, these masters? The history of England for hundreds of years was written in these walls. Did monks build their own priories? How much there was to learn.

And I am living in this building, Grace said to herself, and even though it's the servants' quarters, I'm glad, and I'll remember it always.

Her euphoria wore off as she remembered that Lady Alice had sent for her. Her stomach churned, the palms of her hands began to sweat, and she felt sick.

'Oh, there you are, Grace. Why are you dawdling? Come in. I have a message for you and there's news I want you to tell the others.'

A message? Grace seemed to feel her heart, or at least some internal organ, lurch unpleasantly, but she followed Lady Alice into the house.

'Sit down on the window-seat; it's padded and therefore comfier than the wooden ones.' Lady

Alice walked across to the stone fireplace, where a small fire burned and a coffee pot stood on an iron trivet. There were two cups and saucers on her desk and she poured coffee into both. '*There's an enticing smell, don't you think, Grace?*' she asked as she handed Grace one of the cups.

Surprised, Grace said nothing but waited until her employer was seated and had picked up her own cup. 'Very,' she said, 'although I think I've only ever had Camp coffee.'

'Poor you. So far, I haven't been quite so desperate. I'll get straight to the point. Arnold Archer has been arrested, and, I'm sorry, but this time you will have to appear in court. I'm not sure about Eva; it's perfectly possible that every word of English she's ever learned will drain out of her at the thought, poor girl, and I'd quite like to spare her such an ordeal – we have no real idea of what these Polish refugees have experienced – but it's up to the police. I know you'll help her as much as necessary, if it comes to that, and there's Katia, such a brick. But the other matter refers to you. Your Sam rang late last night; he's on his way up to see you – don't spill coffee on that carpet, please.'

She stopped, waiting until Grace had rescued the cup. 'You are pleased, Grace. I told him we'd give him a bed for the night. He can use the rooms Jack and old Harry used. He didn't want to, of course, very proud and I like that, but...'

She did not finish her thought and Grace had a shrewd idea of what she had been about to say and liked her for it. Sam, Sam coming up. Was it possible that he drove? No, the old van surely would never make it. He must have taken the train.

'Mr Tiverton rang first. It was lovely to speak to him again. Sends his best, of course. Then Sergeant Petrie came on and said he was being given a lift; some military vehicle and he asked very nicely if he could interrupt your work.'

Grace smiled. 'That sounds like Sam, Lady Alice. He's thoughtful and kind, very kind.'

'You do want to know when to expect him?' She took Grace's lowered head as an answer and continued: 'He hopes to arrive about four, military needs not withstanding, whatever that means. You should be at the house about that time, no matter what you are doing, Grace, and Mrs Love will give you a pot of tea in the kitchen. She will remain. Hazel will come in and take Sam to the rooms where he will spend the night. Then he will rejoin you, and if I may suggest, the two of you might enjoy wandering around the grounds until your evening meal is ready. You and Sergeant Petrie will have a tray in the little office; that will give you some privacy but, I'm sorry, Grace, I have asked Hazel to return at nine. You need your sleep and there's a wireless in Sam's quarters.'

'I don't know how to thank you, Lady Alice.'

'Don't be silly. I'm thinking only of our returned warrior. Now off you go and do try to get some work done.'

Grace thanked her and walked as calmly as she could from the beautiful room with its splendid paintings and heavy carved furniture. It was called an office in this twentieth century but, she was quite sure, it had once had a much lovelier name. She skipped a little with excitement. Sam

370

was coming to talk to her. Why? Oh, Sam, he could not have gone to all this trouble to tell her that now, some weeks since they had walked in the Dartford park gardens, he no longer saw her as his 'lovely Grace'.

She looked up at the sky. How blue it was in this lovely time of late spring. Her simple, little watch told her that she had spent too much time with Lady Alice. She was supposed to be planting seed with Hazel and Esau and she would not have anyone think that she expected special treatment. Grace ran.

Hazel and Esau accepted her late arrival in their usual manner. 'Let's get on with this, Grace. I've had that inspector telling me the government expects even more acreage under the plough; we'll be planting wheat in holes in dry-stone walls next. Could you get your plough and start trying to make something of those verges leading to the estate cottages?'

That was a surprise. 'Of course I can start ploughing on those narrow strips, Hazel, but who's going to do the harvesting if there's anything to harvest? The nettles and brambles will strangle everything before it has a chance to sprout.'

'Would you give in to government inspectors, Grace?'

'I suppose not.'

'Good. Now plough the verges – that'll keep them happy – and we'll try to deal with the weeds.'

Grace went off and worked hard all afternoon losing all track of time. The verges were almost impossible for a small girl to plough. She was not nearly strong enough to force her plough through the earth, the weeds, the great strong roots of brambles and other plants. Her back breaking, her hands almost raw, she was startled by a familiar voice. 'Grace, it's me, Sam. Where are you?'

She turned, her heart seeming to swell in her body, joy, in place of blood, coursing through her veins, and looked for him but, although she heard vague noises, Sam was nowhere to he seen. As loudly as she could, she called, 'Sam!' The strange noises stopped and there, on the other side of the stone wall, was Sam, every bit as real and solid as he had been in Dartford. A barber had been busy on his hair, which was now as soft and fair as it had ever been, that stray lock falling over his forehead as it had always done. She started to run towards him.

'Don't come over the wall, Grace, love. I'm afraid I've been well and truly welcomed to "England's green and pleasant land".'

And then they were laughing, for Grace could smell exactly what had welcomed Sam.

'Not a good shortcut to take; we put the cows in that field after milking yesterday,' said Grace, as she looked over the wall to where Sam stood, up to his ankles in a cow pat.

'Have you the faintest idea how long it takes to get my shoes as clean and shiny as the shoes of a sergeant in the British Army should be?' Sam looked at her, giving her what she was beginning to call his special smile, and bent again to his task. 'I'll wipe it off with grass, but I think your friends will smell me coming a mile off.'

'We've all stepped in them, Sam. It's a sort of baptism of fire. We land girls cheat, though.'

He looked down at her tall black Wellingtons and back at his one pair of civilian shoes, and laughed. 'This is not what I thought I'd be doing when I finally found you. Quite a walk from the house. It's a really big place, isn't it?'

Grace was still hearing the interesting words about what he expected to be doing. 'If you're not climbing over from your side, I'll climb over from mine, Sam, but I think you can see this is a nice grassy field, not a sign of a cow anywhere.'

Sam bent down and pulled off his shoes and, shoes in one hand, he looked over the wall and then vaulted into Grace's field. He scraped the soiled shoes against thick tufts of grass, before straightening up. 'Well, it's very nice to see you at last, Grace Paterson.'

Even shoeless, he towered above her. For a second, she was afraid, not of Sam but that she would not see in his eyes what she dreamed of seeing. She looked up and, her heart full of love and her eyes shining with happiness and love, threw herself into his outstretched arms. They stood for some time, saying nothing, simply holding each other, each feeling the other's heartbeat. Grace, scarcely daring to believe that she was actually in Sam's arms, was the first to break the spell. 'You'll get pneumonia, Sam Petrie, standing in your socks.'

'Small price, Grace. Come on, though. That Mrs Love said she'd have a nice cup of tea ready for us and I bet she'll have newspaper I can use to clean off these shoes.' Seeing permission in her eyes, Sam bent again and kissed her, very gently, on her soft lips.

Hand in hand, Sam hobbling occasionally as his stockinged feet landed heavily on a stone, they walked back across the estate towards the house.

'You'll never get newspaper, Sam; we save every bit of waste paper we can get our hands on, but Mrs Love'll have an old duster she can spare. Better not bring them in the kitchen; you'll be really welcome but the smell won't.'

Most of the other land girls who had been able to leave their tasks, had hurried in from the fields, supposedly to have a five-minute break but really to take a good close look at Grace's friend. 'And very nice, too,' was the general consensus. Also, 'He's ever so tall,' or, 'There's something really nice about fair-haired men,' and even, 'But why is he suddenly popping in; she didn't know he was coming?'

'He is pretty to be Polish,' Eva assured them, but Katia was harder and told everyone, 'This is not business of us.'

They were disappointed when Mrs Love, seeing the unexpectedly large group of girls who had found time to pop in for a short break, suggested that Grace and Sam take a tray of tea and bread and butter into the small office, where she intended to serve their evening meal, leaving the other land girls in the huge kitchen to think romantic thoughts.

'Do go and remind Grace to leave the door open, Liz; girls can't be too careful,' said Mrs Love.

'But Mrs Love? They're in love; can't they have a few minutes?'

'They can have fifteen,' said Mrs Love

brusquely, as she measured out a reasonable quantity of last year's apple-and-bramble jam, 'but with the door open. And anyway, what makes you think there's anything between them. He's her best friend's brother, that's all.'

'Oh, how dull.' Susie comforted herself with a small extra spoon of jam. 'There was a wedding at the first farm I was on down in Somerset. Everyone was invited and we saved up for months to rent her a wedding dress from a real bridal shop in London – no need for coupons – and we had masses of cider, and fruit cup, and music and dancing in a clean barn. Took us hours to clean the floor, mind you, and almost the same after the wedding.' Susie finished by saying, 'There's some people as shouldn't ought ever to touch cider,' leaving the girls to deal with the pictures and situations her chatter had created in their heads.

'Sounds fun, Susie,' said Connie, earning herself a smile from Liz. 'Oh, they're coming back. Pretend we hardly even noticed they weren't here.'

Sam carried the tray, which he set down beside the great stone sink. He looked as if he was all set to start washing dishes.

'Just leave those, Sam, waste of water to start when, in five minutes, there'll be more, and, besides, you'd best go and clean those shoes.' Mrs Love turned to Grace, who was looking rather subdued. 'All right, Grace? There's cleaning rags in the wooden box in the pantry. Give Sam two of those and tell him I'll get rid of them when he's done.'

'Thank you, Mrs Love,' said Grace, quietly, as

she walked out, leaving the others to look at one another and wonder about the change of atmosphere.

TWENTY

Grace stood watching as Sam cleaned his shoes. She was sure that she knew what he was going to say and she did not want to hear it. The silence stretched between them as Grace struggled to find things to say that would keep him from telling her.

'You must meet all the girls, Sam; they're all terrific. It's almost like being with Daisy and Rose and Sally. The Polish girls are my favourites.'

She continued to chatter, telling him about the crashed plane and the wounded Polish pilot. 'I think Eva, she's the one with the golden hair – and a golden voice, actually – well, I think she really likes him, the pilot, I mean. He said he had been rescued by angels. She does look like an angel. Won't it be nice if – well, she's a refugee and has no family.'

'We have to talk, Grace,' he said gently. 'This won't go away. I'm being allowed to rejoin my regiment. The medics say everything is functioning properly and so there's no reason to keep a man who's fit for duty, doing nothing useful all day long. I needed to tell you to your face, sweetheart, not in a letter. I asked them. They called me in and had doctors of all sorts question me, examine me inside and out, and I'm fit for duty, and I'm pleased, really pleased.'

Grace listened to him, each word he uttered seeming to strike her as the hammer strikes the nail. She felt that she might very well come apart at the seams. Despite his letter, she had never seriously considered that Sam might return to active service. Had he not done enough for his country, more than enough?

'You won't go back to the war. Please, Sam, your mother won't cope.'

He walked over to where she stood beside the little telephone table, her arms wrapped around her body as if, indeed, she feared that she might fall apart. 'There, there, my little love,' he said as he held her stiff, resisting body in his arms. 'You're not thinking, Grace, not with your brain, you're not. I'm a soldier; it's all I've ever been, since I was sixteen years old. Fourteen years, little love, it's what I do, what I'm good at.' He kissed the top of her shiny brown hair. 'Relax, my Grace. Come sit down here with me. No need to be tense, sweetheart, it's me, Sam, and I want to tell you when it got through my thick head when I knew that I was in love with Grace Paterson. I suppose I loved her since she landed at my feet in the playground, but being in love with her? That's a whole different thing.'

She relaxed but decided that she would not make it easy for him. 'Mrs Love went to a lot of trouble to make this tea.'

'And we can sit and chat over the teacups and think of all the things we've missed.'

Wrong thing to say.

'And will miss again and again if you go back to the war, Sam.'

'My little brother's dead, Grace, and only God and the British Navy know where Phil is. Can you really see me in the front room eating home-baked scones instead of doing my bit to end this madness?'

She cried then. 'You've more than done your bit. You fought, you were wounded, imprisoned. Dear God, Sam, from the little I've heard, it seems you walked across Europe and back again.'

He lifted his arm as if to brush all such trivialities aside. 'One day, I'll show you Italy, the farms I worked on, the *contadini*, that's the country folk, I lived with. It's the most generous of countries, Grace. You can't believe the beauty, and the people, a few ears of corn in the store-room and they share it with a hungry stranger. There was a girl, a small girl with lovely soft brown hair. She reminded me of you, although her eyes were brown, not blue-grey or grey-blue. Her parents had this small stone house and, believe it or not, a cow shared it with them.' He smiled. 'Helped keep us all warm in the winter.' Obviously deep in memories, he stopped and, then again aware of her presence, started talking again.

'They hid me from German patrols, Grace, they let me take shelter in their loft. They fed me and, in return, I worked with Aldo in the fields. I learned all about foraging for food in the woods – mushrooms, truffles, nuts and berries – and I worked his little bit of land. The things that man could get to come up from fairly inhospitable soil.

378

Would you believe, tomatoes grew outside? I've never tasted anything like them, unbelievable. All the men of the area helped one another out with seeds and cuttings, and the women and children worked, too. I found myself getting closer and closer to … I almost said "Grace" there. Her name is Lucia. One blistering cold January day, we were all in the woods trying to collect firewood and I remember thinking how glad I was that she was there. My heart lurched. Daft thought, that, but it's certainly what it seemed to do and suddenly everything made sense. She's Lucia, I said to myself. She's lovely but she's not Grace.'

He hesitated as he looked down into the eyes that he had dreamed of in his darkest moments. 'And I'm in love with Grace.'

Grace felt herself trembling. She tried to stand up and he reached out to help her and, for a long moment, they stood looking at each other.

'I love Grace,' Sam said. 'I'm in love with Grace.'

She could feel tears trembling on her eyelashes. 'Oh, Sam, do you mean it?'

In reply, he drew her into his arms and kissed her. They were not the gentle tender kisses he had dropped on her lips before, but a kiss that grew in passion as, with no thought of Jack or anyone else, she responded to him.

Eventually, he drew back. 'Since I was about fourteen, a little girl with soft brown hair, a very pretty face and the sweetest, giving nature, that girl has held a special place in my heart.'

Grace lifted her head and was almost dazzled by the intensity of his look. 'But you never said, never wrote…'

'A soldier waiting for the war he didn't want but knew was coming? What right has he to tie down a lovely girl? And remember that I only realised that my feelings for you were stronger than just a brotherly affection when I was an escaped POW, relying on the kindness of a family of poor Italians scraping a living in the Italian Alps.'

'When you came down to visit me, I could hardly breathe for loving you. You had to be free to choose, Grace, to look for the special someone.'

She relaxed and leaned forward so that his body supported her. 'I had already found him, Sam.'

He held her close and Grace had never felt so safe, so cherished. How could she have mistaken the feelings aroused by Sam's body so close to hers with the feelings that she had experienced when being held by Jack. She should have waited. She knew that now. It was a girl desperate to feel loved who had responded to Jack. His arms about her, as surely her mother must have held her, had made her feel cherished and safe.

But she had made a mistake and had suffered for it and she feared that she might still have to pay.

'Sam, are you saying that you love me, that you want...?' She stopped. How could she be bold enough to ask?

He took her in his arms again. 'Marriage, Grace, that's what I want, but not with any available girl, but with wee Grace Paterson, who took on the chin everything the world threw at her and never complained.'

'You want to marry me?'

'Well, I quite like Lady Alice, but there's a

picture on her desk … happen she's spoken for.'

Grace had begun to laugh but stopped as she took in what he was saying. 'Oh, I do hope so. She works so hard and, as far as we can see, she never has any fun.'

'Could we get back to Grace and Sam? I want to marry you, Grace. I love you very much, but, sweetheart, we're still in the middle of a world war. I want to ask you to wait until this insanity is over but…' He reached into his pocket and took out a small box. 'I'm selfish enough to want the world to know that I'm the luckiest man in the whole world. Will you marry me, Grace, wear my ring?' He held out the box, which he had opened, and Grace saw a small ring with a lovely blue stone in it. 'I tried to match your lovely eyes, but emeralds were too green. This sapphire came closest.'

Still she said nothing and he looked at her in dismay. 'Don't you love me enough, Grace?'

'Oh, Sam, with all my heart, and I'd be proud to be your wife and to wear this beautiful ring, but I'm not, I've been, I met–'

He reached out and put his fingers on her lips. 'Ssh, my little love. Grace, do you love me? Do you want to be my wife?'

Eyes bright with unshed tears, she nodded, and he took her hand and slipped the little ring onto the fourth finger of her left hand.

'What's past is past, Grace. I'm looking to the future, a future that I want to share with you. It won't be easy. We'll be separated again, but only by land and sea, and one day, when the war is over, next year maybe, we'll be married – perhaps by Mr Tiverton – and then we'll never be separated.'

He put his arms around her. 'I bet if I kiss you, those girls will come rushing in to say our tea's ready. I'm willing to risk it, if you are.'

Feeling that she might explode with happiness, Grace nodded, and he bent his head, his eyes looking into hers, and kissed her, a kiss that seemed to pull her heart straight out of her body. It was his now. So simple. It had always been his.

The publishers hope that this book has given you enjoyable reading. Large Print Books are especially designed to be as easy to see and hold as possible. If you wish a complete list of our books please ask at your local library or write directly to:

Magna Large Print Books
Magna House, Long Preston,
Skipton, North Yorkshire.
BD23 4ND

This Large Print Book for the partially sighted, who cannot read normal print, is published under the auspices of

THE ULVERSCROFT FOUNDATION